AARON L SPEER

UNDEADLY SECRETS SERIES

DAY DREAMER

BOOK TWO

License Notes

DAY DREAMER (Undeadly Secrets, #2)

Email: info@aaronlspeer.com
URL: http://aaronlspeer.com/

ISBN 978-1508895817
Cover Art by Deranged Doctor Design
Formatting by Deranged Doctor Design

Other Works By Aaron L Speer
NIGHT WALKER (Undeadly Secrets, #1)

‘You’re never safe ‘till you see the dawn
And if the clock strikes past midnight
The hope is gone
So move under the moonlight...’
Lyrics – “Carry On Dancing” Savage Garden

This work is dedicated with love to Sally May McCanna.
Your life was not measured by the tears after you'd gone
But by the smiles you created while you were here
Keep shredding, beautiful

CHAPTER 1

WEREWOLF

"Are you serious?" Alex pressed the cold compress to her head. The effect of Dante's bite hadn't worn off. She felt giddy, slightly feverish. Although her brain felt like concrete, she had heard him very clearly. Dante had uttered the word she had always associated with vampires but had never mentioned until now. Truthfully, she had always put the two together because of books and movies, but never had she imagined that vampires and werewolves actually existed in the same place. But then again, if one existed, why not the other?

"Very" Dante peered out through the wall of glass, looking over the glittering city skyline.

"Fuckety…How come you never mentioned anything before?" Alex asked.

"There was no need. There haven't been any in Sydney, not that I know of. I've never faced one, only heard stories from other countries."

"How do you know there haven't been any here?"

"Vincent's law forbids it. They were said to reside in the Canadian Rockies, Northern America, Alaska, Britain, Sweden, and Greenland from memory. Cold places. Places with forests and open, wintry landscapes."

"So what are they doing here now? What do they want with Matt?"

"I have no idea." Dante walked to her and placed his hands on her arms. "There are a few hours to go until sunrise. Stay here. With the security system activated, you'll be safer here than anywhere else."

"Where are you going?"

"Vincent must be told. As I said, he has strategies in place to keep Lycanthropes out of Australia. But I need to see the haematologist that compiled this report first. I need to know what more he can tell me."

"I want to go with you."

Dante smiled. "Stay here and sleep. I won't be long."

"I don't want to sleep. I'm going with you. I want to know what happened to Matt too. I'll always care about him."

Dante paused and gave an impressed raise of his eyebrows. "Very well then."

* * *

4 Months Earlier – Switzerland

Nick Slade sat on the hard brick stairs leading into Albert Hall, watching the other students laugh and chat before the day's classes. Suddenly he heard a piercing wail and the doors that lead to the day spa behind him, smacked open. Two girls ran out, designer hand bags swinging with the effort of moving, stopping just in front of Nick.

"Oh my god, I'm going to kill that bitch!" the one in front screamed, through lips trembling with rage.

"Oh my god, you should! Take a selfie first," the friend replied.

"What?!"

"Evidence for the Police! When they see what she did to your brows you'll get off."

"Oh yeah..."

The two walked off, leaving Nick alone, shaking his head. *Yep, this is my school.*

He twirled a rose in his fingers, resisting the urge to smell it yet again. He swept his hair back, yet strands still fell about his forehead, the two wailing wenches put out of his mind.

He spotted his intended recipient, Belinda Madden, approaching. The first reason he'd found to really appreciate being away from home.

He smiled, hopping to his feet and slinging his bag over his shoulder.

He wanted to give her the rose as a short goodbye gift, seeing as though today was the last before the end of year break.

"Hey. Can we talk?" She spotted the rose in his hand just as she finished.

"Sure," he said, expectant.

"No, not here. Alone." She indicated the toilets to their right.

He walked with her in silence, trying to shake the feeling in his stomach that he was about to receive some very bad news. Put to rest once they reached their destination.

"Nick, you're really great…" Belinda started.

Oh shit.

His father had once told him that anything someone said before the word 'but' should be ignored.

"But…it's just not working out."

Nick shifted uneasily. "Did I do something wrong?"

"No," she replied quickly. "Look, don't make this harder. I told you, you're great. You're sweet and everything but just not my type, that's all."

"You just figured that out now?" Nick replied. He wasn't angry, at least not openly, but he could sense she was partially lying.

"Yeah. I gave you a shot, ok? I just don't feel the same anymore."

"You said you really liked me not two weeks ago."

"Yeah…I did."

"I know you're not being straight with me. If I haven't done anything wrong, what changed?"

"Nothing changed!" she replied sharply. "That's the point. You didn't change! I thought you would roughen up a bit, but you didn't. You are too nice, ok? Too sweet. I want a man, not a chick with a dick, no offence. You hold the door open for me…you hold my hand…you give me light kisses…you send me goofy text messages."

"Amazing how you never mentioned any of this bothering you before…like when we're in bed…"

"That's because I thought you'd pick it up! Look," she said, pointing to the flower in his hand. "Perfect example. The rose…is just too much. Why would you give me a flower? I haven't done anything for it."

Nick looked at the rose. "I just thought you might like it."

The line did make Belinda pause before she continued. "It just feels like you're pushing it. Forcing it down my throat."

"What if I stop being sweet to you then?"

Belinda genuinely smiled at this. "Nick, you're just a nice guy, and you'll always be only…just a nice guy. I know you. You don't have a mean or malicious bone in your body, and that's not a bad thing. It's just not who you are inside. And you're just not what I want." The bell sounded its gong. "Look, I gotta go. Don't be sad, ok? Like I said, you're a great guy. You have that whole blonde hair and blue eyes thing going for you. You'll find someone really nice, *someone you deserve* and we'll still be friends, yeah?"

She had started backing away by the time she finished 'ok'. Being friends after a break up was like saying "honey, the dog died, but we can still keep it." Nick had plenty of things he wanted to say—to yell in fact. But what was the point? He saw Belinda run up to Jericho Piers and nudge him, smiling as they walked side by side into the main entrance. Jericho gave her a once over before tossing his cigarette away as one of the teachers rounded the corner, just missing the act. Belinda giggled, as if admiring him. *"Look at how macho and brave Jericho is,"* Nick imagined her thinking.

What would Belinda have wanted, what would she have expected? Should he have smacked her around? Beat Jericho down? Get drunk and piss on something?

He could handle being told he wasn't good looking enough, not sexy enough, but she had complimented him on his looks. Then called him a chick with a dick. Too nice? What a bunch of horse shit.

Nick leant against the toilet wall, taking one more look at the rose and dropped it to the floor. She was right, he liked being nice to people, though on days like this he wondered why. He straightened his bag strap again and headed to the main doors of Albert Hall, pushing them aside with renewed hatred. Fucking Switzerland. He just wanted to go home.

At least he wouldn't have to deal with anything shitty for a while. He'd be finally home soon.

* * *

Nick woke from his nanna nap later that day aboard his father's private gyrocopter, a retired Sikorsky X2. Expertly manufactured piece by piece in England by designers imported from America, Wilson Slade's aircraft was a modern marvel. Two passengers only ensured a top speed of almost 290 mph. In truth, though he loved the feeling of roaring through the sky, Nick felt like the plane was a huge waste of money. He was slightly uncomfortable with the lavish lifestyle his father expected him to live. Most thought Nick was insane, constantly looking gift horses in the mouth, but they didn't understand what secret his family harboured. Very few did. And those that did served his father as friends.

Well most of them anyway.

Nick shook his head and stretched, when his eyes locked on to the mother moon. Only half, yet lighting up the sky like a jewel. His mother called it the pearl of the sky. His father often referred to it as his beautiful lady, toasting to it almost every night.

Nick tried not to wonder what his father called it when it was full, when the family secret revealed itself.

Wilson had hidden nothing from his son since he was old enough to learn the Slade legacy. Just like Nick had not hidden the fact that he, much to his father's disappointment, had been deprived of his birthright. Fate had seen to it that his father's legacy had skipped a generation.

He was well into puberty and had still exhibited none of his ancestors' abilities. Perfect hair to skin ratio, nails normal enough to be bitten every few weeks, no change in eye colour and the only howling and slobbering he did was when presented with one of his mother's home made chocolate cakes.

The copter began a rapid descent towards the helipad on the grounds of the Slade estate.

"Welcome home, Master Slade," Sam said pleasantly, powering down the vehicle.

"Thank you, Sam. But it's Nick, ok?"

Sam chuckled as he got out. "Very good, sir. Uh, Nick."

Sam rounded the craft and opened the door for him. "That's all right," Nick said hopping out. "We'll work on it."

He stared up at the huge house hoping it was exactly how he remembered it, without the weight of expectancy. At times, he felt like a pregnant woman, under constant watch to see when she was going to deliver.

He had been a little disappointed early on, when he learned that he wasn't like his father. But really any regret was because Wilson had been so determined that his son succeed him, always saying it was just taking its time. Denial 101. Now Nick just rolled with it. There was no point in wishing and hoping. Facts were facts and Nick could live with them. If this what his life had in store, Nick didn't think it was so bad. He just hoped in the time he had been away, that his father had begun to feel the same.

Chapter 2

Great Expectations

The dining hall of the Slade estate was crowded. Dozens of men had convened to hear what their Alpha had to say. The word was he would be naming his successor, but so far, nothing the men had heard made any of them happy. Everyone invited were Wilson Slade's lieutenants or underbosses, and they had brought with them any sons whom they felt deserved the right to be considered.

They had been talking, arguing, debating, for hours. A decision was never going to be reached this night, and anger and frustration were clearly on show. In exasperation, Wilson turned and looked out the windows to the helipad. The copter was almost a mile away and closing, yet his hearing picked it up clearly. Wilson smiled. Finally, this pointless farce could end, temporarily at least.

"Gentlemen, thank you. That will be all," Wilson stated, not turning away from the window.

"What?" Tobias Lee, his youngest lieutenant, shouted. "With all due respect, the situation isn't nearly over."

Wilson gave a sharp nod, eyeing Tobias. Wilson had noticed over the last year the gradual change in the young man. Tobias seemed disgruntled with an ever-more cynical view of the world—Wilson's world. The world Wilson had built and provided for Tobias and everyone else in this room. Tobias had been made a lieutenant as a teenager by the former Alpha, Wilson's father William. Wilson had never understood why. William had clearly seen something that Wilson missed. Tobias had been a meek, docile boy who barely uttered a peep and had grown into a man without much change. He only showed a fool's courage when prompted by others. Such as now, Wilson thought. "The situation of succession is and has always been closed, but I must adjourn. My son is home."

Many grumbles erupted behind him. "What are you talking about, closed?"

"You can't be serious!"

"When will a decision be made?"

Wilson rose slowly and the shouts died down. In a voice that was nearly a growl, he said, "When I am good and well ready."

"You are deliberately stalling. You're the Alpha of Britain, and you know your son is not one of us." Tobias had risen to his feet, a sneer of disdain on his face. "And you just can't face that fact."

"Show some respect." This came from Damien Creed, Wilson's oldest and most trusted advisor.

But Tobias was not ready to stop. "You know, I wouldn't be surprised if he was a faggot, too!"

A vicious snarl erupted and Wilson found himself surprised it hadn't come from his own lips. The words had in fact stung him into momentary paralysation.

Tobias fell to the floor revealing Wilson's wife, Alicia Slade, standing over him, her fist still in the air. "I will remind you that you are in my house, and you speak of my only son."

"So?" Tobias spat.

"So, watch your fucking mouth. I know gays that have bigger balls than you do."

Wilson, recovered from the shock of Tobias's accusation, began a slow clap. A few others joined in, though they looked uncertain as to what they were applauding. "My wife, lads. In all her Australian glory." Wilson wrapped an arm around Alicia's waist as she returned to his side, and brought her in for a short, passionate kiss. When they broke apart, Wilson turned around to address the room. "What are you waiting for? A peep show? Get out of here!" he bellowed. "Didn't you hear what I said? My boy's home!"

There was a sudden hustle towards the door, but Tobias lingered a moment. Keeping his eyes on Alicia, he backed out of the room slowly. "You're lucky you're the Alpha's wife."

"What's that now?" Alicia whipped around, eyebrows raised.

"You heard me," he replied bitterly, still backing toward the door. "You're lucky it's only halftime too," he continued, flicking his eyes outside to the half-moon, just visible in the afternoon sky.

Alicia abruptly put her fingers together and slowly cracked her knuckles. "Don't let halftime stop you, Tobias. You know what the English say." She took a few steps forward, opening her arms and beckoning with the fingers on both hands. "Come on… IF YA THINK YOU'RE 'ARD ENOUGH!"

Tobias lunged toward her.

A cracking sound cut the air and Tobias stopped short, clutching at his throat. Gagging and choking, he fell to the floor yet again, scrambling to pry away the end of the bullwhip that encircled his neck.

"Aw hell, Damien." Alicia huffed. "Why did you have to ruin my fun?"

The bullwhip's wielder walked forward to the struggling form of Tobias, still trying to get his fingers under the tight leather of the whip. Creed knelt by Tobias's head and removed the whip with deliberate slowness.

"You're pissing everyone off today, aren't you, Tobias?" Wilson raised a wine glass in a feigned toast.

"Think about how you address the Alpha's wife next time," Creed growled. "Now get out of here, you little shit."

Wilson could see the veins in the young lieutenant's temples almost popping as the blood rushed back into his face, but Tobias would know better than to swap un-pleasantries with Creed. He scrambled to his feet and marched out of the room without another word. The only thing following him was his humiliation.

"Drive carefully, Tobias." Wilson waved, finishing the last drop of his wine. "Don't run over any landmines or anything." He turned toward his advisor. "Damien, well done and thank you. If you could please escort my boy to the parlour, we will be waiting there for him."

Creed gave a gentle bow and swept out of the room. Alicia and Wilson walked side by side towards the opposite door and along the vast corridor leading to the parlour.

"What are you going to do about all this?" Alicia asked, concerned.

"Whatever I have to until Nicholas is ready."

"Will, stop." She grasped his arm, halting him. "We have been over and over this. I know it isn't something you want to hear—"

"You're right. It isn't," he said, walking away from her. He *had* heard it for the last few hours. The meeting had been called by his lieutenants to discuss the rumblings in the pack. The rumblings centred on the notion of succession, something Wilson had made clear in no uncertain terms, time and time again. Still, the sycophants who called him Alpha to his face—yet old and weak behind his back—continued to bring their standard, off-the-rack offspring for his consideration. Nothing about them sparked Wilson. They were nothing more than pretenders compared to his son, Nicholas. Had he mentioned this, of course, the theory of nepotism would've taken over all discussion. So instead, Wilson humoured them, though it was becoming tedious. "My Alpha, may I present…" Or, "He experienced his first woman at fourteen…" Another, "My son killed his first foe before even I at the same age…" On and on it went. Wilson had kept them alive, prosperous and safe for almost twenty years when packs around the world were destroying each other, and now they were circling his leadership like hyenas over a carcass. Fuck them.

"You can't keep ignoring this. It's not anyone's fault. These things just happen. Why can't you accept that Nicholas is different?"

"I am the Alpha. Like all my ancestors before, I will choose who will succeed me. And I have. Our son *is* one of us; he just doesn't know it yet. And I will be damned if I am going to let some piss-ant son of an underboss take the title away."

They continued towards the parlour and stepped inside, finding it still empty.

"Let them fight over the title," Alicia said. "You have said before you no longer want it. You are still many years away from stepping aside, but isn't that why you want to train Nicholas now? I know how desperate you are. I understand. But they are desperate too. They want to plan…and to brag. This is all about ego, yours against theirs and is doing nothing but damage. Why can't we return home Will, and just forget about all this?"

Wilson studied his wife carefully. Time as a werewolf had not been the most kind to her, not that it made him love her any less. With her too-sharp chin and wide-set eyes, she'd never been beautiful in the conventional sense, but Alicia had always had a certain striking quality about her that had attracted him from the very beginning. As they do with everyone, the years had weathered and muted her features, but her dark-blue eyes still sparkled fiercely from beneath her fringe. Normally, an Alpha's wife was not permitted to question anything the Alpha said or did, but Wilson and Alicia had never had a by-the-book relationship. He had long relied on her wisdom and her temperament, which counter-balanced his own. Her advice often led to him debating issues internally, and frequently to him changing his mind. This had included situations involving their son.

Typically, if an Alpha married a human woman, he would turn his wife before she conceived a child, for the mother's wellbeing. Werewolf pups had caused havoc on the human uterus in the past.

In his case, however, Wilson had discovered Alicia's pregnancy months after they had spent a lone night together. Afraid of losing her humanity, she had argued relentlessly with him for fear of possibly endangering her son, and she'd refused to be turned until she was almost to term. An Alpha could bite his intended with force and would face no punishment, but this equalled rape in Wilson's eyes. He just couldn't bring himself to do such a thing.

While Alicia was turned before she gave birth, the fact that it was late in the proceedings had always haunted Wilson. Had it been so late that Nicholas's development had been unaffected? Wilson was no geneticist. Why couldn't he stop thinking about this? It was not as if he wouldn't love the boy regardless. So why couldn't he move on? Because if the notion that Nicholas was not an Alpha—perhaps not a wolf at all—got into his mind, he would have to accept it as being his fault. Or worse, hers. And that idea was abhorrent.

They had never been able to have another child and Wilson had most certainly wanted them. He couldn't shake the fact, after all these years, that he had been too soft on Alicia because he loved her, and now was facing the consequences. It also meant that maybe, just maybe, the words spoken in hushed whispers that no one thought he could hear were true: that if Wilson could not father a wolf and let his wife dictate terms, he could not possibly be an Alpha of any worth. Wilson did not fear any challenge. He feared having to submit to the will of the pack as a failure, and break his bloodline for the first time in nine generations. He could not, he *would* not allow it to happen.

"To Sydney? Aside from the fact that you have never known me to run from anything, why do you think?" Wilson sighed. "Even if I were to consider it, you and I are too well known there. We would have to make concessions to the vampires that would shame us. Sydney is their city."

"It may be their city, but it is my home. I know it's been years, but I could contact my cousin for help. I could protect us if you'd let me." Alicia said softly, her hand resting on Wilson's arm.

"Protect us from something I can't? What is that exactly?" Wilson replied, his voice rising.

A knock stopped the argument. Wilson growled. He sniffed in the direction of the door and it opened to reveal Creed.

"My Alpha, my lady, forgive me. Young master Slade has requested some time to freshen up before greeting you."

"Is he all right?" Alicia asked, frowning.

"I believe so. Yet I asked if he was glum as I suspected, he replied only with 'Girl trouble'. I daresay he is nursing a broken heart."

"Ah, my poor darling. We'll need to treat this with care," Alicia said.

"With respects my lady, teenage hearts mend faster than we do." Creed replied with a tiny smile before leaving the two alone.

"Well, at least that gives us some extra time to discuss what to do about this." Alicia said.

"There is nothing left to discuss," Wilson replied.

"Of course there is! I want us to both sit down with Nicholas over the next few days and chat about what *he* wants in all this. Have you even thought about that?"

"Of course I have. But how would he know what he wants when he has no idea what he is capable of?"

Alicia put her head on her palm, exasperated. "Oh for fuck's sake, Will! Why can't you move on and see what's right in front of you?"

"One could equally ask why you are so quick to dismiss it." Wilson grumbled and opened the liquor cabinet.

"Don't you think you've had enough?" Alicia asked.

Wilson appeared to consider this as he poured himself some scotch.

“I am not nearly drunk enough yet to forget I have wasted over six hours with a bunch of greedy fools, only to keep wasting my time with my lovely wife on the same pointless subject.” Wilson punctuated this with a cheeky grin and gulped the contents of his glass in one.

“You’re not taking me seriously. You’re not taking anything seriously. You always do this.”

Wilson sat on the edge of the table and upturned his hands as a sign of seriousness. “What do I always do?” he offered, stifling his grin and attempting to really listen.

“Make everything out as if it’s a joke. I have something important to say and then we just go round and round in circles. You just don’t see the danger. Your underbosses are getting restless, more so with each passing day that there is no decision from you. Tobias may be a pathetic excuse for a wolf but he is correct. You are stalling and causing more and more strife. Is this really about Nicholas, or is it about you?”

The words washed over Wilson like a chilled breeze. Did Alicia have a point? Should Wilson have given his son a wide berth to become his own person, not to live in Wilson’s constant shadow? How could a boy hope to grow and expand, werewolf or not, without the guidance of his father?

Wilson rose and walked towards his wife. “I will tell you this: the full moon is in just over a week. If this doesn’t work, if at the end of these holidays I see nothing different in him, then I will choose a successor and let Nicholas go his own way.”

Alicia looked at him suspiciously. *Why the change of heart?* He could hear her practically think it. In many ways, Alicia was perhaps the true Alpha of the relationship, a fact that made him love her more and hate her as well. “I will even send a message to Vincent in Sydney in the morning.”

“Asking what?”

“If Nicholas does not become an Alpha, I will ask out of respect what it would take for him to grant just the three of us entry into his city. I hold little hope that he will even reply, and if he does, I doubt we will be able to come to an agreement both of us finds suitable. Don’t forget this is all only applicable if my vision for Nicholas does not work out. But I will keep my mind open to the possibility. I promise you this.”

Alicia considered her husband for a few seconds. “Will, I swear…

Even with the situations surrounding him, our history, the violence and all that, Nicholas is a good kid. The best. If you even think about putting any kind of pressure on him…"

Wilson shook his head. "No, no. This is merely just a test of my judgement, to see if I am right. He is my son no matter what."

Alicia nodded tightly. "It might be a good idea to tell him that occasionally. Also, let me write the email? You suck with technology."

"Deal," he said, brushing his fingers across the fringe he loved so much.

"I don't know why you changed your mind. But thank you," Alicia said, taking the hand he used, kissing it and continued to hold it in her lap.

"You continue to teach me ways to be a better Alpha and father. I would like to think being good at one, helps me be better at the other. If I have forgotten reason and compromise, you remind me. Without it, we are nothing but the mindless beasts the movies say we are."

* * *

Alicia did not wait for the next morning; she just waited for Wilson to fall asleep. Her email to Vincent was short and to the point, but with a rather massive yet deliberate omission. She asked him for allowances for two werewolves to occupy asylum in Sydney. Her judgement call could prove costly, as the last thing she wanted to do was lie to the Sydney vampire king and get caught, but it was important to her that Vincent not be told of her son's existence just yet. Something—call it mother's intuition—told her Nicholas might end up being used as a bargaining chip. She took her time in turning the computer off, knowing it was early morning in Sydney at this time. The soonest Vincent would likely read it would be when he woke up that evening. Alicia went to bed very apprehensive, but daring to dream.

* * *

I promise nothing. Send your envoys with your proposal if you wish, before or after the full moon. Do this and I will grant them the courtesy of an audience.

H.R.H Vincent Kent.

Alicia stared at the email reply. She did not know what to make of this. To most, it would seem just a begrudging invitation. Alicia sensed there was more to it, however. She sensed something else, too. If not danger, then something close akin. Vincent didn't want a proposal via email. He was actually inviting members of the pack to present it in person. She would have to be extremely careful, and yet she didn't know exactly why.

The last confrontation between werewolves and vampires had occurred long ago, but neither side had forgotten nor forgiven. The two species maintained an uneasy peace out of hatred, respect and also because war did not accomplish anything. Both species needed to live and needed to do so without stepping on each other's toes.

Australia was the last country that had enough overwhelming vampire presence to be able to refuse entry to werewolves. Vincent Kent was at their head, citing a concern for human welfare. All who knew him knew full well that was a farce. Still, Vincent's word was law for Australia. Each state had its own governance, Melbourne even had its own monarchy, but they all answered to Vincent. Now he was accepting a request to talk things over, even possibly accepting the Alpha and his family. Perhaps the criticism he had received from other heads of state internationally had finally gotten to him?

No, Alicia didn't believe that. Vincent did not bow to pressure. There was something more to this. She would organise her envoys, a handful of werewolves, and humans as well, to offer a proposal of asylum. She would inform them of the exact proposal. She would also inform them of a plan B if everything went to hell.

CHAPTER 3

WHO'S AFRAID?

Present Day – Sydney

Alex walked alongside Dante into the Raven Apartments block, located in Surry Hills. They passed four armed guards patrolling the outer perimeter and another two just inside the entry doors. The doors and an entire awning-like entryway around and above them were made of glass. Inside was dark, lit only by the moon shining through the glass.

They strolled into the spacious lobby and up to the reception desk. Alex could smell rich leather, and noticed the tidy two-seater couches set in squares all around her. A tall woman stood behind the desk. She looked austere, her hair in a tight bun and her business suit neatly pressed. Alex guessed she was maybe in her mid-fifties. She looked up as they approached.

"Good evening, Dante," the receptionist said in the most put on, velvety soft voice ever.

Dante nodded in greeting. "Samantha. This is Alex. I'm here to see Herschel."

"I don't suppose he knows you're coming?" Her velvet tones had hardened, leaving Alex to wonder if she was the reason.

"No," Dante replied.

Samantha sighed as if it was a huge effort, yet smiled as she picked up the phone, eyeing him. Dante for the most part was just friendly to her. Alex thrust her hands in her pockets, noting that Samantha was completely ignoring her. *Seems like it is me.*

"Good evening, Mr Rasmussen, I— Well, yes actually. He just walked in. That's why I am calling. Yes, of course."

Samantha hung up. "He was expecting you. I'll escort you to the elevator."

"It's really not necessary," Dante said. But she obviously wasn't listening, walking behind the desk and over to the lift buttons, waiting beside yet another guard. "How've you been?"

"Very well, thank you," she replied, with a huge smile showing all her teeth.

Somewhere, an angel must be getting gonorrhoea, Alex thought. She flicked her eyes over Samantha, who looked ready to pounce and devour Dante. Was she a vampire? How did she know Dante? Alex tensed and with a sickening feeling in her stomach, wondered if maybe they had been an item once. The thought bothered her more than she wanted to admit.

The elevator arrived and the doors opened, not really relieving the tension.

"Thanks for the help. Take care," Dante said simply, leading Alex inside.

"The offer for my number is still wide open, Dante," Samantha said with a smirk, turning on her heel just as the doors closed.

Alex snorted. "I think somebody has a crush."

Dante tensed his jaw. "She is a vampire groupie."

"There's such a thing? How long have you known her?"

"We met several years ago, at a nursing home."

"A nursing home? What were you doing there? What was *she* doing there?"

"Visiting an old friend. She was a former high-end call girl sent by Vincent to lure me back to the fold. At the time, Vincent thought because of her circumstances, I might be swayed in trying to help her—she had been bitten by one of her clients and became obsessed with finding more of us. This caused her to come to the attention of Vincent, who put her to the test: get me back into the family and he would make her immortal."

"Ah… So she failed then?"

"Yes. And though he didn't turn her, as per his law, he obviously thought she would be of some use, so put her here. These apartments have always had my kind living in them, and Samantha is their liaison."

"Is that why there are so many guards here, to protect her?"

"It's a good question. There was never this many before. Must be a recent development."

Alex glanced instinctively at the ceiling of the elevator. It's not like she expected something to crash down onto the roof, but the feeling that she was surrounded by hundreds of the undead at this moment made her feel uneasy. She tried to talk to keep her mind occupied. "So, Samantha wanted to be your donor?"

Dante breathed out sharply through his nose and made a face like he was tasting something bitter. "She wanted me to feed on and sleep with her, but I politely declined. Though unfortunately this didn't stop her getting what she wanted."

"Wait, what?"

Dante sighed, obviously not happy to reveal this particular memory. "I was weakened after a fight at the home. Samantha found me and gave me her wrist. As I frantically fed, I became aroused, as all males of my kind do, and she used this to her advantage."

Alex took a second, before touching Dante's arm. "Are you telling me you were…raped?"

Dante met her eyes briefly before looking down. "I suppose I was. She pulled my pants down around my thighs, hiked her skirt and straddled me, pinning me down in my weakened state. Thankfully, I do not believe I was all that memorable for her. She tasted vile. I wasn't erect for more than a minute, though it was just enough for her to be sated."

"It's still a violation!" Alex was disgusted but could see Dante didn't want to talk about that aspect. She steered toward a more obvious question. "What *did* she taste like?"

"Ashes and salt," he said, without thinking.

"Can I ask what I taste like?" Alex asked.

Dante turned to her and looked her up and down, thinking. "Have you ever tasted a physalis? They're sometimes called an Aztec berry or cape gooseberry."

Alex shook her head and Dante continued. "When bought in a store, they're typically larger, and very tart, because they've been bred for size and are harvested early for shipping. However, if you grow your own and pick them when they're ripe, they're smaller, but the sweetness that bursts from them, touched with just a hint of tanginess... That's what you taste like."

Caught off-guard by Dante's answer, and now interested in trying to find a physalis plant at the local garden centre, Alex hardly noticed when the lift came to a stop and the doors opened not onto a corridor, but a huge laboratory.

Dante touched her arm and got her attention. They stepped out of the lift and into the enormous space. To her right she spotted an entire desk space dedicated to a clear vat of a bubbling, bright blue liquid. There were tubes connected to the vat's sides dripping the liquid into small vials lined up along the desk. *I've seen this before. Where?* Then it came back to her. She had seen the exact same vials in a pantry of the Kent Estate not two weeks ago. Two men had been counting them, discussing whether they had enough. It must've been something important. Alex realised that Dante hadn't seen it. Instead he was focused on a figure at the end of the room.

An elderly man in a sweater vest and brown slacks sat at a computer in the far corner. She could tell by the whiteness of his hair and huge bald spot that the man had to be in his late sixties.

"Welcome, Dante my friend," he greeted, still watching the screen. His voice was rather wheezy, and he had a harsh accent that was difficult to place. *A cross between German and Russian maybe?*

"Hello, Herschel. What can you tell me?"

"Very strange. Very disturbing. Werewolves in Sydney—who would've thought?"

"So you're sure it's wolves?"

"Oh, yes. Quite sure. I had to double check, as my DNA files did not include a Lycanthrope sample, but once that was done there was no doubt."

"How did you get a sample if they are banned from Sydney?" Dante asked.

"Samples are easy to come by. When I say sample I mean several drops. Anything more would alert "our" customs and therefore Vincent."

"Sorry," Alex interrupted, "What did you mean by *your* customs?"

"We have agents quite high in border protection, one that happens to be an old friend. I contact her when I am expecting something that might attract the attention of humans, and it simply bypasses them. Where did you get it your sample from?"

"I found it on the sheet of a hospital bed. This is my donor, Alex. It was her ex-boyfriend's bed. A vampire had injured him, making him a paraplegic. There was a power outage at the hospital. When the lights came on, he was gone. Clearly taken from his room, since he couldn't have left on his own."

"That's interesting."

"Why is that?" Alex asked.

"Because the sample you supplied me was not pure werewolf blood. It was mixed with human blood and human saliva."

"I don't get it. What does that mean?" Alex asked.

Herschel finally turned around and faced his guests. "It means that the ones who took your ex-boyfriend gave him weakened werewolf blood and most probably made him drink it. Enough to heal him."

"Heal him? Like the way vampire blood can heal? Does that mean Matt can walk again?"

Herschel nodded. "Probably. Werewolves heal themselves better and faster even than vampires, in fact, or any other species on the planet. What you need to ask yourself is why. These people were not amateurs. They knew exactly the amount to give him so his system would not be overrun. Perhaps they planned the blackout to coincide with their kidnap mission. That's an awful lot of trouble to go through for some random human."

"He does have a point," Dante agreed, looking at Alex.

Alex shrugged. "I don't have any answers, that's for sure. Although… Matt did get some phone calls for a while. I don't know who it was, but I guess they told him about the existence of vampires and how to kill one."

"Yes, I remember you telling me about the calls."

"I was convinced it was Julian who had phoned him. I mean, he hates Dante. But seeing as how Matt wasn't told the truth on how to properly kill a vampire, then maybe it wasn't Julian after all?"

"I don't know. That certainly sounds like Julian's style," Hershel nodded. "And she's right, he does hate you."

"The feeling is more than mutual," Dante replied.

"Well, I'm afraid I can't be of any more help to you. If you want to find your friend Matt, you'll have to find these werewolves. And to do that, you'll have to determine why and how some wolves have snuck in to Sydney. And do it fast before the pieces start piling up."

"Pieces?" Alex asked.

"You think vampires like Julian are the worst you have ever seen? Think again. Werewolves do not hunt for blood, they hunt for meat. Vincent made a lot of enemies worldwide for his stance on them but in my opinion, it's one of the few things he has done right. Unless they are driven out of here, when the full moon rises, believe me they will come. They cannot be reasoned with, and they will not stop. They do not feel fear or remorse. Fast and brutal. Swift and cunning. Soulless, viscous, primal predators. Yes, we can be cruel in taking blood, but they eat humans alive. I have looked into the eyes of only one before I killed it, back in Germany during the second World War, and could swear I looked into the eyes of evil itself."

Alex thought about Herschel's history lesson and wondered what werewolves could want with Matt. Why heal him if they were going to eat him? Why were they here? What was going on?

"What will you do?" Herschel asked Dante.

"The only logical thing to do: speak to the last person I want to see. I have to tell Vincent that Sydney has need of exterminators."

"Good luck," Herschel chuffed.

Dante shook his head once and made a face. "I guess it's the necessary thing to do." He bid Herschel farewell and walked back towards the elevators.

Alex wasn't quite done, though. "Excuse me, Mr. Rasmussen, can you tell me what this is?" Alex asked, pointing to the vat of blue liquid, curiosity getting the better of her.

Herschel lowered his face, and looked at her over the tops of his glasses. "It's just an experiment I'm working on," he said with a smile that chilled her to the bone.

Dante still hadn't bothered to notice, as he was facing the lift doors. He was probably too busy dreading the trip they were about to make. "Well…good luck with it."

The lift dinged its arrival and Alex stepped inside, relieved to be exiting the lab.

CHAPTER 4

WHO'S PLAYING WHO?

As the elevator doors closed on Alex and Dante, the doors to the lift next to them opened. A boy of no more than nine stepped out, walking hesitantly forward.

"Ah, Zachary, right on time! Come in, come in." Herschel beckoned eagerly.

Zachary did not move.

Herschel turned to him. "You do want me to help your father get better don't you?"

Zachary gave a barely noticeable nod. In response, Herschel patted the medical chair. Zachary reluctantly walked towards the chair and climbed on top, while Herschel busied himself by preparing a syringe of the blue liquid. He flicked it to remove the air bubbles. "You remember what to do don't you? Hold out your arm."

"Please, I don't want to." The boy was on the verge of tears. Herschel might once have felt pity for him.

* * *

Zachary and his father Dean were some of the few humans living in the apartment blocks, moving here after Zachary's mother Jasmine had been claimed by lung cancer. A short time later, Dean had been diagnosed with late-stage lung cancer and given a prognosis of just a few more months. In desperation, he had begun to seek out alternative medical treatments, and this is when Dean came to Herschel's attentions. Herschel needed more test subjects for his experimental tincture, and here was an opportunity that could not be passed over. He administered a dose of Dream State and instructed Dean to relax and imagine himself getting better. The drug put Zachary's father in a deep peaceful sleep, and when he woke, he claimed to indeed feel better. However, after a few days, he was struck by a violent coughing attack, filling tissue after tissue with blood-flecked phlegm.

"Find Herschel," Dean had instructed Zachary between coughs.

A frightened Zachary dashed upstairs to Herschel's apartment, begging for help. Herschel administered another, larger dose of Dream State. When Dean woke, he said he felt better than ever and declared himself in remission.

Herschel shook his head. "I'm afraid you'll need much more than a dose here and there, Dean. You're going to require regular injections for at least some time."

"No problem, doc. This stuff is worth any price you ask."

"Nonsense," Herschel chuckled. "I'm happy to continue helping in any way I can. Why not send Zachary up for your shot whenever you're ready and I'll come administer it for you."

"Really? I don't want to put you out." The gratitude on the man's face was a clear sign to Herschel. This would work out nicely.

"Oh, it's no trouble at all. Really, it's only a few floors down, and just minutes out of my day. I'm more than pleased to do it."

"Well, all right then!" Dean thrust his hand out and shook Herschel's vigorously. "I really appreciate it, doc. I wish you'd let me pay you."

"My father always said helping one's fellow man was a reward in itself."

Dean's smile faltered and Herschel hoped he hadn't gone too far. But then Dean shook his hand once again and Herschel knew it was fine.

"Thank you again. I'll send Zach up…?"

"Er, this evening would be fine. And then, let's say every third day after that," Herschel finished.

Dean gave an affirmative nod and Herschel departed.

That evening, Herschel had prepared an extremely large dose for Zachary's father. After several days, it was true that Dean was not getting worse, but nor was he getting better. In fact, he never even woke up.

In truth, the drug was not a cure for anything. Herschel had designed Dream State to allow vampires to dream. With brain activity unlike living humans, REM sleep was something the undead were unable to achieve. Herschel approached Vincent with his idea but needed one vital ingredient that could stimulate a non-living vampire brain: werewolf blood.

In humans, Dream State had an unforseen effect—the ability to control their dreams. All one had to do was think about what they wanted and when sleep claimed them, that is what they would see. Dream State created opportunity to live out any fantasy. Dean was imagining his life to be as good as it could possibly be, cancer free and no problems.

Zachary had initially been in a panic, but Herschel reassured him that his father was simply "sleeping off the cancer" and that he himself would take care of Zachary's needs while his father slept. Samantha ensured that Zachary received cooked meals and got to school on time, and in the evenings, Hershel invited Zachary up to the lab.

"How would you like to help me in an experiment?" Herschel decided it was time to begin. The boy had been coming to the lab for several weeks now and the fresh smell of his young blood was irresistible. He couldn't wait any longer.

Zachary nodded. "Will it help my dad?"

"It most certainly will. Hop right up into this chair." He patted the seat of a retrofitted dentist's chair and Zachary eagerly did as he was told. Herschel smiled. This was going to be easier than he'd first imagined.

* * *

"Now, Zachary, don't be selfish. I thought you wanted your father to get better. Were you lying?"

"No I wasn't," Zachary replied, shaking his head as tears began to trickle out of his eyes and choked-back sobs started to rack his body.

"You know what happens when he doesn't get his medicine. You remember don't you?"

"Y—yes."

"And there is a price for everything. Nothing in this world is free. This is how you can help your father. You don't want your father to die, do you?"

Zachary shook his head. Taking heaving breaths as he still struggled to stop his tears, he offered his arm, turning his head away.

Herschel's lip curled, his fangs extended and his eyes turned black. He bit down into the boy's tender wrist, growling and clamping his fangs down hard. He feed deeply, salivating over the boy's delicious virginal blood.

Zachary screamed. The louder he was, the harder Herschel drank.

CHAPTER 5

MOTHER KNOWS BEST

Five days previously

Alicia stared at the computer screen. Nothing. No news from the emissaries she had sent to Sydney. No news from the vampire king. She had sent multiple emails, each more and more tense than the previous, and still not one reply.

Her stomach tightened and acid burned the back of her throat. She chewed another antacid tablet, wishing the stress and the fear would go away.

Wilson had spent the last weeks attempting to teach Nicholas the ways of the Alpha: how to hunt and feed, and provide for his pack, as the Alpha was the only wolf that still had some semblance of self while transformed. Nicholas nodded throughout it all, trying to be respectful.

Alicia knew it was pointless. Even before other young wolves had turned, there was no comparing Nicholas's abilities with theirs. Nicholas could not run like the others, he could not climb trees, he was not unusually strong, as they were. Alicia knew Nicholas had no real interest in what his father was trying so desperately to impress upon him.

One evening, Nicholas had confided in her that he felt he was wasting his father's time, and even insulting him by continuing to try. Alicia tried to intervene, calmly asking Wilson to abandon his crusade, but he refused to listen. She knew she had to get Nicholas to safety. And that meant going back home.

Alicia couldn't help but think that something had gone terribly wrong with her envoy to Sydney. Only they knew of what she had planned, and so the thought of sabotage did not immediately come to her—but when it finally did, she did not dismiss it. Was this why she had not heard from the humans she sent along? She had instructed their leader, Calibos, not to alert her, in case their correspondence was seen. She knew if she did receive contact from Calibos, it would be fake, and that he was most likely dead. Any actual information would be gathered from the four werewolves' communication—or lack thereof. It was in her plan that the human contingent remain unseen and unheard, guaranteeing their safety, for a time at least.

Her mind was made up. She needed to get Nicholas out of London at least. Wilson's enemies viewed Nicholas as the reason why no decision had been made. She did not know whom to trust anymore, and with every day that passed, more of her husband's "loyal" men appeared to have their own agendas. If Nicholas was out of the way, Wilson would be forced to name a successor.

There was only one remaining alternative. Family. Alicia penned a letter, not trusting electronic communication. She gave nothing more than an overview of the situation, detailing only the fact that she needed safety for her son. She read it back, wishing she could add more understanding to the direness of the situation, but sealed it.

Who could she give it to? Who could she trust to deliver it to the post office? The more she thought, the more only one name came out to her: Creed.

She had to get the letter to Creed.

Outside the slightly open door of Wilson's study, Alicia heard Nicholas asking Wilson to review the status of the newest foxes—girls who were betrothed to the sons of potential leaders of the pack. She paused to listen before going inside.

The girls in question, Alice and Selena, were childhood friends of Nicholas. On more than one occasion, they had let it be known to Nicholas that they were not comfortable with the idea of their new life. He'd promised to talk to his father on their behalf.

Wilson had had a few too many glasses of wine. Had Nicholas asked her, Alicia would have told him to wait, but it was too late for that. Her husband responded bitterly that if Nicholas was the Alpha he could deal with it himself.

"Dad, enough! I am tired of this. I'm sorry you think I am unworthy of your name and that I've somehow shamed you. But I'm not going to apologise for being who I am. It's not my fault. Look, Alice and Selena are friends. I just ask if you would reverse the pairings of the foxes. They don't want—

"What? To live a life of luxury? To give their families a life free of debt?"

"They want the freedom to live their lives the way they choose them," Nicholas countered.

"Oh dear. Poor foxes!" Wilson mockingly lamented. "People around the world are starving, poverty-stricken, living off scraps and living paycheque to paycheque, flogging their guts out. All they have to do is what all women are built for. What they are good for."

Alicia, overhearing from the open doorway, bristled. This misogyny was not typical of Wilson.

"And what is *that* exactly?" Nicholas sounded offended, which gave Alicia a tinge of pride.

Wilson drained his glass and slammed it down on the table. "To stick their pretty little arses up in the air and give the world sons."

Peeking through the open door, Alicia saw Nicholas set his shoulders, jaw hard.

"And what exactly offends you about that, my dear boy? Have you forgotten you are a man and this is what we do? We conquer and possess. We purge and fuck."

"So you're saying you think of mum as nothing but a toy?"

Wilson faltered momentarily, alcohol preventing him from associating his wife, a woman he loved, with every other female he had generalised.

"Your mother's…different."

Nicholas had begun to walk toward his father and Alicia was prepared to interrupt the situation. What Nicholas would've said, what he would've done, was anyone's guess. But before her hand had reached the doorknob, Damien Creed—by his Alpha's side, as ever—stepped forward and placed a hand on the young man's shoulder.

"Easy, son."

Nicholas looked at his father's face, tired and red from drinking, and shook his head. "And you wonder why I don't jump at the chance to be like you." He turned on his heel and headed straight for the door. Alicia ducked quickly into another room.

"I will make sure the young man is all right," Creed said, leaving without giving Wilson a chance to stop him.

* * *

Creed caught up to Nick. "You should try and be more tolerant of your father."

"He has plenty of people being tolerant and not enough telling him what an arsehole he can be."

"Master Slade, I am serious!" Creed whispered harshly, stopping Nick. "Your father is desperate for you to claim your birth right because he is losing his support and the factions under his rule are headed for civil war. All of it hinders on the right of succession, and who he chooses."

"So tell him to just choose then! I could understand all this pressure if I was one of you, but I'm not. I'm so sick and tired of feeling like I am constantly pissing him off when there's nothing I can do to change it."

Creed considered this. "You really have no abilities? You're not just pretending?"

"No, Creed. I am seventeen and haven't had so much as a supernatural hair out of place. I'm sorry if that means I am less of a man in everyone's eyes, but that's the way it is."

Creed nodded. "Forgive me. I for one am only disappointed because you would have made a wonderful Alpha. Your temperament and maturity for your age are exceptional. Regardless, know that I am proud of the man you are becoming."

Creed offered a hand that Nick shook, and then continued toward his room. Creed did not follow.

* * *

Alicia opened the door of the room she had ducked into. She wanted to catch up with Creed before he got back to Wilson's study. Suddenly, the window beside her shattered, and bits of flaming glass flew in all directions. Alicia gasped in alarm. The shards struck wood and leather, and smoke began to penetrate the room.

In the corridor, she could hear sirens, curses and shouts. From outside came the Crack! Crack! of rifle rounds followed by screams of pain.

The estate was under attack.

* * *

Wilson heard them approach for about two or so minutes, but paid no attention, thinking it was all a drunken nightmare. Intruders and traitors! They were also cowards, attacking without the full moon where the Alpha is strongest of all. Then he heard a crash close by and jerked his head up, listening more intently. He recognised several of the shouting and cursing voices; one of them was Tobias Lee.

"The little shit." Wilson would make sure he had his head before morning. He opened his weapons cabinet. The door to his chamber opened and Wilson smiled without even looking, keeping his eyes on the various blades and rifles. Creed loved battle just as much as he did. They would have to choose some appropriately frightening weapons in order to scare Tobias and the others back into submission.

"Yes, Damien?" Wilson asked casually, slurring his words slightly.

"We have guests," Creed replied, hurrying quickly toward the cabinet.

"So I see. Well we knew this was coming didn't we? Still nothing like a good—" Wilson jerked with what felt like a hard punch to his spine. He slowly looked down to see the blade of a machete poking out of his chest.

"I agree," Creed hissed. "Why do you think I let them in?"

As Wilson fell to his knees, he gazed up at his friend. Words of hatred and shock were not enough, even as the life and strength to speak them poured out of Wilson. "Do not look at me like that. You think I have betrayed you. *You* betrayed *me*, and all of us, for years. I am taking what is rightfully mine. I have cleaned up your messes, *kept your secrets*. Should you have done your job and produced a worthy heir… but nothing from your balls resembles anything like a wolf. Yet you still would never think to announce me as the Alpha?" Creed leant back and removed his head with two swings.

CHAPTER 6

IT'S NO SACRIFICE IF YOU LOVE THEM

Alicia sped along the corridor, heart pounding, running past men going the opposite way—into the battle. "Defend the perimeter! Snipers to the windows and distribute the silver rounds! Time your shots and aim for the head only!" she cried.

Alicia stopped, closed her eyes and concentrated. Her sensitive ears picked up something beyond the fight outside—a slow but increasing swell of sound.

Thudding footsteps, bullets hitting flesh and pavement, barked instructions and exclamations from Wilson's men in the distance.

"They're everywhere!"

"I got one! Only a hundred more!"

"They're not stopping!"

Rushing to a window, Alicia saw the silhouettes of hundreds pouring over the perimeter wall and into the courtyard of the estate. Even with no moon, their wolf abilities propelled them along at impossible speeds. The two sides—those loyal to Wilson, and those not—clashed in a flood of screams and howls.

She hoped that Wilson had a plan, or Creed. She shook her head and started moving again, dodging the last of the men charging past, before barging into Wilson's chamber.

"Wilson, what—" She stopped abruptly. He was lying on the floor. The iron smell of blood and bone drifted into her nostrils. Alicia covered her mouth with both hands and turned around. She scrunched her face and pressed her palms into her mouth, willing herself not to gag or scream.

She took a breath and tamped down the sudden shock. She needed to determine what was going on here. The metallic smell had permeated the room to such a degree that Wilson must have been killed at least several minutes ago. That made it too early to be an intruder. Her instincts were right. They *had* been betrayed.

Clenching her jaw and balling her fists, she walked with quivering legs back towards the weapons cabinet, sniffling back tears, determined not to look down. She located an M16 rifle and extra magazines. When loaded, she slammed the cabinet closed.

Don't look down.

But her heart would not listen, and her face lowered to view what remained of her husband.

Her Wilson. He had not been what people would call a good man, but neither was he bad. He was…complicated. He'd been a friend, a fierce opponent, and a trusted confidante, and she had loved him. From the moment she looked into his eyes until now. Seeing them forever closed, when she still had so much to say, so much to regret. The pain ignited anger. She reached down and closed his eyes, saying goodbye with words she knew would bring him comfort, wherever he was.

"I'm going to carve your name into whoever did this to you."

"Mum?"

Alicia snapped her head around and ran to embrace Nick and keep him from seeing his father in this way.

"What the hell's going on?" Nick panted. "What happ—"

"We need to get out of here. Come on." She shoved Nick out into the hallway, slung the rifle over her shoulder and closed the door behind her. The two of them tore through the long hallways, Wilson's men turning their necks to watch them fly past.

"My lady…!"

"Alicia! What do we…!"

She ignored them all. The battle raging outside did not matter to her now. She could trust no one but the love of her life running next to her.

"They're inside!" a voice echoed.

* * *

Nicholas felt himself slammed against the corridor wall. He was about to protest, when a man, bounding along on all fours rounded the corner, heading straight for them. At least he appeared to be a man. Except his movements were much too fast for a human.

Alicia stood her ground and unleashed a furious spray of bullets that tore into the man's body. He straightened involuntarily and his pace came to a grinding halt, yet Alicia was relentless. More and more bullets pumped into him, blood flowing freely from his various wounds as he fell lifeless to the floor.

Breathless, Alicia said, "Remember, the only thing that can stop a werewolf is what?"

"Silver bullet," Nick replied without thinking.

"And why is that? Why not simply a knife or sword made of silver?"

"Because the silver must be heated. A blade would only work if you managed to remove the head."

"Very good," she replied, reaching into the back of her jeans, "Here is your prize."

Nick caught the pistol his mother threw at him one handed.

"Ever used one?" Alicia asked.

"We did shooting ranges," he replied, staring at the weapon. "They taught us the basics in school."

"Hope they taught you never to hesitate."

Alicia shouldered the rifle and marched forward. Nick, his mind a whirlwind of emotion, took a deep breath and followed. The woman that sung him nursery rhymes as a baby, that tenderly kissed his face no matter what age he was, had just brutally murdered a man in front of him. A man that would've ripped both of them to shreds given the chance. Nick moved past the splattering of blood on the walls and up to the dead man's torso.

At first, he thought he tripped, but as he went down on one knee, he felt a tugging on his leg. Digging into Nick's ankle with his fingers, the man opened his mouth. Two sets of fangs on the top and bottom of his jaw extended, inches away when the bullet fired from Nick's pistol pierced his skull, leaving a gaping hole at both ends.

Nick wrenched his ankle free and rose to his feet.

"Nice work," Alicia said.

"I thought he was dead."

"These," she replied, holding up the rifle, "Are not silver. Yours are."

Nick took one last look at the now-dead man. Eyes closed, fangs gone, a soft sizzling sound coming from his wound.

Mother and son continued. Bodies fell around them. Plaster and cement exploded on all sides, but they did not halt, sticking to the shadows and out of enemy sight. Nick did not need to ask where they were going. As they passed the long line of windows leading to the garage, Nick could see their target: the helipad. The Sikorsky, their best chance of freedom, looked untouched so far.

Alicia was careful not to fire at anything now, trying not to draw attention to them. When they finally reached the garage that housed Wilson's collectable cars, Alicia did not take long before spotting the one she wanted.

"Here!" she exclaimed, leading Nick to an armoured truck. She hopped in the driver's seat, finding the keys under the chair. "Someone is bound to spot us, so this is our best chance."

The engine roared to life and Alicia floored the accelerator, bursting through the garage door and speeding for the helipad. Within seconds, they heard the outside body of the vehicle pummelled with bullets; so many it could've been mistaken for a drum roll.

"Don't worry!" Alicia screamed over the noise. "I'll stop the truck right in front of the Sikorsky and block the gun fire from the chopper. Just jump in when I say!"

Nick nodded, gripping the door hard. The truck reached the plane and turned it broadside toward the estate and the shooters aiming for them.

"Go!" Alicia screamed.

Nick vaulted himself out and swiftly leapt into the cockpit.

"Nick!"

Alicia was on the ground, grasping for her dropped rifle, an arm wrapped around her throat. The attacker must have been on top of the truck. Nick jumped out and aimed his pistol when he felt a stinging blow to the back of his head. He fell and rolled several feet from the impact, his pistol flung away. Getting to his feet again despite the throbbing pain, he rushed to his mother to stop the man choking her. The one that had struck him belted him again and knocked him back hard.

"Pitiful weakling." His attacker turned his attention to Alicia and crossed his arms. "Snap her neck."

Two quick shots rang out. Both attackers fell down dead. Nick turned to find Sam the pilot leaning out of the Sikorsky's window with Nick's pistol in his hands and a dozen men far behind him pouring out from the estate on all fours, closing in fast. "Get in!" he yelled to Nick, sprinting to the driver's side. Alicia coughed, trying to get her breath back.

"Mum, come on!" Nick said, helping her to her feet as the plane powered up.

"The chopper only seats two."

"What?"

With no time to spare, Alicia pulled out the letter from her pocket and thrust it into Nick's hands. "I'm sorry it had to be this way. Sam will take you as far as he can. There is a bank card in the envelope linked to an account no one knows about. Use it to get to Australia! You'll be safe there."

"Australia?"

Alicia took cover from behind the van and unloaded the rest of her magazine at the oncoming horde, felling several but not slowing the rest.

"Be your own person. Know I love you."

"Mum…I—"

"Go!" Alicia screamed. Nick turned and did the hardest thing he'd ever had to do. He ran, diving into the passenger side of the rising helicopter, the sight of his mother reloading getting smaller and smaller. He looked up towards the house to see more and more men pouring out through the doors, heading straight for her.

"Sam, we have to help her!"

"We can't go back there. It's suicide. Her orders to get you safe are my priority."

Nick grabbed Sam by the front of his jacket. "She's my priority!"

* * *

Alicia tried to time her shots when they were in range, but she knew it was hopeless as she fired at the windows of the estate as well. All she could do was draw their fire away from the plane, still rising higher and higher.

She chanced a look at the oncoming enemy and emptied another clip; the ones behind the fallen just ran over the top of them to get to her. The ones she had shot originally were beginning to rise. She did not even have enough time to reload her last magazine when she heard several of them jump over the van's roof. They picked her up roughly, shoving her against the wall of the van.

"I bet you taste good," one said, licking his lips as the rest of them came into her view.

One beside him screamed and ran for cover, followed by the others as they scrambled. Alicia shoved the first away and leapt into the armoured truck, slamming the door.

The Sikorsky had returned, tail up, side propellers inches off the ground as it rocketed into the group of fleeing men, cutting their bodies to pieces and sending them sailing across the grounds. After a final sweep, the Sikorsky rose again and headed away from the estate, disappearing quickly.

Alicia opened the truck door and stepped into nothing but remains of the attacking werewolves, scattered around her for yards. She looked up into the sky, at the speck in the distance that carried her son.

"Goodbye," she whispered.

Two more men, one she knew quite well, approached her from the mansion. Both covered in blood that did not appear to be their own.

Alicia, feet set, glared at them.

"The new Alpha wants to have a word with you." Tobias Lee grinned. "So what's it going to be, bitch?"

Alicia lowered herself like a sprinter, snarled and charged towards them.

* * *

Nick leaned back in the passenger seat, relieved to know his mother was still alive, but he couldn't help wondering for how long. He took out the letter and studied the addressee, realizing it had been written out when intended to be sent via mail. Now it showed him who it was he had to count on for help. The one person in the whole world Alicia trusted with his safety.

Ms. Alexandra Hensley
4/2 Macintosh St, Mascot
Sydney NSW
2020
Australia

Chapter 7

Return Of The King

Present Day – Sydney

Dante wrapped his arm around Alex as she looked up at the mansion and gave an involuntarily shiver.

Dante gave her a comforting squeeze-shake. "You could wait in the car if you like."

"I'm not waiting out here alone for you. Besides, this whole thing concerns me too."

"It'll be all right."

"Are you sure? After what happened last time, don't you think it was a little too easy to score an invitation again?"

Dante shrugged. "That's Vincent for you. He probably couldn't resist knowing why I wanted to see him so soon. Curiosity is one of his defining characteristics. As well as arrogance."

He stepped forward and knocked. *Strange that there's no guard.* The door opened and Dante nearly started when Vincent himself stood there.

"Ah, Dante. Still as beautiful as ever. Come in."

Dante led Alex into the living area. Vincent indicated that they should sit before himself sinking into a huge leather armchair. He crossed his legs and put his chin on his fist. Waiting.

"Thank you for seeing us," Alex said quickly.

Vincent stared at her, appearing to be taking her in. "Well, someone's found her voice since the last time she was here."

Alex opened her mouth to speak but could think of nothing to say, embarrassment silencing her.

Vincent looked amused. "Or perhaps not. How does it feel to be finally *penetrated*?" he asked.

"Enough," Dante said, stepping in front of Alex. "Where is everyone?"

"The night is young. Melina is out hunting with Julian, I suspect. I believe it is their anniversary. They love to feed before returning here and pleasuring each other."

Dante closed and opened his eyes slowly, trying to let go of the anger Vincent was toying with. "I have important matters to discuss with you."

"So discuss them." Vincent waved his hand with a flourish, as if he had merely been patiently waiting for Dante to begin.

"What do you know of werewolves in Sydney?"

Vincent cocked an eyebrow. "You know my stance on them."

"That wasn't what I asked."

"True. Well if you must know, several weeks ago Clive received a computer letter from the Alpha of England, seeking asylum for two of the beasts. The letter proposed a meeting here with a small group of representatives."

"You surely didn't say yes?"

"I saw no reason to not at least hear the proposal. As you may or may not be aware, the British wolves are extremely wealthy."

That was one bit of the puzzle solved for Dante. *Money troubles.* Perhaps reducing expenses was the reason the guards were not at the door. Pausing to listen, he could also tell that the mansion was almost deserted. Some slaves must have been let go as well…or killed.

"I hope your payday was worth it," Dante said bitterly.

"Oh, get down off your high horse. The meeting never took place. The beasts never arrived."

"Either your measures to keep them out have failed, or you're lying. They are here, Vincent."

"What?"

Is it possible that he doesn't know? Dante quickly told the story of Matt's disappearance and the knowledge gained from Herschel Rasmussen. Vincent listened intently, his face getting graver and graver.

"Filthy dogs," he seethed. Rising, he moved to stand beside the fireplace. "They will pay for their deceit."

"What were your measures for keeping them out, by the way?" Dante asked.

Vincent turned his head so that he was looking not quite at Dante, but near him, as if visualising his answer. "Fear. Any that were found here were executed. My stance has seen a ripple effect across the country. There were a few cases in Alice Springs and one in Melbourne, from memory. The way we left their corpses sent shockwaves and outrage even through our world. Australia is a dry desert in their eyes anyway, which meant the threat of revenge was minimal. Most would never think about coming here for that reason, but it intrigued me to be asked permission," Vincent turned around and placed his hands behind his back. "You will be rewarded for bringing this to me."

"There's no need for that. I would settle for you using your influence to keep the authorities off Alexandra. She was questioned about her ex's disappearance."

Vincent nodded. "It will be taken care of. What else?"

"Other than that, you have been told, my duty is done." Dante tucked his hand inside Alex's and headed towards the door.

"Dante," Vincent called. "This may lead to war. I will do what I can to stop it before then, but if it does, do I have your support? Let us not forget, the vampire is their natural enemy, but not their source of food," Vincent said, eyes flicking to Alex and then back again.

Dante recognised the manipulation. Still, war with werewolves was a matter to be considered seriously. He did not take his eyes off Vincent. Finally, without delivering a verdict, he walked out.

* * *

Vincent smiled and jabbed the elevator down button. Stepping inside, he thought about what consequences a war could have for all concerned—especially humans. Yet he would not be a vampire king if he empathised too much with them. The best thing right now was that Dante had not refused him flat out. Though he had not agreed either.

Vincent might finally have his chance to ensure his best soldier returned to the barracks. Dante's usefulness—besides being able to feed off vampire blood, thus ensuring Vincent's ways of intimidation—lay in the fact that he would never be merely a yes man. These were invaluable when it came to maintaining power and control. So even if Dante's only reason for returning to fight alongside his king was to prevent any harm coming to his precious humans, Vincent would accept that.

He exited at the lowest floor, deep beneath the mansion. He walked along the corridor to a metal door twice the height of a typical one, and placed his hand on the palm reader beside it. After scanning his hand, the door slid up, opening into a pitch-black room. Only when Vincent walked in did the fluorescent lights switch on, revealing four occupied beds positioned in a star-circle.

All four occupants were in induced comas, IV tubes leading from a medical bag directly into the arm of each sleeping man. Vincent approached and ran his eyes over them. It was because of these four that Dream State could be made at all, because of them that the money would pour in from selling it. It needed one main ingredient for it to work, the only thing that could heal a vampire brain long enough to give it life before sundown bade them wake: Werewolf blood.

Herschel had first brought his idea of a dream-inducing serum to the king years ago. Vincent had been sceptical, but listened. Herschel maintained it could be made with the addition of pure, live werewolf blood. Importing such a thing, however, would raise too many suspicions. Vincent put the idea out of his mind, but when funds had diminished recently, the once repulsive idea started to generate appeal.

Then, as if on cue, he received the computer letter. The Alpha wanted to send peace envoys? *Werewolf* peace envoys? *Of course* Vincent would meet with them.

Not only had the werewolf representatives met with Vincent, they were still here.

Vincent had wasted no time in getting blood samples to Herschel, and Herschel did not disappoint. When Vincent experienced for himself the effects of Dream State, he ordered mass production.

When Herschel had told Vincent of Dante's inquiries, he had given Herschel permission to reveal what the sample was. He counted on the fact that Dante would be so consumed with concern for his beloved humans that he would come to him for further information. The story of just how Dante had obtained the sample of werewolf blood, and the disappearance of this Matt person from the hospital, was something Vincent had not previously known. This, he hadn't seen coming.

"Well played, Alicia," he breathed, running his fingers along the bag. "You sent more representatives than you led me to believe. You lied to me. Rest assured, I will find the rest of your mutts and spend a month breaking them into Schmako dog treats. Sydney is mine."

* * *

Dante pulled up outside Alex's apartment.

"Well I suppose that wasn't too bad, huh?" Alex asked.

"I'm not so sure." Dante turned off the ignition and looked pensive.

"What do mean?"

"Vincent was a little too casual about the whole thing. I think he knows more than he's letting on."

"Hardly a surprise. What will you do now?"

"There is little I can do. When they are not transformed, a vampire can't tell the difference between a werewolf and a human. The scents are the same. Only a werewolf can recognise its own kind."

"What else do you know about them?" Alex unbuckled her seat belt and turned sideways in her seat, facing him.

"Only what I have read. Werewolves can be born or bitten. Apparently, those born as werewolves have stages of development. They don't 'become' at a specific point in time; it is different for everyone. Generally, though, it coincides with puberty. Those created by biting, on the other hand, have exactly one month before they change. The next full moon."

"And what do they change into? Actual wolves?"

"Hardly. Such creatures are known as shifters."

Alex swallowed. "So…what do the werewolves change into?"

"The nearest I can place it, is neither wolf nor man, but what happens in the middle where they meet. An oversized human body with hair, claws, teeth and a vicious streak."

"Lovely," Alex muttered.

"There are different classes of werewolves. The lowest is the humans that have simply survived an attack and transform within a month. From what I've read, they simply go to sleep and wake up with renewed agility and an unshakeable need to hunt. They don't die easily but also don't have a werewolf's full healing powers, so with enough bullets, they can be killed. Second are those born with Lycanthropy. It manifests itself during their teenage life, settling on them without warning when they sleep. They wake up with incredible strength, agility, and animalistic facial features and enlarged canine teeth. The next class seems to have all the strengths of the previous classes, but also much more body hair growth. This is a mystery class. The theory is that these are made up of those created by being deliberately bitten but not attacked."

"Why is that one mysterious?"

"Because once the full moon rises, all classes but one are slaves to their instincts and desires. They think of nothing except eating, mating and survival. Once their first change occurs, all of them can call on a few of their abilities whenever they wish. The strength and speed will always be with them, to serve and protect their pack, for example. But when the moon is at its highest, they are at their strongest. When the literal teeth come out, all sense of compassion and reason leaves them. They would not hesitate to rip their loved ones to shreds. This leads me to believe that the only class that could possibly bite without attacking is the last. This means that we really don't know that much about them, other than they have the added strength as well as full control of their mental capacity. This makes the final class by far the most dangerous."

"The Alpha class?" Alex asked

Dante nodded. "The deadliest of all werewolves. The longer the bloodline, the stronger they are. I have read about sixth generation Alpha's that could out run lions, for example."

"Sounds like fun," Alex whispered to herself. "And this is what Vincent wanted to bring in here?"

"Doesn't make sense, does it? That's why I believe there is more to this than we know."

Alex looked at the car clock. "You want to come up?"

Dante smiled. "I'd love to, but I have some research on this to do before sunrise."

"Kay," she said, leaning in. Dante closed the distance between them and she wrapped her arm around his shoulders. Her nose scraped the edge of his earlobe and brought in that amazing, citrus scent as she felt his fingers grip her hips. She twirled her fingers through his thick hair and planted a light kiss on his cheek. Dante pulled out of the hug, but paused as he came past her face and continued to hold her close, looking at her eyes. Then her mouth. Alex instinctually ran the tip of her tongue over her lips, "You sure you don't want to come up?"

Dante took a second, maybe two, but shook his head politely and backed away into his seat. He gripped the tips of her fingers and brought them to his mouth. With a small smile, Alex got out of the car.

"Tell your mother I said hello," Dante said, before driving off.

Alex reached inside her pocket for her keys. She didn't think it was a good idea to tell her mother much about Dante, actually. Even though Margaret had been a donor for Dante once, Alex hadn't felt comfortable admitting the entire truth about where she and Dante now stood. She admitted to herself that that was partially because she still didn't really know *how* to classify their relationship, and also because of the way Margaret had warned her about getting too close. Alex was now his donor, sure, but she couldn't help wanting more.

She hadn't stopped thinking about that bloody dream. It had felt so real at the time, and she was shattered to learn it was only a side effect from Dante feeding off her. Even though nothing happened, the fact that Alex had been visualising Dante doing things to her that no one else had ever done, and that *she was letting him*, both freaked her out and made her smile to herself.

Alex had always enjoyed sex with her first guy, and then again with Matt, but it had never really been something she *craved*. It was only ok. It had never been mind-blowing the way Lauren used to describe it, or that she had read about in those crappy BDSM *Twilight* rip-offs that were all the rage with housewives. She could ramp things up on occasion, and would do different positions, but kissing in missionary with someone she really loved was what she liked best. It was nice, and safe. The idea of danger and just being "fucked" like Lauren enjoyed, had always been weird to Alex. Or so she thought.

The things that Dante did to her in that dream…with his tongue…his fingers…the way her body shook from the force of his thrusts. Alex shook her head to clear it. Too much thinking about that might get her a little weak at the knees. But knowing it wasn't real made her wish all the more that it was.

Alex knew Margaret was just worried about her, which is where the warning came from. But even though Alex's mother had never had a sexual relationship with him while she was his donor, could it be possible that she too had desired Dante the way Alex did now? Alex knew her mother loved her, but she also realised there was a lot she didn't know about Margaret.

She looked around, breathing in the still, peaceful night air. Strangely enough, she didn't feel frightened for herself, but she did fear for the rest of the city and the chaos that would ensue if the werewolves were not found. And what the hell did any of this have to do with Matt?

She approached the outer door and stopped. A young man was sleeping on her doorstep, his shoes under his head. He didn't look homeless, not by a long way. He wore a leather jacket and jeans, and the shoes he wore were actually Colorado boots. She looked again at his rather boyishly handsome face, twitching in his uncomfortable sleep.

Alex knelt down over him, feeling an irrational feeling of warmth over this boy, this stranger that looked so familiar. "Hey there. You lost?"

The boy woke and looked up at her. At first, he made to return to sleep but then woke properly and sat up, taking in Alex's face and hair.

"My apologies," the boy said with a cute little proper British accent. "But would you be Alexandra Hensley?"

"Yes," Alex replied, slowly. "What can I do for you?"

"I uh…was asked to give this to you," he said, handing her a letter.

"I don't understand," Alex said, taking it from him. "Asked by whom?"

"Alicia Slade."

"But I don't know anyone named—" Alex stopped trying to open the letter. "Oh my god," she stared at the young boy carefully, barely believing she was going to ask the question.

"Nicholas?"

He nodded. "Actually, I prefer Nick."

* * *

Nick devoured the second of two toasted ham-and-cheese sandwiches as Alex read the letter.

Dear Ally,

I can't begin to describe how sorry I am that I let things go so long between us without contact. I'm even more sorry that the first time I do comes with my asking for your help. I wouldn't if it weren't an emergency but really it's for Nicholas. Things are bad between Wilson and his associates. Really bad. I can't really go into detail, but it's gotten so that Nicholas is in danger and you're the only one I can trust; the only family he has away from all of this. I need you to look after him for a while. I've organised for him to start year 12 at St. Andrews and wired them the full year's tuition fees, but hopefully it won't take that long to sort this out.

I know I'm asking a lot and being cryptic—once again I'm sorry. It's better for everyone if you don't know everything about what's going on.

Please try to understand.

I love you cuz,

Alicia

Alex put the letter on the table. "You must've been hungry."

"Haven't eaten for a while," Nick smiled. "Thank you."

"Shhh, not so loud. You're welcome."

"The other woman who lives with you?"

"Yes, my mum. How did you know?"

"I will have to apologise to her as well. I used the intercom and woke her up. She wasn't pleased to have an unknown male downstairs at four o'clock in the morning asking after her daughter."

"Did you tell her who you were?"

"Seeing as though it wasn't you, I didn't know what to say. How do you and my mother know each other?"

"She's my cousin. The last time I saw your mother face to face, she was heavily pregnant with you, telling your grandmother, my aunt Maureen, that she was leaving for Europe. This did not go down well as your mum was only sixteen and was asked to choose between your father and her family. She chose. It broke my heart for her to have to leave like that. Even though we were cousins, we were like sisters."

"You lived together?"

"I lived with your grandmother since I was a baby. Back then my mum had to…" Alex trailed off. The memories of what Margaret had gone through, dealing with a vampire killing her husband and having to send her baby away for fear of further attack. How would he even understand without thinking she was crazy? "…Well it's complicated. Anyway, Alicia told me in secret that she'd met a man on a school trip to Melbourne. Then several months after that, she informed your grandparents and me that she would be leaving for Europe with him, the father of her unborn baby. That was over seventeen years ago and I haven't seen or heard from her since."

"I never knew anything about this," Nick said, looking disturbed. "How did you know who I was?"

"Your mum had the prettiest blue eyes I have ever seen. You have the same eyes, same hair. It's uncanny."

"How did you know my name?"

Alex smiled and shrugged at the ease of the answer. "She always said she would name her first son Nicholas."

Nothing was said for some time between the two, but finally it was Nick who broke the silence. "I am really sorry for having this put on you. I know it's not fair and it doesn't make sense."

"It might help if you filled in the blanks for me."

"It's complicated," Nick replied, grinning crookedly and using her own line on her.

Alex nodded, realising that was all she would get. "I understand. Well, look, it's really late. Why don't I make up my old roommate's room, and we can see about getting your school things tomorrow?"

"You're letting me stay?" Nick asked.

The hope in his voice touched Alex. "What else am I going to do?"

"Given everything, I don't know. I'm just…grateful. Thank you so much."

Alex ruffled his hair and the young man giggled, relief practically oozing from him. This really was Alicia's last resort and Nick knew it too. "Hey, come on. Of course! We're family."

Chapter 8

A New Start

Nick walked into the St. Andrew's administration office. The walls had been painted in a teal and pale-green colour scheme, giving the whole room the feel of a doctor's waiting area. As he approached the front desk, the receptionist looked up.

"Yes, young man? What can I do for you?" She folded her hands on top of each other on the desk.

"Hello. Um… This is my first day and I don't know where I have to go." He felt nervous and uncomfortable in his grey tweed uniform. It didn't fit him quite right—too baggy in some places, too tight in others—but he refrained from tugging at the fabric as he stood before the prim woman.

"Oh? Well then, welcome," she replied brightly, thumbing through some files in front of her. "Mister Slade?"

"Nicholas Slade. Nick, actually."

The corner of her mouth twitched upward. "Of course, Mister Slade. Principal Parkins will be right with you."

Almost as if on cue, a tall man opened the office door and stepped out to greet him. Rather heavy and with a thin beard, he looked quite friendly as he offered his hand, which Nick shook.

"Good morning, Mister Slade, and welcome to St Andrew's. Allow me to show you around."

Nick was flooded with relief. The receptionist and principal had been welcoming so far, and it put him at ease. He'd been dreading this day for the past week, despite all the help from Alex and her mother Margaret. They'd been nothing but kind, helping him with registration and purchasing school supplies, but it had been clear they were still curious about what had happened that had prompted his mother to send him to Sydney in the first place.

Nick felt extremely guilty that he could not be entirely honest with Alex and her mother, given they had taken him in so readily. But he knew knowing would cause more harm than good. He also knew that their patience would only last so long, and he would have some tough choices to make when that time came.

Still, right now he had other things on his mind. As he began his tour, Nick took stock of St. Andrew's and decided he could really grow to like it here. With nearly a thousand students, both boys and girls, it was one of the few schools in Sydney that went from pre-school to year 12. This meant that the majority of students who were in his year had been at this school their entire educational lives, which Nick thought was very cool.

He was shown the basic facilities—computer lab, science labs, library, sports field, canteen, or "tuck shop" as the principal called it—and was introduced to various handfuls of students and teachers along the way and so on.

Everyone seemed much less concerned with class systems and much more…real than the kids he'd encountered at Albert Hall. This school had the kind of character and life that he had always wanted to experience. It was rustic, put together in bits and pieces, and seemed to have been updated in the same way, by people with ideas and plans for the betterment of the students, and who did the best they could with what they had. Nick admired that.

"Well, that's about it. Oh, well no, one more thing." Principal Parkins led him to an open door, the last along the corridor he was on. "Hopefully, a place we won't need to see you in much," he said, gesturing to the sign next to the door: First Aid and Counsellor's Office. "Let me just see if anyone is in," he said, knocking on the door. "Hello?"

Nick stepped in just as a happy-sounding voice said, "Hello back."

Nick caught sight of a buxom beauty crossing the room. She swept her long brown hair into a quick pony-tail with curvaceous arms, and then picked up a bunch of files from a low table. She sashayed past the two men and placed the files on the desk before turning around to face them. Nick felt a hitch in his breath as he lowered his eyes slowly, taking all of her hour glass figure in, from her luscious rounded hips and thighs to her lovely full bosom.

"Ah, Miss O'Brien, good morning. Is Mrs. Davies in?"

"Good morning! No, I'm afraid she called in sick today."

"I see. Well, I just wanted to introduce our new student. This is Mister Nicholas Slade."

"Nick," Nick blurted without thinking.

"Sorry?" The girl and principal said nearly simultaneously.

The girl blinked and leant her head to the side, expecting. Expecting what, Nick had no idea, not even aware he had to answer something, staring with his mouth half open. She was all ovals. She had an olive tinge to her skin, or maybe it was a tan, Nick wasn't sure. She continued to stare at him with big but not huge brown eyes and the longest lashes he had ever seen, but she started to smile. It was a curious smile, showing two front teeth that were slightly crooked, through a pursing of the lips. And her eyes sparkled above perhaps the most adorable dimples Nick had ever seen.

"Uh, hello," he said, in a voice barely above a whisper, holding out his hand. "No, I'm sorry. Nick. I prefer— Uh… My name… I'm Nick. Nick Slade."

Her smile grew bigger as she took his hand. "Hello, Nick. I'm Nicole." She spoke slowly and gave his hand a deliberate shake—Nick imagined she was trying to wake him up—before finally releasing herself gently from his grip.

"Ok then, son. Let's see about getting you to class," Principal Parkins said quickly. "And look, it's on right now. Just outside here. Physical Education. Take care, Ms. O'Brien!" he finished, leading Nick out of the office.

"You too, sir. Bye, Nick," she waved, grinning.

* * *

Nick got changed into his sports uniform, a singlet and shorts at lightning speed, not believing how foolish and bumbling he had been. What must she think of him? Hell of a way to make a first impression. But he couldn't stop thinking about her. Surely she couldn't be a counsellor—she looked no older than he was—yet the principal spoke to her like an equal almost. Oh well, regardless of how many questions he had, they would go unanswered. He'd been such an idiot, there was no way she'd be interested in talking to him again.

"Hey, new kid. Wake up!" a voice shouted.

Bugger this. She was just a girl. A very beautiful girl though. Some of the kids at Albert Hall would no doubt have called her fat, as anything above a size twelve was considered obese there. But really, Albert Hall kids shunned pretty much anyone unless they had more money than they themselves did. Even then, they were known to insult anyone behind their backs if they didn't fit their idea of perfection. Beauty there was considered only that narrowly defined "ideal" in the pages of the latest fashion magazine.

Nick felt Nicole had a woman's body, regardless of how thick she was. Hips, boobs and a bum. Nevertheless, he needed to forget about her for the sake of his sanity, and to avoid having a ball smack into his head. As the game continued, Nick fumbled and bumbled his way around. He began to run decoys quite a bit, fooling his opposition classmates if he was actually going to receive the ball or not.

The teacher's whistle blew. "Ok, take five minutes."

Nick jogged to the bubbler and heaped the cooling liquid down his parched throat. As he drank, he could feel both sides of his head pulse with a tension headache. He could've taken his shirt off and wrung it out. The other students were not sweating as much, but they were probably not used to the cooler grey summers of Europe.

The whistle blew again, Nick and his team now running in the direction of the counsellor's office. He found the speed of the game a bit better the more he played, evidenced by the increase in passes he received. When his team had to turn the ball over, Nick noticed they had a spectator. Nicole was watching the action, taking sips from a coffee mug.

It went back and forth for a few minutes, nothing really changing but then Nick got his chance.

He got the ball about thirty metres from the opposition goal line, and threw a fake, which his opposite fell for. The spiky black-haired teen was almost twice as broad and a foot taller, but Nick was faster. He dashed through the gap his feign created. Nick easily outran the other boy and scored.

His teammates congratulated him. Even the teacher clapped. Nick looked as slyly as he could to see if Nicole was impressed at all, but she was texting.

There was no time to get shirty about it. The next set, the ball flew toward him, and Nick passed the ball quickly. Just as he let the ball fly, SMACK! He found himself on his back, trying to gasp for air, sharp pain in his chest, the tall black-haired boy standing over him.

The whistle blew. "Hey Miller! What was that?"

"That's how I play football," Miller said, laughing.

"Elbowing blokes in the chest when they're not looking. Yeah you're a real pro. You pull a stunt like that again, you're benched for the finals!" The teacher stood over Nick and held out a hand to help him up. "You all right?"

Nick nodded, accepting the teacher's help to rise. He noticed Nicole watching him with her fingers clasped under her chin.

Nick closed his eyes, cursing to himself. Of course. THAT she witnesses.

"Come on. Five minutes left. Line up." The teacher blew three short, sharp tweets on his whistle.

Nick nodded and got back into line. Finally, Nick's team had the last play of the game. He spotted an overlap and sent the ball soaring out wide. Once the ball left his hands, he noticed Miller charging directly for him again, and time seemed to slow down. Miller had an almost crazed look in his eye as he barrelled toward Nick.

"Shit" he sneered to himself, seeing the taller, stronger-looking boy heading in his direction. Nick made to step aside but regardless, he was going to get flattened again.

Just then a voice cracked through his mind like a bolt of lightning. *No. Stand still.*

Without any real time to think, Nick stood his ground, Miller still coming at him with a full head of steam. The bigger boy crashed into Nick with enough force to send him several feet back. But Nick didn't fall. In fact, he barely felt a thing, while Miller, with a grunt like he had slammed into a brick wall, crumpled to the ground in a heap. With an unfamiliar charge of adrenaline, Nick took his turn to stand over Miller. Surprise turned to a small sense of satisfaction. Nick hadn't been this fired up since Wilson had insulted his mother.

"Ok! Time to hit the showers! Miller…get up."

Nick stepped over Miller and followed the rest of his class to the shower room. A small tiled room with just six showerheads hanging from the ceiling and a tap with a hose attached. The view left a bit to be desired, but Nick didn't care. He stripped and walked in as water poured from each showerhead. He stepped under one and was jolted by the icy water. 'Damn, is this imported directly from the arctic?' He thought.

"Hey, new kid…"

Nick turned as an opposition player stood behind him, extending his hand. Nick shook the water out of his eyes and took it.

"Nick."

"Yeah, okay, cool," the boy replied dismissively. "I'm Jason. Look, I wanted to apologise for Miller out there. I'm his best mate, and I know he can get a little hot headed."

"He sent you to say sorry?"

"They had to help him to the first aid room. He was suffering dizzy spells or something. You got him a good one."

This struck a chord with Nick. "What? I just stood there. Look, I hope he is ok. If you see him before I do, tell him no hard feelings, yeah?"

"Yeah sure, bro. Will do."

Nick stepped out from under the showerhead as Jason took his place. Nick noticed others chancing glances at the two of them, but he just draped his towel around his neck and ignored them.

"Oh, by the way." Jason looked at Nick as he poured shampoo into his hands and rubbed it into his hair. "Just a friendly message that Miller wanted me to pass on: Stay away from Nicole."

Nick stood there dripping wet. "Is she his girlfriend?"

"Not exactly. It's just that he has been trying to nail her for years, and everyone in the school knows it. Thick chicks do way more in bed, they say, right? And Miller wants to tap that and find out if it's true. So, you know, 'bros before hos' right?"

"For years, huh? Sounds like she's not interested. Maybe we should let her decide who she likes."

Jason stepped out of the shower and stared at Nick, no longer jovial. "Kay, maybe you're not getting it coz, you know, you're British or whatever. So I'm gonna make this real clear. Stay away from her. If not, you'd better watch your back. He can get really mean."

Nick snorted. 'Sounds like just the sort of guy she should sleep with,' he thought, but to Jason, he only replied, "Whatever."

"Let's go!" yelled the gym teacher. "Time for your next class! Get a move on."

* * *

As the bell rang for the end of the day, Nick walked out of the grounds feeling that his first day hadn't been too bad. His other classes had consisted mainly of things he'd covered in Switzerland the previous year. His teachers didn't seem to think he'd have any problem catching up with the rest of the students.

He met some nice people, both male and female. Maybe they weren't all friend material, but they could maintain an intelligent conversation without it always referring back to money, which made a refreshing change. And he also met some dickheads. He had not seen Miller or Jason from the time he stepped out of the shower and back to class. He had a feeling that the fewer times their paths crossed over the year would be better for everyone.

"Hey, Nick! Hey!"

Nick turned to see Nicole walking quickly along to reach him. "How was your first day?"

"Ah, good! Thank you for asking." His stomach did small flip-flops as he tried to maintain his cool.

Nicole laughed, giving a little bow and a flourish of her hand. "Oh, well, sir. It is absolutely my pleasure."

Nick giggled, enjoying her teasing. "Yeah yeah," he replied with a sheepish smile.

"See you on Thursday then?" She leant in a little closer. "By the way," she whispered, "that was a sweet hit."

Just like that, she continued on, leaving Nick with that same fluttering rush of adrenaline somewhere in his chest.

Turn around.

That commanding voice again, the same one that told him to take the hit from Miller. Nick listened to it, turning his attention to two figures at the entrance gate. Miller and Jason were leaning against it. Nick made a good bet with himself they had seen the whole exchange. An exchange that pretty much ignored the warning Nick was given. Jason was shaking his head in disbelief; Miller just stared.

Knowing he had made two fresh enemies, and knowing there was nothing he could do about it, Nick just smiled and waved.

Chapter 9

A Dish Best Served Cold

Lauren stared at the ceiling. She had never seen a chandelier with rubies instead of crystal. Red, it must just be a vampire thing. Even though she no longer needed to breathe, let out a sigh anyway.

She had been alive for twenty seven years and dead for about six months. She had never understood the whole vampire craze that gripped women from the books and movies. So many fan girls would love to be in her position, she guessed: immortal, strong and young forever. No sickness, no death. She was probably one of the most enviable women in the world.

I am so fucking bored.

The superpower of newborn vampirism had worn off months ago and, since then, she had spent the majority of her time as a vampire in this room, waiting to be fed from a vein slave. Night after night, her stupid routine never changed.

She had been placed here following her altercation with Matt. Ok, so *altercation* was putting it a bit mildly. She'd broken Matt's back and almost killed Dante with her suped-up newborn rage. That had resulted in an impromptu meeting with Vincent, and he had told her he would find use for her.

He'd seemed pissed, yet impressed. Lauren got the idea though, that it was more the former than the latter. Being locked in here for so long was her punishment. What was the use of eternal life if you spent it in one fucking place?

Her hearing suddenly picked up something now. Footsteps outside. Actually a few of them. Maybe more than ten or so. The house must have guests. One of those guests might be getting closer; she could hear someone coming down the hall.

Her door opened and Clive, the hacker that worked for Vincent took a step forward. He cleared his throat and looked at the ground. "Um… I've been asked to get you."

Oh, great! "So he sends you? What did I do now?"

Clive still couldn't raise his head. "Uh… I—I don't know."

"Bullshit," Lauren spat, rising. Clive, ever the coward, jumped at the speed she used. She smirked and feigned a lunge toward him, making him jump again. "So where are we going then, lackey?"

"Downstairs. The dungeons. That's all I know."

"You're a shitty liar," Lauren said, rolling her eyes. She moved swiftly passed him and out the door. "You better not stand too close. If I die, I'm taking you with me."

Clive heeded her words and walked a few paces back. Lauren walked down the main staircase, turning towards the dungeon. As she swept through the dungeon corridor, she came face to face with Julian. Everything around her was an almost blinding white, walls, floor, ceiling. They stood in a hall with four closed doors on all sides. Clive had not bothered to follow. She was alone with Julian.

"You sent for me?"

"I did."

Lauren stood for a good while, waiting for Julian to break the silence. After several moments, she grew impatient. "So, are you gonna tell me what's up, or what?"

"Kneel."

Lauren gave a whisper like chuckle. "No offense, mate, but the days of me getting on my knees are long gone. Especially not for y—"

He words cut short, Lauren was buckled over by a sharp backhand. It had happened so quickly, she barely noticed blood from her torn lip splatter against the wall. Within seconds, the shimmering red stain was soaked into the whitewashed wall, as if the surface had drunk it in. Lauren scrunched her eyes as the force of Julian's grip squeezed her throat, his strength lifting her off the ground.

"You are an enigma," Julian said, furring his eyebrows as with a more flick of his wrist he sent her into the wall, "Thinking that you can speak to me in such a way, in my domain. I, who have done so much for you."

Lauren gathered herself and wiped some of the blood trickling out of her mouth with the back of her hand. "What the fuck have you ever done for me?"

Julian suddenly had keys in his hand, as if swiped from thin air. He gestured to the door, nearest his right side, "Come forward and see."

Lauren paused as he opened the door.

"If I wanted to kill you, I would have done so long ago. Though it is still very much an option, given your attitude." Julian frowned imperiously at her.

Lauren poked her head around the corner of the doorway. Within the room was a cage, roughly eight feet high and enclosed, filled with three men standing huddled together.

"So what the hell is this?"

"Many things," Julian replied wistfully, glancing over the cage. "Let's start with money for me, revenge for you."

"Revenge?" Lauren asked. "What revenge? I'm not killing some strangers for you to make money."

"Ah, that's right. You've never been properly introduced. But they know who you are. They also knew Ryan Teeran."

Lauren jerked her head back toward Julian, piecing things together. Ryan, her former boyfriend, who had sold her out to the vampire community for money. Ryan, who had filmed them having sex and posted the videos online. Not just any website, his own personal dark fantasy website. Where people would bid on different subjects and what should be done to them. In her case, it was to be transformed, but first being fed on during sex. She remembered something Ryan had said once. "Three guys feeding on you at once."

Lauren focused harder on the occupants of the cage, taking a step forward, lowering her chin.

"Them?" she asked Julian, not keeping her eyes off the cage. She didn't recognise their faces, but something about the way they slinked back, putting more distance between her and them, told her what Julian said was true. Or maybe it was the way they all looked at her, each one with the same sense of rage and yet…regret? *No, fear.* Lauren stepped closer and curled her fingers around the bars.

"It took me a good while to find them all, but once I did, I thought they would do nicely for our little game," Julian said, beginning to encircle the cage, trickling the key along the bars as he went.

"What game?" Lauren seethed, as hatred from the pit of her stomach started to boil. Julian prattled on; he had bet money with the other occupants of the house… These prisoners would be released into the grounds… Lauren would be timed hunting them… Julian had bet seventeen minutes…

Blah blah blah. Lauren barely heard or cared. They hadn't turned her, but they had helped violate her. Fed off her while she screamed for help; salivated over her taste, celebrated her tears as levels of accomplishment. *Only to wipe my memory and have at me again a few days later.* They were predators, having broken her down, viewing her as their entertainment.

Lauren slammed her palms against the bars and screamed as her fangs extended. Her throat ached as a crackling gargle escaped from it, something like the low, rumbling growl of a cougar. The three men gave a short, collective shudder even as their own fangs snapped out, challenging her. The sound strengthened her, reminding her that she was no longer human. Human and society's rules did not apply to her. She was a predator too.

"Ready?" Julian asked.

"Wait," Lauren said, letting go of the metal. "What do I get after this?"

"What do you *get*?"

"Yeah. After I turn these cunts into she-males, what then for me?"

"What more could you possibly want besides revenge and to ensure my happiness?"

Lauren rolled her eyes. "Hey, that's really great. I want freedom. I'm sick of you keeping me trapped in this place and barely feeding me."

"What makes you think you are trapped? I barely feed you? As a human, were you such a useless, disease riddled whore that you can no longer function unless a man presented you with treats after your holes had been used?"

"What the fuck did you just say to me?" Lauren felt her muscles grow rigid with rage.

Julian laughed out loud. "You think anyone will stop you from leaving? You are drastically mistaken. Leave if you wish. Go. The night is waiting for you. So are the sun and the hunters. What will you do? Where will you go? You've lost the only friends you had. Your family thinks you're dead, and to all intents and purposes, you are. But go to them. Go to your parents who have undoubtedly moved on with their lives. They will know what you are eventually, and then we will come for them. My father's word is law; they join us or die. Oh, yes, young one. You will leave and discover you cannot survive without us. This shelter. Our home—your home."

Julian closed the distance between them and indicated the prisoners in the cage. "Destroy them," he whispered hoarsely. "Win my bet, and I'll give you a generous reward."

"How much?"

"Enough!" Julian placed one hand inside his sleeve and pulled out a small wooden container, almost like a small spice rack. In it were four small vials of blue glowing liquid. "All you have to do is take this to Luca at Coffinail. Tell him there is more coming. He will present you with a payment. Bring it back to me and you will have your share. If you survive tonight of course."

Lauren took the spice rack and pocketed it in her jacket as Julian unlocked the cage door. She took a few steps back, knowing she was supposed to give them a head start. With a flick of his wrist, Julian flung the door open and the three inside bolted out, disappearing quickly around the corner. Lauren had barely taken a step when she was halted by Julian.

"What now?" Lauren hissed.

Julian repeated his earlier command. "Kneel."

"Are you kidding me? You want to stop and fuck around with this now? What about your bet?"

"Teaching humility and one's place is worth all the money in the world," Julian replied.

Lauren turned her face to sniff in the direction of her prey. They were still in the mansion as the doors had probably been bolted, but still, she wanted some action. With a grunt, she lowered herself to one knee.

"Is this not simpler, to just obey?" Julian asked. He ran the tips of nails in an almost tender gesture down her cheek. "You have potential, but your *Aussie* spirit will still need to be broken it seems."

He stepped away and Lauren rose, moving towards the doorway. "Seventeen minutes you reckon?"

Julian nodded.

"I'll do it in ten."

You can break my Aussie spirit as it's giving you the finger, arsehole.

Chapter 10

Countdown

Nick sat fidgeting in the counsellor's office. Three days into his new school life, this was the time Principal Parkins had arranged for Nick to meet the school counsellor Mrs. Davies, after missing her on his first day. The door opened and a woman he assumed to be Mrs. Davies had walked in with a small boy.

"Hello, Mr. Slade. I'll be right with you," she said, before turning to the boy, stating gently, "Just sit there next to this young man, Ms. O'Brien will be here shortly."

Mrs. Davies disappeared around the corner, into her office. Nick caught the boy looking at him. The kid looked about eight or nine, no more. He was long in the body but there was nothing of him. Wilson would've said he needed a good feed. Curls of overgrown dirty blonde hair stuck out from under his school cap like weeds, the straps of his backpack were missing buckle, and his black shoes sported one white shoelace. *This kid's parents needed a serious wakeup call! No, I shouldn't judge. It's not my place. Who knows what his home situation might be?*

"Hey, buddy, my name is Nick. What's yours?"

The boy dropped into the designated chair and continued to stare unmoving, merely blinking away the question with the saddest expression Nick had ever seen. Nick didn't think it was that the kid was deaf, because he hadn't been looking at Mrs. Davies when she asked him to sit next to Nick. Better leave him alone. He doesn't seem interested in chatting, Nick thought. Something was definitely wrong with the poor little guy.

"Well hello there!"

Nick looked up from the boy to find the one person he'd been waiting to see, looking at him and grinning.

Like a reflex action, Nick shot up out of his sitting position, and managed to flip his chair over in his attempt at politeness. "Oh…uh…hi."

Nicole simply smirked, and turned her attention to the younger student. "Come on, Zachary," she said, taking him by the hand. She led the boy past Nick, picking up his chair on her way. "Let's go inside."

Just as Nicole disappeared around the corner, Mrs. Davies reappeared with several files and shut the door behind Nicole and Zachary.

"All right, let's see," Mrs. Davies said thoughtfully, seating herself behind the desk.

"I thought your office was in there?" Nick pointed to the room Nicole had just disappeared into.

"Oh? No, that's just an old broom cupboard we've converted into an office for Ms. O'Brien." Mrs. Davies spread some of the files out in front of her. "Well, Mr. Slade, let me first welcome you to the school. And I apologise for starting late."

"It's no problem." Nick smiled.

"It's always nice to have some international flavour to our student body. I understand you're from England?"

"I am, yes, but my mother is Australian."

"Ah, delightful," she replied.

She seemed perfectly friendly, but her words felt more like well-rehearsed lines than sincere thoughts. He got the impression that she had maybe once loved her job, but for whatever reason had perhaps fallen into a rut and now treated every student pretty much the same, just with slightly different, but recycled questions.

"Well, as you may or may not know, this is just a preliminary check to see how things are going with you and if you have any concerns or questions I might be able to help with. Does that seem clear so far?"

"Definitely," Nick replied.

"So firstly, let me ask, do you have any questions before we begin?"

"Actually, I was wondering about Nicole," he said, gesturing with his thumb behind him.

"Oh?" Mrs. Davies looked over the tops of her glasses at him, clearly taken aback. "Uh, I may not be able to help with this particular enquiry. What is it you would like to know? I should warn that I'm not really at liberty to reveal anything about her personally, if that's what you were hoping for."

"No, no," Nick assured. "It's just that I'm intrigued. She doesn't look older than me yet she is clearly not a student here. I was just wondering what her role is?"

"I see," Mrs. Davies said, nodding her understand and relaxing somewhat. "Well, I suppose you could say she is a counsellor's assistant, for want of a better phrase."

"Isn't she a bit young for that?"

"She's nearly twenty. She graduated two years ago and is currently studying psychology. She volunteers here on her days off to gain some experience. She deals only with the younger children in the school, who feel more comfortable talking to people closer to their age. She isn't qualified to diagnose problems, but she can bring potential issues to my attention and I can seek out any required solution at that point. She was one of the most popular Head Girls the school has ever had. The younger children love her, and feel they can trust her. Her initiatives helped raised almost $15,000 for them in her last year."

"Initiatives?"

"Like raffles, talent shows, fetes and the like, to help raise funds for the school. She's actually organising the school end-of-year party, I believe. But she's always gone above and beyond in helping others. Just last year, she called round to some catering and equipment firms and organised for better ovens and freezers for the canteen to be delivered. All in her own time, all for free."

"Wow! How did she manage that?" Nick pressed.

"We called it the O'Brien manoeuvre." Mrs Davies smiled. "She went to see the companies on the half days she had here and took one of the youngest children with her. I was never there, but from what she told me, it was always a lot more difficult to say no to someone face to face than on the phone. Especially if they had a cute child to introduce them to as well—one of the many that would benefit so greatly from their generosity." Mrs Davies laughed. "No one ever said no to her. Most were probably guilt tripped into it, to be honest, or admired her spirit, and others…"

"Others?" Nick asked.

"Were hoping to get a date I suspect. But that's none of my business. Unfortunately when some parents got wind of this, they made a complaint, so we couldn't let her continue." Mrs. Davies stiffened a bit, cleared her throat and jotted down some notes.

It was clear there might be a bit more to this story. Nick said nothing, wondering why at that very moment he felt such a sudden rush of anger.

"Wow," was all Nick could say.

"Yes, but we aren't here to talk about her, are we? Shall we move on?"

Nick felt the heat of embarrassment flushing his face. "Yes, of course."

"So, how are you finding the school so far? It must be completely different to what you are used to. I've only ever heard wonderful things about Albert Hall."

"It was a good school," Nick nodded. "It had excellent facilities, but it was never really my favourite place in the world."

"You had troubles there?"

Surprisingly, Nick found her question to be quite genuine now. Perhaps he had been too quick to judgment. She was likely just tired of saying the same thing over and over. One probably couldn't help sounding robotic and rehearsed. Now that she was faced with a potential problem, Mrs. Davies seemed to liven up.

Nick thought about his wording, trying to think about the things that really pissed him off about Albert Hall. "Annoyances more than anything, I'd say. I find most rich kids to be superficial and boring."

Mrs Davies lifted her eyebrows. "I hope you don't mind me asking, but, aren't you considered a rich kid?"

Nick gave a half-smile. "I suppose so, but I never felt like one, and I definitely hated being treated like one. I think that's one of the reasons I really didn't like going to Albert Hall. Students there are expected to act a certain way, even by the staff."

"What way would that be?"

Nick thought about this. "Like the world owes you a favour, I guess. I never fit in there."

"So are you saying you prefer St. Andrew's?"

"So far, very much so." Nick didn't bother hiding the eagerness in his voice.

"That's interesting. Most people who have had your experience wouldn't say the same, I'd bet."

"I'm not most people." Nick shrugged. "I think those who live with almost everything can learn a lot from those who survive with next to nothing."

The door to Nicole's office opened, and young Zachary emerged, closing it again behind him. Looking as dreary as before, he walked outside without a word. The bell rang signalling the start of the final hour.

"Well, if you could take these forms home with you to fill out and bring them back in tomorrow? Just for our records."

"No problem."

Nick made rather heavy work of leaving. He opened then closed his bag, eyes flicking towards Nicole's door before finally slinging the knapsack over his shoulder and walking out. She obviously wasn't making an appearance just for him. A few steps up the walkway, he found Zachary on his knees, several books splayed on the concrete. The boy's backpack had split.

"Hey there, Zachary. You need help? I hate it when that happens," Nick said, kneeling down without waiting for a response. He reached for the books and Zachary lowered his hands and let Nick assist him. Without a word passing between them, Nick re-organised the books and put them in the second still-intact compartment of Zachary's bag.

"There we go," Nick said, zipping it up for him. "That should hold till you get home."

Zachary took the bag and looked at Nick, confused. To put him at ease, Nick said with a laugh, "Hey, don't worry. It happens to all of us."

Zachary continued to stare with a look that was difficult to place, and then turned around slowly and walked away.

"That was very sweet."

Nick looked up and saw Nicole standing there, indicating to Zachary with her eyes.

"It was nothing," Nick replied earnestly with a wave of his hand, climbing to his feet. "He seems really down."

"Yes, he is down. Poor kid." Nicole walked past him, heading towards the main stairwell. Nick followed and matched her pace.

"Can I ask what the problem with him is?"

"You can ask, but I can't tell you," Nicole replied.

"Oh, of course," Nick said, shaking his head. He should've known that.

"May I ask why you're interested?"

Nick creased his brows. "I just…I feel sorry for him. I was just wondering if there was anything I could do."

Nicole laughed to herself.

"Did I say something funny?"

"You just seem so genuine," Nicole replied.

"And that's…funny?" Nick was thoroughly confused.

"No, just unexpected," Nicole replied. "Especially around this place and for a guy your age."

"A guy my age?"

Nicole nodded.

"Well, I dunno if it means I'm weird or what, but I've always had a soft spot for kids."

"You're not weird," Nicole said, placing a hand on the opposite side of his face, pressing his cheek against her lips ever so slightly. "You're lovely."

She continued on her way, not looking back at him. It was only a light kiss, but he was enveloped with the scent of her strawberry lip-gloss. He stood there in a daze. The adrenaline was back again. It was only on the cheek, but Nick wondered if she was this friendly to everyone she met.

He wandered past the restroom, heavily in thought, when he was blindsided from inside by a punch. Nick scrunched his eyes as the pain erupted and before he knew it he was dragged inside and thrown to the cold floor.

"What a performance!"

Nick struggled to get up but was caught by a kick to the jaw. His body flattened from the hit and red spots floated in front of his eyes. He had barely moved when several lashes connected straight to his ribs and stomach.

"You obviously didn't get the message, so I'll tell you personally. Stay the fuck away from her. That is A-grade pussy and I got it reserved, you got it? I took it easy on you today, so consider this a warning. Next time I won't be so nice. Have a nice day, pommy mother fucker."

Nick rolled slowly onto his back, groaning and coughing. He rose slowly, firstly to his knees, gripping the sink to help him. He got to his feet and looked at himself in the mirror. A massive red mark was already flaring on the right side of his jaw and a small trickle of blood had started to flow from a slit in his eyebrow. Nick dabbed it with water, hissing in pain. He grabbed some squares of toilet paper and pressed them against his forehead to stop the bleeding.

* * *

"Oh my god, what happened to you?" Alex cried, getting a look at Nick's face as he walked in the door, moving over to him, gently checking the damage. The left side of his face was puffy and she saw some remnants of darkened, dried blood on his forehead. "Your school called and said you missed your last class. I knew something had to be up."

Nick waved her off. "It's nothing."

"Nothing, my arse. It looks like someone's been tap dancing on your face," Alex said, beginning to get angry. "Why the hell didn't the teachers do anything?"

"No one saw."

"Well, they will hear about it tomorrow! I'm going to go straight up there—"

"No!" Nick shouted, and then took a breath. "Please, no. It'll just make things worse."

"Don't worry. Alex will do the right thing," Margaret appeared from the other room. She turned to Nick. "Why don't you run yourself a shower, dear. The steam should help reduce the swelling."

Nick nodded to Margaret and squeezed Alex's hand briefly. It was only when he had closed the bathroom door did Alex reply to her mother.

"What the hell? Do you expect me to do nothing?"

"Of course not," Margaret replied, taking a seat. "I expect you to do the right thing."

"What is that supposed to mean?"

"You were going to do what? March up to the school and demand punishment? How often does that actually solve anything? Nick is right. All that would do is make things worse. You're a teacher yourself. You must recognise that."

"Yeah, ok, you're right. But there must be *something* I can do? I'm—*we're* supposed to be looking after him!" Alex hissed.

"Yes we are. My guess is it's over a girl and it isn't the first time Nick has had a run in with the guy. Nick seemed embarrassed but not surprised. In which case, it won't be stopping anytime soon. If we involve the school, Nick will look like a sook and he will lose the fight and the girl probably. We need to think outside the square to help him. I think you know who I mean."

"Dante?" Alex didn't understand how that could possibly help. "You want me to get Dante involved?"

"Of course," Margaret replied quickly. "Nick may need help from someone with a bit more…how can I put it, bite to them? Sometimes threats are all these teenage bullies understand."

Alex stared at her mother in amazement, having never heard her speak like this before. She didn't know whether she should be worried or inspired. A vampire against a teenage boy and her own mother was insisting on it? Margaret thumbed her daughter's hand with a coldness in her gaze as she continued, "No one messes with my babies."

* * *

Who the hell is Dante? Nick wondered, turning on the shower. *And why is Margaret so sure he can—or will—help me?*

Chapter 11

Blue Moon

The wolf opened its eyes and smiled. It was the dead of night, and the women in the house were asleep. The wolf could hear their steady breathing from here, which meant it was free to move about. Walking slowly over to the bedroom window, it looked out over the city, seeing the image of Nick Slade looking back. Small waves of sounds reached it, dogs barking, car alarms, idle chatter, all at once as its eyes roamed, looking through the reflection in the window. How the wolf wanted to open it, to run through the streets, to smell the scents of Sydney, to taste the air and the morsels.

The night was calling, yet the Slade boy resisted. It was too soon. If the wolf were to leap from the window, the fall would most probably break the boy's ankles.

The wolf had remained dormant inside for his entire life, waiting, calculating. Never having an opportunity to reveal itself, as the boy had never hunted, had never wanted, for anything—until now. His sudden desire for the female, and the rage at the school ruffian had awoken the wolf within him. For the first time, Nick craved something.

The wolf backed away from the window and returned to the bed. Now it was out, there was no going back. But until the boy was ready, it would have to be content to keep watching from afar, inside yet not in control. Waiting, ready for the day when Nick would embrace the beast and become who he was born to be.

* * *

Alex turned the sizzling bacon over and grabbed a plate for the toast that had just popped. She plopped cartons of fruit juice and milk on the dining room table, and thought about what her mother had suggested the night before. She had deliberately kept Nick away from Dante, but for the life of her, she couldn't even understand why. She had told Dante about Nick and the circumstances surrounding his arrival, and his reaction was hardly unexpected: one of surprise. He had said he would like to meet the young man, yet she kept on putting it off. Did some part of her want to keep the supernatural and natural parts of her life separate? She convinced herself that that must be it.

Despite the fact she agreed with her mother in principal about bullies needing a lesson from intimidation, she wondered if getting Dante involved would be stepping too far.

"Hey, hun, breakfast is ready," she called down the corridor. "Come and get it or you'll be late."

It wasn't long before she heard the sound of movements from behind Nick's door. She expected him to emerge half asleep, still stiff and sore from the previous day's fight, but he was quite springy when he entered the kitchen, and the swelling was surprisingly diminished. Could she have convinced herself it was worse last night than it really was?

"Smells great. Thank you," he said, sitting down and helping himself to some bacon.

"You're welcome." She put down a plate of toast and lifted his chin to get a closer look.

"Is something wrong?"

"No," Alex replied slowly. "Did you put anything on that bruise yesterday?"

"No, why? How bad does it look?"

"I can barely see it."

"Oh?" Nick replied. "Good! Maybe he didn't get me as hard as he wanted to, huh?"

"I guess so. I thought it looked pretty bad last night. Like some blood vessels had burst, maybe. Now it looks just a bit yellowish. You sure you're feeling ok?"

"Maybe it was the light. I feel great, I promise. Had the weirdest dream, though, but I can't quite remember it."

"Ok, look, I promise I won't nag, but did you want to stay home today?"

Nick shook his head. "No, really it's fine. It's only a half-day today, anyway. Don't worry so much. Don't you have to be at work?"

"My class is at camp for a week. I went last year, so I'm off this week."

"Ah, ok. Well, I'd better go. See you later." Nick rose and picked his bag up from the back of the chair he sat on. He kissed Alex, thanking her again for breakfast and left. Alex poured some coffee and sat down at the table. She laughed to herself. There was cereal, fruit, toast, bacon, eggs, milk and orange juice on the table and the only thing Nick had touched was the bacon. All of it.

* * *

Though he had seen Jason in the halls from time to time giving him triumphant grins, Nick had survived for the entire day without running into Miller. He had no Physical Education classes and hadn't ventured near the bathroom either. He was making a few friends, at least. Several of the boys he'd played touch football with on his first day had welcomed him tentatively into their group. He had seen Zachary as well, watching him from behind a pillar at lunchtime. Nick beckoned him over gently but Zachary had refused to move, staring with that same confused look.

No one had yet asked him about his bruise, which he found surprising. Either bruises were commonplace around the school or no one cared. Either way, he was grateful to have gotten through the half-day without needing to explain. He reached into his pocket, to grab his phone to check the time when he felt the forms Mrs. Davies had given him.

"Aw, crap!" He filled them out in a rush and dashed across the quadrangle to the counsellor's office.

"Hello?" Nick said, as he knocked.

"Well, there's a familiar voice."

Nick stepped inside, determined not to make a fool of himself in front of Nicole this time.

"Hi. I needed to give these to Mrs. Davies," he said, holding the forms up.

"She doesn't usually work the half days. But I can take them and give them to her for you," Nicole replied, holding out her hand.

"That'd be great, thanks," Nick said, handing them over.

"So, what happened there?" she said, leaning back into her chair, tapping her chin.

"I fought a door, and the door won."

Nicole pursed her lips slightly, "Must've been one hell of a door."

Nick smiled nervously as the silence between them grew. "Well…" he said, trying desperately to think of something to say, anything really. The school bell rang. If he was going to do something, he had better do it now. "Are you…busy tonight?"

Nicole looked slightly taken aback. "Yes, actually. Family dinner."

"Any chance you could skip it this once?" Nick winked, trying to be playful.

Nicole looked at him, raising her eyebrows disapprovingly.

Whoa, clearly not funny. "Ok, well, I will see you later then. Enjoy your dinner."

Once out of the room, Nick slapped his forehead with his palm. He clearly was not being very successful at this *not* making a fool of himself business.

He stopped in to Home Room, spending the requisite ten minutes at the end of every day so his teacher Mr. Daniels could see he *hadn't* skipped off early. Once he was dismissed with the rest of his class, Nick found himself in a hurry to leave. As he descended the winding staircase to the ground floor, he was shoved into the concrete wall.

"Should watch where you're going, dude," Jason said.

"Yeah, fella could get hurt on these stairs," Miller agreed.

Both of them chuckled and continued on past Nick. Nick remained in the same spot for several seconds as the rest of his classmates filed past him. No one bothered to ask why he was just standing there, but if they had, Nick couldn't have answered them. He could only stare at his right hand, balled into a fist so tight he was unable to open his fingers. His knuckles had turned bone white, and his muscles tingled from numbness. His hand began to ache heavily and he still could not release the pressure.

Hit something a voice said, the same voice that had told him to stand still when Miller had charged at him during the game. Nick struck his fist on his thigh with no result. *No, you have to HIT something. Something hard.* Without hesitating, without really thinking, Nick buried his fist into the wall next to him. His hand sank into the brick as easily as if he'd punched a cardboard box, the cement crumbling to form an almost perfect circle around his fist. Nick breathed in relief at the release of the cramping pressure. He pulled his arm back, finding he was able to flex his fingers freely. The only pain he felt now was from his scraped and bleeding knuckles.

He walked out of the school in a daze, trying to understand what had happened. His fist had curled the instant Miller and Jason had shoved him. He'd been completely unable to uncurl it, waves of rage rippling through him. The only way to release it had been to strike something, and that something had been solid brick. His hand should be broken, or at least bleeding a lot more than the slight abrasions on his knuckles. It made no sense.

Several car honks beside him halted his trail of thought. Nick turned to see a small, black WRX with tinted windows rolling along beside him. Nick walked over to the passenger side as the window rolled down.

"You off in your own little world there?" Nicole asked laughing. She had taken her sunglasses off and stuck one earpiece into her mouth. "I've been trying to get your attention for about ten seconds."

"Yeah, sorry," Nick replied, shaking his head before eyeing her again. "So…uh…what's up?"

"You wanna go for a coffee?" she asked.

"What, you mean now?"

"Well, as it turns out, my dinner was cancelled."

"Oh, cool!" Nick placed his bag in the back seat and climbed into the car.

"Buckle up!" she said, replacing her sunglasses in a smooth movement and sweeping out of the parking lot and down the street.

Chapter 12

Let The Beast Run Free

Nicole and Nick sat down at a café table in the local shopping centre, Westfield Eastgardens. She set her mocha down carefully, and he slurped a chocolate milkshake.

Nicole grinned. “Seriously, how old are you? Six?”

“I haven’t had one for ages.”

Nicole shook her head slowly, still smiling. “So what brings you to Australia?”

Nick grimaced a little. Did he want to talk about this already? He decided it wasn’t the time. “Family business. Troubles back home.”

“Really? What kind?”

“The kind that requires someone to travel half way around the world to escape, I guess.” Nick shrugged.

Nicole put on a heavy voice, “Sounds so serious.”

Nick looked at the floor between his shoes.

“Wait… *Is* it serious?” Her tone was concerned now.

Nick sighed. “Yes, unfortunately it is. It cost my father his life and I don’t even know if it’s over yet.”

“Oh my god. Nick, I am so sorry.”

Nick waved a hand. “Don’t apologise. How were you supposed to know?”

There was another wave of silence, but Nick did not pay any attention to this one. He could see Nicole taking it in, not merely waiting for him to say something.

"What did you mean by you don't know whether it is over?"

"Well," Nick began softly, holding his cup with two hands. *Maybe we're doing this now after all.* "I know what happened to my dad, but I don't know what happened to my mum. She could be dead or alive and I would have no idea."

"You can't contact her at all?"

"It's too dangerous. It's to do with my father's associates. They killed him and I don't know whether contacting her will put her in more harm's way."

Nicole leaned forward, placing her hands under the table. "Would they ever come after you here?"

"No. The whole situation started with the fact that I was not qualified to take over from my father, even though he insisted I was capable if not ready. This pissed off pretty much everyone that worked under him, since they all thought they were or knew of someone better qualified. But dad didn't listen, and that cost him everything. I'm still not qualified, though, so no, they won't come here. Whether in England or here, I mean nothing to them."

"So, if you don't mind me asking, what was the family business?"

Nick took a big sip from his milkshake. *How to answer this one...* "To put it in simple terms, he was looked upon as a kind of royalty, so I would've been following him into that."

"And you didn't want to do that?"

"The choice was taken out of my hands, so to speak. It was just never for me so I never even considered it an option. Instead of studying at the best schools money can buy to learn about leadership and responsibility, I learned what I could to help me become a paediatrician."

Nicole smiled. "You want to help sick kids?"

"If I could. I have a soft spot for kids. I would love to have at least four of my own one day."

"Good luck. Finding the right man can be hell." Nicole winked.

Nick snorted at her joke and finished his milkshake. "Now to you. How is it that someone so charming and intelligent is single? What dickhead let you go?"

Nicole frowned. "There isn't much to tell. My parents are Aussie but my grandmother is Greek. She set me up with my first serious boyfriend. I was with him till the night before graduation when I found out he had been cheating on me and even had a two-month-old baby with the other woman."

Nicole sipped her coffee, taking a moment. "Ever since then, I focused on my career, moving on and burying myself in work. It would be sad if I didn't love what I do so much."

"Mrs. Davies said you study Psychology?"

Nicole nodded.

"Tell me about that," Nick said, adjusting his seat and studying her carefully.

"Well I suppose you could say I have always wanted to help people with their problems. I think being any sort of medical practitioner is amazing," she offered, gesturing quickly to Nick. "But they mainly focus on the body, where I have always been fascinated by the mind. The examples I have read about which fuels the debate over the mind's power over the body is unbelievable. Mind over matter, as they say, turns out to actually be true. For the most part, western medicine and scientists are only just starting to catch up to what the eastern mystics have known for over two and a half thousand years."

"And that is?"

"That it's not our brain that gives rise to our consciousness, instead it's our consciousness, or mind, that creates everything that seems so real to us."

Nick winced. "Ok, look I know it would be a lot more dashing if I knew what you meant, but…"

Nicole grinned. "I'm not boring you? You really want to know?"

"I wouldn't ask otherwise."

"Ok," Nicole said, pulling out her phone. "Come here."

Nick got up and sat in a chair next to her. He put as little space as possible between them but enough so she wouldn't feel uncomfortable. To his surprise and delight, when she had found whatever it was she was looking for, she leaned against him, eager to show what was on the screen of her phone.

"This should help," she said, handing him the phone. "It's only short, but it is to the point."

He read.

We are all co-creators and fellow shareholders in the universe. We

have collectively created our circumstances through the medium of our own individual minds and under the dominion of the Universal Mind. And the play is woven so cleverly that we do not realize we are taking unreality for reality. We are lost in the world of our five senses and know of no other reality. We have performed the ultimate conjuring trick – we have deluded ourselves. Like the images formed frame by frame in celluloid upon a movie film and projected onto a screen, our life's destiny in the world is projected from within us. But we take the image on the screen as real and do not perceive the inward source. There is no without. What we see doesn't exist, what we don't see really does exist.

From The Secret of The Creative Vacuum by John Davidson

"That help?" she asked.

Nick took a deep breath. "Uh… Not in the slightest."

They both laughed in unison.

"Ok," Nicole began. "What it is saying is that the mind is an untapped resource. We believe what we see and that's all. There are so many things going on that people are just unaware of. I find a lot of the people and patients I talk to have come to me and said that if their psychologist helped them in any way, it was by letting them know they had the power to heal themselves. Most people don't know humans have that power. I honestly believe that we know very little of what goes on in the world, but also of what goes on inside *us*, which I find a much more interesting topic. Western society like I said is only just starting to catch up on things like meditation, the power of positive thinking, animal spirits, and such."

"Animal spirits?" Nick asked, his interest piqued.

"Native Americans believe that an animal spirit, like a wolf or an eagle, descends upon everyone at birth. It determines their personality. Its job is to keep the person safe, strong and wise as to excel in matters of attributes given to that animal."

Nicole finished her mocha and looked to Nick who stared back at her. "I can't believe you need to know all of this to be a psychologist."

"I believe I should learn as much as I can about all cultures and beliefs, even the things bordering on the supernatural. I think it would be hypocritical of me to dismiss anything. Besides, I'm a bit of a geek at heart and I find all of it fascinating."

"I find you fascinating."

Nicole turned to him. She gave a hint of a smile as she rolled her eyes and waved his statement away with a hand.

The sounds around Nick went quiet except for one noise pounding in his ears. A quick *thump thump* sound. Nicole didn't seem to hear it. Nick moved his gaze from the side of her face to her throat, where he could've sworn he saw a vein flare. Yes! There! The smell of strawberry lip-gloss and peppermint shampoo swelled around him as the vein flared again. Nick's mouth moistened as he continued to stare, unmoving otherwise, at her neck as the thumping continued and he realised it was her heartbeat. In his mind, Nick saw himself moving closer to her, smelling her even more deeply than he already could, letting her intoxicating scent overwhelm him as he moved his lips to her neck. He could see them interlocking their fingers, grazing her neck with his mouth and the tip of his tongue, and Nicole letting him. Closing her eyes, letting him taste her, really taste her, even as the urge to bite her supple flesh grew…

"Well, fancy seeing you two here!"

Nick was awoken from his fantasy sharply. He blinked several times, unsure of what the hell he had just seen. He had no idea why he would fantasise about eating Nicole. In other ways, most definitely, but actually wanting to consume her? And the fact that he was so turned on, he was glad his legs were underneath a table. The animal spirits that she had talked about, that had to be it. He had gotten caught up in her intelligence, her stories about the animal spirits, and with his family history, he had put two and two together and gotten fifty. It was a dream. That must be it.

"Hello Mr. Miller," Nicole greeted unenthusiastically.

"I've told you before, Nicky. Call me Trent." Miller grinned at Jason who had come up behind him.

Nick groaned inside. *Just my luck*, he thought.

"And I have told you before that I would call you Trent when you stop calling me Nicky," she replied smoothly.

Miller turned his head slowly and deliberately to Nick.

"You two know each other?" Nicole asked, eyeing one then the other.

"We've met," Nick stated, curling the fingers of his right hand down the edge of the table.

"Oh, that's right," Nicole said breezily. "I forgot. Young Mr. Slade here put you on your arse last week in...*touch* football, was it?" Nicole gave a deep, poignant sigh.

Miller laughed, but Nick could see it was false. "Well, we should be going. Enjoy your beverages, kids."

Jason and Miller took off behind Nicole and Nick watched them go. Miller turned around and walked backwards as he stared back at him, shaking his head slowly, mouthing the words, "You're a dead man."

"What a dick," Nicole said, not even seeing the exchange. "We better be going"

"Really?" Nick asked, not trying to hide the disappointment.

"Yep. I don't have the dinner to go to, but I do have to study."

They both got up and Nicole bent down to pick up her bag. She looked at the table leg where Nick had been sitting. "Hmm, didn't think these tables were as old and worn as that," she said, almost to herself as she turned and began to walk.

Nick looked back at the leg. Four deep greaves in the table ran several centimetres in and to the edge, just in front of where Nick sat. Nick had not noticed them when she had called him over to view her phone, and then as if a lightning bolt hit him he looked at his own fingers. *Did I..?* His fingertips looked perfectly normal. *Relax man, relax*, he thought to himself. He quickly caught up to Nicole, shaking the memory of scraping the edge of the table in fury when Miller had appeared. *Stop it. You don't have claws.*

* * *

By the time Nicole pulled up to Alex's apartment, it was well after sunset.

"Thanks so much for everything," Nick said.

"You can thank me by telling me the truth," Nicole said.

"I'm sorry?"

"Do you really think I'm that dumb? I study the mind. Body language is a part of it. I saw the way you looked at Miller. That bruise wasn't from a door was it?"

Nick breathed out slowly. "No."

"Why didn't you just tell me the truth?" she asked, a hint of disappointment in her voice.

"It's not exactly something one wants to admit to a girl."

"Oh, come on. I thought you were better than that macho bullshit. This is serious. You have to talk to someone about it, so why not me?"

"Because…" *We both want you. Macho bullshit is the sole reason,* Nick thought. "It's not a really big deal. It was an argument. I'm fine, really."

"Nick…" she said softly, touching his bruised chin with just her fingertips. Nick was perfectly still, trying not to concentrate too much on the warm feeling he had from her slightest touch. "He has heaps of enemies and for good reason. You don't know what he is like, what he is capable of. You don't have to do this alone."

Nick leaned across and aimed for her lips, he couldn't help himself. He was inches away when it looked like she was coming forward to meet him but all his lips met were the tips of her fingers. "Too complicated," she whispered.

"I'm sorry, that was totally crazy," he said, leaning back. He felt his cheeks warming with the blood that was rushing to his face. *Dammit! What'd I have to go and do that for?*

"No," she smiled, "It's fine. It's actually flattering, but technically you're a student and I'm staff, so...."

Nick held up a hand. "I totally get that."

"Look, even though it's not exactly within the rules, we'll be friends, yeah?"

"Of course." Nick nodded. *Yeah, because friends is just as good when you're falling for someone.* He was in the dreaded friend zone. Again. Fan-fucking-tastic.

She gently moved his chin to one side and planted yet another rather slow kiss on his cheek, twice. She even added a tiny 'mwah', which to Nick, sounded like a little moan. She had no idea how much it drove him crazy to feel those soft lips. Or maybe she did, which was why she held his face away from hers so he wouldn't be tempted again. But he couldn't help but wonder, why was she so affectionate with him?

"Look, as long as we are talking about honesty, there's something you deserve to know," she said.

"What's that?"

"My dinner didn't get cancelled. I called and said I wasn't feeling well."

Nick didn't know what to say, what he was supposed to do with that information. He merely said as seriously as he could, "Thank-you."

"Anytime," she replied with a smile. "Well…maybe not anytime."

Nick put his hand on the door handle. "Can I get your number?" he asked. "As a friend, you know?"

"Sure. I'll message you when I get home."

"Did you want mine then?"

"I already have it. I put it in my phone from the forms you gave me for Mrs. Davies."

"That is…very unprofessional of you," he said, sounding very much impressed.

"What are you going to do? Tell on me?"

"Nope, but you will have to buy me a coffee to ensure my silence," he replied with a grin.

"Sneaky!" Nicole placed the tip of her tongue on the roof of her mouth, looking at him.

"Can't blame me," he said as he stepped out of the car and leaned into the window. "How else am I going to make sure I get to see you again?"

Nicole started the car and turned to him. "Just ask."

She drove off and beeped him.

Just then, a huge roar erupted behind Nick. He turned to see a gleaming red Maserati turn into the driveway. The driver shut off the engine and stepped out. A tall, broad and tanned man stepped out and walked forward.

"You must be Nick." The man's voice was surprisingly deep. "It's a pleasure to meet you." He held out his hand. "My name is—"

"Dante! Nick!" Alex ran outside, clearly shocked to see both of them standing together.

Nick turned to face the man again. So this was Dante.

"Hey, hun," Alex said, addressing Nick. "Everything ok? You're a little later than usual."

"Sorry, I lost track of time. Was chatting with a girl, you know?"

"Well, we can surely forgive that," Dante said.

Alex laughed nervously. Nick did nothing. He was unsure why Alex appeared so uncomfortable and decided it must be because Dante was here. Nick guessed he was her boyfriend, and he seemed pleasant enough. But something about him was vaguely disturbing. Something he couldn't quite get his finger on. Strangely, his close proximity to Dante was making him tense, so much so that he had to take two steps back just to feel more or less ok.

"Well, we'd better be going," Alex said. "There's plenty of food in the fridge, and mum's upstairs. She raided the video shop and has heaps of R-rated action movies for you guys to watch. I swear, you would think she was a bloke given how much violence and gore she likes."

She hugged Nick and almost jogged to the passenger side of the Maserati.

"Nice to finally meet you, Nick," Dante said, holding out his hand again. Out of pure politeness, Nick shook it. In an instant, his hand was enclosed in an icy grip. The chill ran up his arm and through his body.

"Take care," Dante said with a smile, letting go of him.

Nick was breathing heavily and turned around so neither Alex nor Dante could see his reaction. What was that? Nick didn't know, but he was having a hard time catching his breath. He looked down at his trembling hand. *What I do know is that I never want to touch that guy ever again.*

Chapter 13

A New Dawn

Even for an immortal, there are times when eyes needed a minute to adjust right after waking. Melina had awoken in the same room for over a century, and yet again she felt disoriented, confused. Frustrated. And it was happening with increasing regularity.

The noises were getting louder, worse. For weeks she had been experiencing flashes of sounds, bits and pieces of words and phrases, the beginnings and endings of sentences. They came and went sporadically while she was awake, moving about in the mansion. At first they were merely whispers, as if floating on the breeze, and then they were gone. So fleeting and quiet, she had to pause to make sure she had truly heard something. But over two hundred and fifty years on the planet had taught her to trust herself and be aware of everything.

Even for a vampire, hearing voices you could not place was not a welcome characteristic, and so Melina sought out Sydney's vampire doctor. After seven hundred years, Varis Lintuly believed he had seen it all. Several members of the wider vampire community believed it too and sought out his experience for all manner of cures for the few ailments that could befall the race.

He found nothing wrong with Melina.

Normal people might begin to panic at this stage, worrying they were truly going mad, but Melina was not normal. There was more to this. The sounds, as they were, made no sense. The way they came to her did. As a vampire with the particular gift of communicating with animals, she recognised that the manner in which the sounds appeared to her was similar to when birds, dogs, cats, rats, horses and so on would share conversations with her. She heard the same hum and soft crackle of, for want of a better word, magic. Yet instead of peaceful, she felt constrained and vulnerable, as if the noises were attacking her. However, she was Melina Garcia, member of the Kent vampire family and flashes of noise wouldn't undo her. She did not know where they came from, but she did know what they were. Cries for help.

She lifted the lid on her coffin and stepped out, suddenly aware that all members of her adopted family still resided in theirs, curiously still asleep. Even Julian, who made it a habit of *always* being there to hold her hand as they moved along to the crypt's elevator, as if she were a two-year-old that might fall.

Melina yanked open the top of his coffin, revealing what she already knew but could not fathom. Julian lay there, presumably like the rest of his family, as good as a corpse, cold, still and beautiful. The way all vampires looked while the sun was up. Melina felt a strange twinge of unease in her stomach, a very human emotion of anxiety. She rushed to the crypt wall where a tiny gap existed and stopped still. A barely visible ray of orange had filtered through the gap, leaving a perfect circle of light on the floor. Melina could not believe it.

She scrunched her eyes as a flash and another partial scream blazed through her brain. Without thinking, she rushed back to her coffin and replaced the lid, sobbing before she could even stop herself. Something was wrong with her and her situation had turned from intriguing and frustrating to desperate. She had to find the cause of these sounds, she had to find what was so powerful that could do the impossible—awaken a vampire during daylight.

* * *

The streets of Sydney in the CBD during the day were a fairly safe place to be, all things considered. And surrounded by office buildings and retail outlets along with pubs and clubs, the area offered a great many chances for people to come to your aid if anything did happen to go wrong. At two o'clock in the morning, however, with only scatterings of people about and only a few establishments open, the danger was significantly higher. Unless you were a vampire.

Lauren approached the Coffinail club with ease. She hadn't been here before, but she'd followed the faint scent of decay from over fifty meters away until she faced the structure. It looked like a run-down apartment building, two storeys with a set of iron stairs descending under the pavement into darkness. Lauren looked left to right. The streets of Newtown had scatterings of drunks and junkies filling them and not much else at this hour. For Lauren, this really was the dregs of the city.

She ventured down and reached the bottom of the stairs, spotting the door to a cellar. This was the entrance to Coffinail. *Fuck. How is this place not under the watch of the cops? Who the hell would go to a club through a cellar and not think it raises a red flag?*

She eased the cellar door open and climbed into an elevator. Well, half an elevator, and pressed one of the only two buttons there. As she descended, she looked up, seeing the cellar door close automatically. Had she still been alive, it might have given her a shiver. The trip only took a few seconds, but she could hear the dull thump of music straight away. The elevator stopped in front of a grate. She pushed it open and stepped into a smoke-filled corridor. Whether from cigarettes or dust she wasn't sure, but the place stunk like Granddad's balls. Yet the place was full, and no one seemed to mind.

She moved into the main auditorium, which sported the strangest assortment of decorations she had ever seen. Dimly lit strippers shook their stuff on small stages with their personal poles, but to Lauren they all looked like the B crew; one or two even had bite marks very noticeable. Ancient weapons adorned the walls, some with caked-on blood from their last battle. Red and purple drapes were hung as far as the eye could see. An arch was set up over the main stage where a band was playing. Grungy, gothic I-hate-the-world crap.

Lauren could smell both vampires and humans in the place, though she couldn't tell who was who without getting closer to the patrons. And that was the last thing she wanted to do. She just wanted to get the hell out of here.

Fuck this. Lauren moved up to the bar, pushing aside the waiting customers and rapped her knuckles on the surface.

"Oi, where's Luca?" she asked the bartender.

A male voice behind her said, "Oi yourself, bitch! Wait ya' fuckin' turn!"

The bartender looked like he was about to answer, but Lauren placed her hand in his face. "Hold that thought."

She turned around and faced the speaker, looking him up and down, sniffing. Vampire.

Lauren smiled. Good. She unleashed with two quick punches. The first broke his nose, the second split it across his face. He stumbled and fell back, pitifully trying to contain the damage and blood loss with both hands as the others surrounding him took a step back from Lauren.

Lauren peered down at the man, writhing slowly on the club floor. "Sorry, do you mind if I cut? No? Cheers, mate."

Lauren returned to the bartender and furrowed her brow. "Now what was I saying?"

"Luca's not here. But you can leave your stuff. He left the payment with me."

He lowered himself behind the bar and came up again with a briefcase, placing it in front of Lauren. A young girl took his place and began taking orders.

This was the second deal Lauren had done and it was the same briefcase Luca had presented to her containing forty thousand dollars. Or ten for each vial.

"What, you want to do the deal here?" Lauren said, glancing from side to side.

"You honestly think this is the worst thing people see in here?"

He had a point. People had been murdered here on the dancefloor and no one had squealed. Well not to the cops anyway. Coffinail was under Vincent's jurisdiction and therefore had his protection.

"Whatever, just hand it over."

The bartender gave her a swift nod. Lauren took the briefcase and reached into her jacket pocket for the vials.

"You should really count it, you know," came a voice from behind Lauren.

"What are you doing here, Clive, you lackey?" she asked, turning to glance at Clive. He had cut his hair. The curls were clipped shorter, but he had kept his mini sideburns. He wore a thick, black woollen trench coat with its collar upturned. If he didn't remind Lauren of the black character in Spy vs Spy, he might have looked half decent. "I didn't pick you for a fang banger."

Clive repositioned his glasses on top of his nose. "Count it."

Lauren snorted. "Sure," as she put the briefcase into Clive's hands. "Hold it for me."

She clicked it open and took note of the contents. A single layer of twenty dollar note bunches. The last exchange was two layers of fifty dollar notes.

"What the fuck is this?" Lauren asked the bartender. "This is supposed to be forty grand!"

"Eighty, actually," Clive corrected her. "Sell price has gone up."

"I don't know anything about that. All I know is that's what Luca left," the bartender shrugged.

"It's enough for one vial, if that," Clive said.

"He's expecting four," the bartender replied.

"Vincent expects to get paid. Which do you think is more likely?" Clive asked the bartender.

"You want four, you pay for four," Lauren added.

"Look, give me one, and come out to Luca's safe with me. He'll kill someone if he doesn't get four. Most probably me. He has to have some spare cash around."

"You're going to steal from him?" Lauren asked.

"I said Luca will *probably* kill me, but I'm fucked if I get on Vincent's bad side."

Lauren and Clive followed the bartender into the back. They walked through an abandoned, darkened kitchen. This part of the club had an overwhelming stench of damp dust. It clearly had not been used for months, if not years.

Lauren gazed at the greasy ceiling hoods and the dusty grime of the grill. The only light came from an old cool room, its door slightly ajar. Something about this was starting to make Lauren uneasy. Clive was giving off vibes that indicated he was feeling the same.

"Where's this safe, again?" Lauren asked.

"Round the corner," the bartender said, as he moved around the corner he spoke of. Clive moved a hand to slow Lauren down, making him reach the corner before her. Lauren was about to fling his hand away when Clive gasped, pulled aside and disappeared from Lauren's view around the corner.

"What the fuck?" Lauren yelled. As she followed them, she heard a door slam, and sounds of struggling. She had come full circle—she faced the same elevator she had arrived in.

The bartender had jumped through the cellar opening with Clive in his clutches. Well if it was good for one…

Lauren burst out of the cellar door, landing a little unsteadily, but she didn't have far to chase. The bartender faced her with his fingers clenched around Clive's windpipe. Clive had a fresh bite on his neck, and blood was dripping from the bartender's mouth. He had given Clive a taster.

The streets were deserted; they were alone. Lauren was reminded of facing Alex in a similar situation a few months ago. Yet Lauren had been the one with the hostage on that occasion.

"I'll kill him," the bartender said.

"Yeah, so I see. I don't give a shit. Kill him."

The bartender laughed. "If you didn't give a shit, you wouldn't have followed. Give me the Dream State, and I'll let him go."

Lauren looked down at the briefcase. Something was off about this. "You just want the Dream State? Don't you want Luca's money back too?"

The bartender sneered. "Luca is an idiot. He has no idea what this is really worth or how many people are using. That money is nothing compared to what I'll get on the street. Demand is growing and the net outside of Vincent's jurisdiction is widening. Vampires might be going through it daily, but humans are injecting this shit like there's no tomorrow."

"Are you crazy?" Clive coughed. "You can't give it to humans! You have no idea what it will do to them."

"You're right," the bartender shrugged. "And I don't care. All I know is they are paying more than vamps do. It helps that they have regular income." He winked at Lauren. "So what'll it be?"

Lauren weighed up the options in her head. She shouldn't be in this situation and didn't really care if she lost the Dream State *or* the money. In fact, she didn't care if Clive got his throat cut either.

"You know what?" Lauren set down the briefcase and picked out the vials. "Take 'em," she said, throwing them to the bartender.

The bartender caught them and released Clive at the same time. She should be worried about what Julian would say, but she hadn't signed up for this. What did she have to lose, her life? Julian couldn't take that from her. She was already dead. "Do what you want. I'm out of here."

Lauren turned and walked away. She heard the bartender gleefully gather the Dream State and scarper, leaving the briefcase.

"Are you crazy?" Clive screamed after Lauren. "We have to get it back! We can't let it get out into Sydney!"

"Sorry, can't hear you, lackey," Lauren said, pointing to the night sky and marching forward. "Behold! All the fucks I give!"

The echoing thunder of a gunshot made her pause however. For a split second she thought Clive had fired a warning shot at her. But there was no way he had the balls to pull the trigger.

Lauren twisted around, frantically looking left to right. She saw Clive with his back to her, staring at a body around fifty meters ahead of him. The bartender was dead, half his brains coating the road.

Lauren reached Clive just as the sound of clapping reached her ears. A few cheers as well. Four men came into view from the shadows, three congratulating the fourth. They stood over the body, kicking the corpse.

"Stupid blood sucker."

"What a shot!"

"Now that's how ya do it!"

Lauren grabbed Clive by the shoulder. *Hunters*. Lauren's fangs flared, ready for a fight, as the shooter came into her view. The red hair was completely shaved and he looked like he'd aged thirty years since the last time she had seen him. If she'd needed to breathe, she would have gasped. *Matt!*

The yahooing continued, but Matt was like a statue. His face was expressionless and ice cold. He clocked his gun as if hypnotised, lowering it back down to his side.

One of the three bent to pick up the vials of Dream State the bartender had dropped. Lauren felt Clive tense but not move. He kept flicking glances at her

"Calibos, how long do you reckon this amount of Dream State will last us?" he said.

"I'd say only about a fortnight," the one called Calibos replied, placing his arm around Matt. "As long as our new friend here keeps improving, we'll burn through it! Still, that just means more vamps to kill and less of it on the streets, aye?"

The others cheered the words, but Matt remained still and silent. Yet Lauren could swear he turned a fraction and stared right at her. "For the honour of the Alpha and our lost brothers, we will find them!" Calibos roared, bringing a louder cheer as they all moved in Lauren and Clive's direction.

"Lackey, run!" Lauren hissed through her fangs.

She kept her eyes on the group and had almost lifted her hand from his shoulder when, with surprising speed for a human, he grabbed her wrist. "I'm not leaving you," he whispered, with soft conviction. Lauren was about to retort, maybe shove him out of the way when Calibos said, "Did you hear something, lads?"

The group stopped their gleeful giggling to look around, slightly confused. And they weren't the only ones. Lauren and Clive stood not eight feet from them. Yet the men acted as if they were… Lauren herself looked over at Clive in confusion, about to ask what the punks thought they were up to, but suddenly realised she couldn't see him. At all. She still felt her hand on his shoulder, but she was looking straight through where his body should be to the pavement and buildings behind. *Invisible?*

The men continued on, marching straight past Lauren and Clive, confirming her bizarre conclusion.

Lauren waited for about thirty seconds before letting go of Clive and he reappeared before her. "Fuck me. What the hell was that?"

"I think," Clive said, trying to get his breath back. "We just discovered your power." He gave an impressed nod before adding, "And we should use it to follow them."

"Why are you so desperate to get that stuff back? It's not worth getting killed over."

"It's not just that. I think they are what Vincent has the Elements of Night looking for. The wolf pack."

"Can't be," Lauren said. "I smelt them as they walked past. They were all human."

"What? How else would they know about Dream State? They called it by name. You and I are two of the very few who know exactly where it comes from. It has to be them. We have to follow them anyway and report back. If what that bartender said is right, and Dream State *is* spreading beyond where we can control its circulation—if it's getting into the hands of human drug dealers. That's bad. Very bad."

Lauren felt his conviction, but couldn't understand what the big deal was. "Why?"

"Just trust me. We have to find out more. Sydney is fucked if this gets outside vampire control, but it looks like it already has."

Lauren studied Clive for a few seconds. To give him even minimal credit, he could've run when the men came towards them. But he didn't. He stayed. Maybe the lackey wasn't so bad.

"Fine. Was gonna be a boring night anyway."

CHAPTER 14

PEACE OF MIND

Nicole twirled the biro in her fingers. The pen that refused to write. Her notes for Zachary were getting smaller and less in depth every session, yet never had she more reason to be concerned, because he still refused to talk. There were only so many times you could write that over and over.

She sighed and leaned back in the chair, interlacing her fingers across her abdomen. It wasn't that he didn't talk, that was cause enough. But the boy just seemed…lost, emotionless and drained.

She flicked through his file, yet again. Trying to find anything she may have missed. The only thing that glared at her, was his telephone number. She had asked Mrs. Davies how to go about contacting his father, but was flatly told that even if she was a teacher, under the school system, it would be extremely difficult without appropriate cause.

But what was appropriate cause, she wondered. Something was troubling him, and it was her job to help. That was appropriate enough. For her.

She picked up the handpiece and ignored the tension in her stomach as she dialled the number. There was only one ring.

"Good afternoon. Raven Apartments, this is Samantha. How may I help you?"

Nicole cleared her throat. "Hi, can you put me through to Dean Page please?"

There was a rather long pause after Nicole finished. “Hello?”

“May I ask who’s calling?” the receptionist replied.

“Yes, my name is Nicole O’Brien. I’m calling from St. Andrews.”

Yet another pause. “And what would this be pertaining too?”

“It is in regards to his son.”

“Clearly,” Samantha snapped. “But what specifically is the problem?”

Seriously?

“Well, as I am involved with the counsellor’s office, it would be rather inappropriate for me to relay the message to you. I would just like to converse with Zachary’s father, please.”

“Unfortunately he is out at the moment, so I’ll have to take that message.”

So why didn’t you just say that in the beginning then? Nicole pulled a face at the telephone.

“I’ll call back later, then. Thanks very much.”

Nicole clicked the phone hard, gathered her things and headed out. Her mind raced as fast as her feet, moving through the kids rushing towards the exit at the end of the school day. Frustration turned into anger. *Who the hell was that bitch?* Nicole rummaged around for her keys in her bag as she approached her car.

“Shit…”she said under her breath. “Where are they?”

“Looking for these?”

Nicole turned around to see her keys being held out to her.

“You dropped them back there.” Nick gestured vaguely behind him. I would’ve called out but you looked really pissed. I wanted to make sure you’re ok.”

“Yeah, I…thanks,” Nicole said, taking them. “Just a really rude woman on the phone, nothing major. I’ll live,” she said, forcing a smile. “Can I offer you a lift home to say thanks?”

“Oh, you don’t have to thank me. Normally I would say yes to a ride, but today I have to head up to Eastgardens and meet my cousin at about seven-thirty or so.”

“That’s four hours from now. You sure?”

“Yeah, she’s a teacher. She has work to clear up. I don’t mind. I was thinking about treating myself to a movie. I’m curious to see what the theatres are like over here.” Nick stopped and looked at her with a slight uncertainty. "Would you…care to join?"

Nicole thought about it. She really didn't have anything else on tonight. Plus as she glanced over the blue of his eyes, and glanced again, there were definitely worse things she could spend her time on.

"You know what? Sure, why not? Only one condition. I pay for my own ticket."

Nick bobbed on his feet briefly, hands behind his back. "Counter proposal; you buy the tickets and I pay for the snacks."

"Deal," Nicole said, holding out her hand.

"Deal." Nick smiled, giving her hand a single, firm shake. The good hand shake wasn't the only thing she noticed. The moment their skin touched, a pleasant warmth spread over her, numbing her anger. She was feeling better already. Much better.

Her grandmother's advice popped into her mind before she could stop it. "Nothing like a good man for what ails you" Grandma was old-fashioned, but she also had her share of wisdom. Nicole grinned in spite of herself.

* * *

True to his word, Nick had bought the snacks only. There were no tricks like the coffee, and she appreciated that. She had chosen a "safe" movie—action comedy, which they both enjoyed.

She noted the way he ate his popcorn. Grabbing it in one hand as soon as they sat down and using the other to pick and pop it in his mouth. During the trailers she whispered, "Is that how you always eat it?"

"I didn't know how you were with sharing food."

She rolled her eyes and placed his hand into the box, which rested on her lap. "It's ok, I don't have cooties."

Nick snorted and tossed a few kernels of popcorn at her. "Maybe I do."

She feigned offense and threw some back at him, laughing. "Now you've done it. This means war!"

Then the trailers started and they settled in to watch. She felt hyperaware of her breathing, of the people around them, of his face as he reacted to scenes in the movie.

They walked out of the theatre with a faint hint of buttery salt smell over them, and Nicole couldn't quite remember the plot of the movie. It had been ages since she had just…been silly. And she loved it.

And then she spotted Trent Miller on the other side of the snack bar, the centre of a group of girls and of course, Jason. Nick had seen them too, and his body had almost frozen in place. Nicole held his hand briefly and tugged him away. "Your cousin will be here soon. C'mon, if we're lucky they won't see us."

"I hope they do," Nick said darkly.

"Why?"

"I don't like the way he speaks to you. What he says to you. The way he carries on."

"He's an arse. He's the type that will never grow up. But listen, I don't want or need you to pick fights in order to defend my honour. Better we just avoid him. Besides, I don't want you to get hurt."

"So…you can protect me but I can't protect you?"

Nicole turned to him, trying to judge his expression. It was curious, not arrogant. "Why must we protect? Protect is a strong word. I can care, I can advise, but ultimately it's up to you."

"I just think he is dangerous."

"I don't disagree with you there," Nicole said as they entered the car park. "But you know what he isn't? Worth it. He is obviously very unhappy and makes others want to be the same. Just try and forget him." She continued toward the car and muttered half under her breath, "Besides, he's not the only one who's dangerous."

"What's that? What do you mean?" Nick asked.

She'd said it louder than she'd intended. "You're dangerous too."

Nick looked taken aback. "I don't understand,"

"I didn't expect you to."

He was dangerous for *her*. He was charming, very much so. At first she was sure he was deliberately being that way, trying to get her attention. But lately she wasn't so sure he was even aware of it. He was simply being himself. Like paying for the coffee as a treat for her, honouring his word to buy the snacks, not trying to impress her in a fake, overbearing way. Holding doors open, wanting to protect her from Trent.

Even though she didn't need or want all of it, she was realising this was him, it wasn't an act. That made it somehow more appealing.

Nicole got on tiptoe and kissed his cheek. And another peck before she flattened her feet. Before she knew it, their lips were touching. She barely knew what was going through her head as she continued kissing him, gently cupping his face as his hands found her waist and brought her closer. His lips were so soft, his kiss was so gentle, Nicole felt completely at ease. It was when the tips of their tongues met that she stepped back.

Whoa.

"I didn't plan to do that. Sorry."

Nick nodded. Thankfully, he didn't say anything.

"Thank you for a great time. Hope we can do it again," she said.

"The movies?"

"Yes. The movies."

She smiled as she stepped into the car and drove off, trying not to go too quickly. As she looked in the rear-view mirror, she saw him give a small wave.

Chapter 15

Turn Of The Tide

Alex and Dante stepped into the elevator of Raven Apartments. She jabbed the down button impatiently. Herschel Rasmussen and Dante had just engaged in a long q-&-a session, but as far as Alex could tell it was all mumbo jumbo. But why had Lauren's name been mentioned? She had not heard from her ex-bff and never asked either, but was it possible she had something to do with the wolves?

"Hey do you think—"

Alex was stopped from finishing her question by Dante almost crushing her lips with his own, pressing her body hard into the wall of the elevator. He broke the kiss to seek her jaw and neck, his cool mouth leaving wet kisses and sending tingles over the skin he touched with it.

"Dante…" Alex smiled, "Where did this come from..?"

"Forgive me…" Dante breathed, gripping her body tight, using his tongue to trail up her neck, taking her ear lobe into his mouth and sucking it in. Every kiss gave Alex tingly goose bumps. "It's time."

"Time for what?" Alex whispered, eyes closed, head back.

The elevator shuddered to a halt. Alex snapped her eyes open and saw that Dante that had hit the emergency stop button. His green eyes blazed. "I need you."

Alex wrapped her arms around his neck and covered his mouth with her own. She embraced him with enough force that he had to take a step back, but regained himself to push her into the wall again. With only the briefest of efforts, Alex felt Dante un-button her jeans using a mere flick of his wrist as he returned his kisses to her neck. The groan of the lowering zipper was one of the hottest sounds that had ever reached her ears.

She caressed her tongue over the tips of the three fingers he placed just inside her mouth so that they glistened when he removed them. She was so wet he didn't need to lubricate his fingers, but found sucking on them so he could use them on her too hot to stop him. He reached inside her panties and growled into her neck. With his first and third finger he held open her folds while flicking her slippery clitoris with his second. Every flick caused her to bump against the wall, her body giving involuntary jerks, before he finally inserted them.

She opened her eyes and looked into his. Without thinking, she pulled open her collar violently, exposing her neck for him. Dante sunk his fangs into the flesh connecting her shoulder and neck, pressing his body into hers, locking her in place. Alex grabbed his hair and pulled his face closer, wanting him to take more as he wriggled his fingers faster. She could feel her blood slowly trickling out of his mouth and down her chest, staining her shirt and bra but she didn't care, the pain excited her. Dante released his bite and proceeded to stroke his tongue along the wound, partially sucking the droplets still oozing out. Dante's saliva and her blood mixing on the tender skin of her neck combined with Dante twisting his fingers into her was too much for Alex.

Her eyes fluttered as the elevator's lights flashed.

"Alexandra…" Dante whispered.

"Hmm?" She didn't want to move.

"Alexandra, wake up."

Alex opened her eyes to see Dante staring curiously at her, but they were no longer in an elevator. She was in Dante's bed, just a sheet covering their otherwise naked bodies. "Are you all right?"

"How did we get here?"

"We've been here for hours. We haven't left."

Alex fell back onto her pillow. No. NO. "I was dreaming wasn't I?"

"So it seemed. Quite intensely, I would say," Dante replied, handing her a bottle of water.

"Fuckety." Alex sat up and twisted off the bottle cap. She took a deep swig and felt the water ease her parched throat before swallowing.

She tried to wipe away the wonderful images from the dream and let out a frustrated sigh.

"What is it?" Dante asked.

"Where do you see this going? What is this to you?" she asked, pointing at the freshly healed bite on her neck and then sweeping her hand down and around the whole room, as if to highlight the entire situation.

"I don't understand what you're asking. It's a donor relationship," Dante replied.

"Yeah but, could it be…anything more?"

Dante considered her for a moment, "More?"

Alex raised her eyebrows. "Dante you can't be this dense."

Dante looked her up and down quickly, "Oh. You mean sex."

"Well…not just that," Alex replied quickly. "But just, a little more closeness, I guess. I mean…I've never been in this situation before. I have these feelings, and urges. It seems the more blood you take from me the more I want other things to happen."

"You wish for me to make love to you?"

The word was out so fast before Alex could even think. "Yes."

"I see," Dante frowned. "Forgive me. I never even thought that to be an option, given my history with your mother."

"But you said you two never…"

"We didn't. But I wonder if she had similar feelings, despite the fact that she was married. Which makes me wonder about Michelle…" Dante trailed off just before Alex leaned her head to the side. At the mention of Dante's previous donor, she didn't know what to say.

Michelle Davidson had been with Dante for several years, they were best friends and lovers, but not in love as she had explained once to Alex. Nevertheless, when Vincent had stripped Dante of his right to be with her for breaking vampire law months ago, both had taken it badly, but none worse than Michelle.

Dante sighed and turned away from Alex.

"You haven't mentioned her in a long time," she said softly. "Have you tried speaking to her?"

"Several times, but she still won't answer her phone or return my messages. It bothers me more than I would like."

"I feel so bad. I haven't tried to contact her for ages. With you and

Nick and mum and teaching, things have just been crazy."

Dante nodded his understanding. "I'm sure you miss Matt too."

Alex was again surprised at a name Dante mentioned. "Well, yeah of course. I mean, I wish I knew where he was, obviously. We didn't end on good terms, but I will always care about him."

"Have you thought about dating anyone else?"

"What do you mean?"

"Well only you will know when you're ready, of course. But I just don't want you to waste any opportunities to be happy, if and when they come along."

"So what am I doing here with you then, if this isn't an opportunity to be happy?"

"Alexandra," Dante stood, hands out in a pleading gesture. "I care about you, more than you will know. What we have is something special, but I will not be the one to stand in your way when a real relationship is on offer. That would be selfish and ridiculous."

"So my feelings for you are ridiculous?" Alex asked, anger building.

"You have to understand the difference between having feelings for a human and having them for a vampire. What you're feeling is not real."

"Don't talk to me like I'm a child. And don't tell me what I feel! You've had relationships with humans before. Why not with me? Look, I know that I'll age and that you won't. And I know that my relationship with you would have to end. But it's my life and my choice. Why can't you see that?"

"Alexandra, I am not trying to hurt you. You're taking this too personally."

"You're damn right I am. First, you treat me like an idiot and act as if I have no right to my feelings. So much for someone who cares about me!"

"That is not what I was saying," Dante replied, getting angry himself. "And you know it. I have seen this time and time again. Humans think they fall in love with a vampire, but it is only hormones and curiosity, not love. Love is with someone you can walk in the sun with, someone you can have children with, grow old, and be happy. Vampires can't do that. We are freaks of nature. We cannot give a human the love and life another human can give."

"What if I don't want any of that? What if I just want you?" Alex said thickly.

"I wouldn't give you the choice for the very reason that I do care about you."

Alex took a deep breath and stepped forward. "I need to know right now… Forget everything else, and this caring about me bullshit. Do I mean anything to you?"

"You are a very dear friend."

"No, dammit. You know what I am asking you!"

Dante took a good few seconds before answering. "Yes."

"Then why can't you let me in?"

"Because you're after something I can no longer give to a human. You deserve better than the life I could offer."

Alex drew in a breath and began silently collecting her things. Not until she reached the other side of the front door did the tears come.

* * *

Dante had stood and watched her gather her belongings and go. He'd wanted to stop her, to comfort her, but knew no matter the outcome it would not help. He hated hurting someone so wonderful, feeling he had to remain strong for the both of them. It wasn't the relationship she wanted, but it was the best he could do. He didn't want her to go, but he let her. Just, he thought, lowering his head, as he had had to do a few times in his life with the women that held a special place in his heart. A handful after his heart stopped beating, but only one while it pumped life and love for her through his veins.

Andalucia, Spain 1764

"Alejandro, por la prisa de dioses!" *Alejandro, by the gods, hurry up!*

He paid no attention. He was busy kicking the sand of the beach with his foot and trying to catch it. How he loved the beach. The warm sand, the feeling of jumping and sinking into it, running his fingers through it, then splashing his feet in the cold sea, shrieking with delight. What did he care that his town had been busy preparing for weeks for this very day.

He wasn't even seven yet. Why did he need to behave himself and watch his step and tendency to swear, using the words the sailors used so freely around him, just because the town was expecting a visit from one of the richest men known? Raphael Alvaro, the man who owned several of the houses in Andalucia, had announced an unexpected visit to the city of Cordoba and everyone Alejandro had seen was in a flurry of panic. Alejandro found it strange that the adults he knew were so afraid of Alvaro, yet he, at only four was not. He had heard the stories, but that didn't mean he believed them. Alvaro was known as *El Cuervo*—The Crow—a man who had made his money in blood. These were only some of the stories about him. Others claimed he was a man that had the power to summon demons against those who stood against him. Several people known to have had quarrels with him were never seen or heard from again, the only evidence of foul play were whispers of screams in the night, but these were never spoken of openly.

Alejandro had his hand snatched from his side and his whole body half dragged up to the town centre by Esmeralda. He called her aunt, although she held no relation to him. He was an orphan, and had been found on her doorstep when he was only a few days old. Normally, she enjoyed his games and sense of fun, but not today.

"Alejandro por todos que es bueno y Santo te ruego de comportarse. Sólo por esta vez, para mí! Por favour!" *Alejandro, by all that is good and holy, I beg of you to behave. Just this once, for me! Please.*

Alejandro did not like the rushed way his aunt Esmeralda spoke, clearly upset.

"Aunt, what is wrong? With everybody? Why is this man coming? Why is everyone afraid?"

Alejandro noticed the population of the city lining up at the main gates, standing in welcome. Raphael was close.

"He wants a son," she replied bitterly. "It doesn't matter right now," she said, replying to the child's uncertain look. "What matters is you behave. This man is very powerful. If he sees you do something he doesn't like, he will hurt you. Do you understand?"

Alejandro frowned. Of course he understood the words, but not the reason behind them. How could a town of so many be so deathly afraid of just one man? He looked around as Esmeralda led him into the line at the front of city's inn. Fear was power, and he was beginning to understand its emphatic effect.

The ground beneath his feet trembled, but instead of looking down, he looked up. Coming to a stop just outside the city gates was a four-horse-drawn carriage. The side door opened and slowly, very slowly, a man stepped out. The man Alejandro knew to be Raphael. Large flat nose, greasy, stringy hair and thin beard. He paused when on the ground and looked left and right with a scowl. He approached the line of city folk who bowed in turn as he passed. He walked several steps before stopping and retreating back to stand in front of a young woman, dressed with a shawl over her head.

"You will do nicely," Raphael said, quickly removing the shawl and flicking it to the floor. Whatever the grave-faced girl was supposed to do, it did not seem to please her, even as she curtsied and walked into the inn. Alejandro did not know who looked more devastated, the woman or her young husband. Raphael continued to move along the line, picking a further two girls who followed the first into the inn, all with the same serious and sad looks on their faces. Raphael stopped when he came to Alejandro and Esmeralda. He looked first at her, then to Alejandro.

"I don't like the way this one is looking at me." He sneered. Aunt Esmeralda squeezed Alejandro's hand ever tighter as Raphael asked her, "Is it yours?"

She shook her head. "Forgive him, Lord. His name is Alejandro. He is an orphan, not yet capable of understanding basic manners. The fault is mine for not teaching him."

Raphael grunted as a response before asking, "Han sido aflojados sus lomos?" *Have your loins been loosened?*

Esmeralda faltered slightly as she replied. "No, my Lord. I am not able to have them. I have never been able."

Raphael considered this for a moment. "Esto significa que usted está intacto entonces?" *You mean to tell me you are untouched?*

Esmeralda swallowed. "Yes, my Lord."

"Luego le tendrá primero" he said, turning his back on her. *Then I will have you first.*

"Hey, wait a minute!" a man in the line shouted. "The agreement with our town was you get our women to give you a son. This woman cannot have them yet you take her as well."

"Su punto de ser?" Raphael asked very slowly.

"My point is, I don't think I like the fact you can change the terms any time you feel like."

Without warning, Raphael turned his wrist up and shoved it into the man's chin. As he removed his hand, Alejandro saw a hidden blade in Raphael's glove and a river of blood poured from under the man's jaw, bringing him to his knees and eventually the ground. Despite the horrified cries that followed his action, the line remained intact. Raphael calmly continued on, and ventured into the inn.

Esmeralda made to follow him but first turned to Alejandro and whispered, "Stay out of trouble."

As soon as she disappeared, the line of people dispersed. To his surprise, no one went over to the fallen man, still breathing yet raspy and shaking. Slowly, Alejandro crept forward. When the man saw him coming, he beckoned weakly, pulling out a rather long blade of his own. He held it out to Alejandro. "He is hurting your aunt," he choked out. "Avenge her one day… And me… Please."

He rested his head and said no more.

Alejandro held the dagger in two hands, studying it, marvelling at its beauty. He was certain no one had seen the exchange. If they had, surely someone would have taken it away.

Alejandro stuck the dagger in the side of his pants and placed his shirt on top of it, completely obscuring the handle. He looked up to the inn, suddenly determined to get in there. Going in the front seemed like a bad idea, so he crept around toward the back. Alejandro moved past the massive carriage that had brought Raphael here and walked along the side of the building. He began to hear whimpering and crying. Creeping closer, he chanced a look towards the back of the inn and saw a young, red-haired girl with her back to him, crawling backwards away from a slowly advancing wolf. Without even thinking, Alejandro drew his new dagger. He ignored all manner of common sense and the thought of danger, instead running toward the wolf. Alejandro sneered and growled, acting crazy, trying to get the wolf's attention. The wolf's head went from left to right, uncertain what to do. Finally, it focussed on Alejandro.

"Qué estás!?" the girl squealed loudly. *What are you doing?*

The wolf growled, baring its teeth. Alejandro pointed the dagger and it pounced. The girl beside him screamed with all her might as the snarling wolf leapt on top of Alejandro. The girl's screams were heard by those on the other side, who had come racing around the building to see what the commotion was about.

"Oh my!"

"Someone get a gun!"

"Wait look!"

Alejandro could not move, the weight of the beast pinned him down. Those same rushing feet that came around the corner, he imagined, were frantically trying to remove the wolf from him. Finally managing to do so, the viewers saw the dagger plunged into the wolf's chest, straight through the heart, no doubt killing it instantly. A million to one chance.

"What's the meaning of this?" Raphael said, racing out of the inn, re-doing his trouser buttons. His eyes fell on the scene too, but focused on the young girl, sitting on the ground, openly weeping. "Lita! What is going on?" he shouted. "I told you to stay in the wagon!"

As he approached his daughter he picked her up and hugged her.

"I think you have something to say to the boy," an onlooker said.

"I have nothing to say to a child that does not belong to me," he replied.

"Even one that saved your daughter's life?"

Raphael turned to face the speaker, a stout, elderly woman. "You lie. Surely one of you men killed the beast?"

"No" a man said. "By the god in heaven, it was the boy. I have never seen anything like it."

Raphael was dumbstruck. "A child kills a wolf?"

"An Iberian Wolf to be exact. Quite fierce. Young Alejandro is a natural born killer," the elderly woman replied.

Raphael turned to Alejandro, assessing his small stature. "It appears I owe you thanks." Raphael said. Alejandro said nothing.

"I believe I have the proper way to reward you," Raphael continued, returning his no-longer sobbing daughter to the ground. As he did this, Alejandro plucked his blade from the body of the wolf. Raphael made a mistake; he had turned his back on a natural born killer. One with a weapon.

Remembering the dying man's earlier words, Alejandro twirled the dagger, also remembering the rush he felt as the blade sunk into the coarse fur and then soft flesh of the wolf. He wanted to experience it again. He took one step only, before being almost knocked off his feet a second time as a blur of red hair rushed at him. Lita had wrapped her arms around his, virtually pinning them to his hips, such was the desperation of her hug. She turned her face to the side, rested her cheek on his shoulder and whispered, "*Gracias*."

"Boy." Raphael pointed a finger at Alejandro. "You will be rewarded for saving my daughter. You will be my ward. I will treat you as a son until one is born, then you will be trained by Andalucian's finest masters. You will hereby be known as Alejandro Alvaro."

There were several impressed and even shocked gasps at this news, yet Alejandro remembered the dying man's words. He focused on those words, and not Lita's smile of gratitude, when he agreed to live with Raphael Alvaro.

CHAPTER 16

HUNGRY LIKE THE WOLF

Nick had had to wait until late to get it, but finally Nicole texted him her number. A short, simple message, yet one that made Nick smile at his phone until his cheeks ached.

`Sweet dreams xxx`

Nick debated whether he should reply. He wanted to, but the message was one that didn't require an answer. Did that mean she didn't want him to reply right away, that she hoped he would keep a respectful distance? Why had she waited a whole twenty-four hours just to give her number over? Why send a text just before midnight? Had the message been sent in a rush, or was she thinking of him at that exact moment?

Nothing about this girl made sense and it was driving him crazy, both in a good way and a bad. It was only a message, for god's sake. He had never lost his cool over a girl before, and so far it was proving to be a confusing pain in the arse.

To hell with it. If I continue like this, I'll drive myself around the twist.

He thought about his reply and sent it, just before turning in. `You too. About time btw`

Sleep claimed him quickly, yet as soon as he woke, his hand reached for his phone. Sure enough, there was a message, sent about twenty minutes previously.

`Good morning :).`

Good morning back. Shall I be seeing you today?

Uni today. Sorry to disappoint you.

It's cool. Not like I was really hoping to see you or anything. Nick sent that and waited for a few seconds before sending, Busy tonight?

Lol. Yes. Sorry.

Another family dinner?

No, I'm the guest speaker at a lecture on the power of the mind. My first one!

Guest speaker? Seriously? This girl kept ticking boxes for Nick he didn't even know he had and continued to impress him. Nick thought she had a magnetic personality and he loved talking to her and hearing her ideas. It seemed there were plenty more people that wanted to do so as well.

Wow. That's amazing. Where is it? Will your family be there to cheer you on?

My uni. No they can't come unfortunately.

Nick wondered why her family wouldn't be there? It seemed strange to him that something like this would be done without any sort of support.

That's a shame. Where is it?

Look it up lol. Heading into the car. Talk soon x.

Look it up? She had never told him where she attended university, and he had never asked. Did that mean she wanted him there but wouldn't say? Nick smiled and wondered if this was a playful challenge? He wondered if she wouldn't mind a bit of moral support if he could provide it? Besides hoping to make her smile, he genuinely wanted to know what she had to say.

He received another message, one with a more serious tone. Don't do anything stupid like get yourself hurt today.

Worried about me?

Just don't want to fill the extra paperwork. ;)

He showered and dressed, unable to stop grinning, and headed to the kitchen, feeling hungry for sausages and steak. He'd really been craving the meatier foods lately.

Nick walked to the disappointingly empty table and only then noticed Alex lying on the couch, curled up in a blanket.

“Hey there,” he said. “I was wondering why I heard you come in and not go into your room. Everything okay?”

“Sorry if I woke you. I was trying to be quiet.”

“Nothing to apologise for,” he replied, eyes glancing over the box of tissues on the coffee table. “Did you want to talk about it?”

Alex gave him a sad smile, patting his hand. “No, it’s fine. You’re a sweetie for asking though. Just relationship stuff.”

“Well, even not knowing what it is, I’m sure you two will work it out. He’d be crazy to let you go.”

Alex snuggled into her pillow. “Such a charmer.” As she lay onto her stomach she winced. “Oooh, my back,” she moaned. “Need a new couch. This one just isn’t as comfy as it once was.”

“I have an idea,” Nick said, turning and making his way to the kitchen.

“Oh really, and what’s that?”

Nick came from around the corner and held up a carton of eggs in one hand and a packet of bacon in the other. “I can’t cook worth a buggery, but at least you know there is something else in this world worse than relationship stuff. That’ll make you feel better.”

Nick turned the stove on and placed the bacon inside. For split second, he felt he had to check the expiry date, as he smelt something strange. It wasn’t a usual ‘off’ smell, and Nick couldn’t place it. It was then he realised Alex had risen from the couch and was watching him, leaning against the kitchen door.

“Thank you for doing this. You didn’t have to,” she said.

“Hey, come on. After everything you have done for me, it’s the least I can do. I’m more grateful to you than you could ever imagine. Besides, when can someone take care of you for a change?”

Nick cracked two eggs into the pan and turned briefly to give her a wink. Alex made a hard, tight smile. The one you make when you were holding back tears. “You’re very sweet.”

Nick listened to the sound of her voice, the underlying sadness as he flipped the food over. The smell was getting stronger. Somehow, he could actually give the sensation a name; sadness. “So, if you don’t mind me saying…it looks like he really did a number on you?”

Alex shook her head. “No. It’s not really his fault. Sometimes, two people just want different things.”

“Or maybe they’re wrong for you.”

Alex gave a short laugh. “Oh yes, that too. He’s definitely wrong for me.”

Nick placed the bacon and eggs as delicately as he could on a plate. “I didn’t think you were into the bad boy type. They usually tend to be tools in my experience.”

Alex gave him a curious look and yet tried not to smile. “You don’t like him, do you?”

“Honestly, no. I know I don’t know him and I’ve only seen him once. But that was enough. Something about him just, I don’t know, gives me the creeps. I can’t explain it. Anyway, he made you upset and that’s enough for me,” he said, placing the plate on the table. “Hope this makes you feel better though. If you survive eating it.”

Alex held her arms out and Nick walked in to a soft hug. “Thank you very much. I’m sure it’ll be lovely. It’s the thought that counts anyway.”

Nick kissed Alex goodbye. The scent he caught was still there, but it wasn’t nearly as strong. Weird.

* * *

So far Nick had done what Nicole asked and avoided trouble. The day had gone well in terms of not running into Miller. Nick had seen him several times, but never in a way where Miller could get him one on one. With that out of the way, he knocked on Mrs. Davies’s office with five minutes to go before the end of the day, eager to conclude the last bit of business.

“Hello, Mr. Slade. Can I help you?”

“I was wondering if I could ask you a question?”

“By all means. Fire away.”

“Where does Nicole go to university?”

“I’m sorry?” Mrs. Davies’s voice took on a hard tone.

“She told me she is lecturing tonight at her university, but she didn’t tell me where. I thought I might pop in to listen. I was wondering if you could tell me.”

Mrs. Davies folded her hands over one another. “Have a seat, Mr. Slade.”

Nick found the reply curious but did as asked, taking the same seat he had occupied with her previously.

Mrs. Davies quietly cleared her throat. "I think you should put Ms. O'Brien out of your mind. It is quite frankly very unusual, and in fact against the rules, for any member of the student body to ask so many questions about someone who technically is a member of staff."

Nick gulped. Had he honestly thought asking like this would get him anywhere? *What the hell is wrong with me lately?* "I— I'm sorry. I didn't mean any disrespect."

"It's not a matter of respecting her, as much as respecting boundaries. They exist for a reason: to prevent young people, such as you, from getting hurt."

Nick felt himself begin to sweat, feeling uncomfortable and pissed off. All he was doing was asking a question! No, she was right; this was out of line. He should just leave it be and go. So why could he not move? Why, at that very moment, was he even more determined to find Nicole? "I don't see the problem in asking where she goes to school. It's not like I'm asking her address, is it?"

"The problem is there for you to see, Mr. Slade, if you care to. Do you perhaps think there is a reason she didn't tell you where she went to school?"

She's right, he told himself. *Just say thank you and leave.*

Nick held up his hands and said slowly, hesitating, hearing his own voice as if from outside himself. His tone was as angry and frustrated as he felt. "She was the one who told me she was lecturing. Why would she do that and not expect me to consider turning up?"

"Because you need an invitation to get in. As guest speaker, there is only one invitation allocated and she has given it away already."

Nick's heart sank, and even Mrs. Davies noticed.

"I'm sorry to appear harsh, Mr. Slade, but this truly is for the best. I am only thinking of the welfare of both of you. While I am not accusing you of doing anything wrong by or towards her, it is nevertheless against protocols to encourage or even allow this sort of student-teacher fraternisation. Now look, I know Ms. O'Brien very well. She is a delightful and friendly girl, without doubt, but you should not think of her friendship as any more than it is. For your own good, remember…" she said as the bell rang, "boundaries."

She stood and gave him a rather patronisingly sad smile before moving past him to the second room Nicole usually sat in. "Off to homeroom with you, now."

Nick leant his head back, feeling like screaming. He made for the door when he suddenly stopped. He couldn't believe it; was that Nicole's strawberry lip-gloss he could smell? He dropped his bag. Sniffing, turning his head from side to side with an unnatural and desperate urge to find the source before Mrs. Davies returned.

Something she had said finally sunk in. "She has already given the invitation away…"

He went closer to the desk, lowering his head to a stack of papers. Without thinking, he flicked through the pile until he got to the bottom. He pulled out what looked like a large pamphlet, containing the invitation to the lecture: The Power of the Human Mind, and the Tools Needed to Discover True Leadership Qualities. Headed by Dr. Alan Sarsky and guest, Nicole O'Brien.

Attached to the purple coloured invitation was a hand-written note that read:

My first lecture! Well kind of. If you could come for a bit of moral support, it would mean a lot. At the very least, you can brag to everyone that you taught me everything I know. Ha ha.
Nicole

The note was finished with a faded kiss imprint just under her name, the scent which Nick had followed. The note had to be days, maybe months old, yet Nick could smell the lip gloss as if it had been left today.

But this was wrong. He held the ticket to the ball so to speak, but would he, could he, honestly consider stealing it?

Well that depends, said the voice, the same one that had told him to stand still when Miller had rushed him. It had also urged him to punch the wall to relieve the pressure of his aching fist. Nick finally recognised it as his own voice, but there was a cold and coarse sheen to it. *How badly do you want to see her again?*

Nick thought back to their time at the café. He thought about the way her face lit up whenever he said something funny. He thought about the way she looked at him when she smiled, her scent and the feeling of those tender lips on his cheek.

"Fuck boundaries," he said to himself, stuffing the invitation into his pants pocket as he walked out.

Chapter 17

Fancy Seeing You Here

"Hi, Alex. Glad I caught you." Nick had been hoping her phone would go straight to voicemail where he could leave a message. Oh well, no turning back now. "I wanted to let you know that I'll be a bit late tonight."

"No worries, kiddo. What's up? Hot date?"

Nick felt himself blush and was glad Alex couldn't see him. "Um, no, uh," he stammered. "Just, uh, showing a friend some support. It's a big night for them."

"Uh-huh." Alex clearly was not buying it. "Have fun, but not too late, ok, hun?"

"Ok."

Nick jammed his phone in his pocket and stepped into the auditorium of the University of New South Wales. He showed the invitation to the door attendant, who took it and waved him through.

"I wonder if I could have that back?" Nick asked.

"What, this?" the attendant asked, showing Nick the invitation.

"Yeah, as a souvenir. If you wouldn't mind."

"Sure mate. You're in seat C7."

Nick nodded and made his way into the auditorium. He looked at the invitation, staring at Nicole's name in print, remembering how excited she seemed in her letter to Mrs. Davies about tonight. The fact that he had managed to be here on a night that meant so much to her, meant even more to him.

Nick almost bumped into someone and looked up. The place was packed. At the back of the room, crews were setting up cameras, journalists were preparing their recorders and note pads, and regular attendees were being ushered into their seats. The evening, according to the invitation, would start promptly at six, which was in two minutes. Nick found his seat, only three rows back from the front. Not bad at all. Nick looked around and felt a sense of pride for Nicole that she was a big part in all this.

"Hello, you're rather a pup to be at one of these aren't you?"

Nick turned to see a large woman with a round face. She smiled at him, and looked at him with an air of amused curiosity. Nick quickly glanced around the room, which was filling with primarily older-looking people, professors mostly, Nick guessed. The average age of the room must have been close to fifty.

Nick laughed. "Yes, I suppose I am. Well it is my first."

"Welcome. It's about time we got some young blood in these lectures. I'm Jenny," she said, holding out her hand.

"Nick," he replied, shaking it.

"May I ask how you got an invite? These usually go out to teachers and journalists and what not."

"I actually know the guest speaker."

"Oh, wonderful. I'm curious about her myself. Is she your girlfriend?"

"No, just a friend."

"Oh. Well, don't worry, you seem very nice. Keep working and I'm sure you'll get through."

That's weird. Does she talk to everyone that way, or are my intentions just really that transparent?

"You mentioned you were curious about her too?" Nick asked.

"Oh, right, yes. See, I'm an old student of Dr. Sarsky. Known him for years, and any guest speakers he uses are usually earmarked for big things. When word got around that Miss O'Brien was only nineteen, people came up with all kinds of stories. Like he was losing his marbles or fooling around with her. Oh, don't you worry, dear," she said, patting Nick on the leg, lowering her voice to a barely audible whisper. "Alan Sarsky is a screaming queen. Looks better in a dress than I do," she chuffed.

"Oh…" Nick looked around, not quite comfortable with the turn this conversation was having. He couldn't tell if this lady was being offensive or trying to seem accepting.

"He is also brilliant when it comes to the working of the mind and thought process," she continued. Nick relaxed a little. "He is convinced humans can learn more about the world, the sea and the sky when they better understand the limitless potential of the brain. This lecture will likely be used in schools and universities around the world, dissected and critiqued, argued over and praised. That's why there's all the cameras, you see. It is a huge opportunity for your young Miss O'Brien. I hope she does well."

The audience began to clap and Jenny quietened and turned to the stage. A man in roughly his forties stepped up to the podium and positioned the microphone towards his mouth.

"Good evening ladies and gentlemen. My name is Richard Curtis, a director here at the University Of New South Wales, and it is my pleasure to welcome you all here this evening. Our main speaker tonight, Dr. Sarsky—" He paused as the audience applauded the doctor. "—will appear following his young protégée Nicole O'Brien. This young woman has caused quite a stir in recent weeks after being named one of the youngest guest speaker's Dr. Sarsky had ever chosen. Intensifying the intrigue of this young woman is that she is not yet a graduate—she is still studying the course she will be speaking on this evening. What was going on, people began to ask me. What had Dr. Sarsky seen in this student? What made Miss O'Brien so special? In preparation for this very speech, I asked Dr. Sarsky all of these questions. His reply was simply, 'Let her talk, and they will see for themselves'. Which is indeed what I shall do. Ladies and gentlemen, please give a warm welcome to Nicole O'Brien."

A warm if not enthusiastic round of clapping welcomed Nicole as she calmly and confidently, Nick thought, approached the podium. He couldn't tear his eyes away, and he did not want to. She wore a short white dress and matching heels, and her hair was clipped and swept up. Nick couldn't smell strawberry lip-gloss tonight, but he could smell… something fresh and clean. He couldn't quite place… *Soap. Yardley's English Lavender.* His mother had often placed bars of the soap among her clothes to infuse them with the scent. His head spun. Nicole was beautiful. She felt so perfect to him right here, right now. He realised she was speaking, and shook his head to clear it. *Focus! Listen.*

"Thank you, Mr. Curtis, for that very kind introduction, and may I also take a minute to again welcome everyone. This marks Dr. Sarsky's first lecture in New South Wales for almost fifteen years. During that time, he has given talks and taught in Italy, Brazil, Korea, and most recently the United States where he shared ideas with the top neuroscience and behaviour research institutes at Harvard, Stanford and John Hopkins University. In all that time, as has been previously mentioned, rarely has anyone still studying shared the stage with him. So why did he pick me? Any of his students will tell you, one of his first lessons is to be honest. With yourself, your surroundings, and any endeavour you choose. Speak up if you don't understand, admit when you are wrong and stand your ground when you believe your actions are just. So let me be honest with you; I have no idea why he offered me this opportunity. When I asked him, he told me it didn't matter why, only what my answer would be. Though I couldn't get the yes out fast enough, I, like this audience tonight, felt the curiosity grow. I knew that if I couldn't give a reason why a nineteen-year-old was standing here talking to you tonight, all credibility, mine and his, might be tarnished. Truthfully, all I can offer is the occasion where I may have surprised him for the first time in many years. He was our guest lecturer via satellite for my class some months ago. Our online assignment was on leadership and its values and how these relate to psychology and human behaviour. We were to give opinions and, where possible, supportive facts about how two people can do the same job, say the same thing, yet get different results. He asked us to offer insight on what it takes medically and psychologically to be a 'true leader', to use what our experiences have taught us to inspire and teach. And most importantly, to analyse what it is about the human mind and its power when it comes to helping enhance and stimulate others."

Nicole paused and sipped a glass of water from the podium. Nick used the opportunity to take a quick glance around the room. Everyone, Jenny included had their eyes seemingly glued to the stage. Nicole held the room so far. She certainly held him and he eagerly waited to hear her continue. He had grown up around forceful men. Killers even. Wilson had been a leader. An Alpha is the definition of a leader. But a true leader? As much as Nick fought with him, he loved Wilson, but he did not believe Wilson was a true leader. He was now definitely curious as to what aspects of the brain constituted true leadership.

"The reason I say to you that I surprised him is because I received a

High Distinction on the theory I presented in the assignment, something he told me he had not given to students for many years. Therefore, what I would like to do is tell you about that theory tonight, as a way of possibly giving you insight into why I was chosen to be here."

Nicole reached down and pulled out her notes from a shelf in the podium. As she did so, her eyes flicked up momentarily, and caught his. He gave a small smile and wave. Just for a second, her eyes widened and her mouth gaped, but then all was normal.

Nicole cleared her throat, looking like she was fighting the urge to laugh. "…Excuse me. The theme of the assignment is entitled, What Makes A True Leader? Don't worry, I'll only give the highlights. I won't bore you with the statistical details."

A few chuckles followed this.

"True leaders and what makes them are a discussion that has been taking place since the dawn of civilisation. Ancient China, Greece, Egypt, all of these societies had theories about what made a true leader. They knew that a man could not simply name himself a true leader and believe that others would automatically follow. But how do we today begin to understand their brains? What is it truly about the human mind that defines whether or not someone is or can become a leader? The study of the theory of leadership in psychology has often been in a class of its own, independent of other psychological studies. This may be because it is an issue that affects us all. There are a number of theories that have attempted to explain our presuppositions about leadership and its effectiveness, or to categorise aspects of leadership itself, such as 'influential', 'visionary', and so on, and in what contextual settings a leader's actions take place, such as military, politics, or business.

"After dissecting leadership traits, styles, situations, behaviors, and more, it was perhaps only a matter of time before leadership psychologists focused on the 'self' in their theorizing of leadership. One theory shows how leadership is a process in which leaders can change the way followers feel about themselves in order to elicit their best performances. Another theory shows how leaders must know their true selves in order to be able to judge themselves and their own actions consistently before they can begin to judge others. And finally, there's the elusive charisma and its effect on followers. Even still, we have trouble defining it. While the other qualities can be learned, can be developed, it is charisma that just might be the one thing that a true leader, *must* be born with.

That charisma is what separates true leaders, or the Alpha's, from the rest of the pack. Historically, the word *charisma* was associated with supernatural elements, seen as a gift or talent from heaven that gives an individual the ability and the authority to rule others. While that may seem strange or even ludicrous to some, there is still little to no explanation how some people possess that magnetism, that charm, to influence others.

"So what does this all mean for the study of leadership? Remember that true leaders know themselves and make decisions in difficult situations based on that knowledge. When a 'leader' is acting only to please others in order to further their own status, they are no true leader," Nicole looked up and scanned the room. "Let me just pause here and ask you all, do you know any true leaders? Don't worry if the answer is no. The only one I know is your main speaker tonight and it brings me to my next point.

"True leaders are like eagles. They are unique and rare, and must possess or develop all of the characteristics I've spoken of. And until recently, it was nearly impossible to pinpoint exactly which individual could turn out to be a true leader. But now, with devices such as MRIs and CT scanners becoming more and more common, determining the source of charisma is within grasp. We also know more about the brain than ever before, and have come to understand better its internal workings. I believe that we can learn exactly which chemical is the neurotransmitter responsible for true leadership skills, and which provides us with genuine charisma."

The audience began to whisper behind Nick. It seemed that this theory was indeed something that made them all abuzz with interest.

"Everyone has a leadership capacity in something," Nicole went on. "If you want people to perceive you as charismatic, to embrace you as a true leader, you must also display attributes such as empathy, good listening skills, eye contact, enthusiasm, self-confidence and skillful speaking. These are the attributes social scientists have long spoken of in their attempt to fully understand charismatic communication and leadership. But until now we had not embarked upon an attempt to single out the exact neurotransmitter, the exact brain chemical that is responsible for this elusive charisma needed for true leadership.

"If we can do this, we can begin to predict charisma, and determine in advance whether one has the capability to become a true leader. And furthermore, we may be able to utilise this chemical and enhance its presence in order to create more true leaders. Perhaps we can help shape true leaders of today and tomorrow, because we need them, now more than ever. Thank you."

Nick thought a bomb had gone off in the auditorium, such was the roar of applause Nicole got as she stepped down. Nick stood and clapped along with many others.

"What a breakthrough," Jenny said, amazed. "Wouldn't that be something?"

Nick didn't feel he had to agree, he felt the look on his face would've said it all. Even he knew the look of awe he was giving her. She gave small head nods to the applause she received and focussed on Nick, finding him again in the crowd. They locked eyes and neither looked away. Nicole shook her head slowly as a man walked onto the stage behind her. The applause increased and Nick guessed this must be Dr. Sarsky. Nicole jabbed at Nick quickly with her finger, mouthing, "Stay," as Dr. Sarsky kissed her on the cheek and joined in the applause as she walked off the stage.

The applause died down and Dr. Sarsky approached the podium, smiling triumphantly.

"Speaking of charisma…!"

* * *

The night was over. Nick had bid Jenny farewell and remained in his seat as the audience moved slowly for the door.

Nick sat for over an hour after the room had cleared, going over the things he had heard. Dr. Sarsky had spoken at length about factual paranormal activity concerning brainpower. Dr. Sarsky's theory, was people that had learned how to unlock rare parts of the brain in order to accomplish these things, were true leaders. It was fascinating and while he agreed with Dr. Sarsky that these were the people that should grace the covers of magazines and rather than which B-grade celebrity had slept with who, no matter how many facts and figures put in front of him, Nick just couldn't buy the things he was told. He did not think anyone could actually move objects across a room, read minds or sense injuries from thousands of kilometres away, or levitate, all because they had harnessed the power of their mind. The mind could not be plugged in to a wall socket, and he didn't believe it could pick up paranormal wi-fi.

Strange you can't believe that, but you of course believe the unusual fact that you were born from two werewolves.

"Shut up," Nick breathed.

"Who are you talking to?" Nicole asked. Nick looked up to find her walking towards him. She bent her knees and sat on the lip of the stage, legs crossed and dangling over the edge. She wore a light coat over her dress, her hair was no longer up, so it hung, wavy and full, around her shoulders. Just the way he liked it.

"Oh…no one," Nick said, leaning back in his chair. "I have to say congratulations. You were amazing."

"Thank you. But *I* have to ask, what are you doing here?" she replied softly, leaning her head to the side. "That invitation was *supposed* to be for Mrs. Davies."

"You told me to look you up," Nick crossed his arms and raised his eyebrows. "Are you sorry it's me instead of her?"

"I didn't say that," she replied carefully, again looking as though she was trying not to laugh. "I just want to know how you got it."

Nick got up and walked closer, stopping a few feet in front of her. He placed his hands on either side of her legs. "It doesn't matter."

"Nick… It *does* matter. It matters to me." Nicole barked. "I gave that to Mrs. Davies for good reason and I know for a fact she wouldn't have handed it to you. Did you steal it?"

"Before I answer, can I ask you something? When you saw me, were you happy?"

Nicole didn't answer right away. She stared at him, giving off the impression she was thinking of what to say. Finally, after giving a quick glance to the ground, blinking away with those damn lashes, she said, "Yes."

"Then what does it matter how I got it?" he shrugged.

She grabbed his wrists and looked him dead in the eyes. "Do you realise how much trouble you're in for this?"

Nick laughed. "You're worth it."

Nicole was no longer amused. "Nick, stop. Be serious. You stole from a teacher."

Tell her some of what she means to you. That any threat to you means nothing compared to being able to make her happy.

Nick raised his hand and then quickly lowered it. For an instant, the desire to touch the supple skin of her face was irresistible. To clasp her warmth in his hands and touch his forehead to hers, having her hold onto him in return.

"Hey… I would do a lot more than that if it meant being here to support you on the biggest night of your life so far."

Nicole opened her mouth to reply, but whatever it was about to say, it appeared that she changed her mind. Instead she said, "I can't help you when you get back on Monday," pleading with her eyes for him to understand.

"I don't want your help," he said.

"What *do* you want then?" she whispered.

Nick looked into her eyes, then moved his face, seeking her lips. She waited until the last possible second but pulled away.

"Nick…it's not that I don't want to…" She sounded exasperated.

Nick cursed his lack of patience and the fact he just couldn't help trying, given what she did to him in so many ways. He stepped back from her. This was not going how he planned at all. But had he really planned anything? This wasn't him. What was he thinking? He was trying to do something nice for her. Spontaneous. Wasn't he? No. He had taken something Nicole had purposefully given away and took it upon himself to show up uninvited, maybe even unwanted. Was it any surprise she wasn't exactly jumping for joy?

"Nicole…I'm really sorry. I don't know what…" Nick struggled for the words, shaking his head. All of a sudden, the realisation of what he had done washed over him, as if the last few hours had been out of his control. "I just thought…you might appreciate a bit of support from someone else that is really proud of you, that's all."

Nicole sighed helplessly. "You are…impossible to figure out. I will give you that."

Nick winced. "Well, I guess that's not the worst thing you could say after all this."

“No it’s not. You’re also infuriating as hell,” she replied, hopping down. “Now, stand still and close your eyes.”

Nick frowned but did as he was told. “If I open them and your gone, I’ll underst—” His words had halted as her hands grasped his collar, and her lips touched his. In only five or so seconds, she let him go, but stayed close enough to breathe her in yet again. “You should be sorry,” she whispered. “But…it was really sweet too. I will admit that. But that’s all you’re getting.”

She turned and picked up her purse from the stage. She took his hand as she said, “Come on, I’ll drive you home.”

Chapter 18

Heart Strings

Nicole tried to keep her eyes on the road, but couldn't help stealing a glance at Nick. His presumptuous actions had really irked her, and yet… He currently looked lost in a daydream and wore the most unashamed grin she had ever seen. It didn't seem arrogant, though. That seemed to have disappeared after her kiss.

Another kiss. Was that why he looked so happy now? The thought both warmed her heart and gave her a chill. It was meant to be a thank you, a full stop on the "Let's just be friends" point she'd been trying to make. But it seemed he, and if she was honest with herself, she, had felt something more than she had planned. She could still remember the goose bumps spread over her forearms as their lips touched.

This wasn't good. She shouldn't be kissing students. She needed to keep her wits. There was no way that this was a good idea. Maybe if Nick had been ten years older. Maybe if she didn't happen to work at the very school he was a student at. Maybe if the whole episode in her past had never happened. But she couldn't afford this hiccup in life right now. Anyway, it would be completely unethical. Things were complicated enough as it was, and there was no room to even *begin* to think about what else he could do with such an amazing mouth. *Stop it!* she screamed at herself.

"So…what did you think of my speech?" Nicole asked, trying to change her own internal subject.

"You saw the standing ovation you got, didn't you?" Nick replied.

"I'm asking *you* what *you* thought."

"I'm not sure. I mean I thought you were great, but some stuff you said about leadership I didn't understand."

"Oh really? Like what?"

"Well, you remember how I told you my dad was sort of…nobility, so to speak? I suppose in his surroundings, he could've been considered one of those true leaders you were talking about. I mean, admittedly I was at boarding school for most of my life, so I never really saw him conduct business, but he must have had that charismatic spark you spoke of. The commanding presence. After all, he was responsible for dozens of men, but also their partners and children. His choices affected more than just the people under him, but also generations after as well. And he was really successful for a lot of years. But in the end, those people he had looked after for so long ended up killing him. He was even warned before it happened, and I guess he just ignored everything. It seemed like he'd maybe lost the spark? He certainly didn't have any of the likeability he'd once had. In fact, I'd grown to hate him and his oppressive attitude. But after hearing your speech…I'm wondering if it's possible for someone to become a bad leader, after supposedly being a good one?"

"I don't know how well I can answer that since I don't really know all the circumstances. But from my perspective, it doesn't necessarily make him a bad leader. Maybe a less good one. Anything that rises can fall, yeah? Studies have shown that people can't really lose charisma just like that. It takes something more. Like maybe the individual is struggling with conflicting values within themselves. There was an article I quoted on one of my assignments, from the Charisma Today website. I remember it well. "*It is quite possible that charisma could become latent over time, but not lost, if the charismatic has a paradigm shift in beliefs and motivation.* Perhaps that's what happened with your dad? Maybe he really was listening to the people around him, but doubted himself? I can't say. But it sounds like he was a great man in his way, even just for a time."

Nick seemed to shift uncomfortably in his seat. "Surely a *true* leader can confront their own weakness and defeat something like that?"

"I wouldn't say it works that way. You might have the wrong idea of power. A true leader knows what they oppose and stands up to it anyway. It can be a range of things, even if it's their own weaknesses."

"So weakness lies inside true leaders as well? I know you said earlier they aren't perfect, but that's not the same thing, right?"

The tone of his question was puzzling. She got a hint of desperation in there. *Wow...he must really have loved and lost faith in his father*. "Of course it does, and no it's not the same thing. Well, let me ask this. How would you want to be remembered by your loved ones after you've gone? What do you want your legacy to be?"

Nick pursed his lips, contemplating his answer before answering. "I just want to mean something to someone. Of course I want to travel and build a career and all that, but really isn't that just icing on the cake? The real life essence is finding something or someone that ignites your passion for life."

"Nick, believe me, that's all very nice but you shouldn't be thinking that way, in my opinion anyway. A loving partner is a wonderful thing, but if you're not comfortable within yourself, no other person is going to be able to fix that for you."

She looked sideways at Nick and he nodded, understanding. "You're right, you know. This counselling thing has worked well for you, I think," he replied with a little smile.

Nicole snorted. "Heh, thanks. I *did* work really hard on it."

"Your advice just really rings true to me. I guess the thing is, I am afraid of becoming like my dad."

"You mean taking over the...family business, or whatever it is?"

"No." Nick shook his head. "That's never been in the cards and never will be. I mean having a situation be right in front of him, or all around him and him being totally unable to see it. I don't want to end up blind like that, having never taken a chance to break free, take a risk. I don't want to wake up as a lonely old man with nothing left to give to the world."

They came to a red light. "My personal trainer used to say, it's ok to be defeated by your opponent. Don't get defeated by fear."

Nicole patted Nick's hand in comfort. "If you don't want to be your father, you don't have to be. All you have to do is figure out who you are, what you stand for and what you don't. I have faith in you."

Nick had gently gripped her fingers. She now found herself in a strange position. They were both stroking each other's hand with their thumbs.

The car behind them beeped loudly, waking Nicole up from her semi-trance. She snatched her hand out of his and put the car into gear, accelerating rapidly. *No. No!* She had to correct this.

"Look… About the kiss."

Nick folded his hands in his lap and grinned dreamily. "Don't worry, I won't tell anyone about it. I mean I will tell myself sometimes, but I won't believe it."

"I just mean…I shouldn't have done it. I think it was a mistake. *They* were a mistake."

"A mistake…"

"I feel like I've been leading you on, even though I explained why nothing can happen. Like I said before, we're just friends and that's all. But friends don't kiss, not like that. It was wrong of me to be putting out such mixed signals. I can't expect you to forget about me if I keep going on like that, so I'm sorry."

"No need to apologise. If you hate something, don't want something or are afraid, it's all the same outcome isn't it?"

"I don't hate you," Nicole said.

"I meant if you hated kissing me. If it wasn't as great for you as it was for me. That being the case, it hurts the old ego, but at least it's true, which is what you were talking about tonight. It's cool, I get it."

"That's got nothing to do with it." Nicole stopped the car just outside the driveway of his cousin's apartment. She needed him to understand. She liked it. Ok, she loved it. The fact is that he gave her butterflies. But she had been hurt before. The way she had gotten out of that is by living her life to a schedule and with focus. Work. Career. Study. Achieving her goals. She had avoided all distractions, namely dating, ever since. The best part was, it wasn't something she felt she missed. Until now. She would never forget the way he looked at her that first day. She had never felt so beautiful before, and he couldn't even utter a cohesive sentence. It was just his eyes. People can go their whole lives without experiencing a moment in time like that.

But still, it made no difference. She would most probably be fired for just kissing him, let alone anything else. Why the hell can't she just cut loose?

Hell, she already knew the answer to that. She didn't really want to.

She turned in her seat to talk to Nick properly, but he had already undone his seatbelt.

"It's fine," he said, but he certainly didn't look it. His eyes were closed so hard they almost looked clenched. He looked strained, struggling the way her mother did, to get the words out, when she was suffering from a migraine. "Thanks for the ride. Congrats on the night. You should be proud of yourself. Take care."

And he was gone. He did not slam the car door, but something about the click hit Nicole very deeply.

What was all that about? she thought. *He couldn't even let me explain?*

It seemed pretty clear that Nick was in pain. There was obviously a lot of inner turmoil he was dealing with after the death of his father and the unknown whereabouts of his mum. It was more than understandable. Plus, she felt he had a severe guilt associated with the death, even though it was in no way his fault. He probably needed some professional counselling. Maybe she could make some enquiries to help him, but he would need to ask for that, she wouldn't push. He had taken a big step by trusting her with that information.

But she would have to be more careful. Even if she did have feelings for, and could have considered being with him under other circumstances, she should cut him some slack. She felt she had unconsciously toyed with his emotions, and as her father would say, that wasn't cool. The fact he had this effect on her though, troubled her more than she liked.

No, the best thing she could do now was to offer simple friendship. It was the best thing for the both of them. She told herself that again as she turned the ignition on.

* * *

Nick waited until he heard Nicole's car start and drive away, then he walked out and sat on the steel letterboxes. He didn't want to deal with Margaret or Alex, and the questions they would ask when they saw the look on his face.

He did understand where Nicole was coming from but it made him angry, frustrated. Maybe he had been too quick to leave the car, but it was better than a long, drawn out goodbye. Really, what was the point? She didn't want him.

She wanted to be friends, but that wasn't enough. Why should he torture himself?

You are a fool. She would not have given you a second tender moment if she did not enjoy the first. Do not give up. She can still be yours.

"No," Nick mumbled aloud to himself. "I won't hound her. I'm not going to be that person. I can't believe I made such a huge deal about getting out of the car! Anyway, I would just be making a fool of myself going after her. I tried and failed. Maybe I am a true leader after all. The best thing I can do is just let her go."

A sharp pain in the back of the head, and Nick found the sidewalk coming rapidly toward his face. He quickly thrust his hands out to stop his forehead from smacking the concrete when a kick smashed his cheek. He rolled sideways, and masking tape was rapidly plastered over his mouth.

Dizzy, Nick tried to grab at the tape but both his arms were grabbed, stretched over his head. His chest and stomach were being repeatedly stomped by a heavy foot. Despite his agony, Nick did not need much to figure out who the two were.

"Hullo, muffin," came Miller's coarse whisper beside Nick's ear. "You really aren't a good listener, are you?" He brought his fist smashing clean into Nick's open face. He drew back and hit him repeatedly. "I… told…you. She's…mine!"

Nick felt his nose split with a searing pain as if a hot knife had sliced through his face and in desperation, he kicked both his legs, trying to get them back over himself. The strike wasn't hard, but it was enough to send Miller into the one that held Nick's arms. It wasn't difficult for Nick to figure out it was Jason.

Suddenly freed, Nick got onto his hands and knees, letting the blood of his shattered nose pour onto the ground, lest it choke him what with his mouth covered. His legs were like jelly. He tried to remove the tape but his hands felt numb. He tried to call for help, to run, to crawl even. But his limbs weren't really responding.

Within seconds, his arms were pinned behind him again, and Miller walked into his view.

"Cute," Miller said softly, backing up two steps, measuring. "I couldn't stop you arseholes from taking my bro…" He punctuated the sentence with a front-facing side kick. Nick's head felt as if it would burst open. If Jason hadn't been holding his arms, Nick would be on his back. He couldn't feel his legs at all now. "But you're not fucking getting my girl. Take this as your second warning. And believe me, you won't get a third. She's mine. Stay the fuck away, you fucking pommy cunt."

"Hey! What the hell is going on out here?"

Miller and Jason scarpered off into the night. Nick fell backwards and began to fade. He heard Alex's voice but not the words. He heard sirens, coming closer. He felt hands probing his face, a light shining in his eyes and his body being lifted onto something stiff. After a sting in his right arm, he felt nothing. Heard nothing, but silence. Saw nothing but darkness.

* * *

Alex could not believe the broken and bloodied person under an oxygen mask, the mammoth amount of bandages and wires was her cousin's son. She and Margaret remained in his hospital room, praying that he would be ok. The surgeon had told them Nick had suffered from internal bleeding, a broken nose, and his jaw and three ribs were fractured. He wasn't out of the woods, as they were still concerned about things like potential brain damage and blood clots. It had been touch-and-go, but now the surgeon declared him stable. He would likely recover, but it would be slow going.

"We have to do something," Alex said, exhausted.

"I agree," replied Margaret, never taking her eyes off Nick, leaning forward and stroked what part of his hair was not bandaged.

"I should've gone to the school when I had the chance," Alex said.

"It wouldn't have made a difference. Not with boys like that."

"It would've been something!" Alex yelled, before forming a fist, smacking her thigh and leaning back, closing her eyes.

"What about the police?"

Margaret shook her head. "We have no idea what these little brats look like, so the police can't help."

Alex sighed. This was getting nowhere. "So what do you suggest we do?"

"Wait."

"Wait? Wait for what?" Alex cried.

"For me," Dante answered her question.

Alex felt like her heart would jump through her chest. "Oh my god! You scared me! What are you doing here?"

"I called him," Margaret said simply.

Dante moved closer to the bed, examining Nick from head to toe, taking in the severe bruises and his general condition.

"This was your plan? This *again*?!" Alex shot at Margaret. She hadn't told her mother about the fight she'd had with Dante. Nor had she spoken to Dante since it happened. She felt the need to apologise, but now wasn't the time. *Whatever. Better to focus on Nick.* "Can you help him at all, Dante? Please?"

Dante opened his mouth and his fangs flared. He bit his right wrist and used the fingers of his left hand to smear small amounts of his blood onto Nick's limbs, neck and face. Alex watched in awe as Nick's bruises disappeared before her eyes. "I can only help with the wounds on the surface," he said quietly.

Suddenly, Dante bent over Nick and appeared to be inhaling him.

"What—" Alex began before Dante grimaced.

"Rancid cowards," Dante muttered angrily before turning on his heel and walking out. He gave Margaret a slight nod as he went.

Alex narrowed her eyes at her mother. "Where is he going? Never mind. I think I know already." Dante would have picked up the scent of whoever had attacked Nick. The sudden thought of what was coming after Nick's attackers chilled Alex to the bone.

Chapter 19

Revenge or Justice?

"Special drink for a special girl." Jason handed Lucy a bottle of Jack Daniels. They sat in the swings opposite the Coogee Bay Hotel, the usual hook-up place for all the kids in their area. Though Jason had "booked" it for them, it wasn't uncommon for other kids to show up from time to time and have their own fun. Girls asked guys there, and vice versa. Everyone knew what it meant.

Lucy gave a smile she hoped couldn't be seen through. It was weird to be having sex and potentially be spied on by people she went to school with, but she was used to it. It was always dark, and she could make out a few people, but mostly all she saw was vague flashes of bums and boobs in the dark. Faces were mostly obscured by shadows. The problem was she *hated* screwing Jason Trod. Foreplay meant rubbing her raw, kissing meant his tongue trying to choke her. He was endowed well enough, but he just has no idea how to use it. Lucy had joked with her friends that he had lost his virginity to a patch of wet sand and treated pussy like that's all it was ever since.

Still, it was exciting fooling her parents into thinking she was just hanging with friends. Plus, in return, he supplied some decent booze, ecstasy and pot that almost no money, and quite a bit of stealing could get him. "You know you're getting into my pants, Troddy. Why bother with the small talk?"

"Just trying to be a gentleman," he replied, stroking her neck with his fingers.

“Please, with Trent Miller as your best friend, the last thing you are is gentle. Why are you friends with such a prick?”

“Better to be the beast’s best friend than to be its enemy. Anyway, just be thankful he doesn’t know about this, otherwise he would want to join in, and I ain’t saying no to him.”

“I wouldn’t let him near me,” Lucy said, taking a swig of whiskey. The guy she did want wasn’t here. She had watched the new kid, Nick, for a while now and she thought he was seriously sexy. He had the blonde hair with the hot just-a-bit-too-long-fringe look, along with the big blue eyes, and an even bigger smile.

She had fantasised about what he would be like several times, and it looked like she would again, seeing as though the thirty-second tank was revving his engine. Lucy gave an internal shrug and started unbuttoning her jeans. *Might as well get him over with.*

* * *

“Melina!” Julian hissed.

She had almost completely forgotten she was not alone. Julian had taken her hunting “to improve her mood,” he’d said. They stood on the roof of the Coogee Bay Hotel, watching over the scene below in the small, dark playground in the park. Melina turned to him, eyes weary. “What?”

“I said, do you now see my genius? I told you how easy it was to hunt in Coogee,” he growled. “Tell me how you will tear them apart.”

Melina looked away, rubbing her temples. Tight due to lack of blood and exhaustion. Tonight was their hunting night; yet another activity Julian insisted on joining to direct her as if she was a newborn. “Not tonight.”

Julian was insistent. “You know what it does to me to hear how you will kill. You have never denied me anything before.”

“There is a first time for everything,” she replied, keeping her eyes on the children. Stupid as they were, they did not deserve to die. Not tonight anyway. Besides, the amusement of watching youngsters try to fuck when they still had no idea how, was the only reason her heavy eyes hadn’t slammed down.

Julian crossed his arms, scowling. "You are still on about your ridiculous theory that you woke during the day?"

"I *wake* during the day. It's happening more and more often. But I know I'm wasting my breath. You don't believe me."

"How can I believe something I know to be impossible?"

"That's the same as calling me a liar. And then you run off to tell your father."

"Which is what I told you to do in the first place was it not? He thinks the same as I do, you are just dreaming."

"We don't dream."

"We do now," he corrected.

Melina shook her head. "I haven't taken any of that shit. Dream State is an abomination."

"Father's theory is you don't have to take it to feel its effects. With the number of us using it in the mansion, it is quite possible you are experiencing side effects from the air. This is what he believes."

"It *must* be true then," Melina moaned.

Julian's head whipped around to face her. "Did I just hear you insult my father, the king? What the hell has gotten into you?"

"I'm just…tired. It must be from all my *dreaming*. Does he have any idea what to do based on Clive and Lauren's near miss?" She tensed, hoping the subject change would be enough to calm him.

Julian stiffened. "He and I both admit this is a problem. That greedy fuck at Coffinail slipped underneath Luca's gaze. But he's dead now and Luca has assured us it's nothing that cannot be rectified."

"You make it sound so easy."

"Why wouldn't it be?"

"Because there is clearly more to this than meets the eye. The pack possesses the once paraplegic human that was taken out of his hospital bed some months ago. He can now walk and is being trained to hunt us. Not only that, but they have taken refuge somewhere in the one place our kind would be in danger. Where Vincent's authority is not recognised, much less feared."

"Redfern," Julian spat.

"If Clive hadn't halted Lauren from following them, she would've been killed the other night. Do you not think it strange, even unnerving, that the pack knows to use Redfern as a base?"

"So the coons have some friends around while they sniff some petrol. What of it?"

"The pack is receiving help!" Melina hissed. "Werewolves have never been here, yet they hide in the one place Vincent has declared a no-go zone due to the Aborigine population. Can you not see it? Can you not feel it? A force is gathering. Something is coming. Unseen and unheard, but it's coming after us."

"Don't be so melodramatic, woman. Trust us. My father and I know what we are doing."

"Trust you?" Melina scoffed. "You still refuse to tell me where you get Dream State from. Does it not seem obvious to you we have only had this wolf trouble since it came into our lives? What was it, a few weeks only, that we heard there was a werewolf presence here? No one else knew of it, correct? Well obviously not, and you still hate me asking questions! You won't tell me what's in it, only what it does. Either you know or are being lied to, but somehow you've pissed them off! Why can't you just stop selling or buying it? It's what they are here for!"

"You have no idea what you are talking about!" Julian fired back. "We are the dominant race. We will not back down from a challenge. The mutts will be found and put down. End of story."

Melina wanted to retaliate; she sensed she was hitting a nerve. It pleased her quite immensely, but she just didn't have the energy. Julian knew m9re about Dream State than he was letting on, and whatever it was, Melina imagined connected it with the wolves. And that was what scared him. "Can we just eat and go?"

"Fine," answered Julian, becoming even more livid by the second. "Which one is for you then?"

"Actually, I'm not hungry," Melina replied.

Julian lowered his head after throwing it back dramatically. "You won't tell me what you would do, and you won't let me watch you feed. You still refuse to fuck me. How am I supposed to be kept happy?"

"You're the prince of Sydney, why wouldn't you be happy? You've been busy slamming the slave girls, so I think sex with me is the last thing you should be worrying about."

"Men have needs."

Melina looked at him briefly up and down. "So do women," she replied slowly.

A sudden noise brought their attention back to the campfire. They had heard the same thing, but only Melina recognised the scent immediately. She couldn't see him regardless how desperately she tried, and she had no idea why he was there, but it didn't stop her smiling. An act not lost on Julian, she hoped.

"Alejandro," she whispered.

* * *

"Did you hear something?" Lucy asked, coming up for breath after Jason's expected round of tongue boxing. She heard a loud twig snap as if someone had stepped on it.

Jason's hand moved to guide her mouth back towards his. "Don't worry."

Lucy held his hand at bay. "I'm serious. I heard something."

"You always think you hear something. Come on, I'm horny."

Jason pulled her on top of him, lifted his head, and began kissing her again, his tongue continuing its frantic work. Jason's hand wandered up her thigh, found her rear and squeezed tight. With the other hand, he pulled open her jeans.

"Let's swap. It's more comfy on my back," she said.

"Just hurry up."

On her back, Lucy removed her jeans and panties, Jason didn't even bother, merely unzipping himself and holding his erection ready as he knelt in front of her.

"Open them," he grunted, swatting her knees apart with his hand. She handed him a condom, which he put on. Just like that, he was in. Lucy scrunched her eyes, praying it would be over soon. One thrust, then two, then…nothing. She could no longer feel him. She chanced a look and screamed. Jason was dangling above her, upside down.

The other kids nearby finally heard Lucy's screams and looked over, gasping at the broad figure holding Jason up by the leg as if he were made of paper. The figure turned his attention from the cursing and struggling Jason to Lucy.

"Leave," the figure stated. Nothing happened. Lucy was terrified, and felt frozen to the ground. The figure gave a hiss and his eyes changed to black and…good god, fangs appeared instead of usual teeth. "I said… FUCKING LEAVE!"

Lucy scrambled, grabbing clothes she ran, wanting only to get away as fast as humanly possible.

* * *

Dante dropped Jason unceremoniously. "You have a wonderfully loyal girlfriend."

"Keep away from me, you freak!" Jason shouted, rising to his feet and making to punch Dante. Everything Jason threw, Dante blocked with hilarious ease, finally bringing him to his knees with a stinging slap. The blow cut the boy's cheek in three places from Dante's nails. Jason tried to run, but Dante bit him from behind. The bite was quick, a scare tactic, drawing blood only. He had seen bullies like this before over the years. The only way to respond to their form of attacks was controlled brutality. Showing them the strength they believed they wielded, even in numbers, was a fallacy. That there were things in the world stronger and scarier than they were.

Jason screamed and began to whimper after Dante let him go. "What do you want, man?"

"You attacked a boy tonight," Dante said, licking his fangs and spitting the putrid muck back over him, circling Jason, who stayed in the one spot, breathing rapidly, petrified into stillness. "But you weren't alone. Where is the other?"

"Miller? At…at home."

Dante scowled. So that was why he lost the scent. The scum had gone indoors. "Where does he live?"

"If I tell you…will you let me go?"

"It may help," Dante replied, his lip twitching.

"Sixty-four Bellevue Crescent," he rattled off. Dante grabbed Jason by the throat and held him aloft. "You said you wouldn't kill me!"

"I said it may help," Dante replied, launching Jason into the campfire. The boy quickly rolled over it and along the ground, putting out the small flame that had stuck to his shoulder.

"Oh, Jesus… Someone help me!"

With a swift kick, Dante launched him briefly into the air until he landed on his bony arse and squealed.

"That's right. Scream, beg. What does it feel like to be brutalised with no one to save you?" Dante approached and placed his foot on Jason's neck. "You are a coward who hides behind a stronger accomplice to take on one boy. This is the reward that has gotten you. Are you proud of yourself?"

"No!" Jason blubbered. "Please, I'll do anything! Just don't kill me."

Dante roughly dragged Jason to his feet. "I'm not going to kill you. Not if you do as I say."

"Anything, dude!" Jason's eyes were filled with panic. He wouldn't be able to hang onto even this much calm for much longer. "Please. Name anything, I swear I'll do it!"

Dante grabbed Jason by the throat and gave a squeeze he knew would frighten the boy, but not cause any lasting damage. "First, never call me dude. Second, tell your friend, this Miller, that you want no further part in hurting Nick Slade. Tell him you know for a fact he is protected, and that those protecting him came after you. Say you don't know who they are, but they sent you as a warning."

Jason coughed and writhed in Dante's grasp. "You don't know this guy. Miller won't stop. The more obstacles that get put in front of him, the harder he goes for them. This whole thing started because of a girl at school he wants to fuck. The girl hates him! But he's convinced he will get her and will let no one stand in his way. Plus he hates Brits! Loathes them for something their commandos did in Iraq that got his brother killed. That's why he's after Slade. If I say that stuff to Miller, he's probably going to come after him harder just to spite you."

"That's where you come in, you see," Dante explained pleasantly, as if he were the most patient man in the world. "Do everything in your power to stop him. I don't care what you do. Tell your teachers, the police, other students, fight him off yourself. If he ever comes near Nick again, not only will I come back for Miller, I'll come back for you. You are now responsible for what happens to him. If Nick dies, I will kill Miller, and make you watch what I do to him. Then, I will pluck your still-beating heart from your chest. I have been alive for over two hundred years, I know how to kill quickly, and I know how to kill slowly. For you, I'll be pleased to take my time."

"If I help you and protect this kid, Miller is going to kill me. If I don't protect him, you're going to kill me? What kind of a fucking choice is that?"

"The right thing is rarely easy. Welcome to the real world, kid."

Dante released the boy's neck, turned around and walked away.

"Why is this kid so important to you?" Jason called out.

Because the women who love him mean everything to me. Dante answered in his own head. He did not stop or turn as he said aloud, "He's family."

* * *

Melina stared, not believing what she had just witnessed. The caring and sweet Alejandro, who stood up for human rights, was threatening a teenage boy? The anger she heard in his voice was something she had not witnessed for centuries. She found it exhilarating. For only a few moments, Alejandro was not the human-lover he claimed to be, not the pathetic pansy he was taken for. He was a vampire, doing what comes naturally. He was bold, fierce and intimidating, unleashing only a part of what he kept hidden inside.

Melina had only realised then the sudden heat of the night. She held the backs of her hands to her cheeks and found them warm and flushed. If she didn't know better, she would swear she was aroused.

"So the vampire wannabe finally shows some backbone. Big deal, he chased away our supper. Still, we can snack on the one he left behind."

"No," Melina said. "I want to see this play out. I also want to know what's so special about this boy Alejandro is protecting."

* * *

Julian watched Melina leave and turned back to Jason, who had sat down on the ground and begun to cry out of fear and relief.

Let Melina follow Dante. Julian couldn't care less about that. He wanted to know more about this Miller kid. If Dante hated him, Julian decided he was someone he had to meet. If Dante was personally protecting this kid, Julian just might, put his weight behind Miller and even the odds a bit one day.

This could be a lot of fun, he thought, as he teleported away with the sound of a whip crack. Melina could walk home. Fuck her.

* * *

"The person you are calling has their mobile phone switched off, or unavail—"

Nicole flicked the phone away with her hand and it toppled onto the floor. She'd sent three texts to Nick already, asking if she could call and explain the situation, but after no response, she'd finally decided to bite the bullet and call. Lot of good that did her. She could not believe he could be so childish and not answer his phone, switching it off so he didn't have to talk to her. She put her head in her hands, lamenting to herself. If this was a ploy of his, sadly, it was working. What bothered her more than his behaviour is why she cared so much, and how badly she wanted to talk to him.

* * *

Dante stood opposite the fibro and brick house located on sixty-four Bellevue Crescent. He couldn't smell anything that might verify Jason's story, but he could hear everything. He listened to the sounds of snoring in the front rooms, but also of a bedspring rocking back and forth. Grunting, gasping.

"Trent…fuck… slow down!"

"Shut up."

"God…if Adam ever finds out this happened…"

Dante heard skin clapping against skin. Miller had put his hand over the girl's mouth.

"If you don't shut up, I won't come. If I don't come, I get the shits.

When I get the shits, I start punching things."

"No…wait. STO—"

Dante did not listen anymore. He didn't want to, or need to. What he did hear was too much: three quick slams of a fist into a face and Miller removing himself from the bed, muttering obscenities and cruel taunts, pulling back on his trousers. Crying, whimpering. Fear. Worse still, there was nothing Dante could do to help her from out here, and he could not enter without an invitation. One of the more annoying vampire "rules".

Jason had said the trouble had started with a girl both Miller and Nick wanted. But here Miller was, screwing some unknown girl who clearly meant nothing to him, which indicated that the girl Nick liked also meant nothing to him. Miller had beaten Nick down and would've killed him if given the chance, merely because Nick was an obstacle for this obnoxious kid getting his dick wet. From what Dante just heard, Miller was also a girl basher and probable opportunistic rapist.

Dante had given his word to Dougie that he would never kill another human. His mentor had always told him it was easy to take a life, but saving one was where real power showed itself. Whatever happened with Jason, Dante would ensure Nick's safety. That was paramount. But this Miller kid was having a greater effect on him then he was worth. For the first time in almost a century, Dante was not resisting the urge to kill, and that didn't bother him.

Chapter 20

Alpha Centurion

The wolf opened its eyes, scanning left to right. Straining. Sensing. Struggling. Weak? Yes. The eyes alone were free to move without pain. The chest expanded slightly. The nose and ears absorbed the atmosphere. Chemicals, unpleasant. What were they? The wolf concentrated. Morphine. Disinfectant. Urine—its own, collected in a bag nearby. Saliva on graphite. A human was near, taking notes. Lights bright. Sounds, distant steady beeps. Mumbles of television coming from a far corner. Quiet, calm human voices in the corridor. Good sounds. Safe sounds. Hospital.

Stupid, stupid boy, Nicholas. The wolf could've been in control of the boy's body by now. But the boy had rejected the wolf by giving up on his mate. The wolf had to be patient; these were the actions of a boy, not quite a man. The beating? Another unfortunate lesson. A hunter does not give up. A warrior never retreats. An Alpha never quits. Nicholas could not deny what his heart wanted. Neither could the wolf. Nicholas could also no longer stray the line between who he thought he was and who he was destined to become. The girl was key. The passion of the wolf was always its greatest strength. But Nicholas continued to ignore its existence, disregard its importance. The wolf yearned to break free. The boy's resistance was waning, the wolf knew, yet time was running out. The wolf could sense the danger to Nicholas.

The wolf would try again. The wolf would not move from the

bed, focusing its energy to heal him. It would *push* him. It would *help* Nicholas one more time. The rest was up to the boy.

* * *

Alex hunched over the kitchen table, thumbing through Nick's phone to see if the pricks who had beat him to a pulp had left him any threats.

Margaret stepped out into the hallway midway through a stretch. "Morning," she mumbled through a yawn.

"Hi." Alex was not in the mood to be friendly with her mother right now. She still felt betrayed with the way she had contacted Dante without even talking to her first. Dante was NOT Margaret's hired thug.

"Where did you get Nick's phone?"

"I took it when we left yesterday. It was in an envelope with his watch and wallet. I'm looking through his messages."

"Whatever for?" Margaret asked.

"Evidence. For when I go to the cops."

"There's no need for that. They would've been taken care of by now," Margaret replied, more than a hint of pride in her voice.

What the hell is wrong with her? Alex thought. If she'd believed in body snatchers, she might have accused them of taking her mother and replacing her with this callous creature. "Dante would never kill a teenager."

"Who said anything about kill? He'll surely have scared those little bastards out of their minds, though. There won't be any need for police involvement because they wouldn't dare touch Nick again."

Alex hid her distaste at Margaret's overly confident tone by swallowing the last of her coffee. She deliberately slid her chair back as noisily as possible and got up to refill her mug.

"Did you find anything else on there?" asked Margaret.

"Yes." Alex frowned. "Some missed calls last night from a girl called Nicole."

Margaret looked thoughtful. "Didn't he say this whole thing was about a chicky babe?"

Alex rolled her eyes. "'Chicky babe'? Really, mum? But yeah, it's got to be her." Alex reached for the milk. "What if she's been playing Nick the whole time?"

"We can cross that bridge when we come to it. But right now, I think we should give her the benefit of the doubt. Besides, I don't think Nick would be stupid enough to fight over a girl that wasn't worth the pain and effort." Margaret held out her hand for the phone. "You go have a shower and get ready for work. I'll call her."

"Why would you call her? It's none of our business."

"Rubbish. He's in hospital, how else is she going to know what's happened? She can't be mad at him if she knows he's unconscious."

"We don't know that she's mad at him at all!"

"No woman leaves that many missed calls if she's not mad. But, still. This might be a way for him to get a mercy hump if she doesn't have any real feelings for him."

"Ugh, mum. Don't be disgusting."

"Just kidding."

Alex was certain she wasn't.

* * *

Nicole stood dripping on the bathroom tiles when she heard her mobile tinkle. She barely managed to wrap the towel completely around herself as she dashed across the hall and into her room. When she saw 'Careful' as the caller, she knew it was Nick. She felt a sudden wave of exhilaration and anger, both in equal measures. For a split second, she thought about ignoring it, or hanging up. But she couldn't help herself.

"So you can talk to me now?" she asked lightly.

"Hello, dear," a light voice answered."Oh, uh—hello… I'm sorry, did you have the wrong number?"

"Not if I'm talking to Nicole?"

"Uh, yes you are. Who's this?"

"My name is Margaret, Nick is my niece's son. The reason I'm calling you is to explain why he hasn't been returning your calls. You see, he is in hospital."

Nicole felt her knees go out from under her. Fortunately, she collapsed onto her bed.

"What? Is he okay?" She heard her own voice and how shaky it sounded.

"He is a sorry sight, but he will be fine. They need to keep him here for a few days though."

Nicole sniffed and blew a slow breath out. Her mother came around the corner and was about to ask what was wrong, but a wave of Nicole's hand silenced her. "Can you tell me what happened?"

"Well, it seems some scoundrels attacked him outside the building. Fortunately, my daughter Alex found him and called an ambulance right away."

"Thank you for telling me. At least I know what's going on. I'm very sorry to hear it. He's such a lovely guy. I don't know who would want to hurt him."

"Neither do we, dear,"

"Can he have visitors?"

"Of course. He is in R.P.A. Just be warned about looking in on him, as it's a bit of a shock. Hopefully he will be awake when you're there. It would mean a lot to him to see you I'm sure."

"Thank you again." Nicole hung up and made her way dazedly back to the bathroom. She looked at herself in the mirror and burst into tears, which just made her angry at herself. *Get a grip! Just get through the day. Just stay calm. He's okay. You'll go see him in the hospital after school today, and he'll be fine. This is not your fault.* But as much as she tried to tell herself that, the more she felt she was to blame.

Nicole swiped the tears from her eyes with the heel of her hand and opened her make-up case. She dabbed the sponge but didn't even make it to her face when her head lowered again. She thought of what he must look like given what Margaret had said. Nicole was stuck with images in her head, making them probably ten times worse because it was the guy she…appreciated a lot.

* * *

Nicole was proud of herself, she had made it all the way to lunch without breaking down a single time. She'd known if she could just get through the school day, she would be able to get to the hospital before visiting hours ended if she hauled arse. She didn't care if Nick was asleep; she would be happy to just sit with him.

She picked up her lunch from the school canteen. It was among the staff lunches as usual, but she felt like she was twelve again when she realized what she had ordered earlier that morning: chicken nuggets, a can of Coke, and a chocolate doughnut. Her typical personal-crisis meal.

She carried her lunch across the quadrangle toward the office she shared with Mrs. Davies, thinking it would be good to talk and joke with her mentor about the lecture and why she wasn't there. Something caught her eye and she slowed.

Jason Trod and Trent Miller were standing nearby, and that wasn't unusual. But Jason's cheek was immensely swollen and purple. The bruising was so fresh that it was clear the injury could only have happened very recently. Like last night. She looked at Miller, who was deep in conversation with Jason. Miller's eyes flicked to and fro suspiciously, as if he were afraid someone might overhear. Just then, everything came together for Nicole. Margaret had said scoundrels—plural—so Nick had likely been beaten by more than one assailant. Now here was Jason, a face full of evidence showing a whole heap of damage. But Jason never did anything without Miller, Nicole knew. She remembered back on the first day of Nick's arrival and the touch football game, the cold way Miller had addressed Nick at the café. Suddenly, it all made sense.

She was not aware of when her hands became empty, she did not know what was propelling her forward, she did not have an inkling as to what she was doing. But she was closing the distance on them fast.

Jason was the first one to see her approaching. Maybe it was the look on her face, maybe not, but something told him to back away. Nicole let him; she only had eyes for Miller.

Before he knew what hit him, Nicole had unloaded with a fierce slap across his face. So hard and unexpected that Miller actually staggered. Not even thinking that all the students were watching or that Miller was three times her size, Nicole struck again with a fist. Someone whistled and cheered, but soon they all grew silent, watching the events unfold before them.

"YOU SON OF A BITCH!" she shrieked. "YOU FUCKING LUNATIC!" She had never been in a fight in her life, but she had never felt so uncontrollably livid before either. A left haymaker clocked him on the side of the head and a right uppercut grazed his temple before Jason grabbed her from behind, trapping her arms.

Miller laughed, taking his fingers from his nose and flicking some drops of blood to the ground. He walked closer, and whispered in her ear. "Nice going, Nikki. Fucked your career now, haven't ya? And for what? You put up more of a fight than he did."

Nicole broke free of Jason's grip and began to launch more furious strikes at Miller. It *was* him! He had admitted it; he had been the one to ambush Nick. She wanted to hurt him in any way she could. Miller could've pummelled her but seemed too shocked to do anything but squint and try to put his hands up to protect his face.

"Nicole, what are you doing?" Mrs. Davies shouted from her office before rushing over. "Have you lost your mind?"

Nicole stopped struggling when Mrs. Davies pulled her back toward her office, but Nicole did not move her eyes away from Miller. A hatred filled her that was not simply going to go away. "You're going to pay for this, Trent. I swear to god. You too, Jason. I don't care what it takes, but both of you cowards are going to get what you deserve."

As she was led away, Miller shouted after her, "You're getting a little worked up, Nikki. Dunno what is wrong with you. You'll be all right, baby! Try a heavy flow pad!"

The other students laughed. Nicole seethed.

* * *

"What evidence do you have that Mr. Miller was responsible?" Principal Parkins asked.

"Jason's bruises. They are very new, and today Nick is in the hospital, what do you think?" Nicole fidgeted. She knew this evidence didn't sound as rock-solid as it had when she'd come to this conclusion earlier.

"They are rough kids, Nicole. Always have been. They are always getting into fights inside and outside of school. That doesn't prove a thing."

"But look, Trent has been eyeing off Nick from the day he got in." She told them about the touch football game.

"I admit, that I heard the same from Mr. Schubert, he was refereeing and saw the whole thing," Mrs. Davies said to Parkins before turning back to Nicole. “But that is nothing compared to what he has done to other kids over the years. He is a creep, Nicole, yes, but you completely humiliated yourself, not him, out there today. Nothing you have said gives us any possible reason we can use to defend your behaviour.”

“What about the fact the he admitted having done it to my face, right out there?” She pointed back toward the quadrangle.

“Nicole, it’s not that I don’t believe you,” Principal Parkins said. “Of course I do. Normally I would back you with anything, but I just can’t. We have no way of proving he said this. If Trent presses charges, if his parents find out, if the board of education come down here, you’re finished, and I can’t help you. How am I supposed to explain the reason you went haywire is because of a scenario you put together in your own head? What makes matters worse is the situation raises the question of why you took this particular incident with Mr. Slade so personally in the first place.”

Principal Parkins studied her as if he already knew the answer. “Something that caused you to become violent with a student,” he added softly.

Nicole felt her cheeks burning. Even if she liked Nick, she hadn’t done anything with him. Trent was going to get away with this! “It’s not like that. I am sick and tired of Trent Miller having his way around here. What about all the times he has come on to me, and made unwelcome advances? Pinching me on the arse, trying to grab my breasts and all that? Doesn’t that count for something?”

“No because this was you against him, not the other way around. That happened a year ago so it’s very difficult for us use that to form a defence against this.”

“Excuse me? I told you about it!”

“Yes, and I’m sure you remember what I advised you?”

“You advised me not to make a formal complaint and to think of myself, and the school.”

“That’s right. As a junior counsellor it is a bad look for you to be making accusations against students for something like that. You’d be seen as a troublemaker. Now if it was physical violence you reported—that is another thing entirely. We could perhaps have gotten pictures of marks and bruises. But unwanted groping, as bad as it is, would have dragged your name through the mud, as well as his and the school’s for months, even years. In all that time, you might have been in and out of potential lawsuit offices instead of actually learning and studying your trade. Now this isn't my personal view, but I have seen it happen to others older than you, and I would hate to see you go through it."

"Are you serious?" Nicole asked. "You're telling me that you won't do anything about this, again?"

"Again? What do you mean, again? We are talking about different things here. The first incident, no matter how inappropriate, was a separate issue to today's. That was you and him. No witnesses and no proof, just your word—and yes that is good enough for me, but a claims officer? I don't think so. *You attacked him in front of the entire school!* His case is won without lifting a finger. Even if I presented your case to the board, they would be treated as separate incidents. Yours is violence. You could've been arrested!"

"Nicole…" Mrs. Davies started.

"No! Wait a minute, are you saying you agree with this? You're protecting him!"

"We are protecting *you*!" Parkins replied. "For god's sake, he is a teenager running on testosterone and whatever other junk he has been putting into his system. You are older and I thought more mature than he is. You are supposed to be the bigger person."

"So that's it? Just forget it? Let it go? *Apologise to him* maybe and hope he doesn't sue me?" Nicole said, pinching the bridge of her nose before almost jumping out of her chair. "You know what? I don't have to stand for this. Goodbye!"

"Nicole, wait!" Mrs. Davies reached out a hand.

"No!" she said, facing them both. "This is such bullshit. I listened to you before and I shouldn't have. Now I have to go through this again? Is this the system I'm trying to enter into? One where we look out for the abuser first?" Nicole didn't wait for an answer. She whipped around and grabbed the doorknob.

"Where will you go?" Mrs. Davies asked.

"Who knows? Maybe I'll go find someone who actually cares about me more than themselves. Wouldn't that be something?"

She left, not bothering to close the door.

* * *

Alex was surprised to see Nick sitting up in bed. "Hey there! How are you feeling? The doctor told us you were unlikely to be awake until later!"

"I'm a little sore." Nick began removing his head bandages.

"I don't doubt it," Margaret agreed. "Hold on, there. I don't think you're supposed to be doing that."

"What are they going to do, arrest me?" Nick pulled off the last of the bandages and opened his mouth wide, flexing and moving it around. He was sporting heavy stubble and his hair was beginning to cover his ears.

Alex thought she remembered his hair being quite short merely two days ago. "God doesn't that hurt?" she asked. "With a fractured jaw I mean?"

Nick pressed his fingers along the jawbone. "Yeah, it's a little sore, but I don't think it's broken. It doesn't feel that bad. God, it's so boring here. Can we go home now?" he moaned.

Both women laughed and sniffled a little. Only last night Nick looked like he was on death's door. They had no idea what state he would be in when he woke up, what medication he would need. And now, he was suddenly fighting fit. He looked renewed and energised.

Alex was amazed. *Wow, Dante's blood sure did the trick.*

Chapter 21

Goodbye, Farewell, Amen

"Hey, Charlie! You in, mate?" Senior Constable Solomon Crane wheeled the heavy gurney into the morgue.

"Shop's closed. Come back in the morning." Charlie appeared from around the corner and when he spotted the full body bag, his eyebrows shot up. "What have we got here?"

"Belinda Normacky…Normakai?" Solomon peered at his notebook. "I dunno. Seventeen. Another overdose. Parents found her in her bed this morning, thinking she was asleep. They tried to wake her, but she was already as cold as a witch's tit."

"Fourth one this fortnight. What are these kids doing to themselves now?" Charlie shook his head. "Why'd you bring her here to the university and not take her to the piggy bank? I'm not your coroner; I can't do a proper examination."

Solomon ignored the pig reference. "I'll tell you in a minute."

Charlie waved him over and they lifted the body bag and placed it on the main surgical table.

Charlie might have learned not to take work too seriously after working in the morgue as long as he had, but Solomon could never quite stomach the death of the young. Particularly when it was clear they'd just done something stupid.

Charlie unzipped the bag. Solomon looked down at the body of the girl. Being dead had not diminished her youthful beauty. At least not yet. He ran his eyes over her slightly podgy body yet pert breasts.

“That was considerate of her,” Charlie mumbled grimly.

“What’s that?”

“She even trimmed her hedges.”

“Trimmed her…? Oh Christ, Charlie.”

“Hey, I’m not like you old farts that needed bush to keep warm in the forties. I hate having to go to the dentist for a haircut.”

“Can we get back to the job at hand? Look at her arms.”

“Sure.” Charlie shrugged, snapped on a pair of surgical gloves, and bent over the body, examining more closely. He lifted her arms, turned to check both sides of her neck, opened her mouth to gauge her throat. “Looks like a typical OD,” he said, removing the gloves. “There are several puncture wounds that match something like heroin or meth. I still don’t get it. What am I missing? What do you think I should be looking for?”

“This wasn’t any regular drug overdose. Don’t ask me how I know, I’ll get to that. I’ve seen a heap of drug deaths over the years, but in the last two months they have spiked. I’ve been on the force over eleven years and seen some shit, but I think this goes deeper.”

“What do you mean?”

Solomon took a deep breath. He looked around, though he knew no one could be eavesdropping. “This is going to sound stupid. First of all, this is not something I’m telling anyone else in the department, but I need to tell someone and I know I can trust you.” He paused again and indicated the corpse. “I think whatever this is, there’s something bigger to it. The department is covering it up, and other things as well. A few months ago, I was involved in a missing person’s case, after two detectives were taken off it. A recent paraplegic just went missing from R.P.A hospital after a blackout. So either he miraculously healed, or he was taken. A few weeks later the call came down. I was off the case too. No reason, no cause and I didn’t hear who it was assigned to.”

“Ok, I can see how that would piss you off…”

“The case went cold!” Solomon replied. “No one was assigned to it in my area. I did some checking, and saw it was passed on to a Victorian branch. What would they do with it? Surprise, it’s just sat there for months and still is. I kept track, and called them two weeks ago and got fobbed off. My superintendent found out I called and had a go at me. Said I was causing trouble and not focusing on the cases I *was* assigned.”

Solomon let a huff of breath out. “So I did. I landed a few of these drug overdoses. All of them the same type of thing, except for this—” He pulled out a vial from his trousers and showed it to Charlie. The liquid inside still glowed a bright, luminescent blue.

“What the…?”

“Damnedest thing I’ve ever seen. It definitely ain’t heroin or coke. I would’ve handed those in, but this shit *glows*. Plus, I’m pretty sure I’m being lied to.”

“You want to leave it here?” Charlie asked.

“I want to find out what it is. From someone not linked to the police. I know you’ve still got your connections.”

“Mate, I gave that up ages ago.”

“Charlie, please. My gut is telling me something is up. I’ve had five of these cases in the last fortnight. Exact same MO. This is the first one I got to early and I found the blue stuff. Maybe it’s all a coincidence, I don’t know. I can keep toeing the line of obedience at the office as long as I know something is being done, somewhere, somehow. I really don’t think the department is doing the right thing here.”

Charlie seemed mesmerized for a moment. “Well, let’s figure out what this stuff is, then.”

* * *

Melina moved through the Hall of Relics, struggling on shaking, disobedient legs. The Hall was basically a corridor with rooms leading to various treasures Vincent had collected over the centuries. Snapped awake by the visions, she rose to find the source. This time, they continued after she’d woken, calling to her. The flashes were coming more rapidly now, and Melina suspected she was getting close.

She passed a plinth displaying the pistol thought to have killed the great Pewmulwuy in 1802, one of the most skilled Aboriginal vampire hunters. Some said his descendants were the current leaders of the Forgotten, the group based in Redfern sworn to defend their tribe and land from any who would prey on them. *Faceless*, *Fearless*, was their mantra.

The more recognised and valued treasures were kept hidden in a vault far below the room in which Melina now stood. She recalled once hearing Vincent tell about a sword with an almost white blade. He had bragged it was the oldest Australian artefact, that it dated back to hundreds of thousands of years ago. It represented an ancient society, before recorded time, or lost from history. The myth of the sword, he'd said, was that it had been cursed and could only be wielded by one warrior. This individual, whoever it was, had disappeared and the legend was that the weapon would lie unused and unknown until they returned. The only wielder now was Vincent's ego.

Melina drifted past more displays: a broken sceptre belonging to Queen Elizabeth I, a breastplate of a Roman Legionnaire from Gaul, several other items she did not really pay attention to. Finally she stopped before a steel security door with fingerprint analyser. *This wasn't here before.* She had not been in this part of the mansion for months, but there was no way anyone could have installed this door unless Vincent had ordered it done during the daytime. She looked back at the other doors off the hall. None had fingerprint scanners except this one. *Why? What does he have to hide in here?*

She approached the door and the visions that had been plaguing her grew frantic. This was it. This was the cause of her trouble. The origin of the visions must lay behind this door.

"Melina." Vincent's voice was quiet but harsh.

She started and spun around. So engrossed in how close she was to finding out the reasons for her wakefulness, she had blocked out all other senses.

"What is behind this door?" she asked, turning back to it.

Vincent was silent and the tension grew. Melina was suddenly aware of what she had said and how. She turned and faced him, bowing deeply. "Forgive me, my king. I feel foolish."

"Quite right," Vincent snapped, eyeing her. "It is not your concern."

"Please, Vincent, I need your guidance. It has happened again."

"What has happened again?"

"I woke up today in the sunshine. Again!"

"No, you did not."

"Sire?" *What was he playing at?*

"I have been over this with my son and we both agree that this did not happen. No matter what wild fantasies you cook up, waking up in the day simply cannot be done, my child."

"But the fact that I'm standing here is proof enough! I was already out of my coffin and found my way here, all while the rest of the family slept. The visions I've been having led me to this door. If you could tell me what is behind it, I would have my answers and the evidence you require." Melina looked at the door and ran her fingers up and down the cold metal.

Vincent's hand slammed the door just next to where her head was. His palm and fingers sunk into the steel slightly as if heated. "You have been one of my favourites. It pleases me to look upon you, and your beauty is beyond compare, but you have defied me enough on this matter."

Her ears rang but she was determined not to flinch away. "Defied? I am begging for your help!"

Vincent whipped a stinging backhand across her face, sending her into the steel wall. "You make up impossible stories for attention. You wish to sneak into my private chambers."

He made to hit her again but Melina dodged the blow and struck one of her own.

"Are you insane, woman?" Julian was instantly there behind his father. "What have you *done*?"

Melina could not answer. She had struck the king out of pure instinct alone. Regardless of reason, it was a treasonous act, punishable by death.

In their momentary shock, Melina took what was likely to be her only chance. She sped past them towards the stairs.

Julian teleported into her path. "Really? You're going to try and *run*?"

A furious Vincent appeared behind her. "Put this insubordinate bitch in the dungeons, while I decide what to do with her."

Julian grabbed her arm and marched her towards the dungeons. She had only one small hope. Once she was sure she could whisper without being overheard by Vincent, she leaned into Julian. "Please…if you have ever truly loved me, listen. I need help. Your father is hiding something behind that door. Whatever is beyond it is calling to me. Please, Julian. I need you to find out what your father has in there. That's all."

Julian stopped just in front of a small white chamber with a single lamp in the ceiling. He shoved Melina in and grasped the door. Before closing it, he peered intently at her. "You really mean all of this, don't you?"

"Yes, of course! Please, just ask him. Whatever you have to do. I'm going out of my mind."

He gave a sharp nod. "All right. On one condition. Join with me. I demand *Go deo*," he said, holding both hands up. "Prove your loyalty to me once and for all."

Melina slowly reached out. The Gaelic mystical vow meant she must honour a partnership with Julian forever. Another flash shot through her skull. This pact was her only chance to be rid of these cursed visions. She joined hands with Julian and both sliced the skin of their palms with their fingernails. Each offered the other a palm to drink from. Julian wobbled a little on his feet, as the poison of a fellow vampire's blood entered his system, but only a small amount was needed to make the vow official.

He raised his head and licked his lips, smiling fiercely at Melina, before kicking her inside and slamming the door closed.

"Foolish woman. You think I would betray my father for someone whose greatest skill is sucking cock? And ever since you've been losing your mind and not doing *that* job anymore, I find you completely useless. You forget, I'm not Dante."

Melina spat out the blood she had taken. Unfortunately, it wasn't enough to reverse the *Go deo*.

No, she thought sadly. *You're not.*

Chapter 22

Upgraded

"Hey, Nick."

Nick grabbed his algebra book from his locker for his next class and turned to see who was speaking. "Hey…Lisa is it?"

"You remembered!" The girl giggled and blushed.

"Uh, what's up?" Nick had been getting all kinds of attention once he was discharged from the hospital and returned to school. There had been lots of whispered rumours and unabashed staring, but that didn't bother him as much as he thought it might. It seemed the attack had had a silver lining. He felt more confident now, and more self-aware. And the other students seemed to notice. He'd also let his hair grow since being at the hospital, and had not yet shaved off the sprouting stubble on his face. He couldn't be sure, but maybe that was getting him some added attention too.

"I don't know if you are going to Stewie's party on Saturday but if you do, I think we should totally go together. You know, if you want?"

"Stewie?"

"Oh, he's in our history class. He wanted me to let everyone know. So we are all meeting at the park down in Coogee, at the swings, nine o'clock Saturday night. We could meet and go from there. Let me know, yeah? By the way, don't tell Stacie about it, ok? Stewie doesn't want her there. You look really good today by the way," she said, giggling again and hurrying off to class at the sound of the bell.

She had well and truly motored away before he had a chance to reply. He didn't know Lisa all that well, and he didn't know Stacie either, except that she and Lisa always hung out together. It seemed strange that Lisa would be so willing to go to a party without her friend.

He had just closed his locker when the scent of rosewater soap reached him, and he knew without turning around that he was not alone. This time, he at least recognised the face to put a name to it straight away.

"Stacie!" Nick slung his bag over his shoulder and set off toward his algebra class. *Is this just a coincidence?* he wondered.

Stacie smiled and followed along. "Nick, I'm supposed to invite you to a party."

"I don't suppose it's Stewie's, is it?"

"No, is he having one? Anyway, Pat's having a party Saturday. Ten o'clock at Coogee Bay Hotel. Do you know it?"

Nick raised an eyebrow. "Vaguely. Tell me more."

"Well, I was hoping you would go with me so I wouldn't have to be there all alone," she said, putting her hands together and giving him a pout.

Jesus, Nick thought. *What is it with these popular girls?* He admitted to himself, however, that he didn't know what was worse: the fact she thought that would work on him, or that a few weeks ago, it actually might have. Now, though, he knew better. He could see more clearly; he could see fake.

"Can I invite anyone else?" Not that he had anybody in mind, but he wanted to confirm his suspicions.

"No, it's all hush hush. Not even Lisa, ok?"

Suspicions confirmed. Still, no reason not to push this a bit further. "I would love to go to the party with you, Stacie. But let's meet at nine at the swings, and head to Coogee from there, yeah?" He even gave her a wink to clinch the deal.

"The swings, huh? Sounds like we're going to have our own pre-party." She grinned at him meaningfully and then walked past and moved on down the hall.

Nick pulled a notebook out of his bag and scribbled a note. "Saturday sounds great. Nick." He slipped it through the vent in Lisa's locker. It was a cruel thing to do, but Nick hated the idea of being played by two chicks that wanted to beat each other for him. They didn't care about him. He was a notch on the bed post for both of them. Most guys might like that kind of girl, that kind of attitude. Well, they could have them. Or whatever would be left of them when they got through with each other on Saturday night.

Nick knew he didn't want the things that most guys want. He was not so insecure that he needed as much pussy as he could handle. He didn't want to be a poker machine where everyone got a go. He wanted to be a high-stakes casino, where the best got the jackpot. *Speaking of the best...*

Nick spotted Nicole walking quickly towards her office. She wore all black, including oversized sunglasses. Her body language indicated she wasn't here for a long visit. It was a get in and get out moment. Based on his own experiences this week, Nick could understand why. Several eyes followed her, only to return to their activities when she entered the counsellor's office.

Nick felt the return of the adrenaline. Sensible thoughts about heading to algebra class left him. His jackpot was there to be won.

There had been no messages from her for days. The last ones he got were those she had sent as he lay in the hospital bed. Still, he thought as he walked over, some of the whispers around school were that she had pretty much attacked Miller in his defence. He felt he owed her gratitude for at least that.

He knocked on the door as he stepped in. Both Nicole and Mrs. Davies were in the room, sitting opposite each other. They turned abruptly toward him, both looking flushed and upset. It seemed he'd interrupted something serious.

"Hi, uh, excuse me," Nick said, talking to both. "I'm sorry to interrupt. I was just wondering if I could talk to you, quickly?"

"We're in the middle of something," Mrs Davies said.

"Sure, it doesn't have to be now. Just…sometime today?" he replied. "It's not desperate."

Mrs. Davies was about to retort but stopped as Nicole sighed loudly and rose to her feet. "If it's not desperate, it shouldn't take too long," she said, perhaps more to Mrs. Davies than to him. When she stood up, Nick caught a whiff of her strawberry lip-gloss and started to sweat.

"I want to have a discussion about that invitation, Mr. Slade," Mrs. Davies said pointedly before the door closed.

"Had a lovely night! Thank you!"

Nicole shot him a disapproving look and Nick realised he'd said it out loud. Deep inside his head, he heard laughter; no. More like a mischievous growl.

They found a quiet spot around the back of the school. "Ok, I'm here." Nicole crossed her arms and leaned against the wall. "What is it?"

"First, I wanted to say thank you for sticking up for me the other day. You didn't have to."

Nicole barked a laugh that was anything but happy. "If you don't mind, I really don't want to hear that from you. I screwed up royally and hearing that just makes me feel ten times worse."

"Ok, I get that. I just want to know where we go from here?"

"What are you talking about?"

"The feelings we have for each other," he stated.

"Oh for… You interrupted my meeting for this?" Nicole turned and walked away.

"Nicole, wait! Why can't you just talk to me? I'm not trying to pressure you, really. You attacked a guy heaps bigger than you because he put me in hospital. That was not the act of a friend. That was anger. You were livid because something had happened to me. I know."

Nicole placed a palm on her forehead. "You really are not going to let this go, are you?"

"Maybe the reason you went off is because you feel something that you're not facing. I'm not trying to hustle you. I just want to know the truth, whatever it is. That's all. I swear."

Nicole wheeled around on him. "Ok. I am going to say this once and once only. I swear to god, Nick, after this, you will let this go, or I will make you. Maybe I have feelings for you, ok? But that is irrelevant. It does *not* change the fact that nothing can happen between us. And you already know this, because I have told you plenty of times. I gave into my feelings the other day and it almost cost me my career. In fact, it is still up in the air. That speech I gave—the one you *stole* a ticket to hear—basically means nothing now unless I can set it right. I don't know what will happen to me if Trent or his parents decide to sue or take it higher and I can't control that. I can control this, between you and me. Remember what I said about making a hard call and not trying to be popular? Well, this is it right here. I'm living proof that I practice what I preach."

That's bullshit, said the voice. *YOU are the hard choice. Neither of you understand what you can accomplish together. You need her. She needs you. Make her see that!*

"Stop it!" Nick said, unsure to whom he was speaking.

"Stop what?" Nicole asked, frowning.

"Being with me isn't your hard call. Being with me is the decision that would make people look down on you. The easy way out is pushing aside what your heart wants and choosing the stable, reliable career. If that's the way you feel, I won't try and change your mind. I'm honestly just trying to be honest with you, and I have been." His voice petered out, as did his train of thought. What was he saying? Where was all this coming from. It felt so…familiar.

"Wow, that's some passive aggressive BS you've just delivered there, Nick."

"I—that's not what I meant to say. I'm sorry. I care a lot about you, is all. And I want to say that even if all the stable things you've counted on in your life come crashing down around you, I'll still be there."

* * *

Nicole took a few seconds and tried to judge Nick's face. He was such an enigma. His tone was so genuine, but the look on his face was one that he was almost in pain as he spoke, again as if forcing his words through the veil of an intense headache.

"Thank you. I really appreciate that. But there is nothing you can do. It's my fault and it's my issue. I guess I just have to see how bad the storm will be or wait for it to pass."

"My mum always said life isn't about waiting for the storm to pass, it's learning to dance in the rain."

"Hmm," Nicole nodded thoughtfully. "Even your shadow leaves you when in darkness. That's what my mum used to tell me."

"That's why dreamers, or your true leaders, learn how to steer by the stars. Any good captain would tell you that." Nick cracked a crooked and apologetic smile at her.

She wanted to believe him. "Look, I don't know what my heart may or may not want right now. I only know what I need. And what I need is a friend." There were risks in everything, the difference is what the individual was willing to fight for, and give up. There will always be another career, but maybe only one guy who looked at her like he did. "I'm hoping you can be that, Nick."

Nick closed in on Nicole, who faced him, unmoving. *If he goes in for another fucking kiss, I'll slap him, too*, she screamed in her head.

But he didn't. Nick entwined their thumbs and wrapped his fingers around her hand, bringing it to his lips and then held it against his chest. "I can do that. I promise."

Nicole looked at him. So many things going through her head, so many things to say and yet she felt none of them mattered. She gently let her hand out of his grasp and patted him on the chest as she turned to leave.

She continued on, thinking that he had done a hell of a number on her. He was driving her crazy. Her heart ached wanting to believe in the relationship he envisioned. She had grown up thinking the same way, and if she was truthful to herself, her ex was the reason she stopped believing in romance. Loving someone was like giving them a gun to point to your heart in the hope they would never pull the trigger. She wanted someone to wake up next to, not sleep with.

Who didn't want to be cared for unconditionally, safe in the knowledge that, bar everything else, your heart was in safe hands? But no matter how much she wished it, the world was not like that. And no amount of rising tensions between two people would change it.

* * *

Melina sat with her back to the door. She wondered if Julian and Vincent intended to leave her here to starve. There were only a few ways to kill a vampire, and most of Hollywood lore was bullshit, but starvation was an effective method.

She used her to time to meditate on what she had learned of the situation. Admittedly, it wasn't much. Firstly, Julian was a pathetic little shit. Whatever their relationship (if it even could be classed as that) had been, it was over now. He had betrayed her for his father, Vincent. He must have known whatever was on the other side of that door was the key to her visions, otherwise why would he be so quick to shut her up? Julian, too, must know what was behind the door.

She couldn't find out from here, nor go against the king, not by herself anyway. She rattled off names of the other vampires in the mansion, and not one could she count on for support against him if she survived this shoebox.

"Who's there?" she called. A vampire approached. She heard them stop just outside the door. She couldn't be bothered moving. That, and she didn't have the strength. "If you're going to kill me, get on with it!"

"Melina, whatchoo doin' in there?" came a squeaky voice.

"Nathaniel? What are you doing here, darling boy?"

"I am…not supposed…to…talk to you. Under…any circumcisions," he said. Melina imagined the 90-year-old vampire with the mind and body of a four-year-old boy straining, trying to do his best mocking impression of Julian.

"So then…why are you?"

"Don't you *know*?" He sounded annoyed that she should even ask.

Then Melina understood. "Because he's a boy," Nathaniel's hatred of men was legendary. He and Alejandro were the only vampires she knew of to defy the king. Alejandro was the only male vampire Nathaniel trusted. In fact, he adored him. If Julian had ordered Nathaniel not to talk to Melina, it was the best way possible of ensuring he did. Stupid fuck had proven useful after all.

"Yes!" Nathaniel answered proudly. Again she imagined him with his fists on his hips, staring at the door. "I hate Julian. He's a boy, a bad boy. He can't put a girl in a room. I wanna bash him!"

"No, sweetheart, listen to me." Melina tried to soothe him, making her voice become dreamy. "I have a plan but I can't do it alone. Please, will you help me?"

"Yes," he replied as if in a daze. "Wait…no. Nope nope nope!" he said, stomping his little feet. "I know what you're gonna do! You're gonna go back to him!"

"What do you mean?"

"He's a stupid eshhole! I'll only help you if you never EVER kiss Julian again"

Melina smiled. At four, Nathaniel valued a kiss from a girl the same as someone would a cure for cancer. Which coincidently is what would have killed him had his mother not changed him.

"I promise, my darling. My first kiss when I get out will be you."

Nathaniel gave a guilty giggle. He told everyone he liked her kisses best of all. He told her he loved the way they tickled. Melina heard him creep closer to the door. "What do you want me to do?"

There was only one key, held by Julian. There was no way Melina could see Nathaniel claiming the key to give to her without getting hurt or worse.

The dungeons doors had been specifically designed by Julian. The doors themselves were solid stainless steel, and the inner surface was covered with pure iron, preventing any magical or undead creature locked inside from touching it. They opened inward, and there was simply no way Melina could muster the brute force to break them down. But from the outside…

Melina asked Nathaniel to come down just before sunrise, take a run at the doors and kick them as hard as he could. With any luck, he would be able to break through the deadbolts.

"But you won't be able to go anywhere. Duh sun will be up."

"I know."

"How you gonna get owt if duh sun is up? When it goes down, dey will get you."

"Trust your auntie Melina, darling. When they get up, I will be gone. No one will know what's happened or that you helped me, as long as you don't say anything."

"Can you take me too?"

"I wish I could. But your mummy loves you very much and she would be sad if you left."

"Not forever! Jus a lil while…"

"Once I leave here, I am not coming back."

"You mean…I'm not goin to see you again?"

Melina paused. If Nathaniel thought he would miss her too much, he may refuse to help her leave. "I can't stay, Nathaniel. If I do, they are going to hurt me. You don't want that, do you? Once I escape, it's important they not know where I am, because they are going to look for me. I promise I will try to see you again one day, but never think that I will forget you."

Nathaniel said nothing. Just as she was about to speak again she heard his footsteps disappearing up the steps, carrying her only hope of survival with him.

Several hours later, however as Melina lay almost motionless, she heard the thump-clunk of the deadbolt giving way, and was thankful this room was so far from the rooms the other vampires in the house spent their time. The door swung ajar.

"Nathaniel…" she croaked.

She heard him creep into the room, sniffling.

"Come here."

He lowered himself, squatting by her head, she reached for him and brought him down to her lips, keeping her promise. "My hero. Thank you."

"I don't want you to go," he whimpered.

"I will see you again," she managed, her strength continuing to fail.

"Promise me," he said, wiping one side of his face.

She kissed his cheek, licking her lips as she felt his blood-stained tears. "I…" her head lowered and turned away from him.

"Melina? Melina!" he hissed. "What's wrong?"

She licked her lips again, moaning absentmindedly, trying to get any remaining blood into her mouth. "I haven't fed…in so long."

"Hey…why aren't you sick?"

"I don't get sick from drinking vampire blood."

"Like Dante?"

"Yes."

"Yuk." He looked like he was contemplating something. Suddenly, he shoved his wrist towards her. He said it was still weird to him that a vampire could drink another vampire's blood, but he trusted Melina to know what she was doing.

Melina grasped his arm and bit, too desperate to think about anything else but the blood flowing into her mouth. She let him go, knowing at least not to take too much. Nathaniel wavered a little but steadied himself. Just as he started to walk out, feeling the heat of the sun only minutes away, Melina grasped his ankle.

"One day, I will repay you for this. Run off to bed now."

"I'll miss you, Auntie."

Then he was gone. Melina lay on her back, the weight of the rising sun flattening her into immobility.

She did not believe in god. What sort of god would answer a vampire's prayers? But, she found herself praying none the less for one last vision to wake her. Without it, her plan would come to nothing. Maybe, just maybe if she awoke early again, she might have to rethink this business about a divine being in the universe.

Chapter 23

Position The Pieces

Nick ignored the burning in his legs as he pushed on. The sweat from his brow stung his eyes as trees and bushes smacked his face, disappearing from view as he rushed on. His chest heaved and his breath came in short, wheezing bursts. He felt like he had been running forever, spurred on by panic. The last of his energy reserves was for survival alone. He felt as though struck in the ribs by a blunt object, such was the pain of the sudden stitch but he heard his pursuer right behind him, closing quickly. His knees cracked with each step, the muscles of his thighs tensed with lactic acid build up, feeling like they would explode at any moment. Finally, they gave out and Nick could go no further. He crashed to the ground exhausted, hoping he would have a few seconds to think of something, anything, but his pursuer was already upon him.

"You can't run forever Nicholas," a voice said. His own voice, but not from his mouth.

Nick could only lie there and let the sweat drip from his nose to the soft ground covered in sweet-smelling autumn leaves. He wasn't sure he even wanted to look up. But he did. What he saw, he expected on some level, but he still had a hard time believing it. He was looking at himself. Only this other Nick was walking, no, sauntering around him, sneering and looking smug. This impostor stopped just ahead of him and lowered himself to a knee. Nick recoiled.

"There's no need to be afraid. I am not your enemy."

Easy for him to say. The impostor looked exactly like Nick, except he seemed to be a good deal thicker and bright silver eyes shone in the dark, but the "whites" of his eyes were instead black. When he spoke, Nick noticed two pointy under fangs touching his top lip. He had seen that before. In his father.

"Who the hell are you?" Nick asked.

The impostor tilted his head to one side. "I'm the wolf inside you, the one that changes the course of your life, my friend. The one who has helped you. I am you—well, what you will become."

"No," Nick breathed. "I'm not like my father. I'm not a monster."

"Such harsh words for something you never understood. You can't fight me forever. The longer you do, the worse the transformation will be. You are running out of time as it is."

"I have spent my whole life thinking I wasn't one of them. I had already come to terms with that. In fact, I was happy to not become what my father was. Now you tell me it's not true. How?"

The wolf shrugged easily. "Simple, it's your time. It wasn't before. But now it is. You know what it is now to feel rage, to hunt, to desire, to crave. I am charged with bringing that out in you. That is, unless Nicole can do it for me—"

"You stay the hell away from her! I won't let you hurt her!"

"I would never hurt her. But should you continue to deny who you are, you will. This can only end in one of two ways, Nicholas. You will either become the wolf you should be or the monster you could be. Make your choice."

Nick raised himself into a sprinting position, sneered and charged at the wolf who gave a carefree smile as he closed in. Nick saw the canine fangs in his upper jaw as well when the top lip unveiled them.

"Mr. Slade, will you kindly wake up!"

Nick yelped as he snapped awake. Several members of his class snorted and tittered.

Mr. Shubert, the Physical Education teacher stood over him, looking stern. The class was doing sprint training in the playground in the practical part of the curriculum.

"Sorry, sir." Nick mumbled.

"I should think so. Need I remind you that this," he said, indicating the out of breath students behind him, "will be on your half-yearly exam which is only a few weeks away?"

"Yes, sir," he mumbled. "I mean, no, sir." More stifled giggles. Nick's face felt hot. He really wished Mr. Shubert would take his too-tight shirt and shiny-cranium self-back up to the head of the class and leave him alone.

"Very good. I would appreciate you trying to pay just a little attention. I don't talk just to hear myself think, mate!"

Anger burst through him. "Ok, I get it already! I fucked up! Can we move on, or what?" Several people jumped. Nick realized his voice had erupted into an almighty shout that pierced the air around him.

The giggles stopped and the entire class went silent.

Mr. Shubert dramatically crossed his arms. He simply stared back, not moving for several seconds. The silence was almost as deafening as the lack of movement increased the tension in the air. Nick didn't know where that anger had come from. Was it really necessary? No. But… why did it feel so good?

Mr. Shubert moved away from the class with a determined stride. This wasn't over.

"Come here, Mr. Slade, and bring your bag with you."

Nick did as he was told, beginning to feel even warmer, and now fuzzy in the head. Certainly not in a good way. He faced Mr. Shubert with his back to the class, the inevitable one-on-one confrontation about to commence. Hushed, and away from the others.

"I don't know what you're playing at, or who the hell you think you are, but there is no way in hell I'm going to cop behaviour like that."

"I would imagine so," Nick said slowly, eyes closed, trying to control his breathing.

"Imagine all you like, son. You will learn a tantrum gets you nowhere in this school. I'd expect this from Trent Miller, but not you. You'd especially do well to be reminded not to copy him. You will see me at the end of the day."

Nick couldn't stop the fire building up in him again. He felt his heart threatening to burst out of his chest. "Yes, sir," he said through gritted teeth.

"Are you listening? Look at me."

Nick opened his eyes. Mr. Shubert froze. Nick could smell a hint of urine as Mr. Shubert slowly stepped back, unable to look away from Nick's eyes, keeping out of Nick's reach. "Leave my class," he said, merely breathing the words.

"The end of the day?" Nick asked softly, wondering what had made the PE teacher change so suddenly.

"I don't care where you go, as long as it's not here."

Nick did not hesitate to walk away from the playground, and when he was out of sight of the other students, he broke into a run and dashed around the corner of the main building. He fanned himself with his collar, trying to cool his body already slicked with sweat. He had never lost control like that before, never lost his temper for such a stupid reason. His head was aching from his dream. It had frightened him. Seeing himself like that, as the wolf, wasn't nearly as bad as even the thought of hurting Nicole. Something he could not conceive of doing in any circumstance. It couldn't be the change, could it? He was too old.

His mind, though killing him, began to work through all the strange phenomena he had seen over the last few months as he headed up the stairs, carefully. His quick healing, the nail marks on the café desk, the way he'd envisioned biting Nicole.

Ok, wait, he thought. Besides everything else, that was different. He couldn't explain the other stuff, but the biting he could. That wasn't to attack her, that was just scraping his teeth and tongue sensually over her neck, nipping at her and kissing her softly to give her goose bumps.

Are you kidding me, Nicholas? I was there too, remember? That was the epitome of wolfish love bites. Stop trying to rationalise this. It is going to happen.

Nick held his head, feeling sick. The voice he kept hearing…was that the wolf, that…beast he had just seen? "No," he strained.

You know you want her, Nicholas. Every time you close your eyes, you see her face. Give in to your darkest desire…take her.

Nick wobbled on his feet, everything beginning to go black. "Fuck you," Nick said defiantly, feeling himself heading to the ground. "I'm not going to 'take her'. I love her."

* * *

Nick peeled his eyes open and stared at a rectangular-shaped light in the ceiling, blinking several times as he adjusted to the brightness.

"You're awake," Nicole said. Nick looked around, recognising where he was: the first aid office. Nick also noticed they were the only two inside. Nicole sat on a stool next to the makeshift bed, holding an ice pack on his forehead.

"Well…if this is death, it's pretty good so far," Nick said.

Nicole smiled and shook her head. "You certainly have a flair for the dramatic. The whole school is talking about your fight with Mr. Shubert. After the class, he got in his car and just took off, and then you were brought in here by two teachers. You look like you've got a case of heat stroke," she said, flipping the ice pack over. "But you're still quite the charmer, I see."

"He left? Just like that?"

"Yep."

"Did he say anything?"

"Not a word. He was in too much of a hurry. A few staff tried to call him back but he didn't listen to anyone. What did you say to him?"

"Nothing really. He caught me sleeping in his class and went kinda ape shit. He went on and on and I…lost my temper."

"Ooooh, did you just? Wish I could have been there."

Nick gave her a disbelieving look. "Why?"

"I dunno, I like it when nice guys get angry." She shrugged and winked, clearly pulling his leg.

"Weirdo."

"Drama queen."

Nick playfully swatted her hand away, sitting up. "I'll show you… whoa."

He felt nauseated, warm in the head.

Nicole reacted swiftly, cradling the back of his neck and eased him to his original position. "Yeah, you'll show me what? How good you can throw up? Lie back down."

"Okay, I'm not arguing. What are you doing here anyway? I thought today was your uni day."

"Holidays," she replied like she was reminding him. "So I thought I would come in and have a session with Zachary. I was on my way out when I saw you get carried in here. The nurse got called away so gave me the ice pack and said keep you cool and make you stay lying down. So here we are?"

"How is he?"

"Zachary? Not good." Nicole sighed and shook her head. "I think he is getting worse."

"What's wrong with him?"

"You know I can't tell you."

"But you've just said he's getting worse. Maybe I can do something, maybe I can't, but I'm willing to try. What harm could it do?"

Nicole put the ice pack under the back of his neck and sat back down. "I suppose you're right. Okay, how can I tell you without telling you? Hmm. Well, you already know he refuses to talk, right?"

Nick nodded.

"But only a few months ago he was a bright and happy child, laughing and chatting with the rest of them. Now…" Nicole shrugged. "Everything points to some sort of psychological trauma, but I can't even begin to pinpoint why or what it might be, because he doesn't say anything. He is not rude, he isn't disoriented or nervous. He just simply seems to shuffle on through life as if it's something to get through. But not that he's exasperated at it. More that he isn't even involved in what goes on around him; he's not participating in life."

"Sounds like something is wrong at home, not school."

Nicole nodded emphatically. "Exactly my theory, but when I tried calling his father there was no answer. And since I'm not an official teacher, I'm pretty restricted in what I'm allowed to do. The fact is, apart from the off day when he comes in looking a little pale, he appears to be a healthy boy. No marks or bruises. He is never late. He always does his homework, and his grades are fine—really good, actually. He isn't disrupting other kids, or being bullied. There is no physical evidence or reason that I have to question his dad. He just seems… seriously depressed."

"Can't you speak to his dad when he comes to pick him up from school?"

"His dad doesn't come. He gets picked up by a driver. I only know that because Zachary showed me a photo of a time when he was happiest, and it was a photo of him and his dad on a fishing trip last year. The guy who comes to pick him up isn't the same man."

"So what's your next move?"

"I don't know, I really don't. There is absolutely nothing I can do differently if he doesn't speak. To someone looking in from the outside, there is little to base an action on. It's just me that knows something is wrong with him. I know it."

"If it means anything, I know it too."

"It does," she replied.

"What does Mrs. Davies say?"

"She's concerned too. She's made the same enquiries I have. The only thing is we just monitor him like I'm doing. If something drastic happens, we can call the authorities, but as it is, we have no proof of anything that we could even provide them with."

"Do you think the driver might know anything? Maybe you can wait for him to come pick up Zach and ask him directly?"

"Therein lie some of the restrictions. I can't talk to him about Zach's mental wellbeing. He's not the parent and I'm not a teacher."

"Since when do you take no for an answer? I've heard about your fundraisers! Look, I'll even be with you if you need me. Or if I can help, just tell me."

Nicole didn't respond, just looked to the floor briefly. "You know, sometimes you say things that piss me off, and I think I can see right through you. Then other times you just…I just can't figure you out."

"What do you mean?" Nick asked.

"You can be pushy, childish and a little arrogant. Things that I hate."

"Ok, about that—"

Nicole held up a hand, giving it a second before replacing the cold compress. "And then you show me that you have the kindest heart and think about others. You give me a shot in the arm just when I need it."

"Well…" Nick started, trying to choose his words carefully. "I'm glad I've made a fan."

Nicole laughed. "Don't you think you have enough admirers? I had three girls in twenty minutes in before you woke up, asking if it was true you had punched a teacher and gone to prison. Then two more asking if you had died in the hallway."

Nick rolled his eyes.

"It must be nice," Nicole said.

"What?"

"Having so many chicks fawning over you?"

Nick couldn't understand it, but unless he was imagining it, Nicole sounded jealous. "Yeah, well, I like one of them."

"Oh yeah? Well…lucky her."

"Trouble is she doesn't think she is lucky. She rejected me, saying she just wants to be friends."

Nicole looked at him and blushed at the look he gave her. "Oh," she said. "So…how are you doing with, you know, all that?"

"Can we not do this? Look, you have told me where you stand and I appreciate that. Trouble is, I don't want to be just your friend and never have. You think I care about those girls? I want someone to wake up to, not just sleep with. And that's exactly the opposite of what they want. They don't care about me, so I don't care about them."

Nicole's eyes widened as he stared at her. "Look, uh, you seem better, so I should…probably go. Stay here as long as you need. The nurse will be back in a while."

Nicole rushed to leave, turning around and picking up her bag and coat.

If you will not make her stay…I will. The minute her body was straight and had turned, Nick felt his arm rise.

She is mine!

Nick pulled his arm away violently and crashed to the floor.

Nicole spun around. "What the hell?"

"No…stay back!" he yelled.

"Wha—" Nicole held her hands out, palms facing him. "Nick… listen to me. Talk to me. You're having a panic attack or something. What's going on?"

Nick felt the rush again. The wolf was there, Nick could feel him. He had no choice but to believe. His arm had lifted of its own accord. That was no dream.

"I have to tell you something," Nick said, still pressed against the wall, keeping himself away from her.

"Ok…tell me."

"I wasn't entirely honest with you when I told you about my father. I mean I didn't lie, I just didn't tell you the whole story."

"Ok then." She nodded quickly. "I'd like to hear it."

"My father *was* thought of as royalty, and his position killed him. That along with his refusal to accept the fact that I wasn't like him. Everyone, even my mother and me, told him to forget it. That it was a pipe dream, a fantasy, that it would never happen. He refused to believe, trusting himself, but the people under him grew restless and weary, waiting for his heir to be appointed. But as it turns out…I am like him."

"What do you mean?"

"My father and his associates weren't…normal."

"What do you mean exactly?" Nicole shook her head questioningly, not understanding.

Nick took a deep breath, the pain in his muscles and the heat on his skin reaching feverish levels. "They were werewolves."

Nicole did the exact opposite of what Nick thought she would: absolutely nothing. She stood completely still, with the same face she had before he uttered the words. *I did not expect this from you. An interesting choice to say the least. What will you do now? She doesn't believe you, Nicholas. Convince her? Or backtrack?*

"And you're telling me that…you're a werewolf too?"

"Yes, I…I think so." *You can do better than that.*

Nicole nodded once. "Come here."

"Wait…what?"

"Just come here."

"No, you need to stay away!"

"*Calm down…*" Nicole said, her voice an octave lower. She took both of his hands in hers and looked him directly in the eye. "Come here, I said."

He let her pull him into her arms, embracing him. "Just breathe, ok?"

Nick felt the pain subside, he felt himself cool off as if someone had poured ice-cold water over his steaming body. Being close to Nicole was helping him, more than helping him. He didn't want it to stop, he needed to make sure he was in control. He grasped her hips a little harder then he would've liked, trying to maintain whatever calming effect she had on him.

"Shhh, easy…easy. Just relax," she said, slowly stroking the back of his hair and his back.

How wonderful it is to finally be in her arms. Wouldn't you agree, Nicholas? She soothes me, the beast within you. Remember that.

Nick heard the voice, but tried to focus on the moment. He kissed Nicole on the shoulder as they both continued to hold each other. The wolf was right, though. She didn't believe him. She thought he was probably delusional from his panic attack, but right now, he didn't care. Nick was just grateful to be where he was.

When he had calmed down, Nicole kissed him—on the cheek

again—before she left, promising to call him later that night to see how he was doing. Nick felt good, surprisingly so. After feeling so sick he wanted to throw up, her embrace had enlivened him. It was just a hug, but it had made him feel at peace for the first time in a long time. That in her presence, in her arms was where he was meant to be and nothing else mattered.

He walked, lost in the dream of Nicole, down the winding staircase to woodwork class, along with several other students.

Step to the right. Now!

"Trent, no!" came Jason's voice.

Nick saw Miller barrelling towards him from above, and sidestepped. Miller lost his footing and tumbled down the rest of the stairs to the floor. Thunderous laughter erupted as he came to a stop.

Miller howled in pain. "I think I broke my fucking hand!"

Nick casually made his way down. "Should be more careful, mate. I hear these stairs are pretty dangerous."

Nick walked easily past as Miller raged at him, threatening him. Nick walked on. After the very un-friends-only hug from Nicole, he couldn't even begin to describe how much he didn't care.

Chapter 24

Take Me Home

Melina opened her eyes to darkness. She realised the echo that had woken her was from a vision, not reality. There were no windows in her cell. She had no way of knowing what time it was, but her door was still half-open, which meant no vampire had come to check on her. Perhaps because they were all still asleep? She got to her feet feeling woozy. Nathaniel's blood had helped strengthen her, but it wasn't the nourishment of human blood. She walked as quickly as she could, stumbling up the steps of the dungeon to the outer hall. There was no one around.

As she dared to hope, she spotted it. Streaming through the window, a bright ray of sunshine, and she had never been happier to see it. To think she had feared and even cursed it when she had awoken early the first time, and it had now undoubtedly saved her life.

She came to the front door and flung it open, the light of day drenching her body. She tried to walk down the steps but failed. The sun did not burn her, but after not having seen it for over two hundred years, the light was excruciatingly bright. She could see nothing but a wall of white. She slumped to the ground, fearing that her plan was in vain, dreading the consequences of being found by Vincent when the sun set again.

"My lady? How can this be?"

Melina recognised the voice. Nadia, her human hand-maiden before Julian had dismissed her. Melina blindly reached for her.

* * *

"I'll get you inside!"

"No!" Melina screamed. "A car…drive!"

"I can't leave the estate, my lady!"

"We will both die if you don't!"

Nadia heaved her mistress to her feet. She had no idea what she was in for, what was going on, but she knew Melina was terrified which Nadia had never seen before.

"This way," she said, moving towards Vincent's collection of automobiles, opening the back door of a nearby sedan and helping Melina inside.

Melina sagged into the back seat, unmoving. Nadia felt a heavy painful grip on her arm and stopped, terrified.

"What the hell do you think you're doing, Nadia? Stealing bodies from the crypt?"

"Oh, Damien, it's you." Nadia breathed a sigh of relief. Damien was like her, he tendered to the gardens of the grounds. "Let go of me. I'm not stealing anyone. Melina is awake. She is terrified and very sick. She wants to get away from here."

"Do you think I'm an idiot? The sun is up. You're not going anywhere."

"Take your hands off me!" Nadia half-shouted, half-whispered, before being pushed into the side of the car.

"Got a secret deal going on with a scientist or something? Hmm? Gonna get some money for the body of a vampire? How dare you betray the king's trust. I will—"

A roar of rage erupted from the car. The last thing Nadia heard of Damien was a scream as Melina pulled him partially into the car with her, his legs still dangling off the ground outside the vehicle. Nadia covered her mouth as she peered into the back seat. Melina bit and pierced his jugular. She barely had enough strength to drink the blood spewing from the wound, so she gave a final heave to pull him on top of her instead, letting the thick crimson fountain splash down over her face and torso. When she had drunk and gathered enough energy, she flung him out and he landed in a twisted heap, several metres from the car.

"I think he believes you now," Melina said to Nadia in a dreamy voice before closing her eyes.

Nadia was shaking as she closed the back door and opened the driver's side. She reached for the keys, finding them under the seat. "Where should we go, my lady?"

"Somewhere they can't find us," Melina whispered before finally, Nadia expected, falling asleep.

She started the car and drove, no idea where would be safe when the sunset and the king roused his subjects to hunt them. Where in Sydney could Nadia go that the king had no jurisdiction over? Who would ever help them hide and defy Vincent?

Chapter 25

A Line In The Sand

Werewolf...

No matter how many times she repeated it to herself, Nicole couldn't understand why Nick would make such a wild statement. She had stayed almost an hour past the end of school, mulling it over and she was certainly no closer to figuring it out. It was just so…random.

He wouldn't have meant the physical form obviously—that would be ridiculous—but perhaps he meant the theoretical term of Lycanthropy. The fight between man and beast, the fear of losing oneself? Truthfully she knew very little about Nick's family, so didn't know if this was a natural thing to think of with them. Or maybe it was all just the heat exhaustion talking, and he was just overtired and stressed out.

Nicole sighed, gathered her things and headed out, going over all logical scenarios in her head. Curiously, his revelation didn't make her like him any less. Despite herself, and this was probably the most stupid and illogical thing, she liked him more. It had taken a lot for him to tell her this information, knowing what she might've thought. But whatever was going on in his head could very well explain the strangeness over the last few weeks. The move took balls, and she liked that he could trust her even in all his desperation and fever.

Nicole rounded the corner and spotted something that shook Nick out of her mind.

"Zachary? What are you still doing here?"

The boy was sitting cross-legged outside the ground level classrooms. He had never been here this late before.

Nicole knelt down beside him, “Hey, did your driver say he was going to be late?”

Zachary shook his head.

“Is there anyone else that can come and get you? Anyone that I can call?”

Zachary repeated his move.

Jesus fucking Christ! What the hell is going on here? Who is watching over this kid? “All right, that’s it. C’mon, I’ll drive you home.” She held her hand out to him and he took it.

* * *

Nicole pulled up outside of Raven Apartments. Zachary hopped out of his side and walked alongside her up the path to the huge, rounded glass entrance glinting in the afternoon sun. Strange that someone that lived in such a shiny new place could neglect the greatest asset one could have.

But something about this wasn’t right. Just as they breached the entrance, Nicole heard the rushed sound of clicking heels.

“Zachary! What are you doing? Why didn’t you stay at the school?” the woman screeched. Nicole recognised the voice: Samantha.

“Uh, hello,” Nicole said, moving in front of him. “My name is Nicole O’Brien, and I’m the counsellor’s assistant at the school. We spoke on the phone a while ago?”

“Oh,” Samantha said, faltering slightly before recovering and looking down at Zachary again. “You know the rules! You stay there until someone comes and gets you.”

“Excuse me. First, I think if you’re angry, you should be directing it at the driver who didn’t do his job. Zachary waited well past school hours and no one had come. I decided to give him a lift. A child this age should not be left alone. It was starting to get dark. I insist on speaking to his father about this lapse in responsibility.”

“The driver was taken to hospital about an hour ago. I hadn’t had time to collect an alternative. I see you were inconvenienced. There is no cash kept on premises."

"Wh-what?" Nicole was caught off-guard by this. *What is she on about?*

"Give me a receipt for your fuel expenses and I'll send you a cheque."

What the fuck? "I'm not here for money, thank you very much. I need to speak to Zachary's father. You can't keep fobbing me off. This is ridiculous."

"Fobbing you off?" Samantha said, her eyelids lowering to enhance her crow's feet. "Who the hell do you think you are? This is private property. Leave or you will be escorted out."

"You can't threaten me with that garbage. I can inform the police of the neglect of this child and the entire school faculty will back me on this." Nicole replied, pulling out her mobile. She hoped her bluff would save her. "I can call the police now if you like. Let them come here and question me. Maybe they'll have better luck contacting Zachary's father."

Samantha looked to be weighing up the threat in her mind. Nicole imagined the sight of the police around the grounds wouldn't be a good look for Samantha's bosses. Nicole didn't want to have to put this to the test, but she thought she could at least present a really good case if it came down to it. They would *have* to locate his dad at least.

"Why don't we leave this up to the boy?" Samantha said.

"No," Nicole replied. "We're not leaving anything up to him—"

"Zachary," she interrupted. "How would you like it if the police came up here and interfered in your father's business? How would you feel, letting all that…*added stress* come on to him?"

"Hey, wait a minute," Nicole started, raising a finger towards Samantha. "Don't you *dare* try to emotionally blackmail him. He's a child!"

"And perfectly capable of making his own choices," Samantha replied, not taking her eyes off the boy. Nicole turned, to see his face tense, looking directly back at Samantha. "Do you realise what could happen, Zachary, to your father and also this lady perhaps, should there be any fuss made…where none is needed?"

The reaction was instantaneous. Before Nicole had a chance to speak, Zachary moved forward towards Samantha. "Zachary, no!"

Nicole said, taking his hand and halting him. "You don't have to listen to her. Whatever trouble you're in, I can help you. I can get help. You don't have to be afraid."

Zachary studied her, then turned towards Samantha, whose face glowed with victory. Zachary let go of Nicole's hand and moved back towards Samantha.

"Everything's ok,"

Nicole couldn't believe it. The first words she had heard him speak in ages, and they were a lie. Nicole stood frozen as Zachary moved behind Samantha and continued on slowly.

"By the way," Samantha said. "Your school and the board of education can expect a call from me tomorrow about you. You and your attitude are a disgrace."

Samantha spun around and followed Zachary inside, leaving Nicole there, stunned and silent.

It was a few seconds before Nicole moved, walking back to her car in a fog. She slammed her fists on the roof and screamed. Samantha would follow through, Nicole had no doubts. The career that was hanging by a thread now lay in tatters. She balled her fists in her hair, pressing them hard against her scalp. She wanted to just disappear or go back in time. This was bullshit! She might be able to recover from one complaint, but not two, and both times she had done nothing wrong. No matter what, she would never believe that standing up for what's right should be punished.

Think! What can you do?

There was only one thing she felt she could do right now, and it was the last thing she wanted to. She looked out over the darkening sky and thought it over again, trying to talk herself out of it, but it was no use. If she wanted to save her future, she had to try.

* * *

Nicole gave the door a quick rap with her knuckles after a sighing breath. She heard footsteps approach from the other side.

"Well, here goes."

The door opened and Nicole steeled herself.

"Well, well," said Miller, "Isn't this a nice surprise?"

He wore nothing but golden satin boxer shorts and the biggest toothy grin Nicole had ever seen. Nicole closed her eyes briefly and swallowed, afraid if she took any more notice of him, bile would begin to rise.

"I need to speak to your parents face to face."

"Oh really?" he chuffed. "What about?"

"You know what."

"Um, about the smack down you laid on me? The fact they are suing you? Am I getting close?"

"Yes," Nicole sneered. "Can I speak to them?"

"They aren't here. It's just me. Why don't you come inside and we can wait for them?"

"No thanks. I'll catch them another time."

"It won't make any difference, you know. Whatever you're planning to say. Plead, explain, apologise," Miller waved a hand. "They won't give a shit. I'm their last son. They couldn't do anything to protect or get justice for my brother, but they can do this. Your only hope is to deal with me directly."

"You? What are you talking about?"

"You're a smart girl. I'm sure you can figure it out. You want something from me, and I want something from you."

Nicole shook her head. "What the hell is wrong with you? What is with your freaking obsession over me? I've never liked you. Why do you even care?"

"You don't know? Well, let's just say I was one of the guys that knew your ex before he moved. When was that again? Two years ago? You must be hungry as fuck for some dick. He bragged about you all the time. He said you were the greatest cocksucker he had ever seen. *Gifted* the word was. You were up for anything and wanted it 24/7. So basically, that's my proposition. You show me what he was talking about, I'll make sure these charges get dropped."

Nicole fought the urge to punch him again. She didn't know whether he was telling the truth about her ex or not, about any of it. But it didn't matter. "You are even more messed up than I thought if you think anything would ever happen between us. You sicken me."

"This is a one-time only offer, Nikki. My cock or two years of your life goes wasted."

Nicole turned to leave. "It'll be worth it."

Miller stepped out after her, grabbing her arm. "You think I'm fuckin' around? You think your career is the only thing I can mess up for you?" he growled, his free hand cocked.

"I wouldn't do that if I were you," a voice called from the darkness.

Both Nicole and Miller turned around. A broad figure stood calmly in the street light on the edge of the pavement. His front was almost drenched in black shadow, but despite her adrenaline rush, Nicole could swear she could make out the brightness of his eyes.

"Fuck off, mate. This doesn't concern yo—"

Nicole yelped. The figure had appeared beside her in an instant. She had been pulled free of Miller's grasp and was now standing with the figure by her side. Miller had jumped in shock too and fallen back inside the doorway of his house.

"What the fuck?!" he screamed.

The figure was moving closer ever so slowly to the doorway, like a snake readying a strike. "Cowards that prey on the innocent concern me very much."

The voice was deep. It radiated authority, yet with a sheen of menace that chilled Nicole as well as excited her.

"What the fuck ever," Miller said, trying to sound braver than he probably actually felt, and slammed the door shut.

The figure took a second before turning to Nicole. "Are you all right?"

Nicole had to steady herself. Now she was closer, she got a good look at him. She ran her eyes over his chiselled features and full lips. She noticed a pale tinge to his tanned skin, making the dark circles under his eyes even more prominent, but she stayed fixated on the first things she noticed. The eyes, now she could see them clearly, were a light emerald green. If she had to give them a description, she would have said they were hypnotically beautiful even though the rest of him made her think he was coming down with the flu.

"I'm fine," she said. "Thank you."

"You're welcome," he replied. The voice was warmer now, she noticed. The chilling effect she had experienced before had gone. The excitement however was still there, and also a sense of safety. He flicked his eyes to the keys in her hand. "I'll walk you to your car, if that's all right with you?"

"Sure, that would be great, thanks."

They walked together a few steps and then she could not stop herself from asking, "How did you do that? I mean one minute you were *here* and then you were *there*?"

"I've learned a few things over the years," he replied simply.

"Does that include moving eight feet in less than two seconds?"

"I guess it does." He smiled. "Would you mind me asking you something?"

She shook her head. "No, I don't mind."

"You are an attractive and seemingly intelligent young woman. I do not see why or how you would get mixed up with the likes of that," he gestured his head towards the house.

Nicole sighed. "It's a long story, but believe me I wouldn't choose to be within five hundred feet of him unless it was absolutely necessary. It was his parents that I wanted to talk to."

"Do you not have a phone?" The man asked with a slight smile.

"Yes, I do. Of course." She grinned back in exasperation and amusement. "But I thought face to face would be better seeing as though they are trying to sue me for assault."

"Assault? Why would they do that?"

"Because I smacked the shit out of their son."

The figure raised his eyebrows. "Neat."

"Not really. It's caused me a whole heap of trouble and it's looking I'll be suspended at the very least while the police get involved. If that happens, I can kiss my career of wanting to be a counsellor goodbye."

The man appeared to ponder this, before reaching into his pocket and pulled out a business card. "Take this. If things get really out of hand, feel free to reach me there. I know next to nothing about the education system, but I have many contacts and some of them would. I can't promise anything, but I may be able to help you."

Nicole took the card and looked it over. "You work at T?"

"I own it."

The words sunk in. "Wait. Are you…Dante Delavega?"

He nodded.

"Oh…wow. My name is Nicole. Nicole O'Brien! I've been emailing you, or at least I think it's you, about the—"

"School formal dance," Dante said with a small smile. "Yes, it has been me. I would be delighted for T to host it for you."

"Oh, thank you so much…again! It would mean the world to the kids to have a party like that at T and it would give the school much-needed exposure too."

Dante held up a hand. "Please, it's my pleasure. All that you mentioned is wonderful of course, but this…" he paused gesturing to her face. "Is the best reason. Passion. A love for others and kindness. It's a rarer thing nowadays and I like to help it along wherever possible."

Nicole felt the heat rising in her cheeks. "Well, I'd better be going. But thank you again, for the last time. It means a lot."

Dante made Nicole gasp a second time in the space of five minutes. He had gently taken her outstretched hand and kissed the top of it. It was not the gravely reply of "My pleasure," but she gave an involuntary shiver at the instant hardness of her nipples when he touched her. Strange, as the rest of her body was quite warm. It wasn't a cool night by any standards, but his fingers were like ice blocks. She put it out of her mind enough to wave him goodbye as she turned the car into gear and drove around the corner, leaving the house and Dante behind.

Chapter 26

Help Me

"I demand carnage!" Julian screamed, indicating the broken cell door. "It is impossible for anyone to break out of here from the inside. She had help. I know it!"

Vincent was bored with his son already. He had been for several hundred years, at least. He might have done away with him already, but from time to time, he could prove…useful. "Oh, for fuck's sake. Calm yourself. You sound like the toddler I ate last night…screaming for her mother." He examined the lock and handle. "Did you not follow her advice on how to make these things?"

"Yes. What of it?"

"So did you consider she may have always known of a weakness in the manufacturing? Nothing is foolproof. Especially around you, my dear boy."

Julian's eyes widened, suddenly changing his argument. "I was played. She never loved me. I want her head!"

"No," Vincent growled.

Julian took a breath at this signal and quietened. "She really was waking up in the day, then, wasn't she?"

"Indeed, and getting far too close to our guests upstairs. I should've known her power would draw her to them and vice versa. If she uncovered what we are doing…" Vincent shook his head.

"What harm could she have possibly done?"

"It is imperative that only you, I and Hershel know we are using werewolf blood to make Dream State. The consequences would be diabolical."

These were not just empty words. On the contrary, Vincent truly felt them. His stance on werewolves had prompted an enormous amount of resentment in the greater vampire population. The rest of the world had to put up with them, so why not Australia? Though surprisingly, his actions had gained him an equal measure of respect from the one place he needed it: The Messengers of Osiris, the overseers of the vampire world. They preferred to remain unseen, communicating only through letters sent by falcons that they had imbued with special strength and endurance. Although Vincent had indeed received notification of their approval—or perhaps it was merely tolerance; that was enough for Vincent—via such a falcon, the fact was, he had always doubted the supposed, almost omnipotent aura they commanded. Vincent had long had the view that a vampire's only power was that which was given to them, and further, one could not challenge thin air. But then perhaps it was indeed this distinct absence that made The Messengers of Osiris nigh on invulnerable.

Vincent's position as king was untouchable due to the fact he had been a formidable ally in the war against the wolves. His strength had saved many of his kind back in Innisfree in the late 1600s. Once king of Sydney, he made his choice and stuck to his word against werewolves. Other vampire leaders felt as he did, but due to the hangover from centuries of war all over Europe and the Americas, they relented somewhat and conceded to an uneasy peace in the early 1800s. Vincent, however, had declared that Australia was a free country for vampires only. He would recognise the peace with the werewolves only if they remained out of the country. The wolves were indignant, but could not risk going against Vincent, and more importantly, the newly reached peace.

That's not to say there were not isolated incidents were wolves had snuck in, attempting to undermine him, cause trouble, or to inflict death. They were either quickly disposed of during their second full moon on these shores, or scurried away when they realised Vincent was after them.

It had solidified him as the vampire spokesman for the entire country, although he only officially ruled Sydney. Australia had been cut off and more importantly, left alone, to govern themselves.

This gave Vincent room to move when it came to the biggest nuisance of his entire ruling life: Australian politicians. Gone were the days when all one needed was a pair of fangs to keep the snakes in line. Now, though, there were just a few too many incidents where a feeding vampire was spotted by a member of the general public or captured by police. To keep these events out of the headlines took the one thing Vincent had long had little use for, and it was just the thing politicians seemed to always be in need of: money. Vincent all too frequently found himself "donating" large sums of hush money to the government, who would then distribute this to the media, or the Aboriginal charities—silencing them for a bit longer—as well as other forms of grants or funding. Vincent was fortunate in the fact that Australian politicians did not have term limits. He had only had to negotiate with a few prime ministers over the years. Most were spineless worms. Only one had ever proven to be almost more trouble than he was worth, and that was Harold Holt. He would not bow to pressure, and was not easily intimidated. To this day, Holt was the only Prime Minister to "go missing" and never be found. *And*, Vincent smiled to himself, *he never will be.*

Pride and a sense of caution now prevented Vincent from admitting that funds had run low. It was becoming more and more difficult and expensive to keep their existence out of the news. The fees and taxes gained from vampire businesses were no longer enough. Word was spreading to the far ends of Australia and beyond that Sydney, or Vincent's hold over it, was weakening. The human government was a vacuum of cash, yet within the last few years, Vincent had been forced to destroy more and more of his kin before the government went to him with demands for money. He simply could no longer afford the chance they could re-offend. Dream State was the chance to refill the coffers and re-establish himself as the true ruler of Sydney.

Should the fact that he was using wolf blood to make a vampire drug—one that killed humans, to boot—wind up being leaked to the public somehow, everything he had worked for would be gone. His kingship, his life, would be over. Julian could never take his place; he could never command respect. And Vincent was short on any other underlings who might be able to take command. This was why he had been working so hard to win back Dante. A fact that made Vincent grind his teeth in anger.

"What's the problem? We are making a tonne of money, so who cares? We have paid off our debts. Raven Apartments is now guarded twenty-four hours a day. Soon we will be rich enough to take on the other states and make Dream State available Australia wide. No one will be able to stop us."

His son was never one to be able to see much beyond the end of his own nose. There was no real point in trying to explain to him, though. Better to give him some direct orders. He could usually manage to fulfil those without too many ill side-effects. Dream State was only a short term fix, yet with huge returns. It just needed to keep going for perhaps another twelve months, but Julian didn't need to know that. Hershel was working on other things and Vincent wanted them to continue as soon as possible. "Yes, but I need you focussed on the tasks at hand. The reports come in every night of more vampire bodies found in the streets by our scouts."

"The Forgotten are on the move?"

"The scouts inform me there is no evidence they have left Redfern. There is a new group out there hunting us however. And that group seems to disappear into Redfern as well."

"You think it's the wolves?" Julian asked, eyes narrowed, belying his actual inability to come to conclusions that Vincent had not already placed before him.

"I believe they could be working in unison, and if so, it…vexes me." Vincent turned and left the cell with a flourish, beckoning his son to follow. "The wounds have been knife and bullet related—not a wolf's style. Though I am thinking the pack that Clive and his little blonde friend found are the ones responsible, yet they must be only initiates. Humans wishing to prove worthy of the cursed bite. They may call themselves wolves, but they must be human. It has been months since they arrived, and not once during all the following full moons have I received word of any maulings of the type those creatures can create. This was Alicia's plan all along, I'd imagine. Send wolves to meet with me, then humans as back up so we could not track them as easily. Clever little cunt. I am mobilising the Elements of Night and I want you to lead them. But first, I want you to send what's-her-name, the blonde, back out there first. She has seen them. She will know who you are to look for. Let her do the reconnaissance for this, see if she can handle herself. Wait for her to report back, or if she doesn't, make sure you place a homing signal on her so we can trace her corpse. Do this now. It suits you better than hunting your ex-pain and sex toy."

"The only thing better would be killing her."

Vincent sighed and waved his hand dismissively. "Put the thought out of your mind. She is probably dead already. Besides, who has the kindness to help a vampire and a slave in this city?"

* * *

It was a long shot, but her only shot. It was nearly dawn and Melina was sound asleep. Nadia had parked outside Dante Delavega's place. It was an old three-storey house that had been converted into a number of smaller apartments. It looked like no one was home; she'd have to wait. What if he didn't accept them? But then again, what if he did? Would Melina kill her for coming here? Melina did say anywhere, but even so, asking this particular vampire for help might be too much. Even for her. Would Dante kill Nadia for even daring to ask on Melina's behalf? Though Nadia had been her handmaiden for many years, she knew little about Dante Delavega—she had never met him, only heard his name. Sometimes it was spat out with derision by other vampires in the mansion, particularly Julian. But she'd also heard Melina mention it when it was just the two of them alone. She raged about him, cursing him and telling Nadia how much of a pathetic worm he was, a disgrace to vampires. But one evening, Melina had become sad after a similar rant, and inadvertently let it slip that he was her old love. This gave Nadia enough hope he would hear her out at least.

Finally, she saw him, or at least, she thought it must be, based on the descriptions she had heard. He went inside and she waited. How long to give him? A minute perhaps. She hurried across the road and stopped at his front door.

Nadia pressed the intercom button and did not have to wait long for an answer.

"Hello?" The voice was deep and sounded weary.

"I need to speak to you, Mr Delavega. It's urgent."

"It is very late to be selling cookies."

Nadia faltered. She heard a chuckling on the other end. He thought this was a joke? "I'm not selling cookies…I come—"

"Ah! A subscription to Foxtel then?" he asked, sounding amused.

"Sir! I come in the request and name of Melina Garcia."

Silence.

Nadia felt a whoosh and something heavy landed behind her. She whirled and took an instinctive step back towards the door, her eyes running over his broad shoulders. Years of vampire treatment had taught her to expect punishment, for anything. She faced Dante, faltering momentarily as she stared into the bright green eyes. "How did you…?"

"Jumped out the top window," he interrupted dismissively. "You wear the rags of a king's slave. What message do you bring?"

He was no longer mirthful. He stood before her, imposing, radiating a presence that commanded…respect? Definitely not fear. He wouldn't hurt her, she knew. This was nothing like the royal family. She had served them for years and never sensed anything remotely like this. Yet here, it was obvious within seconds.

Nadia indicated the car. "I haven't brought a message. I have brought her. She…needs your help."

Without a word, Dante was beside the vehicle. He picked up Melina and carried her into his apartment. Nadia followed, watching as he placed Melina gently on his bed. She now felt better about her choice to come here. He held Melina so tenderly and with such care, it was as if she was a delicate crystal that was in constant danger of shattering.

He stared at Melina for well over a minute. Nadia could not place what he appeared to be thinking. His face was expressionless, his body like stone.

"What is your name?" he asked, still staring at the unconscious beauty.

"Nadia, master."

"Do not call me that. You are now in my house, and here there are no masters and no slaves. Please tell me how it is you came to be here." He finally turned to her and looked her up and down. "But first, something to eat. Follow me."

* * *

The wolf licked its lips at the prospect; it was close. It had tracked the teacher to this spot overlooking Carss Park beach. The night air was thick and dark as pitch. The wolf crouched, homing, its senses alive as the night answered its call. There! It was so simple and quick. Bodily fluid, urine, the same Nicholas could faintly smell earlier. The wolf kept low, closing in on the beige-coloured car. Now that the wolf had him here, what to do with him? The wolf found it interesting that despite wearing a wedding ring, the stink of cheap lipstick from at least two females reached it. Clearly, this had not been the man's first stop.

The wolf heard low mumbling from him, babbling even. But there was no one else present except for them. Shubert was obviously drunk.

How easy it would be to break his ribs, one by one. But no. This was not about killing. In fact, it was quite the opposite. Shubert was not the target of this lesson; Nick was.

The wolf leapt onto the front bonnet, its silver-eyed reflection staring back at him. When the wolf gave a smile, all four canines were obvious, sharp and gleaming.

"Can I ask you about getting some more credit, sir?" the wolf boomed gleefully.

Shubert screamed and tried to start the car in a rush. Failing again and again to turn the engine over. His fingers trembled and his hands shook. Finally, the engine roared to life.

The wolf slammed its fingers into the roof of the car and pulled back strips of metal with its thick, sharp nails. Shubert had thrown the car into reverse and was backing as fast as the car could manage. Rather than falling off, however, the wolf smiled just with the corners of its mouth, the bottom fangs noticeable, even from inside the car.

The teacher slammed on the brakes and turned the car, dragging it to the edge of the cliff before coming to a stop. The wolf sailed over the top of the car, landed on all fours, and bolted into the trees and out of sight of Shubert as he sped away.

Chapter 27

Tonight You're Mine

"I don't care what anyone says, this plans sucks donkey's balls," Lauren snapped.

She and some other unknown walked past Redfern Oval. They had been around to a few pubs and she had presented the bartenders with a picture of Matt, taken from a selfie two years ago with her and Alex. It was the best shot she had at getting a lead, but no luck. She also tried showing a half-empty vial of Dream State, asking where she could get more. She had hoped if she could get to someone that knew of it, or a distributor, she could get closer to the guys Clive had called the "wolf pack". It seemed pretty clear they were behind the Dream State somehow, what with the way they had snapped it up from that Coffinail dipshit. If she found a vamp distributor, she'd have to beat the shit out of them for information, which sounded like fun. If it was human, all the more so.

All the bartenders so far, though, had said they had no idea what it was. At least it wasn't like the scenes she'd heard about recently, with the disgusting remnants of slaughtered vampires. Matt and his pals were sure making a mess of the city.

Her companion was a foot taller than she was, a member of the Elements of Night, Vincent's personal strike force, and he refused to give his name. "It's classified," he'd said. Lauren had snorted at this. *Someone's been watching way too many secret service movies.*

It was past midnight, yet true to form, the streets were far from empty. Lauren always thought of Redfern as one of the places where Sydney life came to die. When she'd been human, she had believed that almost no one but drunks, drug addicts and derelicts hung out at Redfern around this time. Now that she could see, smell and hear better than ever before, she knew she'd been right.

"Where are we heading? Or is that classified too?" Lauren scoffed.

"You were told the exact directions."

"Nooo, I wasn't," she explained with more patience than she felt. "I was told I was being dropped off at Redfern and I would have an escort. How the hell am I expected to find anyone here? Where am I supposed to go?"

"Use your ingenuity to get information. We have narrowed down the packs' possible base of operations to this particular area, these particular pubs. They seem to stick to a general radius. So we keep searching the pubs until we find what we're looking for. You and Clive are the only ones who can identify the human pack from Coffinail."

"Don't remind me." Lauren pulled a face thinking about vampire goo. She snapped her eyes left to right and almost crashed into No-name as staggering people brushed past her. "And geez, can you fuckin' keep it down? You won't even give me your name but you practically shout the words *vampire* and *werewolf* at the top of your voice? Where is the sense in that?"

"Make no mistake, those who know nothing won't remember or even be listening. Those we are looking for, already know you're here. It makes no difference."

"Wait…they know? How? Why didn't you freaking tell me?"

"Without a doubt. We are being followed. A man and a woman have been trailing us for some time. I want you to have a look."

"I thought the idea was to never let pursuers know you're on to them?"

"I *want* them to know. I want to see if they change their tactics or if they contact someone."

Lauren turned her head slowly and sure enough, she saw them. An Aboriginal couple, maybe early thirties, dressed in filthy sports clothing and barefoot, walking in unison together. She looked at them for several seconds, but that was enough. The couple stopped when she blew them a kiss. Then gave them the finger.

Lauren smirked. "Pretty sure they got the message."

"Fuck," was the reply as No-name whipped his head back around to look behind them. Lauren followed suit and her mouth dropped open. The couple was gone.

"What the hell—"

"They can do things in Redfern that they can't anywhere else. No idea how. Black fella magic," No-name grumbled. "C'mon. Across the road. This pub will be as good as any."

Lauren definitely wasn't imagining it; the couple was there a second ago. Not even vampires could move that fast. But she also saw a few heads turn towards her. A group of Aboriginal men sat on a brick fence just in front of her, tipsy in delight. Yet when she closed on them, they were silent. Every single one faced her, collective eyes like steel balls of loathing.

"I don't like this…" Lauren said. All of her strength, all of her rage didn't matter right now. The world in general lived in denial about the existence of the creatures of the night, but Redfern was different. The inhabitants seemed not only to know vampires existed, they could sense them. She was not welcome here. There was a reason vampires never came here. Because it was said that none left alive. She now believed that rumour to be true.

"Try here," No-name said as they came to the Dingo's Ditch entrance. He peeked in, "The line to the bar isn't long. Ask the bartender in there if he knows anything."

This was ridiculous. It was going nowhere. She had to get back to basics, back to herself. "Fuck this. I'm not doing it your way anymore. No one here knows Matt. We never hung around this area. And anyway, he's got a shaved head now and in this pic he looks like Raggedy Ann. Just showing them Dream State gets us no answers either."

"Think of something else then."

Lauren sighed and took off her jacket, tossing it to him. "He's a guy, right? Guess it's time to call in help."

No-name watched in silence as she undid the first four buttons of her top and placed the vial in her ample cleavage. Without a word she walked through the door and up to the bar. She stood in line for the first time in ages. When her time came, she placed her elbows on the bar and leaned forward, giving him the best view she possibly could.

He gave her chest two glances, and then a third before asking her what she wanted.

"You got anything other than beer?" she giggled.

"If you ask really nicely," he smiled back. He seemed okay. Young and horny, which was no crime in her book.

"What if I feel like something other than drinking?" she asked, smiling and biting her lip. It was so easy to fool these young things.

The bartender took a second before wincing. "Believe me, I wish I could help you, but I have a girlfriend."

Lauren chuffed. "Ha! Easy handsome. I was thinking of this." She pulled the vial part-way from her cleavage—enough that he could see the tell-tale colour—and then poked it back down again.

Silence. Lauren sensed the instant aroma of salty sweat forming on his body. Exactly what she wanted.

"Know where I can get some? I've got money."

"How much?" he asked.

"Trust me, I've got enough."

The bartender looked sceptical and nervous. "We'll see. Wait here."

Lauren waited for him to leave before giving the news to No-name, who was now lingering behind her. "Bingo. He knows something. But we're gonna need to show we've got the cash."

"Here." No-name shoved a wad of bills into her hand. "It's roughly two grand. That should be enough to loosen their tongues at least. He will try to take you in the rear, and I need you to let him."

Lauren thumbed the money, roughly counting it in her head. "Many guys have tried taking me in the rear. No one will ever get there. The odd finger doesn't feel too bad though, if he knows what he's doing."

"The back of the building! I'll head around to back you up, just in case."

"You E.O.N guys have, like, no sense of humour."

Lauren didn't have to wait long before spotting the bartender beckoning her over towards the staff entrance, slyly showing her two full vials and hiding them quickly. Lauren ducked after him. "Where are we going?"

"You said you had money, right?"

"Of course."

"A lot?"

"Obviously."

"We just got a new delivery. You better not be yankin' my chain," he laughed. As they approached the door to the back entrance, Lauren was suddenly aware they were not alone in the corridor. Two men were behind her and closing the distance.

Shit.

Just as the thought of danger reached her, two taser jolts struck her in the back, bringing her to one knee, screaming. She was strong, but not enough to simply shake off two tasers and a sudden knee to the face from the bartender. Something grabbed her by the head and tossed her outside onto the cold ground, surrounded by rows of industrial garbage bins and kegs.

"Big mistake to come here alone, bitch." That was not the bartender. Lauren recognised the voice but couldn't quite place it. She rose, baring her fangs, and saw the speaker. It was Calibos, the head honcho of the wolf pack she'd witnessed at Coffinail. She guessed No-name and his pals had indeed done their homework in narrowing down the list of pubs that might be their headquarters. Pulling out the wires, she tossed them away from her and hissed, "Who says I'm alone?"

"Oh, what?" Calibos said, pointing up, as more men moved to surround her. "You mean you were counting on him?"

Lauren's stomach felt full of cold lead. No-name hung from a noose on a large hook above the bartender, twitching like a fish on a line, blood foaming and pouring from his neck. It wasn't rope digging into his throat, it was barbed wire.

Lauren cracked her neck and then her knuckles, baring her fangs. There was nothing she could do for No-name, but she still had a chance, even if it was just to kick some arse before dying. "Let's go, fuckers."

Calibos held the others at bay. "She wants to play, boys. I'm game."

There was a crack like thunder and Lauren rocked her head back and screamed again. A bullet had been fired and gone straight through her leg. She grabbed her thigh with both hands and collapsed. Even through her pain, she knew neither Calibos nor the bartender had been holding a gun. And it wasn't the guys behind her, either. Where had the bullet come from?

"Well…that was disappointingly quick." He pouted. "Oh well. Let's see if you can shoot her other leg from there."

The response was another bullet. There were cheers now that drowned out her wails. She scrunched her eyes but could tell there were at least five men closing in on her.

“Two bullets filled with lemon juice and salt. Man that’s gotta sting. Let her have a couple more. She can take it.”

One, two more. One in her shoulder and another in her leg. Lauren’s fangs were piercing her lower jaw, she was clenching them so hard. She tried not to let the tears show, but as the red haze came over her, they could not be missed.

“Sit her up,” Calibos instructed.

Her arms were yanked over her head and she was brought up to a sitting position. The side of her face caved in as several fists pummelled her. She was too weak to use her one defence—invisibility.

She heard the reloading of the gun. The shooter had positioned himself directly in front of her. She fluttered her eyes open. *No...*

“Matt, please stop.”

“Matt?” Calibos asked. “You know him?”

“Go fuck yourself, wolf”

Calibos laughed. “No point in asking him for mercy, babe. Matty is blank upstairs. Healing him up took a lot more from him than we thought. We’ve given him Dream State to enhance his skills when he sleeps. He gets better every day. Now he is a silent killing machine, but that’s the trade-off. His elevator doesn’t go all the way up to the top floor anymore, as long as we keep juicing him up. Ain’t that right, Matty? We only do one thing now, aye? Kill vamps!”

The men holding Lauren let out a unified howl. Oh the irony. She had succeeded in her mission. She had found Matt and the wolves but she would not be able to tell Clive or Vincent or anyone else.

“Who are you and what the fuck are you doing in Sydney?” She shouted a last desperate attempt to find out something, anything. Was it just to buy time? She wasn’t sure. She just knew she wasn’t ready to die.

“I’ll answer yours if you answer mine. Deal?”

Lauren grunted her affirmation.

Calibos squeezed her neck rather tight. “How do you know Matt?”

Lauren tensed her face, yet did not show how much his grip was hurting her. “He is my…ex besties…ex. Then I broke his back. Or I thought so. Couldn’t have done a good job.”

“*You* put him in hospital?! No shit. What a small world,” Calibos spoke up to his pack. “Aye, boys, I’ve just had a thought. Let’s send this bitch back to her king. She can deliver a message for us. Tell me, bitch, where does he live?”

"Darling Point." Lauren didn't hesitate to tell them. Any chance she might live would be worth it.

"Good girl. Now to your question. You will tell your king that my name is Calibos. My men and I are here looking for our friends. Four of them were sent here by our Alpha's wife to negotiate with your king. They were never heard from again."

"So Vincent has obviously killed them!"

"Uh-uh," Calibos said. "We may have believed that, except that this…" he indicated the Dream State lodged in her cleavage, "proves otherwise. It is made with living werewolf blood. Vincent is keeping them somewhere. We want to know where. It's very simple. If he hands them over to us unharmed, we'll go home. If he doesn't, vampire blood is going to keep flooding the streets. He brought this upon himself."

Calibos reached into his pocket and pulled out a switchblade, then knelt down closer to Lauren. "Tie her up to that post, boys."

They dragged her several feet backwards and tied her hands together around the lamppost. "So, you're just gonna kill me now?"

"No sweetness, I'm going to send you home with a message. Like I said. But not just yet. You see, I think you'll be good company for Matty, since you know him so well."

Fear and rage swelled in the pit of Lauren's chest. She steeled herself as Calibos swiped at her top with the blade, clean cutting it and her bra free, exposing her breasts to the cool night air. She had never been demure, but this was somehow more excruciating, more violating than the bullets had been. She clenched her teeth as well as she could with a broken jaw and cheekbone, and swallowed the blood in her mouth rather than spitting it out.

"That's a shame. Best set of tits I've seen and wasted on a dead chick. Oh well."

Calibos brought the knife down and sliced her chest, deep and slow. Lauren heard a horrible shriek and realised it was her own voice. Calibos simply ignored or was excited by her agony.

"Matty needs more practice. Dream State can only take him so far. Every time he ventures out with us, you guys don't last long enough."

Calibos tapped Lauren on the cheek and handed the switchblade to Matt. "Now remember: shoulders, sides, thighs and arms. No face and no chest. Got that, Matty? If you hit the chest, she just might bleed to death before we send her back and you'll break your toy."

Lauren didn't know if Matt even registered he was being spoken to. He continued to stare blankly at nothing. But he did take the knife with four hands. *Wait, four?*

Lauren scrunched her eyes and released them quickly. Her vision was still blurry and skewed. The adrenaline was subsiding and the pain was seeping in. Every bone felt broken. Her chin felt so heavy…she couldn't hold the weight of her head.

"Oi! You better not be dying on me," Calibos yelled. "Not yet. Keep your head up or the first throw will go through your forehead to help you on your way."

Even if she'd wanted to, Lauren could not obey. Exhaustion and pain were overtaking her. Without warning, Lauren coughed and retched as blood flowed from her mouth.

"Jesus Christ!" Calibos exclaimed. "The one time you actually want a vampire to live…"

Belt in hand, he approached her and pushed the back of her head against the pole she was tied to. He clipped it around her forehead and the lamppost, keeping her head upright and in place.

"Doesn't look like we've got long with this one, Matty. She's on the way out I'd say. Let's make it a quick practice."

"Matt, no, please…" Lauren whimpered,

Matt flung the blade directly at her. She wailed at the sickening *thud* it made, and felt like she'd been punched hard in the shoulder. Its aim must have been true, due to the howls and cheers of the wolf pack.

"Nice one, Matty! Clean as a virgin's slit." Calibos wrenched the blade free, ignoring Lauren's sobs. "Let's try the other shoulder."

There was no energy left to protest, let alone fight back. She was going nowhere.

Chapter 28

Lean On Me

"Hey, sleepy head… Let's go!"

"Awwww, come on. Just five more minutes," Nick mumbled in semi-consciousness.

"That's what you said fifteen minutes ago." Alex swiped his pillow from under his face and smacked him with it. "Let's…go!"

Nick laughed into his sheets as he rubbed his rear. "Who told you I'm into that?"

"Oh shut up, you brat!" Alex grinned and pushed his face back down into the mattress. "Jesus, I really have to take you shopping."

Nick sat up and frowned. "What do you mean?" He followed her gaze to his chest. The sleeveless shirt he wore to sleep in was torn from collar to stomach.

"Looks like you're growing out of your clothes overnight, Incredible Hulk! How small is that singlet?"

"It isn't. Small, I mean. I only bought it last week. It fit me fine." He tried to get a look at it and found the bottom completely shredded. He pulled it over his head and it came apart in his hands. "Geez, so much for craftsmanship."

"Weird. Well, I'll try to pick you up something with a bit better quality later today. Meanwhile, in the shower you go."

Nick pulled a face at her, but Alex was not to be thwarted. "Come on, you stink. What the hell have you been up to, running a marathon?

Hurry up. You'll be late for school."

"Yes, dear," he said, kissing her on the cheek as he left.

Nick closed the bathroom door, stripped off his underwear, and checked himself out in the mirror. He had noticed his body changing rapidly over the last few days, but particularly today. He showered and stepped out, noticing his shoulders and chest seemed broader, bulkier. Back when his father still had hope of Nick becoming his alpha heir, he had told him that the body of a werewolf transforms in a different way for each individual, much like regular puberty—only much faster. As the change nears, the body increases in size to deal with the trauma it is to be put through on a monthly basis. Yet again, more proof that this was real. This was happening. He was still unsure how he felt about that. It was frightening, but there was also an excitement that he couldn't quite explain.

Nick dressed quickly and inhaled breakfast. He wasn't sure what it was, something crunchy and fruity.

"Nick, hun? Can you sit for a sec?"

Nick froze. Alex sounded serious, and whatever it was she wanted to talk about, he really didn't feel ready for it right now. Especially if they wanted him to come clean about Alicia. "I'm going to be late."

"We really want to talk to you. Please?"

Nick slumped back down opposite Alex and Margaret and waited with some trepidation.

"Nick, you know we love you and we care about you," Alex began. "But I think the time has come to ask a difficult question."

Nick nodded, barely.

"Now just so you know, no matter what you tell us, as long as you're honest, we're not going to be angry," Margaret added.

Nick let out a short breath, but before he could utter a reply, Alex cut him off. "Are you taking steroids?"

Nick did a double-take. He could not have heard that right. "Sorry?"

"Hun, you have grown something like ten, maybe fifteen kilos of muscle in only a few weeks…"

Nick could not help but laugh. "Ooh, is that what this is about? Look, Alex—"

"You were getting bullied at school, and then that seemed to stop very quick. Plus, it was over a girl, and certain girls like the muscly type. I mean if you put the pieces all together…"

"Alex, I see where you're going with this. I swear I am not taking anything. I couldn't do that to my body, and besides I couldn't afford it." He grinned.

"Ok, then how…?" Alex indicated all his new bulk, eyebrows raised in confusion.

"It's just me," Nick shrugged. That was true. He could not stand lying anymore, but without knowing the full extent of what his body was doing, it was all he could say. After all, it wasn't as if he wasn't in control of himself. He stood, needing to get out of there. He wasn't going to be able to explain anything more to their satisfaction right now anyway. "But I really gotta go now. See you later."

Alex narrowed her eyes, but didn't say anything as he grabbed his pack and made for the door.

* * *

Nick stepped off the bus to flashing lights. An ambulance and two police cars were parked outside the front entrance of the school, and the double doors were filled with staff and students, not yet allowed to go in. It seemed someone was close to being brought out.

"What's happening?" Nick asked a huddle of students at the base of the steps.

"I dunno exactly. I heard Mr. Shubert came in this morning and went nuts."

"What?"

"Yeah, had a gun and everything."

"But why?"

The student shrugged and was about to say something more, but the murmuring of the crowd near the door made him close his mouth again. Medics wheeled Mr. Shubert, tied to a gurney, out toward the ambulance. Shubert was raving. "He's not human. He tried to kill me! Look at my car. Why don't you believe me? Let me go!"

The paramedics loaded the coach into the back and injected him with something that made him immediately drowsy. He grew quieter, but Nick could still hear what he whimpered. "He's dangerous…don't… let him…near…anyone."

The ambulance doors shut and one police car escorted it along the street to the main road where the vehicles turned and disappeared. Two police officers remained behind to take statements from witnesses. A heap of students lined up for questioning, even those Nick had travelled with on the bus, who could not possibly have seen anything.

The boy he had spoken to moments before piped up. "Did you see his car? You should have a look before the cops take it."

"Sure," Nick said. "What does he drive?"

"Some shitty Ford. It won't be hard to find."

They found it parked a short distance up the street. They weren't the only ones who had had the same idea. The vehicle was surrounded by a small-but-growing crowd of students and even a few curious teachers.

When Nick finally got close enough to see the car, he felt a lump rise in his throat. Four gashes about a metre long and a fifth about half that, had been ripped into the roof, allowing streamers of sunshine to pour into the car. The edges were sharp and bent upward, as if pried up by a crazed can opener. The chatter went on around him.

"What the hell could've done such a thing?"

"Aw, come on, bro. Stupid fuck got pissed and hit a tree or an animal last night or something."

"Then where is the damage to the bumper, the windshield?" Nick asked to no one in particular. He tried to shake the feeling he knew exactly what had happened but couldn't remember. Or something wasn't letting him.

Four and a half grooves, just like the table in the cafe.

"I suggest you all get back to school before you spend the next week in detention!"

"Sorry, Ms. O'Brien!" One boy shouted and ran off together with a friend as the remains of the crowd dispersed.

Nick couldn't bring himself to move. Nicole walked up behind him. "Just because I have a soft spot for you doesn't mean you're above anyone else. Come on…"

When Nick still didn't make any motion to leave, however, she changed tacks. "Hey, are you ok?"

Nick had his hands on the boot, studying the roof, not really listening to her words. "I did this," he whispered.

He chanced a look at her. Nicole looked around, making sure no one could see her. She placed her hand on Nick's cheek and turned him around to face her. When she spoke, her voice was soft, not demanding like it had been.

"How do you mean? This is not your fault."

"What?" Nick snapped in shock.

"I know you feel guilty for what happened yesterday, but you shouldn't. He was hysterical when he arrived this morning. I usually wouldn't speak ill of a staff member, but he was absolutely off his rocker. He stormed into the staff room this morning, ranting about a monster and demanding the teachers cancel lessons and lock the kids in their classrooms!"

"Nikki…" Nick said, taking her had from his cheek and holding it tight. "You don't understand. I did this. To him, to his car. It was me!"

"To his car? You mean those cuts?" she asked, her head to the side. "Impossible. If you made them, how did you do it?"

"I don't know. *I can't remember*," he said.

She quirked her mouth. "Doesn't that tell you something?"

"That I am losing my fucking mind or I'm an inhuman beast."

"I don't think it's either of those."

"Nikki, something is happening to me. I wish I could explain it but I can't. I wish you'd believed me before, but I guess it would be strange if you did. You have to stay away from me."

She didn't move. "Nick this is ridiculous. Why won't you let me help you? Friends don't abandon each other."

Nick rolled his eyes. He wanted her to be quiet. He wanted her to kiss him. He wanted her to just shut up about that goddamn "friend" business. "Because I don't want to hurt you! And I don't fucking want to just be your friend. I want… I *need* you." Before anger overtook him further, Nick walked past her and headed to the school. He heard Nicole start to speak, but he ignored it. He couldn't listen right now.

* * *

Nick took several deep breaths and splashed his face with water. Control, he must learn control. No one would believe him, so he couldn't turn himself in. And maybe Nicole's disbelief wasn't so wrong. How was he even sure he had done anything?

Duck. Move your head right now.

Nick dodged a punch that shattered the mirror he had been facing.

"I'm not in the mood," Nick snarled. He turned and faced Miller, hand and forearm clad in a cast. Jason was behind him, looking terrified.

"Good, then just take it," Miller snapped back. He swung with both fists, but hit nothing. Nick moved with his knees, bobbing and weaving away everything that came his way with ease.

"Last chance," Nick barked. "Leave me alone. Or else."

"You just don't get it, do you? You broke my fucking hand. If she's not mine, I'll make sure she's not yours."

Nick grabbed Miller's plaster-encapsulated fist out of the air. "Was that a threat? To hurt Nicole?"

"It's a fucking promise."

Nick sighed. "Stupid choice," he breathed, and crushed the cast and the bones inside. Miller screamed for several long seconds and then slumped to his knees.

"You gonna have a go, too?" Nick asked Jason, who shook his head furiously.

Miller feebly swung his other fist toward Nick's groin, but Nick caught that easily. "Can you think of the one thing there you shouldn't have said, tough guy? Threatening to hurt a girl? Such a big and brave boy you are. Just for that—" He bent Miller's other wrist backward until again the sounds of cracking bones echoed off the tiled walls. "Listen up, *arsehole*… You will not TOUCH HER!"

Nick roared the last two words in a voice that boomed around the bathroom. He let fly with a kick directly to Miller's chest. Miller flew backwards into Jason and the toilet stalls. Both boys cannoned into the cubicles. Dust, wood, tiles, and cement exploded in front of Nick and rained on the two of them, half-burying them beneath a pile of rubble.

A moment of exhilaration passed quickly, before Nick thought about what he had done. The strength…the rage. He really *had* attacked Mr. Shubert last night. He still didn't remember it, but he was starting to believe the voice within him was right. The shirt this morning. The claw marks. If he were a werewolf like his father, that would make all the pieces of the puzzle fall into place. He heard a groan from beneath the settling dust and remembered there were still two police officers in close proximity. Without thinking, Nick turned and ran.

CHAPTER 29

WILL YOU STILL LOVE ME TOMORROW

Good lord, boy. Where do you think you're going?

"I don't know. Away from the people I care about," Nick said, stopping to take a breath. He looked around him and found he was in a golf course that was about a kilometre away from the school. There was no one around, no one to overhear him talking to himself, so he looked for a spot to settle in and gather his thoughts.

Why do you always run from what you are?

"I am NOT that. I will not be evil. I will not be hated and feared."

And running is going to prove that?

"You could've killed Mr. Shubert."

The wolf's voice snorted from somewhere deep within his brain. *I didn't have any intention of killing him.*

"I'm probably wanted for Miller's murder now anyway."

He's not dead, but don't worry. Your confrontation with him will come soon enough.

"I am not a killer!"

Not yet.

"No!" Nick bellowed. "I will not have that on my conscience."

We have no conscience. We defend what we cherish: our loved ones, and our lifestyle. We trample the corpses of anyone who tries to take what we cherish from us. This is the instinct you were born with. No amount of running will change the fact that this is who you are. Just accept it.

"Make me," Nick challenged.

The wolf chuckled to itself. *Very well, Nicholas. If you insist on learning the hard way...*

* * *

Alex knocked on the door of the apartment. She could've called first, probably should've really. But she hoped the surprise would fight off any frostiness accrued in the time of no contact.

The door opened and a bright smile appeared on the face of Michelle Davidson. "Hello, stranger."

Alex embraced her and held on. "I'm so sorry it's been so long."

"Don't be sorry. I haven't called you either. It's my fault too. Come inside."

And so Michelle told Alex of what she had been up to for the last few months. She had travelled Europe with money saved from her years with Dante, visiting Britain and Ireland, taking a break from everything. While she was in Ireland, two vampires had attacked her. Yet once they tasted her Silver Tranite-poisoned blood, they immediately began bleeding from every orifice in their body. Michelle found this wickedly funny, but Alex found the mental image pretty disgusting.

Now, Michelle had been back in Sydney for about five weeks and was looking for steady work. With her degrees, she felt something in accounting, personal assistance, or management for a conglomerate would be worthwhile. "After all, I ran a vampire's life for three years, so I think I can handle anything regular corporate types throw at me." She grinned and shrugged lightly. "But it's not urgent. I still have plenty of cash leftover, so I can afford to wait for something good. Anyway, enough about me. How are you and the big boy going?"

Alex took a deep breath and proceeded to pour out everything that had occurred while Michelle had been gone. Matt going missing and werewolves suspected in his disappearance, Nick's arrival and subsequent problems with other boys from school, and on and on. When she got to the point where she had given an ultimatum to Dante and he had turned her down, Michelle winced but let her continue. She finished with Dante going after Nick's attackers.

"Well, that beats my story, that's for sure. I don't even know where to start."

"I need your help, Mish. You were always so wonderful at knowing just what to do."

"I dunno about that," There was a hint of sadness in her voice.

"Do you have any advice for me on what should I do about Nick?"

"I don't think there is anything you can do for him, hun. Seriously, he is a growing boy and you need to let him stand on his own feet. He'll figure it out. In any case, from what you have told me, it seems that the attacks have stopped for now, right?"

"Yeah, but it's not just that. It's the ease at which Mum called Dante to beat those kids up. Don't get me wrong, I definitely think they needed to be taught a lesson, but I just couldn't send a vampire to do it. It just seems like a serious mismatch, you know?"

"Yeah, I get what you're saying, but I do disagree. For one thing, Dante knows what he is doing. He would've scared the shit out of those little creeps. Maybe it worked and they don't want to hurt Nick again, or maybe Nick has been able to fight back. It doesn't matter really. Secondly, what your mum did doesn't surprise me at all. If you're not willing to go to extremes to protect the ones you love, to make a stand for what you believe in, life's not worth living."

Alex couldn't help but think there was more to Margaret's strange behaviour than just protecting Nick, but she had no way to describe her impression, and no proof of anything sinister from her mother…yet. It was better to save that subject for another day. "So…what about Matt? Why would werewolves kidnap him from the hospital?"

"That, I admit, shocks me. I mean, even just the idea of werewolves. Man, you grow used to hearing about vampires and you forget the other beings out there. I haven't seen or heard anything on the news about any violent killings taking place during the full moon, though. I have no idea why they would be here in Sydney, but I think I have an idea why they took Matt."

"You serious? Tell me."

"Lauren. On the same night she tried to kill Dante, she crippled Matt. Actions like these leave ripples, people talk to other people. Eventually, someone you don't expect is going to take notice. Just because King Fuckwit has a law about silencing anyone who learns about vampires' existence, doesn't mean they catch everyone. I think you'll have the answers to your questions very soon."

Alex nodded, realising Michelle was probably right about that. She hoped Matt would be okay. Despite everything, she didn't wish him ill. "And Dante?"

Michelle straightened, clearly prepared for this. "Oh, honey, welcome to my world."

"What do you mean? I thought you told me you had an easy understanding with him."

"Mm-mmm." She shook her head. "What I said was, our bond goes deeper than love, and it does. Well, it did. But that doesn't mean it wasn't torture, even a little, every day. Knowing no matter what was said, or done, I couldn't be with him. Of course you wanted to, of course you fell for him—how couldn't you, really? That face, that voice, that body…" Michelle grinned, took a breath and raised her eyebrows meaningfully. "Anyway, he gave up on love the day Melina shattered his heart, and he's never let anyone else in. It's as simple as that. Ever since then, he has kept close to humans, particularly females, because he doesn't want to hate all women based on the actions of one. I learnt little by little how to love him and be loved by him without jealousy or expectation. It didn't come easy. But then again, I had no point of reference like you have with me, so I had nothing to gauge our relationship on. You did and I'm sorry about that, but believe me, he would've said the same thing to me had I given him the same ultimatum."

"Really? Because that's kinda what I got most upset with: the idea that he only said no to me because he didn't think I was as good as you."

"Oh, honey, no. God no. You and I are fine. We are both young and hot. He cares for both of us equally. And the reason I know that is because no matter how much sex we gave him, no matter how great our blood tasted, we will just never be *her*."

"But that's just it. There was no sex…" Alex started.

"Alex, it really shouldn't matter…"

"I know it shouldn't. I don't know what's with me. But it was driving me insane, having all these pent up feelings, these…desires. Then to have them just be nothing! I mean, in all the time you spent with him, are you sure the sex was real?"

"I'm sure."

“How can you be, though? Couldn’t it have been in your mind, just like it was with me?”

“Well…there was one time where it wasn’t just us. So there’s that.”

“Wait…what? You guys had a threesome? With who?”

Michelle shifted in her seat. “Another vampire, Kiara. She’d known Dante for a while before I came along. They had an intense casual thing once. Anyway, she came to Sydney in my first year with Dante.”

“So, you guys just…got it on after a few drinks? Look, I know you’re not trying to, but this makes me angry. I mean, it seems that it’s just me that he doesn’t want to be with. I feel like that Samantha bitch.”

“Alex, do you honestly think Dante would initiate it? It was her idea but I was the one who said yes and asked him. He did it for me.”

Alex didn’t know why, but she couldn’t help but smirk. “I didn’t know you were that way inclined, Mish.”

Michelle pursed her lips. She did not return Alex’s light-hearted gaze. “I’m not. Remember when I said I’d do anything for him? Well, just think about this. Dante refused to climax whenever he was with me. Vampire ejaculate consists only of blood. So the idea of coming inside me sickened him, and I’m sure that sounds gross to you too, but I didn’t care. I begged him to. On me, in me, I didn’t care. I felt so guilty that I was getting off left right and centre and he wasn’t. So I know how you feel. But he insisted he would never put me in danger by getting me in contact with his blood. He wasn’t going to take the risk. He said though, that watching me orgasm was enough for him. Pleasuring me, pleasured him.

“Anyway, Kiara came up to me on her last night visiting Sydney and wished me well with him.”

“What was she like?” Alex asked.

“She was respectful, polite, but she snuck in a little comment about how she wished she could taste me. Apparently she had secretly enjoyed watching us the previous night.”

“Watching you—oh…” Alex got the message.

Thinking about it herself, Alex would never admit she could see the appeal. Alex herself had found she could not help but stare as Dante fed off Michelle’s wrist in the mansion a few months ago. Even something so simple was erotic to Alex. Watching Dante with a girl, with Michelle, that knew how to handle him would’ve been interesting. Suddenly Alex shook her head. *What was wrong with her?*

"Anyway, I got the idea that if she could join us for one night, she might be able to allow Dante to enjoy himself more fully, and finally climax. She agreed in a flash, but without seeming creepy, and well, the rest is history."

"Well, what was it like?" Alex asked.

"It was…" Michelle seemed to give up trying to find the correct phrase. "I mean, I don't tend to think about girls that way, but she was a great kisser. And she fed a bit like Dante."

"She bit you?"

"Oh, yeah. They both did. For a while, at the same time. In any case, even if she was terrible, it would've been worth it to see Dante come. It remains the only one I've ever been a part of with him. I told you, as good as it was, I did it for him, and would do it again in a heartbeat. The way he kissed me directly after, I'll never forget."

Alex realized she was getting rather warm and put up a finger, signalling Michelle to wait. With a wink, she went to the kitchen where she knew Michelle kept a bottle of vodka in the freezer. She grabbed some glasses and poured them both a measure. Alex skolled hers and felt the cool burn slide down her throat before refilling her glass and heading back out to the lounge room.

"Alex, I'm only telling you this so you can try and understand a bit where he is coming from. Maybe he's wrong, maybe he's right. But the thing is, he *believes* he has your best interests at heart. My guess is that he thinks that if he just jumped into bed with you, immediately after having been with me, you might view it as him using you. Or, he thinks that you would fall for him and he knows he can't give anything back to you, long term, so he figures it's better to just keep his distance from the get-go."

"And you were ok with that, when you were with him?" Alex asked.

Michelle sighed. "I know you're not gonna like this answer, but honestly, yes. He meant the world to me, and I will never regret any time that I had with him. But I will never try to be someone else or regret that I'm not. But don't get me wrong. I know he didn't love me *that way*. He will never love anyone the way he loved Melina."

"I know. I just don't know if I can be as cool as you are with everything. You're always calm and in control."

"You'd be surprised," she replied softly. "Look, Alex, Dante is great but he is not the be all and end all. If you think you can continue to let him feed, great. If you need more fulfilment in your life, he will understand. The best advice I can give is to talk to him and figure it out together."

"I haven't fed him in ages."

"Well, for the both of your sakes, I hope you get your shit sorted. He needs blood and you need your peace of mind back. So get to it, missy! Go work it out with *our* man. Or I'll kick both your arses."

Alex laughed and hugged Michelle goodbye. She had to get back to prepare dinner, but promised to call in the next few days.

* * *

Michelle closed the door behind Alex and went straight to her bedroom.

From her wardrobe, she pulled out an old jewellery box, carrying it over to her bed and placing it on the bedside table. She lifted the lid and felt the glow of bright blue light from within.

She was almost out. There was only one vial left, enough for two more doses. She would have to get to Coffinail to procure some more. Three thousand dollars' worth would be enough for a month.

But she would worry about that later, she thought, as she began to prepare a syringe.

* * *

Melina awoke for the first time in weeks, at the normal time of sunset. The visions had not come again since her last day at the mansion. Strangely, she didn't know how she felt about that. Should she be happy that her rest was peaceful again? Or angry that the mystery remained hidden behind that steel door?

"My lady, you're up. How do you feel?" Nadia said, holding her gown.

Melina saw her holding it and looked down at her herself. She wore a light blue, silk pyjama top and nothing else.

"Call me Melina. We are not in the mansion any longer, and such a title may expose us." She looked around at the unfamiliar surroundings. "Where are we? Is this a hotel?"

"No, my—Melina. We are in Dante Delavega's apartment."

Melina cleared her throat. "We are…where?"

Nadia repeated herself, slowly.

Melina pinched the shoulders of her top. "Am I to understand, this is his?"

"Yes," Nadia replied quickly, holding up the garment in her hands. "It was all I could find while I laundered your gown."

Melina clenched her teeth and shook her head in disbelief. "And how did you know where he lived? Never mind, it doesn't matter. You told him the situation? He welcomed you? Us? Just like that?"

"He has truly been a gracious host. He carried you into this bedroom. He does not allow me to do any manner of work for him."

"Perhaps because he knew that as my handmaiden, he had no right to order you to do anything," Melina said gruffly.

"Oh, no. It's not like that. He treats me as a guest. I have never met a vampire like him."

"Sounds like someone is infatuated," Melina could not decide whether she was amused or annoyed when she noticed a reddish tinge to Nadia's wrist. "He *fed* from you?"

"It was I who offered! He had collapsed and looked quite sick… It had been quite a while since he—"

Melina leapt to her feet and clutched Nadia's wrist close to her face. "You have been under Vincent's roof for many years and never has a vampire fed from you. You hated the idea, and so I forbade anyone to touch you. Yet less than one night after meeting him, you wanted him to bite you?"

"I…it was…I felt it was an emergency. And he has been truly gracious. He bit out of instinct and didn't take much. When he collected himself, he thanked me but said he promised to only feed from another. He was actually very gentle…"

Melina raised Nadia's wrist and inhaled. "She obviously isn't doing her job then, is she?" Though Dante had healed the wound, she could still smell his mouth on the skin's surface.

Melina's fangs snapped down. "You enjoyed him, then?"

"Oh…well, I—" Nadia said, suddenly flushed.

Melina dropped Nadia's hand with a dismissive gesture and retracted her fangs. "Calm yourself," Melina said, to herself as much as to Nadia. "What once was there is long gone. Destroyed by betrayal. He is pathetic. A worthless human-lover. I would prefer to never see him ever again," she said, turning her head, listening, then snapping. "And just where is he then?"

Nadia frowned. "He had to go to T, I believe."

"So he left us here? He left me all alone? Not even giving me the chance to tell him I do not intend to stay one minute longer? Fucking typical."

"It was an urgent call, from what I gathered. Some kind of emergency. But, my lady, you said you didn't want to see him…"

"I know what I said," Melina snapped, storming out of the bedroom.

* * *

Nicole held the letter tightly in her hand. She couldn't read it again, not the whole thing. She felt tears welling in her eyes but refused to cry them. She ran her gaze over the most important parts.

Department of Education…notification of misconduct…serious allegations…violently abusive…cannot be tolerated…treats cases with the presumption of innocence…suspension must be handed down… investigations will start immediately.

Nicole threw it away. With the act, she truly felt her entire career would follow. No matter what the letter said about presumption of innocence, she knew in her heart her career was over. Everything she had worked for was gone.

She picked up her phone and dialled Dr. Sarsky before she lost her nerve. She reached only his voicemail, and so tried to explain everything she could at a rapid pace. After a moment, she started to apologise, but the words didn't feel right, so she simply ended the call.

No, she would not apologise after all. She did not feel like she had done the wrong thing. Miller had deserved the slap, not that the school board would understand that. The system that she fought for was trying to pin her down, but she wouldn't let it. She would fight to clear her name.

The only thing she regretted was the fact Nick was in the middle of all this. At least he hadn't let her down; he hadn't shunned her. All he wanted was to be closer. So what was she so afraid of? Her reputation? She had ruined that all by herself. He hadn't made her do it. But she did do it *because* of him, that she couldn't deny. She wondered what else she had missed out on because she was so work obsessed. Right now it was a handsome boy that really liked her. Made her smile. Drove her crazy. *Kissed her like she was his salvation.*

A rapping from the door made her jump and march towards the entrance.

She opened the door and was struck momentarily dumb. The figure opposite her was heaving, sweating, looking very sick.

"Nick? Are you all right? You look terrible. And how did you find where I lived?"

"I…followed your scent."

"What? My what? What are you—"

"I'm sorry. Please, I don't know where else to go. I need your…" Nick didn't finish his plea before he tensed, looking past Nicole's shoulder. Felix, the family's white cat stood at the foot of the stairs, back arched and hissing in Nick's direction.

"Don't worry about him. He just doesn't like strangers," Nicole said. She hadn't seen Felix react quite this strongly to people before, but shrugged it off. Maybe it was just because her parents weren't home. "Come in."

Nick took a step toward the door and the cat began to meow angrily, ears pinned back, looking frightened and angry.

"Felix, what's with you?"

Nick growled softly, taking a step back.

"Hang on, I'll just be a second." Nicole moved towards the incensed feline. Felix swatted the air with a paw.

"What the hell has gotten into you, cat? HEY!" she yelled as Felix tried with all his might to fight off her grip. Swatting, kicking, even biting. "That does it," she said, holding him out at arm's length. She went to the back door and dropped him on the wooden veranda, quickly closing the door before he got back inside.

She returned to Nick, who collapsed into her arms, and she partially dragged him inside. As she swung the door closed with her foot, she glimpsed a partially cloud-covered full moon, shining through the treetops.

Chapter 30

I Would Do Anything For Love, Except That

Nicole pulled another soaking sheet off Nick's now bare torso, her hands shaking in unison with the spasms of his body.

"What's happening to you?" she asked despondently, cooling his forehead with a wet towel. Her curtain suddenly fluffed and waved as the clouds rolled outside, thunder not too far away. She moistened her lips with her tongue, tasting several beads of salty sweat. Nicole's first thought was to close her window, but the sudden gust of wind was the only cool air she was receiving. His body was giving off extraordinary heat.

"You…" Nick croaked, trying to find the words or the strength to speak them, Nicole wasn't sure. She leaned a little closer and gently placed the towel over his mouth, before resuming her effort. "Don't talk," she whispered. She continued to cool his head and face, but Nick was determined, breathing, "You are so beautiful."

Nicole paused in her motion of squeezing the towel into the ice-water filled bowl beside her, and lifted her eyebrows in bemusement. "It's a good thing we are just friends, otherwise I might believe you. But you're obviously delirious."

"I'm dying" he replied, voice thick. His eyes, raw and red, leaked tears.

"No you're not. It's probably just a bout of the flu. You'd better not make me sick," she said in a mock threat, forcing another laugh and trying to make light out of the situation that was scaring her more and more.

“I need to tell you…before—”

“Shush! You’re not dying! I don’t care what you think this is, I won’t let you!” She resumed her work with ferocity, clenching her teeth together to keep her lips from trembling.

“I’m sorry…don’t mean to be a…” Nick paused as he looked at her, trying to smile. “Drama queen”

“So you should. You’re a pain in my arse,” she snapped. Her reply was much more forceful than intended, but fear could do that. She slowed her movements with the cloth over his chest and stomach, sliding the damp fabric over his sculpted muscles. The water traces and the low light from the bedside lamp gave his physique an almost luminous glow, the long shadows cast surely exaggerating the muscle definition. She had noticed the past few days how tight his shirts were, but seeing him now, completely naked with just a sheet covering his lower half, she was almost startled at how much he looked like a glossy magazine model whose abs had been airbrushed to perfection.

His body began to twitch again, bringing her attention back to his condition.

“I feel like I am on fire…”

Nicole could no longer joke as she moaned with worry. “Please tell me what can I do.” She was unsure if she was asking Nick or the universe in general. It didn’t matter, as long as she could get an answer. She debated calling an ambulance, but didn’t dare leave Nick’s side just yet.

It took several seconds, but Nick became still. His blue eyes met hers and held her gaze. “Kiss me,” he whispered, a hint of a grin on his otherwise strained face.

“What, now?” Nicole could not help but smile as she shook her head. “That’s crazy. You’re sick. Something’s wrong with you. Besides, it would be…wrong.”

“You’ve done it before.”

“That was to say thank you. This is…very different.”

Nick focused on her, his eyes probing. “You really don’t want to kiss me?” A line of worry appeared on his forehead. It was almost too endearing to resist.

“I…” Nicole said, not sure what this sickness was doing to Nick, but found his newly discovered bravado quite surprising. “You’re not well.”

Nick continued to stare with an expression whose thoughts behind it Nicole could only guess at. What he would've said, though, was drowned by a dry, retching cough. He gave it up as a lost cause, whatever it was, and outstretched his fingers. "Hold my hand?"

She had no idea if he had seen through her response. She denied his request for a kiss, but as she enclosed his trembling hand in both of hers for the first time, and caressed his fingers with her own, the corners of her mouth upturned into a smile. She didn't want to let go.

"What if I tell you a saying?" Nicole asked.

"Does it have mermaids?"

"No."

"Then I don't wanna hear it. I want mermaids...and pixie dust."

Nicole rose and sat beside him on the bed. She placed his hand with one of hers on her lap and ran the fingers of her other hand through his damp hair. "It's about wolves."

Nick looked at her. "You don't believe what's happening to me."

"What I believe doesn't matter," Nicole countered. "You do. You believe you are changing, that you are losing a battle. That something is fighting to come out. But you're not alone."

Nick gazed down at their interlocked hands. "I know."

Nicole smiled. "That's not only what I meant. Shall I begin? Very well. Dogs, even mad dogs, fight, and the losing dog, if he can, runs away. But no wolf runs. The wolf wins every fight, except his last."

Nicole had Nick's complete attention, she was sure, he was now propped up on his elbows, leaning his head and shoulders closer to her. Nicole had kept still as she spoke, then gradually turned her head towards him, unable to ignore her rushing heartbeat. Those lips of his had always looked good, but in the dull light of her room and with his body glistening, they were beginning to look irresistible.

"So...you want me to fight?" Nick asked, inches away from her and closing, refusing to be denied what he wanted.

"I want you to win," she whispered, letting his burning face come closer.

Nick paused. For what reason, Nicole would never know. But a second later, both of their mouths came together.

"Wait," Nick said, pulling away about an inch. "Are you sure?"

Nicole answered by accepting his kiss and returning it with as much enthusiasm. His question showed the maturity and respect she had always seen glimpses of and she realized she had neglected to say the key phrase she'd long been encouraging students to utter when she and the school counsellor's office provided lectures on mutual consent.

Pulling back briefly, she placed her hands on either side of his face and grinned. "Yes means yes!" She kissed him a third time and felt the skin beneath her palms draining of heat. Was he cooling off just by touching her? For whatever reason, the kisses seemed to be helping him. She stopped wondering at it and leaned in. Despite all her attempts throughout the year of deciding this was wrong for her, just now it could not have felt more right, more natural. All reasons for resisting were absent from her mind.

With a ruffle, the curtains blew aside again, and the storm clouds covering the moon shifted. A ray of moonlight shone down on the two of them, and Nick rocked back in an agonising grimace. Nicole screamed.

His teeth flared, his back arched and he bellowed from the base of his spine. Nicole could make out only one word from his roars of pain.

"Run!"

Nick rolled off the bed and crashed to the floor, crawling towards the door. Nicole rushed to his side and found him unconscious, heat once again rolling off his body in waves. She wrapped her arms around him, kissing his forehead. "I'm not going to leave you."

Nick went limp in her arms, suddenly at peace. Nicole bolted to her phone and dialled 000. A new gust of wind brought her attention back to the window.

The storm clouds had covered the moon again. *The moon...what the?* she wondered.

"—the nature of your emergency? Hello?"

Nicole snapped out of her thoughts and brought the phone to her ear. "Hello? Please send an ambulance. I think my boyfriend is dying!"

Chapter 31

Can You Fill Me In

Nick opened his heavy eyelids and spotted a thin ray of black skyline outside an unfamiliar window. As he cleared his head from the fuzziness of sleep, his ears pulsed with the beeps of a heart monitor. Another early morning in a hospital room.

It's a strange feeling indeed when there's no pain in your body, yet you felt weak and stiff at the same time. He leaned side to side to stretch his aching back muscles and saw Nicole curled up on a couch next to his bed. The sight of her sleeping form alone made him think he may be dead and this was heaven.

"You've only been here about two hours but she hasn't left your side for a second."

He jolted toward the speaker and winced at the pain. As it turned out all three of the women in his life were there in the hospital room.

Alex stood in the doorway, paper cafeteria-coffee cup in her hand. "So I'm guessing this is Nicole. You guys dating?"

"I wish."

Margaret patted his shoulder. "You like her, huh? She's very pretty."

"She's the most beautiful thing I've ever seen in my life. But it's her brains and personality that drive me crazy."

"A woman driving a man crazy? Who would've thought?" Margaret laughed at her own joke.

"Why do you say that?" Alex rolled her eyes in her mother's

direction, Nick noticed, wondering what might be going on there. He'd been pretty oblivious to things happening at home lately, he realized. Better to defuse the situation for now, he decided.

"I don't really know where I stand with her. Sometimes she is adamant we can only be friends. I am teacher, you are student." He moved his arms in a jerky imitation of a robot. "Yet others it seems like that's the last thing she wants."

"I'd say she is having a crisis of conscience." Alex gestured to her temple. "You have to understand with her profession, it's hard for her if she has feelings for a student."

"Yes, I would listen to Alex, dear. It may be tough for you for a little while, but hang in there. Don't move too fast as you might scare her off with impatience. I can't speak for all girls, but as one at heart myself, no one stays by a man's side in a hospital room all night for no reason. She obviously feels something."

He glanced over to Nicole who had begun to stir and stretch.

"Oh, I'm sorry. I didn't realise everyone was here." Nicole stammered and turned bright red when she noticed everyone looking.

"Don't fret, dear. We didn't want to wake you. I'm Margaret." Margaret held out her hand and Nicole shook it, and then Alex moved to sit beside her on the couch. She put her arm around Nicole's shoulder.

"Thank you *so* much for looking after him."

"You're welcome, but it's nothing. I was in the right place and just called the ambulance. The doctor examined him and said it was a high fever but it broke almost as soon as he was brought in. It's like the fever didn't want to get examined," she laughed. She turned to Nick. "Well, now you have your family here, I'll…actually, before I go, I wonder… Could you please give us just a minute?"

"Absolutely!" Margaret gushed, whisking Alex away in a flash.

Once alone, Nicole moved closer to the bed and leaned over him, placing the back of her hand on his forehead. "How are you feeling?"

"Better. Thanks to you. But I'm sorry if I scared you."

She took a deep breath. "You terrified me. I was so worried about you. But I wanted to talk to you while we have this time. What do you remember?"

"I don't really know. It's hazy. I remember you taking care of me and I'm pretty sure you've now seen me naked."

Nicole smiled crookedly. "Anything else?"

"Are you asking me if I remember the kiss?"

"No, actually. But now that you mention it, I'm glad you do."

"I could never forget that."

She ran her finger under his chin. "Such a charmer. What I meant, though, was do you remember when you were at my front door, you said you'd followed my scent?"

"Your…"

Oh god. He didn't remember that, yet it made perfect sense. Of course he would go to her, even semi-conscious for help. "No I don't. But with what I think is happening, it makes sense. At least to me."

"Well, that's the point. What you think is happening to you. Look, I'm not going to pretend I understand. But I told you I have an open mind to pretty much everything. When you're ready, I'd like for us to work it out together. What I'm going to offer, is help if you need it. Someone to talk to. I will have a lot of free time on my hands from now on."

"Free time?"

"You deserve to know, that I'm not involved with the school anymore. I've been suspended, effective as of yesterday."

Nick leaned back and closed his eyes. "Oh fuck…Miller."

"It's not just that. I got another complaint when I confronted a woman about Zach. It was vile what she said, but they've taken it on board. I've notified Dr Sarsky."

"Nikki, you can't give up."

She shook her head emphatically. "I'm not. I have every intention of fighting for myself. I just wanted to let you know you won't be seeing me around school and to offer you help with what you're going through."

"Then let me help you too. It's the least I can do."

"Hey, I don't want you to feel guilty. This was all my choice. But, maybe we can help each other, the way friends should."

"Friends?"

Nicole took a breath and cleared her throat. "Look, Nick, I don't know what this is," she said, pointing first to herself and then to him. "But I can't deny it anymore either. I like you, a lot. I haven't felt this way in…I've never felt this way. That really scares me and I don't want to hurt you."

"I don't fancy that much either. But why should that be an issue right now? We like each other, can that not be enough to be going on with?

You know how I feel about you, but I don't want anything you're not ready for. How's about we just agree to take things as they come. Not slow. Not fast. No restrictions, no expectations."

"Ok, I can do that. That sounds nice."

"What I would like to do, is get to know you better, and then maybe take you on a proper date. What about after the dance tomorrow night?"

"I'm not really in the mood for going to the dance. Why don't you come around to my place again?"

"Not going? Why not? You organised it, after all."

Nicole shrugged. "I've seen it all before."

"Ok, how does seven sound? I'll be there with bells on."

Nicole giggled and gave him a peck on the cheek. "Sounds perfect."

Picking up her bag and purse from the floor beside the couch, she made to leave. But Nick grabbed her hand and gently eased her back down. Smiling, she tucked a lock of hair behind her ear and kissed him again, this time on the mouth. A tingling warmth spread throughout her and she wanted nothing more than to stay here all day, but…

"I've…gotta…get…going," she said, giggling in between kisses.

Nick gently held her face in place. "So…stop…kissing me…"

Nicole let herself free and pinched him. "Cheeky bastard. You're supposed to be recovering." She slung her bag over her shoulder and pointed towards the bed. "I'd fix that before they come in."

Nick looked down to where she indicated and turned bright red. He quickly grabbed the extra pillow from behind him and placed on his lap.

"See you later." Nicole waved goodbye.

* * *

"And just *where* the fuck have you been?"

"Ah…you're awake. How delightful." Dante had stepped through the door of his apartment to find Melina sitting in his favourite chair, cross-legged and armed, tapping her fingers. "Hope you had a nice nap. Pity it couldn't have gone on for another few years."

"Shut up!" Melina bolted to her feet. "How dare you think you can just leave me here."

"Humblest apologies I did not seek your permission, Mistress." Dante gave a deep bow. "I didn't realise you had taken my balls with you to the mansion all those years ago."

Melina crossed her arms and her eyes shrunk to slits. "Just who the hell do you think you are, talking to me like that?"

"Should I talk more like Julian? I'll bend over then, while you insert something."

"Don't mention that ingrate. I've moved on to bigger and better things. Well…" Melina paused to look around, as if reminding herself where she was. "Figuratively speaking."

"If the décor does not meet with Mistress' approval, there is the door."

"Oh, but how would you gloat then? Poor Melina had to come to you of all people for help."

Dante unbuttoned his shirt. He didn't have time for this. "You're welcome by the way."

Her eyes darted over his chest. "What are you doing?"

"Getting changed."

"You're leaving again? I'm just supposed to stay locked in this cage, am I?"

Dante tossed the shirt into a chair and grabbed a new one from the closet. "Do what you like."

"I intend to."

Dante realised with a jerk what she was thinking, what she was expecting. "Oh no. Except that."

"I wasn't asking. I'm bored and I'm coming with you." With deft hands, the pyjama top she was wearing was removed over her shoulders and flicked to him. She stood before him, all angelic radiance, and bold in her nudity, but Dante kept his focus on her eyes.

"The last place you need to be is on the streets."

"The last place I need to be is stuck in one place where they can get to me. Besides, I'll have my big strong man to protect me." Melina wrapped her arms around herself.

"You will have no such thing. You got yourself into this mess, you can get yourself out of it."

Melina gave a huff. "So where are we going then?"

"Jesus Christ, woman. Will it shut you up?"

"It might."

"Well then, you will have to get changed too." She could say whatever she wanted but she couldn't hide the truth from him. *Methinks the lady doth protest too much.* Melina wanted and needed no one. Ever. Yet she was no more than a foot from him. Having every opportunity to leave, she stayed. And for what, to trade insults? No, Dante knew better. "Are you coming or what?"

"What the hell do I have to dress up for? Where are we going?"

"To see Sebastian Gould."

"Who?"

"You're still speaking."

"I'm still bored!"

* * *

Dante pulled up outside the lavish two-storey house. Naked and semi-naked men and women strolled uninhibited in and out of the grounds. The air was thick with laughter and marijuana.

Sebastian Gould had his fingers in a lot of pies, as the saying went. His business was sex and drug trafficking. There was nothing illegal that went on in Sydney that he didn't think up, pass up, or hear about. He knew about the existence of vampires and said nothing because a lot of the deals he did were for Vincent and with Vincent's blessing. He was also a bisexual nymphomaniac and a clinical sociopath. And he would be just the one who might be able to help Dante now.

Dante and Melina strolled along the footpath leading up to the front door, as the world of Sebastian Gould moved around them. The lawn was bathed in bright light, supplied by an oversized search light. The pool was crowded in and around with party goers. There were rows of naked women along the deck with lines of coke set up along their bodies. Surrounding them all were separate groups of up to four, each with a ziplock bag of pills. Dante had seen it all before and watched with detachment, but he could tell Melina was thinking with her stomach. "Not here. We aren't here for that," he warned.

"Speak for yourself." Melina replied, looking at a well-built negro walking past, wearing nothing but sunglasses. He carried a lighter and spoon with him, and joined a group of five around a picnic table, topped off with a pipe and crystal meth.

Dante took her hand and pulled her along with him. "Let's go."

"Ice users are scum of the earth anyway. What the fuck is this place? There are more knobs here than a locksmith's gallery and enough clit on show that I should be a sea captain. Why did you make me wear this if I can't join in?"

She looked down at her ensemble. At least it matched Dante's. They were both in leather. He wore an open black silk shirt with leather strips along the shoulders and leather pants, she a jacket that buttoned closed just over her bra, and tight pants, opening at the ankle.

"It's a requirement of those who attend his drug orgies. Either naked or leather."

"I don't know if I want to kill this human or buy him a drink."

"Neither. He has plenty of people giving him things and I need him."

"You still haven't told me what for?"

"And I probably won't."

Dante led Melina up to the front door before he felt her pull back. She was staring at a couple engaging in carefree sex. The gaunt woman though, with sunken eyes, had abandoned her cries of passion and stared at Melina. The partner, that looked to be at least thirty years older than her, continued to plug away.

Breathless, as if in awe, the woman raised her voice to just under shouting. "Who are you?"

"I'm the fuck fairy."

"Join us."

The volume of her voice carried, and several heads turned towards Dante and Melina, noticing them for the first time.

"Come on. You know you want to," she continued, trying to reach for Melina, as if forgetting her partner was even there. "I can't handle the thought—"

Melina clicked her fangs down. "You couldn't handle the ride, junkie slut."

Dante pulled Melina away and through the door.

Melina flicked her face back and retracted her fangs. "Couldn't help myself."

"You could try."

Dante waved to a tanned blonde girl in a bikini standing behind a mini desk just inside the door.

"Whoa…hey, Dante."

"Hello, Stephanie. Nice to see you."

"And you," she purred.

"Where's the boss?"

"Upstairs. Someone else wanted to speak with him, but he has been up there for a while. You should be good to go."

"Thanks. Take care of yourself."

"Call me."

Melina did not wait until she was out of earshot before mocking Stephanie. "*Call me.* I cannot believe you associate with the likes of that."

"Bossy and jealous, what a prize you have become. Although given the way you looked at the dark gent, your taste his improved. From Julian, anyway."

Both of them reached the top of the stairs, and Melina followed Dante to the right.

"My taste? Fuck you! At least he isn't platinum blonde like Miss Universe-reject downstairs. Her roots look like you did them."

"Oh, please!" A short and scrawny man, with thick-rimmed glasses, and curly hair that looked rather lifeless, appeared from one of the rooms. "Will you two kindly get a room and get it out of your system? The sexual tension is killing my party's mojo."

He wore silk pyjama pants and a red silk dressing gown, holding a full whiskey glass.

"Sebastian." Dante nodded.

"My god, the bogan Hugh Hefner."

Sebastian raised his glass to her. "A terrific social scientist, my dear, and I'm not ashamed to say, my inspiration. I see you getting all flustered with the D Man. Have you given any thought to rooting him? The thought of what a video with you and my gorgeous Spaniard here would make us all rich. Well…richer."

Sebastian took a sip from his glass and a young Asian boy appeared from the room and knelt before him. Sebastian raised his eyebrows at Melina. Dante had to nudge her with his elbow. Clearly, the sight was just something she had to deal with, as he was expecting an answer.

"I popped his cherry," Melina replied.

"Oh my god, you lucky bitch!" he giggled. The Asian boy continued his work and Sebastian continued to act as if nothing out of the ordinary was going on. "Come on, just between us girls—Dante hold your ears. How big is he?"

"Sebastian…" Dante really had no desire to banter this night.

Sebastian sighed and reached into his pocket as the boy got to his feet. He slapped the boy across the face. "Teeth! How many times do I have to tell you, no fucking teeth! Here…" he said, dropping a pill into the boy's palm. "Take this and don't come back till you know how to do it right!"

The boy rushed away, swallowing the pill with no water.

"Now we can talk, Dante."

"I had a call earlier from a detective Crane, two of my staff were found dead. Both drug related, although the authorities have nothing to go on. Both of them went the same way. It looked like they had just fallen asleep and didn't wake up. Firstly, I need to know if our agreement is still intact."

"If your staff died from taking, it was from shit I didn't supply. I don't push into T and neither do my dealers, as per your wishes. You know what happened the last time I even suspected one did."

Dante did remember, replying gravely, "You poured battery acid down her throat."

Sebastian looked thoughtful. "I did, didn't I? Thank god. I would've been a father had she lived. Good girl, nice legs. Oh well." He shrugged. "You don't know how the drug scene works. They could've got it from a number of sources. It's a nightclub after all."

"I don't know how it works and that's the point. You are the drug king. Which are the deadliest ones?"

Sebastian laughed. "All of them, if you're talking about overdosing. A hit too big and that's it. You close your eyes and you don't wake up."

"Fine, is there anything new on the market?"

"Well, now that you mention it, yes. Now you have me thinking, my convict friend." He dug in his pocket and pulled a small vial out containing a glowing blue liquid. "Here it is."

"Where did you get that?" Melina asked.

Dante flicked his eyes from the vial to Melina. "You know this?"

"Of course, it's Dream State, a drug created for vampires to let them dream. The mansion is rife with it. I have no idea where it comes from, but I do know it's not meant for humans."

"On the contrary, humans love this stuff. It allows them to dream whatever they want. It is the best high you can get."

"And perhaps the most deadly. Vampires have to wake up at sunset. They have no choice, and it is a natural defence against the major risk of this Dream State, which makes the user not want to stop living in the fantasy world."

"Wow…good thing I haven't done it then, ain't it?"

"You haven't?" Melina sounded sceptical.

"Baby, anything *glowing* I prefer to put in someone else."

"Stop!" Dante gripped him by the shoulder. "Where did you get the Dream State?"

"You know I never reveal my dealers."

"Your dealer is responsible for the death of my staff, even indirectly. You can always get another dealer, you can't get another testicle. Choose now."

"Well, when you put it that way." Sebastian searched again in his pocket. He handed Dante an old business card of an insurance agency. The agent's name and number had been scratched off, replaced with *Luca* and a mobile number. "That's his name, and the address on the card is where he lives."

"Botany. We can make it before sunrise. I'll be seeing you."

"No hug and kiss?"

Dante didn't turn as he and Melina headed for the stairs. "Goodbye, Sebastian."

"So, we gonna kill him?"

"Possibly. As a last resort."

"What an odd couple we are. I have the vagina, yet you're the pussy. Killing is the *only* resort."

"I may be the pussy, yet you're the one running for your life. We will do it my way."

* * *

On the roof opposite the building listed at the address on the card, Dante and Melina stood watch. The scene below them should have been a regular if not sleazy drug deal. But this wasn't regular. A young woman had approached a vampire, who was willing to give her anything she wanted, as long as she gave him the one thing he needed.

"You're Luca, right?"

The vampire nodded.

"I got some money. My friend told me it would be two hundred."

"I don't need money." Luca gripped her chin.

The woman moaned as if coming to a difficult choice. "All right, you got any condoms?"

"You mistake me again. Your friend was clearly not very informative."

"What do you want then?"

He flashed his fangs, hand covering her mouth. "Just a little something I can sink my teeth into."

Beside Dante, Melina leapt off the roof. "To hell with this. *Amateurs*!"

Luca leaned his head back, stopping as she landed. Dante followed a second later.

"Bravo," Melina clapped. "That has to be in the top five vampire attack clichés to use, and ya did. My favourite line when they ask that would be, the salt of your tears on my tongue, something like that."

"Rack off, bitch. Find your own dinner."

Dante moved forward in step with Melina. Her rage could set this off before necessary. "Now is that any way of treating two potential customers?"

Luca looked above and then behind him, several things probably going through his mind. In the end, he went for the more sensible option and let the woman go. She dashed off around the corner of the building as quickly as her legs could take her.

"Ok," he raised and lowered his hands. "Can't say no to two customers. Hope you have cash coz that was my meal. What do you want?"

"Dream State."

"How much?"

"All of it. Why you are selling to humans and where do you get it from?"

Luca chuckled. "Whatever. I don't know what game this is, one of you better start talking sense, or shit is about to get real. You tell me how much you want, I tell you the price."

"The lady already told you, we want all of it." Dante said.

"Yeah," Melina agreed, flashing her fangs and black eyes. "And we won't be paying for shit."

"Ooooh scary." Luca displayed his own fangs. "What you gonna do, ranga?"

"I'm going to rip your cock off!" Melina screamed, before Dante halted her.

"There's no need for this to get out of hand."

Melina balled her hands into fists. "Like hell!"

"Yeah, fuck you, grandpa."

Melina shoved Dante out of the way and onto his back and whipped around to Luca. "Come here, you little shit."

She startled him with a left and right fist combination. Before he could retaliate, she had jumped and launched a kick to his chest, sending him into the concrete wall of the insurance building, shaking the powdered cement out of his eyes. Melina came at Luca again but he ducked her punch and pushed out a kick of his own which she dodged.

"Have to be quicker than—"

But he was, uppercutting her to the ground.

"Have to be smarter than—"

Finally, Dante saw his chance, and thrust his hands around Luca's throat, lifting him high into the air.

"You don't have to die. Just tell us what we want to know."

"Just kill him!" Melina spat out blood, advancing.

"Ok! Ok!" Luca tapped Dante's hand. "My stash is inside, it's all I have got."

"Who told you to sell to humans? After you take your cut, where does the rest go?" Dante said.

"Like I'm going to tell you…"

Dante struck an elbow to his head, splitting the flesh open just under his left eye. Melina smiled. Dante ignored her eagerness.

"Try again?"

Luca did not answer him, just struggling for release.

"Oh my god, you suck at this!" Melina marched over. "Move," she said, standing next to Dante and gripped Luca's groin with the ferocity of an eagle with a fox in its talons. Within seconds, the tips of her fingers moistened with blood.

Luca screamed in agony and croaked, "Julian."

"No fucking way…" Melina released her grip.

"I sell where Vincent tells me. He tops me up every few weeks. At first I started dealing through Coffinail, but then there were rumours going around that a vamp tried it out with his human. Word spread. Soon I found out people were buying off me and then selling it to humans because they have much better and quicker access to cash. The humans think this is just the latest drug craze. It started out as a simple cash cow, but it's getting out of control. I only have a small network but every dealer I know seems to have it. Money is changing hands so fast no one can keep up."

Melina closed her eyes. "Of course, how could I have been so stupid?"

Dante dropped Luca in a heap. "Talk to me…"

"It all makes sense. The drugs and the money. Vincent has been losing money for years. It was obvious to me, but he was too proud to admit it and Julian would never hear anything against himself or his father. They must've came up with this together. Julian always made it seem like he and Vincent were an on seller, a distributor just like this piece of shit." Melina waved a hand at Luca. "It seemed like they were supplying for the mansion only. They aren't just a link in the chain, they are the reason this shit exists. Everything comes back to them."

Dante pressed a fist to his mouth. Staring at the ground, he asked, "When did you first hear about Dream State? When Alex, Michelle and I were at the mansion to be sentenced?"

Melina nodded. "About then, roughly. Why?"

"That's around the time I found the sample of werewolf blood."

"Yes! I asked Julian about the wolves and Dream State, but the limp-dicked bastard brushed me off. I thought they were here because they wanted a piece of it."

"I asked Vincent about them. He told me they never arrived."

"It's bullshit. I heard that baby vamp with the big tits found a group of humans that were looking for their wolf comrades. They had your blonde's ex with them."

"So there is a wolf contingent and a human one, sent as a back-up or rescue. Vincent lied. Not that I am surprised. He must've captured the wolves when they were to meet with him."

"He's got them in the mansion…" Melina clicked her fingers, realisation dawning on her face. "Behind that ugly door. That's what I was hearing! That's what woke me up. I was hearing them behind the walls."

"That could be where he is making it. He must be using werewolf blood in its manufacture. Perhaps that's what he needs to spark a vampire brain."

Melina licked her fingers. "Makes sense. Vincent hates wolves and humans. He wouldn't care how many dogs he has to use and put down to solidify his power. As for humans, he is now rolling in money because of their stupid deadly addiction. Vampires are immune. It's a win-win."

"He will pay for this."

"He will pay?" Luca groaned. "*He will*? You are delusional. It doesn't matter that you stopped me. Someone else will take my place. Dream State is out and the humans will buy it even if it is known what it does to people. That's how stupid they are. Face it, Hansel and Gretel. The witch will win."

With a roar, Dante smashed his entire body into Luca and both men landed on the ground, Dante was on top of Luca, teeth deep in his neck, clasping his scalp viciously and sucking hard.

He sat up. "You want some?"

Melina grabbed his shirt and pulled him up to her lips. She kissed and licked his mouth, smacking her lips and pushing him down to his arse when she was done. "Not bad. But I've got an idea…"

Melina skipped her way to the buildings entrance, ripped the front door off its hinges and returned to Dante, bringing it down onto Luca's neck. His head popped off like a pellet with a single strike.

"And that is how it's done, kids."

Dante took off inside the building. Within a minute he had found the stash of Dream State, in the oven of all places, in the upstairs kitchen. Maybe there was more, but it wouldn't matter. He ripped the main gas line from its socket, releasing it into the room. He picked up a bottle of canola oil spray and placed it inside the microwave. He punched in three minutes on the timer, set it to high. Not taking any chances, he leapt from the window, straight down next to Melina. "Let's not linger."

Melina heard him and bolted to the car, thankfully not questioning him. They raced along the highway, past the airport, when the first of several rapid explosions cannoned into the night, leaving a brief mushroom cloud of fire in the Maserati's wake.

Dante himself looked back in the rear view mirror. "*That's* how it's done, kids."

"Remember," Melina pointed a forefinger covered in glistening blood at his face. "This *doesn't* mean I like you."

CHAPTER 32

PLEASE FORGIVE ME

As night descended on Sydney, T was just coming alive with the build-up for the St. Andrew's – Westmead Ball. This year, the ball had become more significant to everyone involved.

Later, the staff of T would hold a private memorial for Will Hefley and Amanda Riles, the two that had lost their lives earlier in the week due to overdosing. The sudden loss of two cherished friends hit the club hard, and Dante had closed the club temporarily for the first time in its history. Regulars had still come now and then, waiting outside the club just in case there was a change, but it was not to be. The ball would be the much debated reopening.

Dante was caught in a difficult situation, a clear rock and a hard place. Was it too soon to open? Some of his staff thought so and told him to his face. On the other hand, what more could be done for the dead now, except wallow in questions that will never be answered, lives that would never be lived and the unfairness of it all.

A gigantic welcome banner was erected over the entrance to T, which Dante had signed and added the phrase "Honouring The Fallen". He wanted the night to become not only a celebration but a commemoration. A vow that hope and strength would always rule over tragedy and fear.

Death was a part of life, and he should know. But when it was senseless…meaningless…for an immortal creature that cared for humans, it was a bitter pill to swallow. He had debated cancelling the ball, wasting months of hard work the students had put into preparation, as well as costing thousands of dollars in public relations for both the Westmead Hospital and St. Andrew's in the process. People wanted the club to re-open, they wanted the ball to take place. So in the end, he decided to use the opportunity to remember Amanda and Will.

Dante viewed the staff and students of St. Andrews through the two-way mirror of his office, high above T. He would've liked to have gone down and greeted them, but the ubiquitous camera phones kept him at bay. The last thing he needed was photos and selfies appearing on social media with him *supposed* to be in them, yet always mysteriously missing what with that whole vampires-being-unable-to-be-seen-by-manmade-surveillance-devices thing.

T was the biggest target of the new "blame game" in what the papers called The Sleeping Plague, victims old and young dying in their sleep. The connection between working for a nightclub and a drug overdose was hard to ignore and rumours abounded that perhaps the increasingly popular T had a lot to do with the new drug craze gaining momentum. Will and Amanda were the latest additions to the growing list of alarming deaths. Newspapers called up T staff members at odd hours of the day, offering money for interviews. Photographers followed them too. This was the first scandal the club had faced in its short existence and everyone was anxious or at least curious to see how adaptable Dante Delavega was.

By seven-thirty that evening, as the students and staff began to arrive in droves, the change in atmosphere outside the club had been substantial. Tense and sombre had become jovial and light-hearted. Some of the press had remained, but most had left. People had gathered on the opposite side of the street with cameras to catch some of the action. Staff of the school and hospital had gotten into the mood of the night. Giant hats, wigs, and ties were spotted, but the real sight was the younger brigade. They turned up as movie and TV show characters, fairies, leprechauns, angels and demons, pirates, and so on.

"Come in," he answered to a knock at the office door.

Though he kept his face straight, it was the twitch of his nose that made him turn, raising him out of his stupor. *Gooseberry*. "Alexandra…"

Dante closed the distance between them in a heartbeat, closing the door for her. She stood in front of him with a bunch of flowers, the cellophane glinting under the dim light.

"I read about your staff members in the paper. I'm so sorry."

"Thank you. You didn't have to bring these all the way up to me, though. There was a collection booth in the front."

"I know, I saw. These are for you."

"For me?"

"Yeah," Alex scratched the back of her head as if distracted. "Hope you don't think it's weird getting flowers from a girl?"

"It's not weird at all. They're beautiful."

Alex gave a brief smile as Dante took them. "I can't say anything to fix it, but I just wanted you to know how sorry I am, and that I'm here if you need anything."

"Thank you, Alexandra."

"And," she started, before pausing as if thinking of the right way to continue. "That's not all I'm sorry for. I've been thinking about you a lot lately. About us, and what happened that last time we spoke…"

"Alexandra, you don't have to—"

Alex put her hand up and moved closer. "Please don't. I need to do this. I'm so sorry. I don't know what came over me. I've never acted like that. And I don't want you to think less of me because of it."

"I don't. You have thoughts, feelings and desires that were not being met. It's only natural."

"It's not just that. I had expectations. Based on what I knew about your time with Michelle. I thought that sex was what always happens between a vampire and their donor. I was worried that I would need to, just so the bite wouldn't be so painful. I was nervous about being so intimate with you, being naked with you. And then you put me at ease. The bite wasn't really that bad. In a weird way…I like it. You were just as naked as me, and you being calm, helped me. So after everything else being settled and very enjoyable, that just left the sex. I found myself curious as to why it wasn't happening. Then I wanted it, especially after the dreams. All these pent up feelings and emotions, just got the better of me. I thought maybe there was something wrong. I know better now."

"You do? But…you said before that you wanted me. Has that changed?"

"No. I still want you. I think I always will. And I'm not of the opinion that if I grow old without being married with kids it's a wasted life. I might want that one day, I might not. But I do understand that you are trying to clear the path for me just in case. Maybe I'm not ready to sleep with you and vice versa. All I'm hoping, is that if the time comes when we are both ready, that you respect me enough to allow me to make my own choices, and not choose for me. You're right, what we have is special. It's also confusing and complicated. In the meantime…"

Alex took him by the hand and led him towards the red leather couch in the middle of the room, where, on more than one occasion, Dante had listened to her, massaged her feet and put her at ease when she'd been distressed.

She gave a gentle push so he sat and sunk into the softness. Alex took his hand and kissed his palm, before letting it go. She removed her top and bra, flinging it to the desk, kicking off her shoes and stepping out of her jeans and panties. There was no tension from her, no tears like last time. Dante sensed a need to be close. A loneliness. A longing to be touched. All things he knew quite well, as he wanted them too. Standing in front of him, she pulled her hair free from her pony tail and said. "I made a promise to you and I haven't kept it. You look awful. And I…"

"Go on."

For the first time, Dante heard a thickness in her voice. "I miss you."

"And I you."

Alex raised one knee and placed it by his side, then the other. She sat on his thighs and waited. She placed her fingers through his hair, scrunching them. "You've always taken care of me. Let me do the same for you. I want you to touch me. I want you to drink…"

Dante inhaled the gooseberry scent in deep, running his fingers over the milky white of her skin. She leaned in close, planting soft pecks along his forehead, bringing her taught nipples in front of his eyes and the sound of her pulse even closer. The blood in her veins was calling to him as it pumped life and warmth through her young, supple body.

Dante closed his eyes and ran his nose and lips across the face of one breast to the other, gripping her hips, breathing out over them, kissing them lightly. His fangs dropped without a sound, yet Alex seemed to sense he was ready, and positioned herself lower. Dante held her, one hand cradling her jaw, the other caressing and gripping her rear, finding her relaxed and at ease, though she shuddered and groaned as he bit into her neck. The warm, delicious stickiness pooled and then flowed into his mouth. He rocked her backwards and drank deep, letting her moans guide him as to when she had enough. Though that wouldn't be for a few minutes yet.

CHAPTER 33

TONIGHT'S THE NIGHT

"Cheers." Nick chinked his glass with Nicole's and they both sipped. Nick leaned back into her sofa, looking at her side on. She wore a cotton skirt and jumper that covered only one shoulder, leaving the other bare and gleaming. Shadows of the flames danced over her olive skin as she peered over her glass at him, smiling and at complete ease. "Thank you for coming and for this."

She swapped the glass at her mouth for the red rose Nick had brought along, carefully inhaling it.

"You're very welcome. I hope it isn't too much."

"Of course not, why would it be? It's beautiful. But don't think buttering me up will stop me from asking the hard questions, mister."

Nick gave a huge calming breath. "Ask away."

"For starters, something easy. How did you get a bottle of wine when you're not eighteen?"

Nick held his hands up. "I'm innocent on this. This was all Aunt Margaret. She asked me what I was bringing and I said nothing. She put her hands on her hips and informed me that 'anyone who shows up to a woman's house without wine is not a real man.' So there you have it."

"God love her. But tell her she has great taste. This shiraz is delicious." Nicole took a big sip.

And you, my dear are simply resplendent.

Fuck off! Do not ruin this! She's finally relaxing around me! I really like her, and I will not be your puppet.

No Nicholas, you are no one's puppet anymore except yourself. I cannot make you do things. I can tell you are becoming a man. You are where you should be; alone with her. Why would I ruin a perfect moment?

"And how are you doing with…the school and everything?"

"I'm doing ok," Nicole nodded. "Really. Sure I was pissed when I was told that I should forget what Miller had done, again. The inappropriate touching. Which I absolutely refused to do. If I'm being honest, it felt great belting him. That Raven Apartments bitch really got under my skin too. It took a lot of restraint for me not to throttle her. And I'm not even a violent person. I was worried she would cause me trouble, and even when it did, I had a little *why me* moment, but I got over that. Everything that happened was my choice, and I'd do it again. I tend to over think things, but I'm glad I went on my instinct. I'll see whatever avenues are available to me and go from there."

"Zach is lucky to have someone watching over him. That poor kid is clearly having a hard life, and it seems like his father isn't really around to help him."

"I wish I could do more for Zach, but now I can't see him. I *know* something is going on over there."

"If you need me to help, just ask."

Nicole patted his hand and shook her head. "Nothing you can do right now for Zach. Thank you for the offer, and if circumstances there change, well… I'll let you know." She shrugged, then drained her glass and reached for the wine bottle to refill it. "Now comes what I want to ask. I want you to be as honest with me as possible. About this werewolf thing."

Nick gulped. "Ok…shoot."

"Do you mean, an actual werewolf? Teeth, claws and all that?"

Be honest Nicholas. A leap of faith to someone that means you no harm. Nick took a second. "Yes. I mean in the literal sense."

Nicole kept her glass close to her chin. Her expression was calm, her following question was quiet. "Why did your father get killed?"

"Because his time as the Alpha was coming to an end."

"I knew it!" Nicole leaned forward. Nick saw a change in her face, from passive to delighted. "I've been going over and over this in my head. Let me see if I've got this. So, you told me at the café your dad wanted you to *take over the family business*, which now I'm guessing you were to be the Alpha, right? And the men that worked for him hated that, so they wanted their sons to be considered. But you said he refused to listen to them. He only wanted you. So they killed him. Your mum knew they might come after you, so sent you away?"

Nick didn't know what to say. Everything he had worried about telling her, how to explain, had just been rattled off to him in under thirty seconds. She had pieced together the whole story from bits and pieces of information.

And that is why she is worth this. How many more will you find so accepting? So in tune? "That's exactly right, yes."

"Wow..." Nicole looked towards the ground for several seconds, before looking back at him. "So...what you can do?"

Nick placed his glass on the table slowly. "Wait. You...believe me?"

She does. Will you do the same? Will you believe in her?

"I do. I admit I didn't before. The whole idea seemed so preposterous, but I saw something in your face last night when the moon hit you. Just a flash, mind. And it just came over me. This feeling of understanding, acceptance and...I don't know...wonderment. Then I thought about a number of other things that happened. Your behaviour at my speech, the way our cat freaked out, the marks you claimed to have made on the coach's car, the fact that you were so feverish and ill just as the moon was getting fuller. It all makes sense now. This is incredible."

"Well...I guess."

"What's wrong?"

Was he really having this conversation? How was talking to her about this suddenly so easy? He had been going over and over this in his mind ever since he developed more than just a crush on her. Never in his wildest dreams did he imagine having a calm, rational discussion about what he was.

"I just—aren't you...afraid?"

"Of you?" Nicole scooted closer to him and placed her hand aside his neck, making Nick breathe in sharply. "Not at all. You'd never hurt me."

Nick grasped the hand she touched him with and held it tight. "Nikki, it's true I don't want to hurt you, but I'm terrified I might. I wake up without knowing what's happened the previous night. Like the car. The scratches. I *know* I did them, but I can't remember. I have flashes in my mind that gets me up in the middle of the night. Things that I shouldn't know unless I was there. The-"

The smell of the teacher's breath. The alcohol. The way our nails, yes Nicholas, our nails, cut the metal so easily, like foam. The rush we felt as he looked into our eyes and screamed. Your mouth still waters at the taste of the one thing you have never embraced; power. That includes power over me. She gives you confidence, her touch is calming. We can bring men to their knees, or we can help them rise. That choice has never been mine Nicholas.

"-I don't want anything to happen to you."

Nicole shook her head in emphatic denial. "No, nothing will happen to me. You won't hurt me. Think again of Alan Shubert. You could have killed him, but you didn't."

"Yes, but the wolf itself told me I would hurt you."

And so I did, should you not take her. It was only you that assumed I meant the primal fashion. Hold her Nicholas. Trust her. The head has never been the source of our strength. The heart is. What we cherish, what we protect. She is accepting you for what you are. Why won't you do the same?

"You speak to it?"

"Not exactly. It's like a voice in my head, always telling me to go after you and to give in to the fact that I want you so much. Not to quit when you said we can just be friends. Manipulating me. In the nurse's office, for example, I felt my arm raise towards you, on its own."

Nick paused at the grin Nicole gave him. "I'm serious!"

"I know you are. I'm smiling because on that day, I felt you calm down just by touching me. When you felt like you were on fire, I kissed you and you cooled off. I think what you have inside you is very old, very powerful but ultimately, a trickster. And clearly you have some influence over it. I bet you can take even more control if you try."

Nick was grave. "I don't know. It told me that if I don't succumb to my hunger, that transformation will be much worse. I don't know what it's waiting for. I would've thought last night would've been the perfect time, but I'm grateful it didn't."

She calms me. But even she cannot hold me back much longer. I'm afraid the time is coming, and the process will be agonising.

"Me too. I wouldn't have been prepared like I am now. So," Nicole finished her glass and placed it on the table next to Nick's and faced him. "What's this about hunger? Do you *hunger* for me?"

"I didn't mean it like that—"

Nicole flashed a mischievous grin. "I think maybe you did. I think you meant exactly that." She leaned forward yet again and kissed him. Nick felt confused, and he returned the kiss half-heartedly.

Nicole eyed him, repeating his words from last night "You don't want to kiss me?"

She placed her hands on either side of his face and let him come to her. He held the back of her head as he kissed her deep. Her tongue teased his, neither of them getting too close. Nicole slinked off the seat, sliding to her knees on the floor, gently bringing Nick to the same position, opposite her. Nick stared into her eyes for what seemed like entire minutes, before her hands found their way to his top buttons. She kept her gaze focused on him, until his last had come undone, then she looked down. She eased the shirt apart, spreading her hands over his chest and then around his shoulders. That was where her gaze lingered, as she continued to run her hands over him. Her palms, then fingers. Across his chest, up his neck.

This is how it should be Nicholas, touched by a lover. You can experience something that few ever get to. The act of love by someone that truly cares.

Nick closed his eyes and supressed a shiver. They were surrounded by darkness. No window was open. Yet even she had to feel his goose bumps.

Nicole held her hair back with both hands as she left gentle presses of her lips along his pectorals, flicking his nipple with her tongue. Her hands ventured down his stomach and to the belt of his jeans.

"Nikki…maybe we shouldn't." Though his body screamed at him, he felt it had to be said. All this was just too good to be true. Only last night they had agreed to see each other as more than friends. She had just lost her career. He didn't want to take advantage if she wasn't thinking clearly.

"Yes we should," her mouth was only an inch from his. "I'm tired of denying myself what I want for the sake of appearances and protocols. I don't have to follow those anymore. You trusted me just now and told me something that would've terrified you. I can't control the future or the past. Maybe I should be afraid, maybe I should be running, but I'm not. I don't want to. I will no longer say no just because of what other people might think, especially those that don't care about me. I want to be here, now, with someone who does."

She removed her jumper. She slid the straps of her bra down slowly, maybe in her own small way, putting on a show for him. Making him anticipate. She took both his hands and brought him closer, moving them past and behind her. He gazed into her eyes as her cleavage bulged just in front of him.

Her eyes revealed her thoughts. Take it off for me.

He pinched his fingers on her clasp as he opened his mouth and softly licked in between her breasts, leaving small kisses as he went. He felt the slightest touch of her fingers in his hair, partially massaging his scalp as she gave a sharp breath out. No, not just a breath, something else. A word, whispered. His name. He clicked his fingers and the clasp snapped free, revealing her full, rounded breasts and darkened, enlarged areolas.

"Wow" he whispered. She shook the bra off as he cupped the weighty softness in his hand and with only a second's pause to admire her further, he brought her to his open mouth. With his free hand, he kneaded her other breast, carefully pinching and pulling the nub between the tips of his fingers. Nicole closed her eyes, swaying slightly on her knees. The sounds escaping from her throat were a cross between a moan and a giggle. He teased the nipple, flicking it against his teeth with his tongue. He opened his mouth a little wider and rounded his tongue over her areola, sucking and nibbling ever so gently.

Nick moved his salivating mouth from her nipple, glistening with his saliva, and brought it to the side of her breast, and then her ribs. He allowed himself a brief grin as her body jerked and skin tightened after every tender kiss and lick to the area. Only to then return to her original position, ready for more.

"My turn." She said

With her palms and thumbs she massaged his chest, neck and shoulders. He looked at her while she touched him, watching her enjoy using her hands all over him.

"I love your ears," Nicole pressed her mouth close to them.

"My ears?" Nick smiled.

“They’re so cute.”

Nick clenched a fist as she kissed his left ear, his lobe and the skin just under it. Nicole moved her head side to side, slowly kissing both sides of his neck as she continued to press his shoulders. Nick had no idea something could feel so good being only lips and a tongue, slowly teased like this.

She leaned back a little slowly. “Did you just growl at me?”

Nick kept his eyes closed, not certain of whether he had or not. “Did I?”

She laughed through her nose. “Awesome.”

She returned to what she was doing, but with more energy, seeming to enjoy the effect she was having on him. Nick parted her hair and kissed her neck, keeping his movements slow. He ran his hand down her back and with the other, he kept her neck open for him, holding her. Without even realising, his tongue was lightly flicking her as his lips closed.

Nicole released his belt and brought his zipper down. “Off.”

Nick slid his jeans down his legs, kicked them off and Nicole brought him down on top of her. Nick cupped the sides of her breasts with both hands, taking his time to kiss them both as he made his way down her stomach, to her groin. He curled his fingers around her hips, under her skirt and as she lifted her hips, slid it off.

He admired the boldness of her wearing nothing underneath, mouthing the strip of pubic hair he found, kissing just above her opening.

Freshly waxed, just for you. I think you should feel privileged.

He grazed her inner thighs with his teeth, holding her soft skin in his mouth. He put his head to the side, and ran his tongue up and down her entrance, with long, slow licks. She placed her hand at the back of his head and brought him in. He plunged his tongue into her, quivering it, again and again, coating his mouth with her juices. He gave her roughly thirty seconds of this, then sped up, lapping at her clitoris, using his tongue to centre it for his mouth before taking it between his lips. He sucked, pressing it against his teeth, moving it around in his mouth, enjoying the trembling of her knees on either side of his head.

He gripped the tops of her thighs and opened her legs a little wider.

What was one hand at the back of his head had become two, lifting his face. The rising swell of her stomach had become rapid, as her breathing quickened. She breathed a short command, for him to come up.

Nick positioned himself between her legs. Her eyes flicked down, noticing that he held his shaft with one hand, not quite making the fingers touch.

Feel the blood in the veins beneath your fingers. It pulses desire. It feeds your strength. You need her just as much as she needs you.

Their eyes locked briefly before she gave a small whistle, "Go slow…"

Nick nodded, using the tip to nudge her opening and entered, inch by inch. He took his time, running his eyes over her full curves, watching her body shift the deeper he went. A primal pleasure flicked inside his mind, watching her concentrate between her legs, tongue between her teeth, realizing there was still more length, placing her finger tips against his stomach. Nicole closed her eyes and swore softly as her tender, slick folds stretched to accommodate his cock. But Nick could feel she was more than ready for him and brought his mouth to her neck, which she turned to offer him. He kissed and licked the sweet flesh, tasting the tanginess of her vanilla musk body lotion.

His thrusting movements were slow at first, deep, removing himself completely before sliding his full length into her. Her whole body moved with him again and again, bringing a mute, open mouth gasp from her as her fingers found their way to his back and gripped him hard.

Nicole eased him up, until he was removed from her. She moved her leg up and across his body, turning herself over, leaning on her elbows as Nick gripped her hips and entered her again. This didn't bring a mute gasp. The move brought a cry of surprise because he didn't take his time, he buried himself to the hilt with no resistance. Nick took a few seconds, allowing himself a brief pause, getting his mind around how it felt to finally be inside her. Her inner muscles tightened around him, something that must've been deliberate on her part. He felt her squeeze his cock as he pulled himself out, slowly. The further he went the tighter she made herself. He heard her breathing deeply through her nose, noises subdued through her closed mouth.

Treat her like a Queen. Fuck her like an Alpha.

Just as the head was visible, Nick sunk himself into her again, with a touch more force. He was done teasing. His grip on her hips was gentle, his thrusts were measured, controlled, loving the feeling of her round, soft arse jiggling against his groin. Nicole moaned, hissing encouragement, biting her lip when Nick reached around her and circled her clitoris with two fingers. She moved her hips with him, arching her back to give him better access.

As his hand continued to bend and press with increasing pressure, she reached underneath herself and rubbed his testicles, massaging and squeezing her breasts with the other hand.

Nick grabbed a fistful of her shiny hair, and even though the pleas came, he did not wait for them, rolling her hair in his hand tighter and tighter, stretching her neck back further and further.

He slid his fingers up her jaw, closing in on her mouth, until finally she took in his index finger, running her tongue over it, sucking hard. It was taken away before he made her see there was a method to his gesture.

He circled over her anus along with his hip movements, matching them in tempo, until finally he dared to insert the tip. Nicole screamed, putting her head down, clutching her hair, cursing her orgasm into the floor.

He shifted, moving faster, rocking her body, as she gripped the carpet in both hands, bringing it closer to her chest and clenching it. Her temperature was rising. He could see the sweat forming on her back.

Nicole yelped as Nick brought her up. She hit his chest with her back. She flicked strands of wet hair off her face, moving the back of her head onto his shoulder, turning to accept his kiss. He wrapped one arm around her waist and his other hand on her hip, keeping her still and locked into him. His thrusts were lighter. On her knees and pressed into him, every one intended for her g-spot. She threw her head back and clenched his forearm tight.

He could feel the end building.

Nick pressed his nose against her cheek. “Do you have any condoms?”

She barked a laugh. “No. I’ve got the rod implant,” she paused to give him a quick kiss. “Now shut up and keep going.”

Nick eased her onto her back and hooked her leg over his arm. Nick took her hand and slammed it to just beside her head and held it still, interlocking their fingers as she gripped his bottom lip between her teeth and gave a quick bite, bringing her free hand to his arse and squeezing roughly. Bringing him in harder, his lightning quick thrusts returned, deeper than before. Nicole stretched her neck back, letting him go, mouth open. She screamed something he couldn't quite make out, but something inside him hoped it was name once more. From the same area that hope came from, Nick's orgasm found him. Sudden and relentless. His body froze, clenching his teeth, before her hands touched either side of his face and he looked down. Looking into her eyes and the smile she wore as they both felt his seed coat her insides over and over, was something he would never forget. He collapsed exhausted on top of her body, twitching with her second orgasm.

It was a few minutes before either could move. When they did, Nick let go of her hand and reached with both arms under her back, keeping still and holding her. In response, she repositioned her legs so he could lie at an angle on top of her, quietly running her fingers through his hair and across his back as the flames continued to flicker and crackle.

* * *

The wolf awoke to find Nicole's limbs draped over its body and her head on its shoulder. She had fallen asleep in Nicholas's arms. The wolf stared at the girl, sound asleep, having been satisfied over a dozen times in the last few hours. *Nicholas has done well.*

How ironic that she had challenged the wolf to emerge and here it was, lying naked in bed with her. The wolf admired her spirit. It lowered its head and planted a delicate lick on her forehead. *I will never hurt this one. After all, she is the reason I was unleashed.*

Very carefully, the wolf peeled itself away, careful not to wake her, breathing in, readying itself. It looked again at the sleeping beauty, then at its own hand. The nails out, sharp and prepared.

The wolf vowed never to hurt *this* one, but others would not be so lucky. Nicholas had solved half the puzzle. Nicholas had claimed his prize but now it was time for the wolf to make its first kill. The time had come for revenge.

It dressed in the clothes Nicholas had worn and walked over to the window. Thanks to Nicole, the boy was strong now, was becoming a man. Their merging would soon be complete. The wolf leapt to the ground and ran as it landed, avoiding the populated streets. The wolf waited until there was not a soul around before breaking into a wolf sprint, all fours racing across the grassy fields.

It had the scent. They were together and isolated.

This was not to be a mere scare tactic like the incident with the teacher. This was not a run through the streets. It was time to hunt. They had beaten Nicholas and threatened his heart's desire, which alone had sealed their fate. *Tonight, I will show no mercy.*

Chapter 34

It's Nothing Personal, I'm Just Taking Your Head

Quiet. Finally it's quiet. The ringing in Lauren's ears had stopped. The cheers had been silenced. Perhaps they had done enough to her. Perhaps she had bled enough for them.

How long had she been here, tied with her hands to this fucking pole? Days, weeks? She couldn't even tell. Looking at the pool of her own half-dried blood below her, it might be close to a month.

She rested her head against her shoulder, hiding her eyes from them. She couldn't look down anymore. Seeing the blood and sores across her chest and stomach was like reliving the events that caused them all over again. Calibos had kept carving a huge 'S' into her torso. S for Slade—Wilson Slade, their Alpha. At least they could've lied and told her it was Supervamp. She didn't need to breathe but she tried to calm herself with a sigh, and gagged as the stench of her own breath reflected off her arm. She didn't want to imagine what the rest of her looked or smelt like.

The cool night air touched her dead skin, from the little sensation she still had in her nerve-endings, she could tell there were copious amounts of caked-on blood drying and crumbling on her face like some kind of horrible mud mask, left on for *way too long*.

A rough pair of hands titled her head, checking if she was alive.

"Matt…" she coughed in a voice that resembled a wheezing croak. "Please…"

"Why?"

Lauren wobbled her stone-like head to look at him properly, or attempt to. He had never spoken back to her before. He seemed as confused as his speech. "Talk. All the time. Me, know? Do you? Do I?"

"That's enough, Matty!"

Calibos led Matt back to his position. Night after night, the same thing. Knives and bullets driven into her, and all by the same guy she had shared numerous drinks with over three years. The guy that made dick and fart jokes. The guy that had dated her best friend. The guy that she had screwed and fed off only last year. Then broke his back and hospitalized him. Now he was unrecognizable to her in every way.

Lauren no longer believed that Calibos would set her free. It had been too long. Only the sun had saved her from *the eternal sleep.* It healed her during the day while she slept, but that just meant she was fresh for another round every night for Zombie Matt to practice his aim. If she wanted out, she would have to break herself out. Or die. That, was fucking well not in her plans.

Her best weapon against men, her tits, were already on show and had been since she was taken. So what else did she have? Her eyes darted back and forth. She had nothing. All she had ever done to get out of and in trouble was use her body. Even if it was just allowing a glance at her cleavage to get out of speeding tickets or sex with a hot guy that happened to be married. She got what she wanted, always. Except for one time.

That memory brought back the image of the one man that turned her down, that never showed any interest in her: Dante Delavega. Now she understood why. Where others saw her as hot with a great rack, worthy of a good time, he saw her as empty, a stock-standard shell. His last words to her flowed through her brain, as if the Spaniard were there, talking to her right now. *"I look at you and I see two people. The woman you are and the woman you could be."*

And he was right. *Fuck this feeling sorry for yourself shit. I'm not an empty shell. I'm a vampire. Think!* She had her invisibility, being so weak she hadn't even attempted to use it, it was time she mustered the strength.

"Now, Matty, you've been a little bit wonky. I know you need some Dream State but there's a shortage. You're starting to talk again, but your skill is now lacking. We will just have to make do for a while,"

Calibos raised Matt's arm directly to where he wanted him to throw. Matt furrowed his brows, trying to concentrate, but it looked like he was dying to piss. *Yeah, this is going to end real well.*

Lauren couldn't close her eyes, she had decided. She had to watch the weapon. She would need to hold perfectly still when the knife hit. No movement whatsoever. That should cause someone to check on her, like the first night. But the way Matt was shaking, that knife could be going anywhere. Matt raised his arm and stopped. Hesitation wasn't doing anything for Lauren's nerves.

"Go!" Calibos said.

Matt flung the knife sidearm, and it thundered straight above Lauren's head. She felt nothing but the thud of the blade into the wood above her. She held herself like a statue.

"Goddammit!" Calibos threw his hands up in the air. *Like he cares*, thought Lauren, annoyed. "Matty, what's going on, bud? I know you're running on empty, but this shit is ridiculous! That wasn't even close to her shoulder." He gestured to Lauren, taking notice of her. He stilled before moving quickly towards her. He clutched her face in one hand and jerked it upwards. She stared blankly ahead, letting her body sag the moment he jostled her. "Bloody hell… Oi! Get me one of those bags."

A blood bag was slapped into his outstretched palm and Calibos pulled the knife from the pole and sliced it open. Tilting Lauren's head back farther, he opened her jaw and tipped the contents down her throat and over her face. She craved all of it, but didn't want to let on that she was not as dead as she was pretending to be. In the splashback she could only afford a generous gulp before letting the rest run out of her mouth, sagging back down as he released her. "Well, that plan is fucked." He punctuated this by shoving the knife blade back into the wooden post.

"I told you we should've either killed the bitch or let her go ages ago!"

Lauren didn't know who the voice belonged to, and didn't care. All she cared about was Calibos. He whirled around to confront the speaker. "What was that?"

"You heard me!"

"Calm down, the both of you…"

Shouts erupted back and forth. This was Lauren's chance. She had no idea if the blood she had taken was enough, but with all her might, she clenched her stomach, let her body seize up. She raised her wrists to give the appearance of slack on the straps. It was now or never. *C'mon... c'mon! Hide me.*

"Oi! Where the fuck did she go?"

Lauren chanced a look down, seeing nothing but bloodied asphalt. *It worked!* She faced the pack. She was right in front of them.

"Are you kidding me?"

"It must be some kind of trick. Find the bitch!"

"You said we were going to let her go anyway, so who the hell cares?"

"I care! She can't have gotten far. Let's go."

All of them left her. This was the worst time. Desperation to escape vied with the fear they were still too close by. She didn't know how long her ability would last. But perhaps luck was on her side. She licked as much blood off her face as she could and glanced up at the knife still in the pole. Completely forgotten by all. Except her.

In seconds her binds were no more. She was free. Although it took two attempts to stand, she did so. She moved like a newborn foal, but still she moved, keeping to the back streets, the dark alleyways. All the while, she remained invisible, the fear it could be temporary gripping her.

There was no way she could travel to the mansion from here, but she had to get out of Redfern. The farther she went, the colder the night got until she saw the only light in the darkness. The train line. She didn't know which direction it was going and she didn't care. Either direction was safety in the short term. Her body was flickering, coming in and out of view. She ran as hard as she could along the length of the fence. On and on she went, keeping to the fence. The stations were fortunately closed, so there were no people so far.

The screech of tires in front of her from a car that almost tipped in its urgency to turn into the street made her stop. She hid against the trunk of a tree as finally her power had worn out and he headlights were the only illumination in the black, deserted street.

"Give me a fucking break."

All notions she may have had that the driver was not looking for her were cast aside as it crept along, closing the distance between them. The driver's door opened. Lauren readied herself, clicking her fangs down.

"Lauren? Are you there? It's me!"

"Lackey…?"

Lauren stepped out from the tree and covered her eyes. Clive rushed to her, wriggling out of his jacket, but before he could reach her, the relief and leftover fear rushed over her and she crumpled to her knees, tears flowing, arms held out. Clive wrapped his still-warm jacket around her and held her close.

"It's ok," he patted her hair. "I've got you."

Lauren hugged him tighter. Kissing his cheek, moving down to his neck. Before she knew it, her fangs were buried in his flesh.

"Lauren? Wait, no, please!"

She couldn't stop herself. She closed her eyes and sucked his essence with nothing more than grunts to match his screams, before her head was yanked off his neck.

"That's enough, young lady."

Julian held her at arm's length, keeping her face at bay.

* * *

"What's wrong with you?" Miller asked through a loud burp. "Your taste is in your arse. I bet she tastes like fruit syrup."

"Give it up, dude. She is not interested."

"She isn't, is she?"

"No. Please tell me you're finally getting that?"

"I guess," Miller replied, taking a swig of beer. "She wants that pommy poof."

"Who knows, who cares? Let's just stay away from them, yeah?"

"After I break his legs."

"Aw, come on. You're talking crazy man," Jason said.

"Crazy? Look at my fucking hands!" Miller replied, holding both his plastered hands up. "You expect me to let him walk away?"

"I told you what would happen if we went after him again."

"Yeah, and what has happened? Nothing! We have gone at him—"

"*You* have gone at him."

Jason was such a whiner sometimes. "Aw, shut up. We have gone at him twice and nothing has happened."

"Look at your hands!"

Miller scoffed. "No freak with fangs has appeared to us, you dick. Christ almighty, sometimes I feel like I am the only person with a brain in a world of shitheads. Hand me another beer."

Miller heard gargling, but no response. He turned. Jason appeared to be levitating, head to the side, choking. Miller took a step forward when a terrible, continuous popping sound like a bunch of bubble wrap being stepped on stung his ears. Jason gave a partial yet harsh scream and his body crumpled over, falling with a gush of blood to the floor. Miller's eyes switched from Jason's body to the person standing over him.

Miller couldn't stop staring at his face. Nick Slade, smiling like a maniac. But it wasn't him…it couldn't be. He was all wrong. His hair had grown wild, and silver eyes glared out at him. The teeth were as sharp as spikes on a pitchfork. He stood straight and proud, holding something out, presenting it to Miller. With a sick realisation, Miller recognised Jason's spine, oozing blood the consistency of syrup.

"Hello, Trent. I don't believe we've had the pleasure."

The voice was Slade's, but with a colder sheen to it.

Miller, eyes locked onto the gory sight of his friend's spine, was paralysed with fear. He spoke as if hypnotised, his voice was merely floating on the crisp cool air. "What the *fuck* have you done?"

"I have given him a quick death. A concession I will not make twice." Slade dropped Jason's spine with no emotion whatsoever. It tumbled to the floor just as Slade crouched low, eyes blazing, and the strange version of Nick advanced on Miller. On all fours.

Miller scrambled backward, nearly tripping over a bench in his attempt to get away.

"It's fun to frighten people, isn't it, Trent?"

* * *

With a short, savage lunge, the wolf pushed Miller to the ground. It did not stop Miller from crawling backwards, frantically putting as much distance as possible between them. The wolf moved effortlessly, however not stopping its slow crawling towards him.

"It's not so fun when you're the one being frightened, though, is it?"

The wolf pounced, driving his foot directly to Miller's fibula, shattering the bone to pieces. Blood seeped from the shards that ripped through the surface of his skin. Miller could barely get the scream of agony out before his bottom jaw snapped into his top. The wolf's viscous kick crumbling it. Miller turned, spewing a fountain of blood, broken teeth, and bone on the floor.

"That's how you kick."

Miller made a pathetic half-gasp sound that brought a smile to the wolf. The wolf grasped his mangled, lopsided jaw, holding him on his back and in place. "You will not hurt anyone anymore."

The wolf dug its nails into Miller's face and ripped its hand down his body, opening his throat, chest and stomach to fresh air. When it got to his groin, the wolf dug even deeper, reaching the pelvis with the tip of his nails and slowly pulled the penis and testicles away from the body. The wolf held its blood soaked hand high and flicked Miller's body. Miller lay twitching, coughing and spluttering, unable to move or even scream.

"I leave you here to die slowly, in your own blood and organs. You should've chosen another life, my dear fellow. Or a safer target." The wolf raised its head and howled to the sky in victory.

* * *

Julian snapped to, listening. The sound was accompanied by a subtle tremor that briefly shook the very ground they stood on. Lauren's words carried his thoughts.

"What the fuck was that?"

Julian let her go. He tilted his head, trying to place the direction. "East of here. No. South-East Not far."

"Was it a bomb?"

Julian ignored her and concentrated, disappearing with his usual *pop*.

Julian appeared in a park, with few lights. Actually only one, and that was flickering. He took a step in the darkness and broken glass crunched underfoot. *So there were lights, but the sound has busted the lamps?* This was almost the exact spot the sound had come from, yet there was no sign of a blaze nor did any burning smell reach him. It definitely wasn't a bomb. What he did smell, however, was the smell of death. Very fresh, too.

And blood as well. So much, that he found to the scene simply by following his nose.

"My, my. You lot are in a sorry state indeed." Julian ignored the spineless one. The other though, was fading fast.

"What did this to you, boy?"

He may as well not have spoken, the boy barely registered. Julian pulled out a vial containing a dark red liquid from his inside pocket and emptied it over the boy's vital organs. *Werewolf blood,* he muttered to himself. *A precautionary measure, should I ever need it.*

The wounds healed instantly and slowly the colour started returning to the boy's cheeks. Not much, though. Werewolf blood couldn't replace blood loss. The kid still didn't have long. Julian picked him up by the collar. "Oi! What happened to you? What did this?"

But there was no response. The boy was unconscious, his breathing ragged.

Julian flung the boy over his shoulder. "Fuckin' teenagers."

He popped and emerged once more beside Lauren and Clive, both also unconscious. Julian rolled his eyes. "Why am I surrounded by a bunch of inept, useless cunts? Well that's about to change."

He flung Lauren over his other shoulder and grabbed Clive with his free hand, popping them all away from this damn place.

CHAPTER 35

A RUMBLE IN THE DISTANCE

Nicole ran her hand over Nick's position in bed, searching for him. Finding only empty sheets and rumpled blankets woke her up fully. She looked to make sure, and in the morning glow from the window, she realised he was indeed gone.

She reached for her phone, hoping he had left a message, and there was one. But not from him; from Dr Sarsky:

`Miss O'Brien, I received your voicemail. This situation is absolutely ridiculous. Don't worry, I'll sort it out. You have my word.`

She sat up and heard footsteps coming up the stairs outside her room. The door slowly opened.

"Hey, you're up! I wanted to surprise you."

He held a tray in both hands. The smell of bacon and eggs, and the sight of a glass filled with orange juice brought a relieved and happy grin to her face.

"You made me breakfast in bed?"

"No, I just bought up a tray from downstairs. I thought it looked nice."

She hadn't even let him put the tray of food on the bedside table before she leaned over and kissed him.

"Good morning," he said.

"This is the sweetest thing ever."

Pulling back, he scanned her features intently. "Wait a second. Did you think I'd left you?"

"Maybe, just for a second."

"Nikki…" He looked hurt.

"In my defence, I've had that actually happen, and no one has ever made me breakfast in bed."

Nick sat on the edge of the bed. "Well, I'd never leave like that. You have my word."

"Ok. It's just, you and me, this is…" she said, trying to gesture the end of her description.

"A big deal for you," he finished for her.

"Huge. And I want to make sure we are on the same page. I don't know where this is going, but I like it. I *really* like it. Last night proved something to me. I want to know what you are, the things you can do. What you see."

"I don't know what I am, or what I can do. Any training I've had, I wasted because I thought it was pointless. Besides I don't want you to be in harm's way."

Nicole shrugged this off. "We never know what life's going to bring us anyway. I could get run over by a car tomorrow. Stepping outside is dangerous. I feel like I am on the edge of something great, something few people ever truly see. And although Dr Sarsky says he can help me…"

"Wait, what do you mean? With your career?"

"Yes, apparently he feels he can fix things. I just got a text message. I don't like to doubt such an amazing man, but it's impossible. There's nothing he can do except let the matter run its course. I would do anything to be a counsellor, of course. For my life to be back on track, the way I planned it. But it's not. So, it's time to start fresh. Whatever this is, isn't a bad plan B."

Nick kissed her hand. "So, would you like to go somewhere for lunch?"

"Maybe I should have breakfast first!" She nodded toward the tray. "And then…"

"Then?"

Nicole brought his lips to meet hers. "*Then.*"

* * *

"To breaking news. The residents of Glebe woke up to the gruesome discovery of a teenage boy's body in the centre of Jubilee Park this morning. Rebecca Zietta is there. Hello, Rebecca. What can you tell us?"

"At approximately 5:40 this morning, a group of girl guides doing a bushwalk came across the body of the boy, who appears to have been killed and left at the scene of the crime. A bizarre incident was also reported last night in the same area: a booming roar that rattled windows and led to a number of calls to emergency services. I spoke to several of the residents of nearby apartments and all are quite shaken by the events, as you can imagine."

"Rebecca, have the police come out with any information on what they think might have killed the boy?"

"The police are playing their cards close to the chest as to what their suspicions are. They will come out with an official statement in a couple of hours' time, and hopefully then they'll be able to shed some light on the many questions local residents have been asking. All we know at the moment is the report from the initial witnesses—and I caution any sensitive viewers who might not wish to hear this next portion—the initial witnesses, who said, and I quote, "his spine looked like it had been literally ripped from his body and tossed to the ground just beside him."

"How horrible. Thank you, Rebecca. And just in on that story, the boy's identity has now been released, as the victim's family has now been informed. The boy was seventeen-year-old Jason Trodd. We will have more news on that for you as it appears."

* * *

“What do you make of this?”

Calibos stepped into the main area of the pub and dropped the daily newspaper on the table. It was late afternoon, so the only occupants were the pack. They were all grumbly about Lauren’s escape and their failure to recover her. They weren’t in the mood for questions and games either.

“We should patrol Glebe?”

“Honestly, yes and no. Do you have any idea the raw power needed to do that to a human body?”

“Vampire,” Matt said.

Calibos wore a bright smile. “Nice try on the input Matty. Not a vampire in this case, though. Werewolf.”

“I don’t get it.”

“We aren’t alone. One of the captives may have gotten free or England sent someone to help. We’re gonna try and find him for when we take the mansion. We’ll need the extra muscle.”

“For when?”

“We make final preparations for the next full moon. It’s time to take back what’s ours.”

* * *

Vincent stepped out of his custom-made security vault, housing his four wolves. “All present and accounted for. No change in readings.”

“Well then, what are we to do make of this? It was clearly a wolf I heard last night, and only a wolf could’ve caused the wounds I saw. If none have escaped from us, and with no incidents at all from the others you say have been here for months’ worth of full moons, then what was it? Last night was only a half-moon. This doesn’t bode well for the full potential this wolf must have.”

“But why now? To what purpose? You said yourself there were no bite marks on either human. And where are the other bodies?”

“Other bodies?”

"Since when have you ever heard of a wolf only attacking two people in a night? This was a public park, and a huge one. They were in the middle of it, no one else in sight. The beast would've had to travel past any number of potential victims to get there, yet left them all alone. It's not typical behaviour."

"You make it sound like a pre-meditated attack, as if the wolf had set out to do this mauling and nothing else."

Vincent turned abruptly.

"Father?"

"That's exactly what it was. And only one class of wolf targets specific prey if it so wishes. We have an Alpha amongst us. Have you succeeded with turning the boy?"

Julian grimaced. "No idea. I ordered the blonde to stay with him until he wakes up. If I'm not mistaken, she is the holder of a record. She's not even a year old and already a maker."

"Desperate times call for desperate measures. We will need the strength of a newborn against an Alpha. It will guarantee victory. Speaking of which, have Clive meet me in my room at once. There's something I need to find out."

"What's that?"

"Whether Wilson Slade had any children," Vincent growled.

Vincent stormed into his room and looked up at the ceiling. A sharp squeaking had gotten his attention. Finding nothing, his eyes fell to his desk and an envelope that lay there. Vincent didn't know what it contained, obviously, but he knew who sent it. The Messengers of Osiris. Over two hundred years ago, when Vincent had still been living in Ireland, he had received a letter like this informing him he had been made a king. He remembered it well as it also followed the sound of squeaking. An angry falcon had nestled in the corner of the room.

Looking up again toward where he'd heard the noise, he spotted it. The falcon, wings curling slowly around its body, could've been identical to that one from so long ago.

The legend was that if the addressee did not respond to the letter's instructions within one week, the falcon would take their soul.

Vincent slit open the envelope with a nail and read.

We are disappointed. You have disgraced yourself for money and tainted your rule over Sydney. Power is not yours to gain, it is ours to give and take. You are blinded by greed and you will no longer be responsible for Sydney. You are ordered to relinquish power by signing your name in blood. Once this is done, the falcon will return with your new instructions.

Vincent looked up at the falcon and tore the letter in half as Clive stumbled into the room. Good thing he didn't believe in myths and legends.

"You are to send a computer letter to the new Alpha of Britain. I need to know if his predecessor spawned any mutts. Do this and I may forget you defied my direct order."

"Vincent, Lauren was going to die—"

"I told you I do not care. She was foolish enough to get herself captured."

"She has had no training! Everyone has abandoned her, yet when she matters to either you or Julian, then you have expectations she can't possibly live up to. You asked me to place a tracker on her before she left. I asked for you to let me bring her home, that's all."

"I denied you. Day after day, when I should only have to do it once, you just up and out. Off on your merry way to be the dashing rescuer, when she thinks you insignificant?"

"That's not…that's not what this is."

"I think it is."

"It's about doing what's right!"

"Enough! I decide what's right. You are fortunate that as of this moment I require your services and Julian requires hers. Otherwise your fates could be vastly different. Send the letter, and one day, you may see her again."

* * *

The Creed Estate – Britain

A loud echoing pounding continued on his bedroom door. "Somebody had better be dead!" Damien Creed roared.

The door swung open and Tobias Lee walked in jauntily, holding a printed A4 piece of paper. "I'm in luck then."

Creed gritted his teeth and snatched the note from Tobias. He really needed to do something about his arrogance. He glanced sleepily at the message and then sat up abruptly and read it again.

"Is he serious?" Creed asked.

"Yep, it's no trick. I just looked it up on the world news and it's all over YouTube as well. Some stupid kid got his spine ripped out in Sydney. It was a great kill."

But Creed wasn't listening. His eyes blazed as he kicked the sheets off himself and almost ran to the button on the wall on the opposite side of the room. He pressed it. A panel in the wall slid open revealing a woman huddled in the corner. Creed raised an arm and walloped her before grabbing the chains holding her to the wall and yanking her across the floor.

"Guess who just sent me an email, Alicia? The vampire king of Sydney. You remember him, don't you? You know that I watched all your communication with him all those months ago? He knew not to worry about the men you were sending because their proposal would be null and void as the British Pack would be undergoing a change of management. Here's what he didn't know: that a second team would be coming along. He was pissed off to say the least, but when nothing happened every full moon following, he realised they were human and no threat to him and his business operation. None of those traitors have been sighted again. They're probably a vampire snack by now, so you fucked up well and truly. But it appears you had more brains than I gave you credit for. Do you know what the current headline in Sydney is today? Imagine the vampire king's surprise when a werewolf attack is reported now, after all this time. You sent a third party along: your only son."

Alicia spat on the floor, blood mixing with the saliva. "Leave him out of this, Creed. He's done nothing to you."

"Shut up. I've had a thought. I was going to kill you, send you off in pieces to him, as a warning and to show him how it's really done, but no. How about a deal? You'll get to go to Sydney and be with your precious boy. On one condition. You present yourself and your son to Vincent and subject yourselves to his jurisdiction."

Alicia nodded, and Creed waved some guards in to take her away. Under ordinary circumstances, the Alicia he'd known would have taken time to think things over, but she'd been locked up for months now, and Creed knew the overwhelming need to see her son took over all else.

When she was out of ear shot, Tobias raised an eyebrow. "So what are you really going to do?"

"I'm going to tell Vincent everything. Nick's name and what he looks like. It's up to him to find him. But I'll tell him that within days he will have the former Alpha's son and wife at his disposal. The wife that tricked him. I'd wager he'll kill them publicly as a warning to other wolves to stay out of Australia."

"Your response will be?"

"That as far as I am concerned, their blood is tainted, therefore it does not bother me the line ends with Nick. I hate Australia, and everyone knows that. There will be no need to even pretend to care about the fact we are forbidden to go there. As long as I still get my cut from Dream State, Vincent can do what he likes."

Tobias cleared his throat. "My Alpha, is that wise?"

"What?"

"Wilson's son is the blood Alpha. Is it wise to let a vampire be seen destroying what is naturally yours to challenge? There cannot be two Alphas. It's not possible."

"In a few days, Vincent will make sure it's not an issue. The boy and his mother are dead. The future belongs to me."

* * *

Alex sat up and rolled her head around, stretching. She got up from the bed and casually searched for her underwear. She and Dante had resumed their naked feeding ritual, and Alex had never felt better. She was comfortable and at ease with him. She loved the kissing of her lips and neck, the licks across her breasts, the gentle sucks and his hands exploring her body. That was still as far as it went, still it was all to turn her on. Doing so, helped make the bite easier, and boy did it.

"Try not to be afraid," Dante said.

"I'm not," Alex got down on her hands and knees to look under the bed, reaching. "I admit the news today shocked me, and now when you're telling me it's obvious a wolf has done it, I agree. I'm not afraid. We knew they were here, so now we've just got to deal with it."

"*I've* got to deal with it."

"Dante," Alex stood and stepped into her panties, facing him. "Let's not ruin this ok? I told you, I want to be with you, as your donor and as your friend. That means taking everything on that you do. I can't do what you do, but I can be by your side and help. I want to smash these pricks back to England, or hell, or wherever. I want to help however I can."

"Very well. Until that time comes, just take care of yourself and your mother. Nick too, of course."

"Yeah, Nick seems to need a lot of protection at the moment."

"I don't understand."

"Well, he went over to a girl's place last night, and he hasn't been home yet."

"Ah, yes. Well, as far as protection goes, I'm sure he'll be responsible. As long as he is making her happy and vice versa."

"He was so happy on the phone when he told me he was still there. I wish Alicia could see him now. It would be weird if the two of them went on to get married. Nick and Nicole Slade… Dante?"

He had jerked his head toward her. "What did you say the name was?"

"Nick's? Slade. Why?"

Dante clenched his jaw but shook his head dismissively. "Oh… I thought you said something else. My mistake."

Alex wondered what the deal really was, but Dante was not going to tell her until he was ready. “No worries. Anyway, gotta rush off. I’m meeting mum for dinner. Talk soon?”

“Definitely,” he said. Alex gripped him in a strong hug and pressed her lips against his.

“Bye!”

* * *

Dante marched to his study and removed a book from the newer part of his collection. Flipping to the index, he scanned down the list and turned to the correct page.

Current Alpha of Germany 1989 – Armin Cordula (2nd Generation)
Omega – Felicie Bauer Cordula (dec)
Children - Franz, Hanz, Angelique, Geert (dec)
Current Alpha of France 1971 – Claude Absolon (3rd Generation)
Omega – Charlotte Christelle Absolon
Children – Eveline, Jaq, Claude Jnr, Jean (dec), Fabien (dec)
Current Alpha of England 2003 – Wilson Slade (9th Generation)
Omega – Alicia Slade
[No children present at time of printing. Maiden name not given]

Dante hung his head. He *knew* he had heard the name Slade before. So much made sense now, though it made it harder to digest.

Nick was the killer of the teenage boy, Jason Trodd. Alex’s cousin, a tenth generation Alpha wolf, and probably not even aware of it or how strong he would become. Dante looked out the window into the darkness, deciding. What to do? His heart and his head were in very different places. He set in mind what he should do, and would worry about the consequences later. He had to do what he believed was right.

“Please, forgive me,” he whispered to the night.

Picking up the phone on his desk, he dialled. “It’s me.” He rubbed his palm across his forehead. “Get Vincent.”

Chapter 36

The Things You Do For Love

"Thank you all for coming."

Alex raised her glass toward Margaret, Nick and Nicole, all seated at Dante's dining table. He had invited them all over for dinner. This in itself was not a strange thing for Alex. What was strange was that Dante was *insistent,* and as long as she had known him, he was never insistent.

It got even stranger when Dante had called her yesterday to check and double check they were all coming.

Still, dinner had been delicious, and conversation interesting. Admittedly, Nicole hadn't taken her eyes off Nick for more than three seconds, constantly looking at him like he was a giant Ferrero Rocher chocolate that she just wanted to attack. And of course Nick looked back at her like…well, Alex didn't want to think about that. Still, all in all, a pleasant evening.

Alex and Dante joked with each other. Just for a minute, Alex could imagine this being a a recurring event. Might be nice to have a "family night" of sorts. Alex appreciated the closeness and the connection to Dante again after making up. He didn't treat her as a boyfriend, because that's not what he was. He was a very affectionate friend. But something was different tonight, despite it all. Off. Forced? Alex couldn't put her finger on it. The lead-up to the night just wasn't right.

Dante had spent a lot of time speaking to Nicole, probably trying to make her feel comfortable. But at the same time Alex couldn't help but feel he was trying to charm her. Which again, was not typical of Dante.

Everyone seemed content, but Alex could sense something was amiss.

"It is wonderful to see you again," Dante chinked his wine glass against Nicole's, and set it down as she sipped. "And looking so happy. Your new…uh," Dante held out a hand, as if uncertain how to pronounce the word, "friendship? Seems to be agreeing with you. He is a fine fellow. May I ask what you see in him?"

Nick swallowed his food rather fast and gave a brief cough.

"Dante…" Alex started. Dante never asked something like that of anyone. He viewed such things as none of his business. Why now?

"No, it's ok," Nicole smiled and held Nick's hand. "He's really sweet. He makes me laugh. He makes me feel comfortable just being me."

Alex's eyes flicked towards Margaret, who said nothing, but sipped her wine with a strangely sly smile teasing the corners of her mouth. Alex swallowed another forkful of her dessert and glanced at Dante, who stared at Nicole, seemingly captivated, even though she was no longer facing him. He seemed to be studying her, hard, a questioning expression adorning his face. Contemplating something?

"Now," Dante said loudly, and the front door burst open. Alex screamed, as did Nicole beside her. Nick bolted upright, knocking his chair over as over a dozen men in riot gear streamed in, drawing submachine guns and pistols out, pointing them all at him.

"On your knees!" shouted one with bleach-blonde hair, and jerked his foot at the back of Nick's leg, forcing him to collapse to his knees. "Where's the other one?" he asked Dante.

"Basement." Dante gestured with his head. Three broke off from the group and jogged in that direction.

"Dante, who are these people? What are you doing?" Alex yelled.

"These are the Elements of Night. They are here for the same reason I am, to protect you all from him," he said, pointing to Nick.

Nick glared at Dante, frozen in anger. "What?"

"Protect us? Dante, what the hell is wrong with you?" Alex screamed.

"He is not what you think he is. He has been lying to you for months." Dante faced Nicole. "Your boyfriend murdered Jason Trodd."

"What? I—I don't believe you," Nicole breathed, eyes wide. She looked across at Nick. If it was a joke, he wasn't in on it either.

"Believe what you want. Nick is a werewolf. And tonight, the moon is full."

Alex felt like the room was spinning. What was he even saying?

Nick? A werewolf? What? It just didn't make sense.

"I already know. What's it to you?"

"What do you mean 'you know'? What the fuck is going here?!" Alex looked all around at every face and no one could or would answer her.

"You will see soon enough." Dante spoke over the commotion.

An angry scream erupted from behind and Alex saw Melina and another woman struggling with the two Elements of Night soldiers who were half-dragging, half-carrying her from the basement, in their attempt to get her out.

"What the hell is she doing here?" Alex asked.

"Alejandro! You fucking traitor! How could you tell them? How could you do this to me?"

The shorter woman burst free and rushed over to Dante. The blonde man aimed his weapon but Dante halted him. She gripped Dante with tears in her eyes. "Please tell me it's not true. Please tell me this is some sort of trick. We trusted you."

"You should choose your friends more carefully, Nadia. I am no longer Alejandro, the boy she loved. I am Dante, the monster she made. I will never forgive her for that." Alex thought she had never heard Dante sound so cold.

Nadia, devastated, allowed herself to be led away.

"Take the rest," the blonde said.

"Dante, where are they taking us?" Alex tried to grab his hand, but was wrested toward the door by the blonde man and another of these vampire thugs. Dante seemed not to notice. He had eyes only for Nick and Nicole.

Nick lunged at a vampire closing in on Nicole. "Get away from her!" He reached back for a full swing when his arm was caught by Dante, who flashed his eyes and fangs at him.

"Don't try it. You're not that strong…not yet."

One of the Elements of Night took the presented opportunity and plunged a needle into the vein in the teenager's neck. The effect was instantaneous. Nick collapsed and the vampire caught him. A terrified Nicole was beside him, fighting a losing battle to extricate herself from another vampire's grip.

"Let's go," Dante said. Margaret moved past him and out the door, not forced by anyone, just followed by a guard with a gun at her back.

Maybe she just couldn't watch anymore.

"Where?" Alex bellowed.

"Vincent is waiting."

Chapter 37

Ask and You Shall Receive

Alex was shoved into one of two black sedans, along with Margaret and Nicole. The others travelled with Dante.

Alex could not sit still, hands held together so tight her knuckles were pale, the ties digging painfully into her wrists. This couldn't be real. Dante would never treat her like this. Nick couldn't be the werewolf he was talking about. The flashes of light from the streetlights were like signals for the memories that flooded her brain, pounding into her skull one by one, fuelling her confusion, her shock and her fear.

Nick smiling at her, such genuine warmth… Dante's kisses, so delicate, so tender… Nick's abrupt weight gain, his destroyed clothing… The cold way Dante spoke to her, to them all. Nothing but contempt.

"Try to calm down," Margaret said, squeezing Alex's hands briefly.

"How can you say that? Even *your* voice is shaking. I can't let this happen."

"Alex, stop and think. You said this was about British wolves from the beginning. Where is Nick from?"

The question hit Alex like a brick, but she recovered quickly. "But they were here well before Nick was!"

"And why do you suppose Nick is here?"

"Because he had trouble! Alicia asked us to help him. You already kn—"

"Why did Alicia send him, Alex? What was the reason?"

Now Alex understood what Margaret meant. He had never told them the reason. To this day, he had kept it to himself. Was it because he feared they would judge him? Cast him out? If so, who could blame him?

Alex shook her head. "I don't care about the reason. What if he didn't know what he was?"

"I wasn't sure either. But I suspected. I said nothing because he hadn't shown any signs. But when he gained those muscles, and then the boy turned up dead on the full moon. As hard as it is, it fits."

"I don't care! Even if it was him, he would never hurt anyone deliberately."

"He hasn't just *hurt* anyone Alex. He has brutally killed a boy."

"And Dante hasn't? If Nick did do something, he couldn't help it. If it was him, he didn't know what he was doing."

"Which is exactly what makes him so dangerous. Look, I love him too. He's family. But we need to do what's right. Even if he didn't know what he was doing, or can't remember, you have to understand he is two people, and we are the ones caught in the middle. You don't think I want to scream and rave too? That I don't want to protect him? But I will not stand by and do nothing with you in danger. Neither will Dante. The needs of the many outweigh the needs of the one. I'm sorry, Alex but you are not thinking logically. As hard as this is for everyone, I support Dante."

"Stop, mother. I can't listen to this right now." Alex couldn't think about logic. Her head pounded, the flesh of her wrists stung. She pressed the fingertips of both hands to her temples. Margaret sat staring out the window now, a vacant expression cemented on her face. Alex realized that both she and Margaret knew Dante, and he had drunk from both, but could either claim to know him better? Margaret had known him longer, but he had been far more intimate with Alex. Did any of that even matter now?

The vans holding the captives pulled up into the drive way of the Kent mansion. Dante was the first to get out of the lead vehicle heading into the already open door. Alex and her group were shoved out and guided just behind him, to be greeted by Vincent who smiled warmly.

"You have done me a great service, Dante."

"I did not do this for you. I did it for my city. I did it for them." He gestured toward Alex and her mother. "These are humans I care for and they would've been in danger had this beast been allowed to roam free."

Alex gritted her teeth. *He forced us out of our home and brought us here because he cares?* It didn't make any sense.

"Indeed. A maturing Alpha wolf is a danger to all. I vow tonight we will settle all werewolf affairs once and for all. This will be an historic occasion."

"Spare me the speech. Just tell me everything is as we agreed."

"The humans will not be harmed. No other vampires are in the house. We are alone."

"Good," Dante said as Melina and the rest were brought inside. "I want no one knowing I helped you."

"You want no one knowing what a traitor you are?" Melina screamed. "What a fucking sycophant you have become? *How could you*?"

"Be silent, bitch!" Dante fired back. Vincent was delighted.

"And here I thought you two secretly still loved each other. Hello again, Melina my pet. I must say it brings me great joy to see Dante be the one to put you in your place."

Melina spat at Vincent. "Put that in its place while you're at it, fucking prick."

Vincent laughed. "Charming to the last."

Dante stepped forward and addressed the Elements of Night. "Take the women to the observation deck and the redhead to the king's office. Bring the wolf and his lover with me."

Alex pulled out of an attempted grasp and lunged for the vampire holding Nick. It was no use. The vampire held her at bay with a mere fend and the first slung her over his shoulder. "Dante, god-fucking-dammit! Don't do this! Listen to me!"

Margaret called to Nicole to be brave, Nadia called for Melina but there was no use. The vampires holding them were too strong, and they all parted directions as per Dante's orders.

* * *

Nicole tried to keep up as best she could, but the men around her moved ridiculously quickly. Her vision blurred until she blinked the tears away. All she could see was a long stretch of tunnel. No doors, no corners. Her plan if nothing else, was to get Nick and bolt. But he hadn't woken. She had no idea what they injected him with, or how strong it was. But there was no way she could carry him on her own.

Ok, think... You need to get out. You have to get Nick out too. Stall for time. "Please, I didn't do anything."

Dante did not look at her. "I know that."

"Why are you doing this to me, then?"

Dante stopped and slowly turned. "I meant it when I said you were intelligent. But I know what it is like to love someone that would only ever end in heartbreak. I am truly sorry about this. It gives me no pleasure."

Dante led them down a corridor lined with nothing but torches and down a short staircase, coming to an open door opening into a large round room.

Nicole looked around at the vacuous space. She was surrounded by walls of brick and cement. No decorations of any kind, only a shiny, silver-coloured box on the floor. Above to her left were three gigantic window panes, behind which stood the shocked, miserable forms of Alex, Margaret and…the other woman, Nadine was it? Nadia. So that was the observation deck. Directly above her, she guessed some twenty feet, was a perfectly circular opening like a skylight. Except this had no glass pane; it was open to the night air. The sky was clearly visible, as were the endless stars. On any other night, it would've been breathtaking and beautiful.

On the other side of the entrance, two chains were bolted to the brick walls. Dante walked over to the box, opened it and pulled out a gleaming pistol. "Put the wolf over there. Make sure he is secure before he wakes."

"Don't hurt him, please," Nicole begged.

"What makes you think I will?" Dante said, holding up the pistol.

"Please don't do this. I know him. He wouldn't kill anybody. It's a mistake."

Dante looked at her. "Is that what you really believe?"

"Yes!" she fired.

"So kind of you to think that. I hope you feel the same way when he treats your liver like chewing gum."

He gestured upwards to an opening in the ceiling. "In about five minutes, the light of the full moon will shine directly in the spot he is standing in. There is no holding him back now. He has claimed his first kill, and is now one with his wolf nature." He stopped and looked up at the observation deck, yelling so the women could hear the seriousness of his voice. "The Slade line has never been broken, meaning he will be a tenth-generation Alpha. This makes him unimaginably powerful. Do you understand? If I hadn't brought you here, he would have killed all of you."

"Dante," came a voice from the entrance. "His Majesty requests your presence."

Dante nodded. "Tell the other Elements guards to retreat."

"We were ordered to ensure the dog is put down…"

Dante whipped his head around and sneered at the guard. "You think your weapons will be enough? You think those chains will actually hold him? By all means, stay here with her. You will be torn to pieces before firing a single, worthless shot."

The guards looked at each other uncomfortably and filed out. Dante returned his attention to Nicole, who was shaking from head to foot. They were going to leave her alone. This might be her chance to get Nick out of here. But then, a voice she didn't want to acknowledge crept into her thoughts.

What if he wants to leave, but the wolf doesn't? What if Dante was right about everything? Nicole believed with all her heart that Nick truly cared for her, maybe even loved her. But what did the wolf want? Did the wolf feel human emotion? Did it care? It had already killed Jason, what was another body to it?

"Why do you want me here? If you think he's going to kill me, why bring me here?"

"You can stop all of this. Here and now. You can save him and yourself. You can save many lives by making a choice."

"A choice to do what? To kill him?" Nicole shrieked.

"To save him." Dante said, placing the gun on the floor in front of her. Behind him, Nick began to stir. "This has one silver bullet loaded and ready. An Alpha can only be killed by a silver bullet through the heart or head. You are the reason he has embraced his nature. You are the one that can stop him."

"Why me?" Nicole cried, tears beginning to fall. "Because he slept with me?"

Dante placed the gun in her hand and replied heavily. "Because he loves you. His fate and the fate of many are in your hands."

Dante walked towards the door behind her and as he passed, he stopped, leaning in to her ear, whispering. "Everything will be all right if you let your feelings for him guide you. You will know what to do. I trust you will do the right thing."

Dante stepped out of the room and closed the door. The loud clang roused Nick. He shook his head to clear the cobwebs, looking around bemused. "Nikki…"

"Nick!" she said rushing towards him. "Come on, we have to get you out of here."

She pulled at the chains but to no effect. In truth, she knew she couldn't break them herself, but she had to do try something.

"Where are we? What's that gun for?" Nick asked softly.

"Don't worry about that," Nicole said quickly. "Come on, pull with me."

"Wait, can't you shoot the chains?"

"There is only one bullet in it."

Nick grabbed her wrist gently that had been pulling on the chains. "Wait," he said. "I remember. Jason's dead… Miller too. I—the wolf—ripped them to pieces. I'm a murderer."

He pushed Nicole toward the gun and the door.

"Get out!"

* * *

Dante walked into Vincent's private quarters. Melina sat with her back to him at a huge desk, Vincent opposite her.

"Ah, Dante, welcome—"

Vincent stopped speaking as Melina lunged at Dante. She was quick, but he was quicker, using her own force and speed to slam her face into the door he had just entered, splintering it. She whimpered in pain, crumpling to the floor. Dante looked at her with contempt and snapped the lock.

"Just in case you get any funny ideas." Dante stepped over her and then lifted her up and shoved her violently back in her seat.

"Dear me, you really can't trust anyone these days, can you, Melina? Imagine the man whose heart you broke having no qualms about giving you up to his king."

Melina said nothing, dropping her face and slowly reaching a trembling hand to her bleeding forehead. She even appeared to be crying.

"Now the time has come for remuneration," Vincent said.

"You know my terms. The humans will be freed after they witness what a monster they have been protecting. The slave girl is not to be harmed as she was forced to do Melina's bidding."

"Wonderful, and the wolf's mate?"

"If she survives, let her go after giving her a memory wipe." Dante shrugged. "If she survives."

* * *

"I'm not going to leave you," Nicole said.

Nick looked up at the opening, and saw the partial moon. Nicole was sure he felt a surge in his stomach as she did, putting the situation together. This could be stopped. She was sure. Just had to keep him calm, focused on her. She wanted to run. She wanted to stay and defend him from anything. Even himself.

"Nicole please...pick up the gun."

Nicole was aghast. "What?"

"Do it!" he screamed.

"No!" she replied even louder.

A stream of moonlight filtered through the opening. As it touched Nick, he tensed and fell forward. Nicole rushed to him and knelt in from of him. She clasped his face, forcing him to look up.

"Nick...baby look at me. Look at me. You have to fight this. You hear me? Remember the story. Don't let it control you."

Another burst of moonlight hit him as the moon rose higher, making Nick scream in agony. Nicole felt his skin begin to burn and quiver. Tears streamed down her face. "Please don't give in."

Nicole was shoved to her back and Nick spoke, in a voice that wasn't his own. It snaked around the room as if made of smoke, rising in coldness to her ears. "Kill me…"

Nicole shook her head, lips trembling. Finally, Nick raised his head and Nicole crumbled to her knees, covering her mouth. "Oh god…no…"

Nick was heaving, staring at her with silver eyes and gleaming fangs.

* * *

"You know, I feel quite joyous!" Vincent paced the room, hands behind his back.

Dante crossed his arms. "And why is that?"

"I have proven my eminence, that's why. Yes, with your help making things a great deal simpler. After all, you practically handed the boy to me once I discovered who he was. But despite receiving a letter instructing me to give up my kingdom, I have managed to fix all the city's problems in one fell swoop. The letter means nothing now, which proves there is no rightful person or way to take away what is mine."

"The Messengers of Osiris?"

"Yes, how did you know?"

"I got a letter as well."

Vincent paused at that. "You what?"

"Yes, this one in fact." Dante pulled a piece of paper from his pocket. "And it reads: You have started a war against Dream State. It is a war we approve of. It is a war begun by the current king of Sydney and his own toxic concoction. Use any means necessary to infiltrate the mansion and destroy the source of the drug."

Dante folded the letter and placed it back in his pocket.

"Is this some kind of joke?"

"You can read it if you like."

Vincent gave a quick roll of his eyes as the situation began to make sense. "This whole thing was a set-up?"

"From the moment I called you."

"I am still the king. What can you possibly hope to match against my power?"

"You tell me. You're the one locked in a room with the two vampires in Sydney that feed off vampire blood."

Vincent looked at Melina who had raised her head and smiled at him, fangs out and looking hungry.

* * *

"Please… Don't leave me." Nicole had tried again to get close to him. A splash of blood had burst from his mouth seconds earlier and sounds of snapping and crunching were echoing all around the room. His body was changing before her eyes. His shirt was in tatters, his facial hair had grown exponentially, giving him thick mutton chops. He held her tight, both at bay and yet still close. His grip dug into her but she didn't care. She felt as if she was his last hope and that he was holding on to her like he was holding onto his humanity.

"The wolf…warned me…the change would be hard…"

Nicole smoothed his new mane of hair, "That's it, just keep talking,"

"It's my…fault. I'm so sorry."

"Don't…don't. It's ok."

"No!" he boomed. Nicole was blown back with the force of his scream. The moon was high, the transformation was nearly complete. He rose to his full height, towering above her and taking a step.

"Do it. If you care about me…you'll help me."

Nicole picked up the gun, slowly pointing it towards Nick, or what once could be called him.

Nick stumbled, the pain reaching its peak. "Please… It's what I want."

Nicole was sobbing, the gun was wavering left and right such was the terror coursing through her veins. "I can't do it."

"You must. Hurry! KILL M—"

The full moon burst into the room, completely bathing Nick. His scream turned into a roar. His shirt exploded off his body as the muscles underneath became instantly over developed. His nose and mouth extended. He rose again a man mountain, even taller than he was before. Nicole knew, even before he ripped both chains out of the wall one by one, that Nick was gone. What stood before her wasn't even what killed Jason Trodd. She stared at the Alpha wolf. And it was coming closer.

* * *

"You dare think you can trick me? Both of you together are half my age. You will fail."

"We shall see," Dante said, but Melina was the one who struck first. She flung herself at Vincent who caught her by the throat.

"Mediocre. Where do you think you're going?" Vincent dropped her when she slashed at his hand with her nails, tearing the skin severely. His blood spat at first then flowed like a fountain. He gasped and held his hand as his head was pummelled with quick strikes from Dante. Vincent swiped at him with a backhand but Dante ducked it. Vincent was about to swing again when Melina slashed at him again with her fingers, this time the side of his neck. He reached blindly for Melina but she dodged his grip as Dante tore more flesh off Vincent's neck and drank. Vincent clawed at him, managing to get a grip with both hands when Melina bit him on the other side of his neck and drank. The double team was working.

Vincent, regardless of his strength, could not get a bearing on either because they alternated attacks rather than coming at him together. Now, he had two vampires feeding off his powerful eight-hundred-year old blood and it was taking its toll. He couldn't keep up. They had betrayed him and he had fallen for it, eager to cement his position. The death curst was coming to pass despite all he'd done to stop it.

All three fell to the floor. Dante and Melina held each of his arms with both of their hands as they tore more of his flesh with their fangs, ensuring more blood poured out of the wounds and into their mouths. Finally, Vincent began to sag underneath them, no more fight in him. Dante and Melina released themselves.

"Apart from everything else, this is for the hundreds of people you've killed with Dream State," looming over Vincent.

Vincent laughed. "You think you've won? Go ahead then, kill me. You have no idea what this will mean for you. Julian will avenge me."

Dante laughed himself. "I truly hope so."

"You did all this for a fucking wolf you don't even know?

"No, I told you, I did it for my city. An Alpha wolf is nothing compared to the plague you have infected Sydney with."

Vincent chuckled. "Plague? Dream State is a blessing. I have blessed an entire city…including your former donor."

Dante knelt down again, picking up Vincent by the scruff of the neck. "What?"

Vincent chuckled, a hollow gargling sound. "Surprise."

* * *

The Alpha wolf stepped closer again, heaving, not taking its eyes off Nicole.

Nicole, tears now flowing freely down her face, stared at the beast before her and then threw the gun away. "I don't know if you can even hear me. But I am not going to do it. God forgive me, I just can't."

The Alpha wolf's gaze followed the arc of the gun, then looked back at her. It held out both of its hands, waiting. Nicole did not think she could possibly move, but somehow she did, closing in on the wolf. The creature took her hands gently before lifting her into its arms. It gripped her securely, and then with a sudden burst of ferocious power, charged at the door and burst through it, racing along the corridor, looking for the way out. Elements of Night members scattered as the wolf blew past them. The world rushed past her as the wolf dashed through the front door and out into freedom, the mansion diminishing behind them.

Chapter 38

Hail

Through the scope of his rifle, Calibos peered into the mansion. He had only just seen the massive blur race far past him and needed a second to both catch his breath, and stop grinning. Not even Wilson had been that developed when fully transformed.

The Elements of Night soldiers picked themselves up and ran for the door, shouting pursuit instructions to each other. A handful clambered into the first black SUV. Seconds later, the vehicle exploded, tossing the remaining soldiers back, scattered like leaves on Autumn wind. The car had burst into flames the instant the driver-side door was shut.

Calibos cackled and clapped Matt on the shoulder. "Good going, Matty."

Matt threw the remote detonator to the floor and raised a semi-automatic. "Let's hunt."

Now that Matt had been without Dream State for a few weeks, his mind and bits of memory had started to come back to him. This meant that his improvement had slowed down dramatically, but thank fully not his enthusiasm.

* * *

Dante heard the explosion, but did not flinch. He kept his eyes on Vincent. Nothing else mattered to him. "What are you talking about? Michelle?" he asked through gritted teeth. Out of the corner of his eye, he saw Melina move towards the window, looking down on the situation below.

"Dream State needed a test subject. I may have anonymously leaked information that there was a cure for Vincent's Bitter. There is no such thing, of course. It's ironic, really. Despite all you have done to keep her safe, she will die and it will be because of you. All so she could see your pretty face again. Still, I wouldn't worry about your former blood-sack. It appears you have more pressing matters... Your Majesty."

"Why should I be worried? From the sounds of it, I'd hazard a guess your mystery wolf pack is eager to introduce themselves."

"So let them find me and be done with it."

"I don't think so," Dante said looking at Melina and then back again. "When you get to hell, I want the devil to know who sent you."

Dante bit Vincent as hard as he could, intent on draining Vincent of every ounce of blood he had left. Vincent's face, frozen in a sneer of pain, was becoming pale and dry. Dante merely drank more deeply. Melina took Vincent's shaking hand and bit his wrist to finish the job. After a moment, Dante rose and peered down at Vincent, who was nothing more now than a skeleton with a thin layer of desiccated, stretched skin.

"You're not thinking of going to her, I hope?" Melina asked.

"I need to." He couldn't let Michelle go without seeing her a final time, without proving to himself what Vincent said was true. The sound of rapid gunfire cracking through the air outside the mansion filtered in to them.

"Are you fucking kidding me? Can you not hear what's going on around you? I need you here."

"This is nothing you can't handle, Melina."

"Fuck you! You can't just cop out on this. You're the king now. Take your damn responsibility." Melina thrust her arm toward the window where more gunfire could be heard.

Dante paused, clenched his teeth. "You're right. Free the women. Explain to them what happened. I fear the sight of me would not go over well with them right now."

Melina snorted. “Imagine that. It only *appeared* as if you were betraying them all, is that right?”

Dante did not gratify her snipe with an answer, but instead made his way toward the door.

“By the way…” Melina’s fist came at him and descended hard across his nose. “That’s for ramming my head into the door.” She swept her long red hair behind her shoulder and exited the room before he stopped seeing stars.

“It needed to look real,” Dante grumbled to no one.

He made his way outside where two soldiers of the Elements of Night were in cover on each side of the front door, blindly firing at anything past the flaming car.

“Cease fire,” Dante said.

“What? Are you kidding me?” one screamed.

“It’s a waste of bullets. C’mon, you can’t seriously see anything out there.” Dante indicated the lawn and driveway of the mansion and then realised he had a better reason. “I order you as the king of Sydney.”

The order gave them pause, but they looked him full in the face at this. Dante knew Vincent’s blood must still be all over his mouth and chin. The two folded into their respective covers and stowed their weapons. Still, they were, perhaps understandably, sceptical.

“We’re just supposed to believe you?”

“Not at all,” Dante said, striding past them and into the open night and gunfire. “I’m happy to prove it to you.”

* * *

The wolf abandoned its journey along the ground. It left barely a sound as it bounded along, leaping sleekly from rooftop to rooftop.

When it reached Nicole’s house, it missed the roof and landed on the ground beside her bedroom, digging the nails of its free hand and feet into the cement to steady itself as it helped her to the window. Her feet touched the ground and in the same movement she turned to face the wolf.

The wolf sensed her fear before she moved to back away. It was only a few steps, but the intent was clear. Her eyes roamed over his frame, taking in the changes.

Changes. To Nicholas. That's what she was used to. The wolf raised its hand and stared. The thick, sausage fingers, the not quite inch-long nails, the overgrown arm and palm hair. Nicole surely did not view it as a hand that protected her, but a weapon used to murder. A peculiar feeling welled inside the wolf that it did not expect. A human emotion. Shame. Not for the attack on the punks. But…for having frightened her. The wolf scraped its nails briefly along the base of the windowsill, keeping its eyes off her. It couldn't speak, but it needed to try to communicate with her in some way. Nicole took a hesitant step forward but recoiled once more at the sound the wolf made.

The wolf was instantly alert. Its senses were alive, giving off signals, no, warnings. Something was tracking them. And closing. The wolf growled and snarled at the audacity. But through the beastly rage was the human concern. The wolf would lead this unknown in open combat, and it would destroy it. But it would do so far away from Nicole.

"Wait! Don't go!" Nicole raised her hand and held it palm out.

The wolf paused, eager to stay but unable to speak of the danger approaching. The wolf pressed its gigantic hand against hers. *I know you fear me, but I would never hurt you. You are too important to me.*

* * *

A furious hail of gunfire pelted and pummelled Dante's body, hot lead ripping his skin to pieces, yet he still stood. He held up his hand, as a submission of sorts. Unexpectedly, the gunfire stopped.

"Thank you." Dante locked his knees, struggling to stay up through the sheen of pain clouding his vision. "Show yourself, so we can talk. I'm sure we can come to some agreement."

One crept out, keeping his gun trained on Dante. "We didn't come here to talk. We want what's ours."

"Tell me your name. Perhaps if you tell me what it is you want, I can help you."

"Don't act like you don't know. We want our comrades back."

"Take them. They were never my prisoners."

"Liar," he spat.

Behind and above him, Melina appeared on the veranda with Alex.

Alex gasped and took a few steps into the yard. "Matt? Matt…is that you?"

Matt stood from among the remaining shooters and joined the one speaking. He used his hand to lower the speaker's gun. "Not now, Calibos."

"Matt, what the hell did they do to you?" Alex took another tentative step.

"They…" Matt began, straining through the words. "F-fixed me."

Calibos stared at Alex for a few seconds. "You're the ex? Alex?"

Alex nodded.

"Matty sobs your name in his sleep." Calibos chuckled, thinking this was somehow quite the joke. He then turned back to Dante. "They went in to broker a deal with your king and never came out."

"As I said…take them. Your missing pack members mean nothing to me. Take them and leave."

"Walk into a vampire stronghold with the king still inside? You must think we're stupid," Calibos said.

"The king is dead. Long live me, I guess, as I am the new king. Search the mansion. If you find them, they are yours. I would hazard a guess Melina might know where to start."

Melina gave a curt nod.

"Now if you'll excuse me." Dante limped toward Vincent's—*Mine*, he reminded himself—collection of cars.

"Dante!" Alex called. "Wait!"

"I cannot wait. Michelle is in trouble."

Alex ran up beside him. "Melina told me. I'm driving."

Dante stumbled and Alex caught him and kept him from falling to the ground. "I think that's a good idea," he mumbled.

"God, you're bleeding badly. Are you going to be ok?"

"I just need more time to heal."

Alex helped him into the passenger side of a rather sleek-looking car and quickly ran to the driver's side and hopped in. Dante found the keys in the glove compartment. Thievery obviously wasn't a big issue in the vampire mansion.

"Here," she said, offering her wrist to him.

"No. I need more than what you can give me, and I need you alert to drive."

She started the car and sped off. "I just wanted to say thank you. But I need an explanation. Like, yesterday."

"I won't apologise for the deception, because it was necessary. Vincent needed to believe it. I am sorry it frightened you."

"Frightened me? You scared the shit out of me! And poor Nicole, what about her? You let those arseholes manhandle us, then inject Nick with God knows what. You chained him up and made her think she had to kill him! Jesus…that poor girl."

"It had to look real…" Dante found himself repeating the answer he'd given Melina earlier and wondered if he'd gone too far. He hated the fact that he'd had to betray anyone's trust.

"Trust me, it did. Too bloody real. But why, Dante? Why would you do this to us, even pretending? You risked a hell of a lot on a very shaky plan, where every little thing had to fall in place. Did you not even once think about trusting me with this, talking to me at all?"

"Yes…but that would've been the surest way to get you killed."

"You don't know that for sure."

Dante sighed. "Please do not misunderstand. I had no desire to hurt or frighten anyone, and I do not doubt you possess supreme deception skills when needed. But you cannot hide the pheromone of real fear. Do you think Vincent believed I would turn on you, when I had done so much to keep you alive and close to me? Sure, he could understand my actions regarding a werewolf in the midst, but to completely fool him, you needed to be terrified. Shocked. Feeling betrayed. He would've sensed if you were in on it, then not only would Nick have died, we all would have been killed as well."

"Did you always know? About Nick, I mean."

"No, not until a few days ago. You let it slip that Alicia Slade was his mother. Had I known that, I might have made the connection sooner. I knew, though, that if I realised who he was, it wouldn't be long before others did too, now the wolf was out. That's when I called Vincent and set everything up. I needed a way to get in and get close to Vincent. I knew I couldn't take him alone, so I needed Melina."

"She was in on the whole thing?"

He nodded. "It was only with the both of us that we had a chance to take him down. So I told him I could give him his fugitive and the Alpha wolf, but only on my terms."

"Which were?"

"That no vampire besides himself, be in the mansion. That the

Elements of Night would collect them at my house, and that I would be the one to handle the termination of the wolf."

"Why would he agree to something like that? It doesn't seem very like Vincent to allow himself to be so vulnerable."

"Firstly, because he thought that capturing the wolf and killing it would end the death curse the Messengers of Osiris had placed on him. Little did he know, he was bringing the curse into his home. Secondly, I had something he didn't have: an actual means to kill Nick."

"I don't— What did you have?"

"Nicole."

"What? How…"

"Vincent has always been cruel. He adored the idea that Nick's lover would have to kill him, with the threat of being eaten alive as a consequence. But I trusted that wouldn't happen."

"That was pretty risky. How did you know for sure Nick wouldn't hurt her when he changed?"

"To be honest, I couldn't be certain of that. But I was certain of her. I knew she wouldn't shoot him because of the way she answered me at the dinner table. It was all down to whether she could just handle the sight of the change. If that didn't terrify her into shooting him, she would be fine."

Alex shifted gears and launched the car onto the highway. Dante calculated Michelle's house at about ten minutes away.

"Thank you for protecting him."

"I didn't do this for him."

"What do you mean?"

Dante looked at Alex pointedly.

"Me?"

"I had one day to organise a plan that would save both of your lives. Once Nick's identity was known, what do you think Vincent would've done to you once he'd captured Nick? Vincent wouldn't have cared whether or not you knew Nick was a werewolf. And even though Vincent is dead now, that doesn't stop the problems, or the enemies. In fact, it may increase them. We are all in great danger. As hard as it is to accept, it would be more convenient for me in many ways if Nick was put down. But I know what that would do to you, especially if there was something I could do about it and didn't."

Alex stopped at a red light, and began slapping her thigh agitatedly, waiting for the light to turn green again. "Dante…we have a long, hard road ahead of us. I don't know what we do or where we go from here. Everything will change. But…" She reached over and clasped Dante's trembling hand, sticky from congealing blood. "I meant what I said. But I will ask this one more time. No more lies, no more deceptions. I want to be there. I want to help. Whatever it takes. But—" Alex turned to Dante and held her gaze. "Don't you ever use my nephew like that again. Ever."

Dante eyed her back and gave a brief nod, before leaning his head back. "Please just hurry."

* * *

The wolf raced along, using an abandoned bridge as overhead cover. It headed towards a football field a few metres ahead. The wolf sensed the other change course, coming from the right, set to meet the wolf head on. Perfect.

The wolf leapt high and landed on the crossbar of the goal posts. Sniffing…listening. A rustling behind. The wolf whisked around to see the unknown pursuer leap from the trees and bolt forward, on all fours. The wolf snarled and jumped to the ground, ready to charge. The other's scent filled the air now. A female. She slowed her pace and began walking forward on two legs.

Her eyes were silver, her features had changed, but the wolf would recognise its own mother anywhere. Alicia Slade stood tall, taking in the sight that met her eyes. And then, in a slow movement, Alicia got down on one knee, bowing her head.

The wolf touched her chin lightly with his fingernails, raising her just as slowly. It would not have its mother remain on her knees.

Mother embraced pup. She smelt his hair, lightly licked his ears, scraped her cheek against his and tightened her arms around him. She had found her pup. The wolf spotted tears in her eyes and a dull whimpering from her throat. So much the wolf wanted to say, but nothing compared to wanting to hear its mother's voice again.

But in the end, the moon, which robbed both of speech when full, showed that sometimes words were not necessary as it gleamed high above their continuous embrace.

Chapter 39

Did You Lose Something?

Dante and Alex burst through the door of Michelle's apartment. There was no time to knock, Dante was frantic. Usually he would need an invitation to enter a mortal's home. But he had been invited before, many times. He had cooked dinner for Michelle in this apartment, he'd made love to her here. Endured her god awful reality tv shows here, on her 'couch snuggle fest' nights she loved so much.

The lights were all out, bits and pieces of clothes were everywhere, the place looking unkempt. That was not like Michelle. They both called out to her yet no sound was returned. But Dante knew she was here. He followed his nose, locating her scent.

He knocked down the door that led to her bedroom, Alex shot in after him.

"Michelle!" Dante yelled.

"Oh god, no," Alex moaned.

Michelle lay face up on her bed, vary pale, with her eyes glossy and open. Alex pressed her fingers against Michelle's throat, feeling for a pulse. She gulped and shook her head. "I think she's—"

"No, I hear her heartbeat, but it is irregular. We need to get her to a hospital fast." He moved to lift her when he spotted a shoebox filled with vials containing the tell-tale blue glowing liquid along with syringe. In a rage, he thrust the box to the floor and stomped down on it. Glass crunched and the floor was flooded with Dream State, which evaporated in a puff of smoke.

"Wow," breathed Alex. "What's in that stuff?"

Dante gritted his teeth and tried to swallow the lump in his throat. He picked up Michelle and carried her out, struggling with his newfound weakness..

* * *

"NO!" Julian screamed. "No no no! How many times do you have to be told, drink slowly! The fear makes the blood taste better"

"Fuck that. I want more." Miller licked his greedy lips.

He had just finished off the second human. At this rate, Julian was going to be out of targets much sooner than he'd expected. When his father asked him to take his new protégé and train tonight, Julian knew it was best to obey.

He had meticulously shown the kid how to plan and strategize his attacks, explained when and where to hunt, demonstrated the best way to feed, but it was all like talking to a brick wall. At one point, they were hidden in a copse of trees, watching people, waiting for appropriate prey when Miller jumped out and ravaged the first woman he saw. Her husband tried to attack him, but Julian belted him unconscious. Miller fed wastefully, spilling more blood than he consumed. Within seconds, the woman was dead, and the idiot kid had only ingested a quarter of what he should have. Before Julian could stop him, Miller had snapped the neck of the husband just as he was trying to get a decent feeding grip on his neck. Julian admitted that Miller was extraordinarily strong, even for a newborn, but that strength was wasted.

"You are too impatient. Even your mother learnt that steady wins the race." Julian gestured to Lauren, who had appeared behind Miller.

The kid flinched, startled. "I hate it when you do that invisibility thing. That shit freaks me out."

"It's called camouflage, and it's very useful when you're hunting. And you should begin practicing using your own power," Julian said.

"Whatever. Woo, I can manipulate shadows," Miller moaned. "Hold me while I think about how shitty that is."

"Every power is useful, everyone has a purpose and you would not be who you are without it. Do you not agree, Lauren?"

"Mm-hmm," she replied in a bored tone. She then perked up with a much happier and far more sarcastic. "I mean, yes indeed, Sir Julian, sir."

"Good, then we are done here."

"What? Already? Oh come on, just a few more. I'm starving. Hey you…" he said, looking at Lauren. "Aren't you like our bar wench? Can't you get us some food or something?"

Lauren glared at him, Julian burst out laughing. "I knew I chose right. Keep the women in line so they never forget their place. And you, my boy, never forget that they crave being dominated."

He placed an arm over Miller's shoulder and looked back at Lauren. "Go back to the mansion and wait there. We shall save you an artery."

* * *

Dante pulled up outside the mansion. He had dropped Michelle off at the hospital and the news wasn't good. She was in a waking coma, completely unresponsive to any stimulation, awake but not aware. The Dream State had eroded her brain to the point where she couldn't fall asleep or wake up. The doctor had only been marginally helpful. *"Mr Delavega, I'm sorry… Just like the other cases… Nothing we can do… Can make her comfortable… Won't be long…"*

Dante got out of the car and took the porch steps two at a time, but paused with his hand on the doorknob. He wasn't ready to enter the mansion, to walk into what awaited him inside, both literally and figuratively. He took a deep breath, steeling himself, when Melina opened the door.

"What's the news?"

Dante shook his head. Alex followed up the stairs. "There's nothing we can do but wait. And even that doesn't seem hopeful," she said.

Dante changed the subject. "What was so important that you needed us back here so quickly?"

Melina led him into the lounge where they found Calibos and Matt surrounded by four Elements of Night, guns at the ready.

"What is going on?"

"They're gone," Melina replied.

"What?"

"The rest of the wolf pack. I knew where Vincent had been holding them, using them for the production of Dream State. The tubes, the cots, all there, but the vat was gone, and the pack was gone, though they must have left quite recently."

"Convenient that you were so willing to allow us to take something that was no longer here." Calibos glared at Dante.

Dante ignored him. "Vincent must have moved them after getting his letter. He didn't want his cash cow scheme to come undone, so relocated it."

Melina looked doubtful. "I don't think so. No one knew anything about it—not even within the mansion. That's why it was so…successful. Anyway, where could he take a production like that?"

"Wait a minute. There was at least one other person who knew about Dream State, that blue stuff. Dante, when you smashed it, I recognised the colour. I've seen it before, being made. In the lab…" Alex looked into the fireplace, forlorn.

"Of course…"

"Who made Dream State? I thought Vincent did?"

"Vincent was no chemist. There was no way he could have done it himself. I'd just suspected he'd brought someone in here. But he wouldn't need to if Hershel Rasmussen was helping him."

"That Nazi scientist?" Melina asked. "Where is he?"

"Raven Apartments," Dante answered.

Melina snorted. "So you want to attack the one place containing heaps of our kind and guarded by a crack security firm that are probably going to be prepared and waiting for us? What do you plan to use? Sub-machine guns, rifles and the like?"

"That's about it," Dante replied.

"Sounds like fun." Melina grinned.

Dante turned to address the Elements of Night, as well as Calibos and Matt. "I would not advise anyone to stay here. Julian may be back at any moment with that teleportation of his."

They did as he asked, moving swiftly.

Alex looked up at him, shook her head at whatever she was about to say, kissed him quickly and hugged him. "Be safe and good luck. I love Michelle too, you know."

"I know, but I am not doing this for her only."

"Yes you are," Melina and Alex said together.

Melina folded her arms and raised her eyebrows at Alex. "Where's my kiss goodbye?"

Alex smiled nervously before Melina cleared her throat. Alex realised she was serious when she stuck her cheek out. "Um…ok."

Alex leaned in to give her a peck and Melina turned her face and kissed her full on the lips. Alex waved her hands in the air, just beginning to close them over Melina's shoulders when Melina broke off the kiss. "Yummy."

Dante rolled his eyes. "For god's sake, leave the poor girl alone." He gently grabbed Alex's arm and took her the few steps she needed to get her bearings back. She mumbled something and pointed to the car they had driven back in before turning and leaving.

"Did you have to?" Dante said.

"Of course. She has a really soft mouth. Like yours if I remember correctly. Anyway, what's good enough for you is good enough for me." Melina walked forward slowly and folded her hands behind her back, looking up at him. "What are your orders for me?" she asked, her voice soft and kind.

It was hard for Dante to know if it was an act. It was harder still for him to see her behave the way he remembered. Apart from her fire, the gentleness underneath it was one of the reasons he had fallen in love with her so long ago.

"I would not think to give you orders."

"Because I'm special to you?"

Dante made to touch her lips with his thumb but dropped his hand. "Because it's a waste of time and you would do your own thing anyway."

Melina followed Dante out, chanting. "Let's go and be the good guys. Let's go fight the good fight and all that jazz."

"Let's just survive," Dante muttered.

* * *

Behind them, back inside the mansion. Lauren shimmered into view, head cocked to one side, and watched them walk away.

Chapter 40

Welcome To Raven Apartments

The moon was the only light shining on Raven Apartments. The complete absence of stars mirrored the atmosphere below. Tense and very dark. Yet Dante viewed the structure with equal amounts of hope and fear. If he could have guaranteed the wolves were here, he could've just told Calibos to "go fetch" them. But retaliation from Calibos and his pups wasn't the only reason Dante felt apprehensive. He needed to find out from Herschel whether there was a cure for Dream State. Dante was not going to let anything happen to Michelle. *Anything else,* he muttered and cursed himself. The wolves were Calibos's problem. Herschel was Dante's.

It looked like every agent ever employed to guard the premises was on duty, giving Dante more reason to believe the wolves were here. Vincent would've increased the security to maximum after receiving his Messengers of Osiris threat. Every floor was covered; from bulky silhouettes obviously clad in riot gear to more tidy figures in suits and ear pieces patrolling the grounds, there was a distinct feel of government protection at Raven Apartments tonight.

Dante could hear them counting off position and clearance checks every five minutes, starting from the roof down. He presumed if any guard failed to report, the place would go into lockdown.

They were good. He could admit that. These guards were well trained and well prepared. But they weren't vampires, at least not all of them. Dante stood with the rest of the group out of range of them and studied their movements, running through a number of scenarios until one stuck out in his mind. Dante eyed the building's employee car park and turned to Calibos. "I don't suppose you have another of those fancy bombs, do you?"

* * *

Julian teleported into the mansion and knew instantly something was wrong. The house was empty and the air smelt of familiar blood, gasoline and smoke. Julian ducked to look out the window and saw the remnants of the car. *Father!* Then he shouted it. "Father? Where are you?"

Julian teleported in a panic. First to the coffin chamber. Empty. The Hall of Relics. The viewing room. He could see the chains ripped from the walls, the moon shining through, the steel entrance crumpled and tossed to the side like cardboard. Julian flashed to Vincent's chambers. He walked forward with shaky steps and then sunk to his knees. He reached out and hovered his hand over his father's pale, dry scalp. "You fool," he whispered through gritted teeth. "Why did you send me away? Is that what *he* asked? You played into his hands. He was always your favourite. *I could've saved you, father!"*

Julian pulled drawers out, looking for anything he could find that would piece together what had happened. The scent of Dante and Melina lingered, but they had existed in an uneasy peace with Vincent for so long, there was obviously some reason. He caught sight of a crumpled up piece of paper beneath one corner of the desk. Kneeling, he snatched it up and realised it looked familiar. The heavy paper stock, the texture and colour, he had seen this stationery before when the Messengers of Osiris had commanded him to retake control of what would become the Eureka Stockade.

Julian smoothed the paper, read.

Miller sprinted up to the door. "There you are…whoa. What the hell happened here?"

Julian flicked up a hand as he finished. "So, we got caught. Still doesn't explain why father even got fucking Dante involved. It was done, there was nothing… What is that?"

Miller had produced another piece of wadded up paper and was reading it. "Another note, I guess?"

Julian held out a hand. Miller continued to read. "Give it here now," Julian demanded, and this time it was presented to him. He would have to teach this boy some respect, but there was no time for that now. Julian placed the two letters side by side on the desk and looked from one to the other. "Very interesting. Dante, what were you up to?"

"Are they supposed to be different?" Miller asked. "This one's a lighter shade."

"No, they are not. This one," he said holding up the one Miller had presented to him, "is fake. Absolutely worthless. Dante wrote it himself. And yet it was good enough to fool my father. At least it would've distracted him long enough that Dante could do whatever he'd had planned."

Julian thought he had the gist of it now. The wolf had been brought here and escaped. Melina and Dante had killed Vincent. *Oh, Father, if only you had accepted me. I would have protected you.* It made him sick to his stomach to think it, but he had more important things than avenging his father to worry about.

Without a moment's further dwelling, Julian marched with Miller to the elevators and took it down.

"You have been…helpful. Calm under fire," Julian addressed Miller, gaze held firmly on the mirrored doors.

"Man, I have no idea what the fuck is goin' on. But you are all I've got. You saved my life. Whatever you need, I'll do it."

"Very good. I will make you no promises save for that I will be a better father to you than mine was."

"So," Miller looked sidelong at Julian. "Why are we using the elevator instead of you just beaming or zapping or whatever it is that you do?"

"My father used the Waratah plant in the cement when these lower rooms were being built. It counters my ability to teleport."

And repel vampires much the way garlic was supposed to. Julian was briefly taken back to early Sydney when the fucking things were everywhere. Hung on door ways and some even around their necks. There was an unspoken myth that when the Waratah was not in bloom, people wound up missing or dead. It was with a sense of disgust, Julian realized that the Waratah protected the people of NSW and vampires were partially the reason for it being the state's emblem.

The doors opened and they both stepped out into the Information Centre. Shelves full of computers and components lined the walls and there were screens everywhere. Many of them showed the various rooms covered by the mansion's security cameras. A glass door showed an inner room with even more computers that Clive kept at a cooler temperature. Julian rarely bothered going in there, but now he strode over and slid the door open.

"Clive," Julian snarled, looking around. "You had better be here, you snivelling coward. If I find out you had anything to do with helping Dante, I will feed your cock to a rabid dog while it's still on your body."

"Doesn't seem like anybody's here. Who the hell is Clive anyway?"

Julian let the server room door close again. "A hacker my father uses…used, for years. I need him to send an email immediately."

"Email? That's all you need? I can do that. It's piss easy."

"How is it you know this?"

"Everyone does these days." Miller shrugged. "I guess you really are older than you look."

Julian grunted and indicated the desk chair. Miller sat and tapped at the keyboard, starting up some program. "What's his user name and password?"

"Vincent and flayed." Julian recalled.

"Sick," Miller smiled. "Ok," he said, scanning the screen. "Here we go. Who do you want to send it to?"

"Look for anything that has been recently sent. There is bound to be something from Damien Creed."

"Yep, here it is." Miller clicked and a reply box opened.

"Very well, write this: Creed, It's Julian. Situation critical. Mansion compromised. Vincent dead. Alpha still alive."

"Ok, sent. Now what?"

"We wait."

"Didn't you say this is going to England? It'll take ages before we get a reply."

"If I know Creed, he'll have this email chain patrolled twenty-four hours a day until he gets news the Alpha has been killed. Now he knows the truth, we likely won't have to wait long at all."

* * *

"North! Hostile incoming!" a guard screamed. The car headed straight for the opening of the apartments and fast. Dante took the opportunity to sprint around the back as the guards patrolling the area scrambled to the front. He leapt high and grabbed a window ledge, steadied himself, then crawled upwards as fast as he could, listening to the alerted guards and judging their positions.

The men that manoeuvred in front of the building stood their ground, pumping every round they could at the oncoming vehicle's windshield. The bullets destroyed the glass it was plane to see there was no driver.

"Take cover!"

Dante heard the car smash into the stairs leading up to the opening and flip forward, crashing into glass and steel before exploding, sending bodies and more glass flying.

As his fingers gripped the edge of the roof, the three men guarding it ran for the opposite end, peering over to see the billowing flames of the car wave furiously up at them. Dante inhaled a second time, these were vampires, not men. Just what Dante wanted.

The leader put his hand to his ear.

"Street team! Does anyone copy? Does anyone copy, over? Level team, we have a situation here. Stay where you are! That's an order. If they get past us you're the only protection for the cargo."

He cocked his gun and placed one foot on the ledge, peering through his scope, then Dante struck. "Right, fellas, this is what we trained for…" Dante snaked behind them, gripped the chins of the men on either side of the leader and twisted quickly. "Look sharp…fellas?"

The leader turned and Dante snatched the gun out of his hand before he had moved his body the entire way.

"I'm so glad this is what you've trained for," Dante said, snapping the gun in two hands.

The vampire stared at Dante and then reached for his pistol, before Dante launched a kick to his chest. A second later his body was hurtling to the ground, screaming as he dropped.

* * *

"And that's our signal," Melina said to the Elements of Night and the pack behind her.

"A frontal attack, are you serious?" Calibos paused while loading his pistol. "Just because we're alongside you, don't think we'll fall for a trap. You aren't trusted."

"Oh my god, let me get you some cheese to go with that whine. I thought you were all bad-arse killers?" Melina scoffed. She stood and faced the opening, spotting the guards form a defensive layout, cocking their weapons one by one. "You wanna see a real killer, I'll show you a real killer," she said as her fangs extended slowly. "Besides," looked up at Dante. "He's at least one up. There ain't no way he is beating me at this game."

* * *

"Ahh, lookie here." Miller rubbed his hands excitedly and clicked on the reply.

"What does it say?"

"He's pissed. The first bit is all in capitals… Wow, so intimidating."

"WHAT DOES IT SAY?" Julian may have to start this kid's lessons sooner rather than later, just to keep Miller from getting on his last nerve.

"Okay, and I quote: You dead shits are absolutely fucking useless. Forget telling you about a plan. I will deal with this myself. I am coming to Sydney with my best men. As the mansion has been compromised, it is not safe to divulge anything further. Find a safe computer to contact me and delete this. If it's not too difficult."

Julian growled. *Smug bastard.* "Let us leave."

They walked into the elevator together, but Miller turned and faced him as the doors closed. "Wait! So what about your dad? Those fuckers killed him."

"That fact does not escape me." Julian countered as the elevator shot upwards. "And they will pay. But the best revenge is the one they don't know is coming."

Julian gripped Miller's shoulder and disappeared with a pop as soon as he was out of reach of the Waratah.

* * *

Lauren materialised as soon as she heard the pop and released her hand from over Clive's mouth.

"Is there any way to stop them sending another email? From contacting him?" Lauren asked.

"No, I'm sorry. They could go anywhere and use any computer, any email. And what good would it do now? This Creed guy is already on his way, he said."

"Fuck. Can you find out when these beasts are arriving? Isn't there any goddamn thing you can do?"

"Look. I, uh, I can't stop them, but I might be able to slow them down. They wouldn't use commercial airliners, not with the money they have. So it would be a private jet. From London." Clive pulled up the desk chair and began a search. "I can monitor air traffic from here. When I see a special clearance request, I can pin them down, but not for long. It will at least give us some indication of how long we have. I can mark their plane for a special check or something when they get here, but they will get in eventually."

"Do it. Do all of it."

"Ok..." Lauren looked down at Clive's trembling fingers. He clenched his fists to still them and started typing again. Beads of sweat were forming on his brow and trickles of blood were running down his neck from under a gauze on his neck. "What's wrong with you?"

"I'm feeling a bit hot. I think the love bite you gave me is infected." He gave a half-hearted chuckle.

My bite? I did that? "Oh shit, lackey. I'm so sorry." Lauren licked a fang, cutting her tongue as she peeled the gauze off with her fingernails. "Come here."

"No, it's ok…" Clive leaned away, but without much conviction.

"Oh, shut up." Lauren held the side of his face with one hand and licked his neck, mopping up the blood and using her own to heal the wound. "Better?"

Clive's heart pumped faster, bringing a delicious smell to the surface of his skin. *Better,* she knew.

"Yes…thank you."

Lauren certainly felt better. "This might freak you out a bit, but boy do you taste good. I haven't eaten in hours but I feel, refreshed."

"Uh… That's nice." Clive peered at her for a moment, but went back to typing.

Lauren planted a kiss on his cheek. "I never thanked you for coming to get me that night. Thank you, lackey."

Clive blushed, making him look even tastier, and was also somehow very endearing. The corners of his mouth twitched and he leaned over his computer with renewed vigour.

After a few moments, he asked, "Do you really think Dante can win? Against Julian and an entire pack?"

"I don't know, but he is willing to try. And I'm going to help him. Dante was the only one to believe in me. He could've killed me last year in the car park but he didn't. Even after everything I've done, everyone else would've dropped me. He gave me a second chance. I owe him."

* * *

Melina took the lead, several steps in front of Calibos and the Elements of Night. On the other side of the flaming wreckage, she estimated twenty guards lay in wait. She heard them, inside what was left of the lobby of Raven Apartments, raise their weapons, expecting the attack, holding steady. They whispered their cute little code words, as if that meant anything. Death had come for them. Melina led the Elements of Night through the flames and into their line of sight, heading straight for them.

"Fire!"

The guards had barely squeezed their triggers when Melina and the Elements took off in all directions. Bullets from the guards flew everywhere, but the only thing they hit was furniture, stone or glass. They were just too fast. The shots from the Elements however found their mark again and again. Guards dropped from bullets to the head left and right. They were the lucky ones.

Melina gleefully laughed, cutting, tearing and biting her way through body after body, too fast for any human guard to see. As the last man fell, Melina was soaked in crimson and not a drop of it was her own.

"Best…shower…ever." She raised her index finger and licked it.

She swore as a piercing pain jolted through her shoulder. A bullet. She turned and faced the shooters direction, finding an attractive middle-aged woman quivering in the elevator, pointing a small six shooter at her.

Melina smiled and placed her hands on her knees, addressing her the way you would a puppy.

"Oh, that's *so adorable*! Do you sleep with that under your pillow?"

Without another word, Melina had snatched the gun and held it under the woman's chin, forcing her to lay down half way in the elevator. "I won't kill you for shooting me, ok?" Melina said, looking down to face her and smiling. "Tell me your name."

"S…Samantha."

"Wait a minute. You're the one that only fucks vampires right?"

"What…no…no…yes."

Melina now recognized her. She had seen her at the mansion once or twice. Samantha. The vampire whore. Now a 9-to-5 switch bitch for Vincent. Well, not anymore.

Melina smiled warmly. "Isn't it true you got Dante to feed off you? Vincent told me you humped him for fun when he didn't really want it."

"Yes…once," she replied. "Does that really matter?"

"Of course!" Melina exclaimed happily, placing her hand on the door of the elevator. Suddenly she turned her expression cold, her true feelings towards this piece of shit. "It matters to me, bitch."

"NO!"

Melina slammed the elevator door closed, crushing Samantha's body so hard the two ends folded inwards. Her face and mouth smacking against the cold metal, as did her knees and feet on the other side, breaking several places.

* * *

Dante crashed through the window of Hershel's penthouse.

"What on earth is going on here?" he demanded.

"I've come for a cure and the wolf prisoners," Dante said, rising slowly, flaring his fangs as he took in the seven vats of Dream State lining the wall, all with tubes containing blood travelling through a hole leading to a back room.

"Have you gone insane? There is no cure. What prisoners? There is no one else here."

"Don't lie to me," Dante roared, lifting Herschel in the air. "I want the cure for Dream State?"

"There is none. It isn't a disease. It was designed for vampires, and we are immune to its ill effects. If humans are stupid enough to take it, they deserve to die."

Dante turned his head, smelling something. He dropped Hershel to the floor and moved towards his desk. Now he could hear it, whimpering, sniffling. He pulled the desk from its bolts with one hand and revealed a small boy in the foetal position, scared out of his mind and sobbing. He was holding his arm, bleeding from two puncture marks near his wrist.

"You feed off children?" Dante asked, still looking at the young boy.

Dante did not wait for an answer, leaping on top of Hershel and beating his head against the floor. Dante heard a pop and blood poured out of a wound he created. He lifted and slammed him into the dentist chair.

Dante walked towards a vat of Dream State and unhooked a delivery hose, bringing it over to Herschel. "Your project is over."

Herschel laughed, coughing and spitting out blood. "You think you're so smart. Do you have any idea how much money I bring in for Vincent? How many projects I have in the pipeline? How many experiments I oversee? How many sinister things I keep under wraps? What will happen to them when I'm gone? Have you even thought about that?"

"Not really," Dante said. "I've really only thought about this."

He plunged the hose as far as it could go into a screaming Hershel's cranium, and kicked the chair towards the window. The brute force ripped the holds off the other vats. They and the table they were on, followed Hershel sailing out the window and plummeted down onto the flaming car, obliterating him and the vats in seconds.

Dante sensed that Herschel was lying about the prisoners, not about the cure. There was no cure. No hope for Michelle. For any of them.

Dante retreated his fangs as he closed in on the small boy, who still scurried backwards to the wall.

"I swear I'm not going to hurt you, and neither will he anymore."

"Stay away from me," the terrified boy screamed.

Dante lowered himself to one knee. "Can you tell me your name?" he said gently.

The boy shook his head fiercely. "Go away!"

"You heard him," said Melina. She had come up the elevator, and shifted Dante out of the way. "Move, you big ugly thing you!"

Melina knelt in Dante's place as Dante backed far away. He knew what she was trying and hoped it worked on the poor boy, although the fact she was covered in blood didn't seem like it would help the situation much.

Melina made her voice go soft, and velvety smooth. When she spoke, she didn't sound like a vampire, but a teenager, as pure as New York snow. "Oh honey, please don't cry. I know how terrible it must've been for you all this time, but that man was a monster and we're…" she paused. "We're not like that. We'd never hurt you sweetie. We just want to get you home. We need to get that bite fixed. You've been so brave through all this. Will you let me help you?"

"Can you find my dad?" the boy asked meekly.

"Of course. Is he here in the building?"

The boy nodded.

"Then we'll go right after I fix that bite for you."

Melina held out her hand, and smiled at him, one that spoke to the boy of trust and love. Slowly, the boy eased his way over to her and took her hand with his injured one. No matter how young, Melina's voice unconsciously drew in all males. A siren song none could resist.

She bit her finger and rubbed his wrist before he could even stop her. She let him go so he could see the instant effect for himself.

"Now that wasn't so hard, was it…?"

“Zachary,” he said.

“Oh.” She smiled. “I love that name. “Look, see? All gone.”

Zachary seemed to brighten up just a little and found the energy to hug Melina. “Thank you.”

She lifted him into her arms and rubbed his back. “You’re more than welcome, brave boy.”

CHAPTER 41

RISE OF THE ALPHA

Dante watched Melina take Zachary down the lift to find the boy's father. Dante needed to find something else. He knew the wolves must be in here somewhere. He scanned the room, somewhat chagrined at the destruction he'd caused. He had not really been acting like himself lately. *What's wrong with me?* he wondered. *What's different now?* As he tried to play the last weeks over in his head, he spotted a portion of the wall that looked…odd. Dante approached the spot, tilting his head this way and that, and tried to determine what was so strange. *Perhaps my temper tantrum served a good purpose this time.*

stayed behind, following the cords that dangled from the hole in the wall. Now the bench was no longer there, Dante noticed the hidden door leading behind the wall the cords were fed through.

A bench had been in front of this wall before, and Dante had pried it violently from its brackets and thrown it across the room to frighten Herschel. Now there was a hole in the plasterboard wall, some dangling electrical wires visible within. He peered closer to see what their purpose might be and when he took a step, shifting his weight from one foot to the other, he felt a small depression in the floor and heard a click. The broken wall swung open.

Dante stepped into a cramped room and saw the four beds and their sleeping occupants, all attached to an enormous vat of Dream State. So that was how Vincent had controlled their monthly shifts: every full moon they had been unconscious the whole time. *Ironic that the drug being used on them is also made from them.*

Dante looked over all of them and then to the vat itself, and a digital read out of Dream State levels.

He could remove the tubes, but there was no guarantee they would live if he did. Vincent had claimed that humans deprived of Dream State would die, but who knew how it would be with werewolves. How easy it would be if they could just die painlessly. He could tell Calibos there was nothing that could be done. Even if Calibos suspected something, he was surrounded by Elements of Night. But that wasn't who he was. And despite the trouble that he was potentially bringing, these men did not deserve to die like that.

"Don't make me regret this," he said to himself as he switched the transfer of Dream State off.

* * *

Melina lifted Zachary's father's eyelids and saw only a man in a catatonic state; there didn't seem to be any hope of recovery.

"Can you help him?" The boy's voice sounded feeble, much younger than his age might otherwise have indicated. Melina wondered just how long this had been going on.

"I don't know, darling, but the man upstairs and I will try."

He nodded, looking up at her, eyes filled with sincerity, hope, longing.

Melina crouched down, cupping his chin with her hands. "Look at me, Zachary," she said slowly. "For right now, I don't want you to worry about anything. You're feeling tired, so you should lie down and have a little nap while my friend and I figure out a way to help you and your father, okay?"

Zachary looked like he had more questions, but before he could shape any of them, Melina pressed her fingers into the back of his neck and caught him as he slumped forward.

"Come on. Lie down next to dad. That's the boy."

Behind her, the door opened. Melina heard Dante's footsteps as he strode in. "Well?"

"It doesn't look good for the father. He won't wake up. We need to get him into a hospital, for all the good it will do. The boy will need to be given to the proper authorities. What did you find?"

"The wolves are here, as I suspected. I need to get them out and back to the mansion before they wake up. Hopefully, they will be more willing to make peace in a less hostile setting. I'll call the Elements to bring vans and stretchers."

"They can help move Zachary and his father too," Melina said.

"So what was all that in the elevator?" Dante asked, jerking his head toward the obliterated corpse of Samantha.

"Art. Do you like it?" Melina asked, raising her hands, spreading them out over her imagined canvas. "I call it Slut Punishment…by Melina."

* * *

Nicole awoke to sunlight streaming in through the window and a finger stroking her cheek. At first she thought she was dreaming, but she gasped and sat upright as realisation came.

"Oh my god. Are you ok?" She grabbed Nick's shoulders. He seemed to be back to his old self.

"I'm fine, but I was going to ask you the same question."

"I was fine, thanks to you, or you know…"

"The wolf, it's ok you can say it."

"You remember?"

"I remembered everything this time."

"Where did you go after you left here?"

"I sensed another werewolf tracking me. I didn't want it to find you so I ran to draw it away. I finally encountered it in a football field about two miles from here."

Nicole gulped. "Did you…kill it?"

Nick laughed at this. "Oh my god, no! It was my mum."

She punched him on the arm then laughed herself. "Don't laugh. How could I have known?"

"Ow!" Nick feigned injury and rubbed his arm where she'd punched it.

"So wow, your mom. She's here? She's ok?"

"She's fine," Nick smiled.

"Where is she now?"

"Well, we were both wolves last night. So of course we couldn't talk, right?"

Nicole nodded.

"Even so, she accompanied me back to the mansion."

"Why would you go back there?" Nicole asked, astonished.

"I had to save Alex and Margaret." Nick reminded her. "But when we got there, it was deserted. There was a bombed out car in the driveway, and everyone had left. And the remaining scent of Alex and her mum told me they weren't there anymore. I doubled back to Alex's apartment and saw lights on there. I got close enough to listen and heard them fighting."

"Fighting? About what?"

"Me." Nick sighed. "Margaret doesn't trust me anymore, thanks to…what I am. But Alex stood up for me. The last I heard, Alex left and caught a cab somewhere. When I knew she was ok, I came back here."

"But you didn't come back last night. I was really worried."

"I did, but I didn't come in. Felix was in the house."

"Felix? Oh, of course!" Nicole said, smacking her head with her palm. "That's why he went so nuts the other night. So what happened?"

"You have a very intelligent cat. He didn't leave his post for a second. I had to wait in the bushes. Only when the sun came up and I reverted back, did he relax."

"Why didn't you wake me?"

Nick shrugged. "You looked so peaceful, so I let you sleep."

Nicole looked him over properly for the first time and realised he was shirtless and his pants were ripped along the seams where his thighs had expanded. She lightly ran her fingers along his shoulder.

"Nikki, we have to talk."

"Yes. we do," she nodded. "You first."

"I spoke to my mum this morning, and she said, well, she thinks that I may have been misleading you."

"What do you mean?"

"I guess there is such a thing called the Alpha Pull. It's something that Alphas use to inspire feelings in those important to them. Loyalty in their Betas, fear from their enemies, and lust from potential mates. Some kind of ultra-pheromone thing. When I woke up this morning, she told me it was very strange that I changed after all this time. Normally, a werewolf shifts for the first time around the onset of puberty." Nick swallowed, looking a bit uncomfortable. "Anyway, one of the questions she asked was whether I had slept with anyone recently. I told her I found someone I love."

"Nick, please don't—"

"Wait, please just let me get this out. She asked me how we'd met. When I told her that you were a counsellor and you'd been reluctant to see me, because of your job and your ethical reputation, she thought there might be a chance I used the Pull without knowing it. Then I remembered that you seemed to come around very quick, going from 'It can't happen' to having eight orgasms. I was so happy that I didn't think anything of it, but maybe I should've. You fought a guy over me, which, you gotta admit, was kinda irrational and not very much like you at all. But—it *is* something a mate would do for their Alpha.

"Look, I don't know the truth, but what I do know is I don't want you by a trick. Mum told me this is how my dad got her, and when she found out, the Pull wore off. She tried to claw his face to shreds. She told me it was up to me to tell you. I know it means I could lose you forever. So I…" He looked pained, trying to get as much out before she lost her mind at him. Little did he know, that was the last thing she was thinking. "I have to be honest with you—"

Nicole seized his hands and shushed him. "My turn now. I spoke to someone last night too. Dr Sarsky left me a voicemail. When I called him, he said he couldn't reverse the Board of Education's decision. Their ruling stands as long as Miller's family say so."

"Oh…I'm sorry."

"But, there's more. He said I can still do my degree and earn even better accreditation through him. I can have just as good, probably better, a career now because he will personally mentor me. The only thing, is…I have to travel with him."

Nick tensed. "Travel? Where would you go?"

"To Europe. For three years."

Nick looked down and nodded. "Well, take the time you need to think about…" He looked up again and caught her expression. "Wait…

You already agreed, didn't you?"

Nicole thought she prepared herself for this, but she did not expect to be struck dumb at that moment. She was doing the right thing, so why couldn't she look at him? She felt the sting of brimming tears fall, unable to voice a response.

Nick placed his hand on her knee. "It's ok."

"No, it's not. You just said the most amazing…that you…" Nicole gestured with her hands, attempting to jostle the word out. *Love me*. "I'm so sorry. You're the last person in the world I'd want to hurt. I thought long and hard about it and there was only one reason I would have for staying—and that's you. But all those years, all that I've worked for, would have been for nothing. I wanted that all the love and devotion I put into this work to not be wasted. I wanted to help people, to share what I've learned. If I go with the professor, all the shit that's happened would be like it never was. Clean slate. The chance for everything I wanted, presented for me there on a platter. Nick, I just…I can't bet everything on a whirlwind romance."

It seemed an age later when she finally got a reply. "When do you leave?"

"The end of the week."

"He doesn't screw around, huh? It's ok. We said that this had no expectations. You always said you wanted to pursue your career, and now you have the chance. Who am I to ask you to stay? All that I am, everything I feel…I have nothing to offer you in comparison."

"Nick, that's got nothing to do with it. Don't be that way. You're better than this."

"I'm not trying to get sympathy, really. It's the facts. Of course I want you to stay. I want us to have that whirlwind romance. I want us to ride into the sunset together. But that's only in stories. This is real. Real life doesn't always happen like that. The reality is that after last night I'm wanted. And I'm a werewolf. Hard to get around that fact."

"What I saw last night, it was…"

"Scary," Nick finished for her.

"Terrifying," she added. "But it was also amazing. Vampires and werewolves. Myths and legends walking and talking. Real. What's happened to you is a miracle."

"I wouldn't count the desire and ability to tear people apart as a miracle exactly." Nick frowned.

"You—the wolf—you weren't like that at all!" Nicole exclaimed. "As the wolf, you held me the same as you do when you're like this. Even the way you looked at me was the same."

"It's because it was me. I could actually control what I did."

"Really? All that was you?" She wasn't surprised really. She had seen it in his eyes.

Nick nodded. "I still can't believe you didn't shoot. You had no idea I wouldn't attack."

Nicole ran her fingertips over his chest. "I think I did. I know what's inside your heart. Never forget, I believe in you."

"Thank you." Nick took her hand and kissed her fingers before rising and moving towards her window. "I should go. I'll contact you before you leave."

And just like that, he was gone.

* * *

Nick pushed through the tree branches and met his mother in the nearby park.

Alicia stroked his face. "Are you ok?"

"No," Nick replied, pulling away, but then flashing his mother a look of apology.

She smiled and lifted her hands. "You're not a little boy anymore. I understand.

They walked side by side in silence for a moment.

"At least I know I didn't have the Pull influencing her. If it was, she never would have been able to decide to leave like that, right? Is that how it works?"

"Yes."

"Well then," Nick mustered a smile. "Silver lining and all that." He reached into his pocket and handed the contents over. "I guess you can take this back."

Alicia accepted the thing she had given him only a few hours before. Her own engagement ring. Alicia had made it clear that if Nick truly felt something for Nicole, now they were mated, he should follow his heart. Just as Alphas all over the world did. Just as Wilson had.

Wilson had come to Australia, a young brash Alpha that wanted to rebel against vampire law forbidding his kind entry. He knew he would be discovered; he simply wanted the vampires to know he had the balls to do it. What he didn't count on was falling in love with a girl on her school trip. Unfortunately, the vampires of Melbourne discovered him on the very night he'd slept with Alicia. So he fled without a word, concerned they would discover her as well, and think they were both wolves. He could leave the country, she couldn't. She would go back to Sydney completely unaware of the world he was saving her from.

When he returned to England, Wilson used the Alpha Pull to great effect, bedding many a hapless maiden. But Alicia had left him with a strange but wonderful scent that night, something he couldn't forget even thousands of miles away. She stayed on his mind. He heard her crying in her sleep, she spoke to him in dreams. He'd had no idea why until he later discovered he had impregnated his mate. Steeled by the strength and determination of a yet-to-be father, Wilson followed his heart and nose to Sydney.

He found her and explained everything. After showing her the things he could do (leaping high, running fast and then the nails and fangs) he professed his undying love for her. Swearing to protect her and their unborn child, but only if she returned with him to England. If she chose to go with him, she must tell her family nothing for fear the vampires would uncover the secret. A wolf conceived on Australian soil was seen as an act of war, and the vampires would take their lives or the life of the child in recompense.

Alicia had made a decision there and then that was both ridiculously easy and heartbreakingly difficult. She had feelings for Wilson, but wasn't as infatuated as he was and would eventually become. She loved her family but would never see them hurt, even if it be just a threat.

In the end, she took a chance on love. Not for Wilson, not at first, but for her baby. The ring was a symbol of, apart from anything else, resolve. That when all else seems lost, crazy or impossible, resolve, trust and love will win out. That was the theory anyway.

"You don't have to give this back. She didn't say she wanted to break up."

"Neither did I. But let's face it, that's what it was. Three years of long distance would be hard enough without my condition thrown in. What *have I* got to offer her? Nothing. Just me, or love, is a nice way of selling romances, but it isn't enough. She's a smart girl with hopes and dreams and she's had them long before I got here. I don't want to take that away from her. This is the best thing."

"Sweetheart, I think you're trying to convince yourself, not me."

Nick blinked several times and shook his head. "Maybe. Look, I know it's time for us to get out of dodge, but can we check on Alex before we go?"

"Alex? I love her and she's family, but we made sure she and Margaret both were okay last night. There is no reason for us to be here anymore, honey. You can't do any more for them, and it's too dangerous."

"I just keep thinking about what she said, how she defended me to Margaret. I have to see her. I… I have to thank her for trying to protect me. For believing in me."

* * *

Nick reached his hand into his pocket for the key, but paused as he heard hurried footsteps on the other side. The door swung in towards the room and Margaret appeared, suitcase in hand.

"You've got some nerve…"

"What's happening?" Nick asked.

Margaret flicked her eyes towards Alicia, before replying. "I'm leaving. Please get out of my way."

"Wait a minute. Is this about me?"

"You know damn well it is," Margaret spat.

"Margaret, you don't have to be afraid—"

"Afraid? You think that's what it is?" Margaret grabbed his arm in a vice-like grip and ushered him inside. "Come here."

Nick was marched towards the TV and Margaret used the remote to turn it on to an already playing news programme.

"…and the latest reports are that the death toll of the Dream State epidemic has today reached over 7,000. Hospitals from Dee Why to Hurstville are reporting a further 1,200 in critical condition. Doctors so

far have been unable to find a cure…"

Margaret switched off the screen. "This is your fault."

"What? How? I don't—" Nick scrunched his eyebrows.

"I know you didn't mean it. That's why your mother should shoulder most of the blame. But Dream State is made with werewolf blood. The only reason it was available is because of the four your mother sent here. The ones you didn't tell Alex and me about."

"I didn't know."

"But you did know what your father was. You knew why you were sent here and eventually, you knew for certain you were a wolf, and you kept that from us as well. Do you have any idea how close we all came to death last night? If Dante hadn't pretended to turn you in, Alex and I would've been beaten and tortured for housing you. Nicole would've received worse. The excuse *we didn't know* wouldn't have worked for them either. Your lying to us would've got us all killed. 7,000 people are dead right now. Alex has a friend in hospital right now. She's saying goodbye to a braindead vegetable, for chrissake. I spent over twenty years in an asylum purely to protect my daughter, and just when I get her back, you come in and piss all over us…"

Alicia roared, flaring her fangs. She had only taken a step when Margaret pulled a pistol from her handbag. "That werewolf shit doesn't scare me." Margaret cocked the gun. "You'll have to do better than that, missy."

Alicia spread her fingers out as a response, her nails curved and sharp, ready to strike.

"Stop!" Nick stepped in between them. "Margaret, please—"

"Don't! Not another word. I will say this, from the bottom of my heart, Nicholas. I love you, your human side, I truly do. You may not understand that, but it's the truth. That's why this is so hard. I could understand the lying and look past it, as I have had to do it myself to protect those I love. But when the lies lead directly to my only child being in danger, when I have sacrificed so much to keep her out of harm's way, I cannot forgive that. It was selfish and stupid. And dangerous. You may think you have your shifting under control, but you don't, and you won't. The beast always wins. Alex doesn't see it, that's why she's kicked me out, but I do. I am asking you to get out of the city."

"Or what?" Alicia sneered.

"Or I will do what I have to. I'm going to come after you, and I will kill that thing inside you."

"We're already planning to leave," Nick insisted.

"Fine. Then so am I." Margaret moved towards the door, still pointing her pistol, until finally she bolted out the door.

"Don't listen to her, honey. She's wrong."

Nick stared after one of the two women that had been so kind, that housed him. Gave him love and kindness. What had he given them in return?

"No… I don't believe she is."

Chapter 42

What Say You?

"What is going on?" Creed pushed his head against the cockpit window of the jet. They were going to miss their spot in the take-off queue if this delay went on much longer.

Tobias waved him away as if he were an annoying gnat and repositioned the microphone of his headset. "Say again, tower? I missed that, over." He spoke the message aloud to Creed as he received them:

"Repeating, you have not been given clearance. We are experiencing technical difficulties. As soon as they are fixed, your flight path to Sydney will be confirmed. Over."

"Give me that..." Creed snatched the headphones and microphone from Tobias.

"What technical difficulties? It's fucking Heathrow! Do they only have one computer?"

Tobias shook his head hard, looking just as exasperated as Creed felt.

The flight controller's voice took on a tone of indignant politeness. "There is no need for the attitude, sir. I can't explain why your details can't be processed. It could be because you only booked this morning. You and your group will just have to be patient. I have been to three computers and my supervisor has been to two and we both get the same error message every time."

"What error message?"

"Sydney says: No dogs allowed. Must be a glitch of some kind."

"No dogs…?" Creed drummed his fingernails along the dashboard. He snorted when he realised, and then couldn't stop a full-on belly laugh. He tossed the headpiece back to Tobias.

"What's so funny?"

Creed raised an impressed eyebrow. "They certainly know how to make their final hours entertaining. I will give them that."

"So…they know we are coming?"

"It seems that way."

"I wouldn't let the men know that. They are willing for the hunt no doubt, but now the element of surprise is gone, coupled with the knowledge of Wilson's son…" Tobias gave a shrug and a sceptical shake of his head. "After all, Wilson was known to be extremely powerful."

"And yet he was beheaded without a whimper. By me. Anything can be stopped. Everyone can be killed. But I do admit this does take some rethinking. If they can hack Heathrow's systems, they will no doubt be able to monitor us from the air. They will attempt any delay they can. Very well…"

"What do you have in mind?"

Creed looked out onto the tarmac under the gloomy sky. The runway looked surprisingly sparse today compared to what he was used to. All those times travelling with Wilson and a few of these same men all across Europe for business dealings. Some exchanged money, others fists and fangs. But they had triumphed every time. Stood tall and won respect and riches. It caused him no grief whatsoever to think of carrying both Alicia and her son's head back with him. They were a stepping stone to his ultimate glory. But if he was honest with himself, a small part of him died when he removed Wilson's head. Creed had loved him as a brother and a son. Mentored him for his duty as an Alpha. That Wilson had foundered in that duty was as much Creed's failure as it was Wilson's. Bitterly, Creed pictured that blonde bitch in his mind. She truly had made what could've been a great Alpha weak. She hadn't been the one Creed had wanted for Wilson.

Creed leant back in seat, his mind ablaze with daring. Could it be possible?

"I will take a page out of Alicia's book. Why didn't I think of this before? I will head to Sydney with my best, except one. You will stay here and do something for me."

When Tobias looked disappointed, Creed continued, "Or rather, you'll go to Sydney as well, but without me."

Tobias remained silent.

"They will know how many are coming, and when we are scheduled. But you, will be my plan B and you will bring my plan C. I want you to go to Rannoch Moor."

"The Scottish Highlands?"

Creed gave an abrupt nod. "I will give you the exact location. There you will find something that the Australians know nothing about, a weapon we can use, stronger than any of us."

"What is it?"

"It's not an it. It's a her."

* * *

Alex blinked through her red achy eyes. Dry from lack of sleep and crying. *How long have I been in this hospital room? A day and a half? More? Fuckety.* Her palm was warm and sweaty from constantly holding Michelle's hand but she just couldn't remove it. She knew every minute that ticked by, she was closer to saying goodbye for the final time.

Kept breathing by machines only, Michelle had been moved from her private room to this ward of other Dream State victims. It was horrible hearing the families, one after another, pleading with their loved ones not to leave them, crying out in anguish when their hearts finally gave out. Every flat line, rush to the body by the nurses, futile resuscitation attempts and finally the silence, before the cries of sorrow, were like knives to Alex's soul.

She knew every life that dumbed down to nothing was like time, ticking away what Michelle had left.

"I don't know if you can hear me," Alex stroked Michelle's face. "But I hope you can. I'm so sorry, Mish. I don't know why you couldn't talk to me instead of turning to this. I should've been there for you..." Alex sucked in her lips as the emotion caught up in her throat. "I'm so lost. I kicked mum out. I have no idea where Nick is. Dante wants to be here, but he's dealing with the wolves and the worst part is that such a wonderful, beautiful person…my favourite person in the world, only has one friend beside her. You deserve so much more."

Alex broke down. She'd wanted to contact Michelle's parents but didn't know their names. Michelle had never said, only that they had been told years before that she was deceased. By her tone, Alex had let the subject drop at the time. But now she wished she had pursued it. Somewhere out there were two people that had no idea their daughter was slipping away. It just didn't seem right. Dammit, none of this was right or fair.

Alex placed her head in Michelle's lap, holding her as best she could, begging her through hushed sobs to wake up, before sleep finally claimed her.

It could've been hours, or it could've been moments, Alex wasn't sure how long she had been out. She felt the tiniest press of lips against her head. *Dante.* It was a relief that he had made it. Exhausted, she remained where she was, eyes closed, still half-drifting. She heard Dante move to the other side of the bed. But he said nothing for the longest time. Maybe the sight of Michelle was harder on him than she thought. Or maybe he just didn't believe his words would reach her?

Alex thought about what to say, or whether anything she could say would even be reassuring to him. It was truly his choice what he should do, but if Alex could comfort him in anyway, she would. They were in this together, and she needed him just as much as he needed her. But then Alex heard something in the darkness she didn't expect. Heavy breathing. Struggling. Pain.

For an instant, Alex thought that Dante had succumbed to tears. But even so, Dante didn't *breathe*. The figure on the other side most certainly was breathing.

Alex slowly raised her eyes and jerked back, startled. She fumbled for her phone and clicked the torch app.

"Oh my god…"

It was Nick. He had taken the IV needle out of the bag and plunged it into his exposed arm. He raised his head, face covered in sweat. His beautiful blue eyes had changed to their silver counterparts, staring at her, his breath heaving like a marathon runner through clenched teeth and four gleaming fangs.

Chapter 43

Anything You Want, You Got It

"Nicholas!" It was not Alex who screamed. Just as she was about to turn, Alex saw someone she hadn't laid eyes on for over seventeen years rush over to her nephew. "What do you think you're doing? Stop!"

"No..." he grumbled, wheezing heavily. "My fault..."

"Don't listen to that old bitch! She doesn't know you. You didn't do this. It's not worth your life!"

Nick's eyes fluttered and Alex gazed down at his arm. Blood pumped out of the hole, oozing steadily. The grip that he had on the needle had faltered, his strength failing him as it bent sideways.

"Maybe not," Nick met Alex's gaze. "But *she* is."

Alex stood with her mouth partially open, watching this unfold. Only when Nick collapsed did she move, joining Alicia kneeling on the floor over him.

"I..." Alex took a hand in both of hers. "I don't understand. What happened?"

"Your mother got to him. He told me he wanted to see you before we left, to thank you for supporting him. If I had known he had this in mind, I never would've agreed. Little shit." Alicia sniffed, brushing Nick's hair.

Alex noted the words were harsh but Alicia's actions were gentle. She was scared for him. *Yikes. Better not to talk about mother Margaret, I guess.* "What was he doing with the IV? Is he ok? What will happen to her?" She indicated Michelle.

"I don't know about her. Check." Alicia's answers were no less curt than before.

As Alex rose and turned to check on her friend, the lights of the room sparked on. A ward nurse stood in the doorway.

"I understand this is a difficult time, but only you were given an allowance to be here after hours." She marched over with determination. "I'm sorry you'll both have to— What is going on here?"

Alex looked over Alicia, who was standing in front of a prone Nick. It looked like she had shoved him towards the wall to disguise him, but not in time.

"Whatever this is," declared the nurse, "you will all need to leave right now, before I call security."

"You'll have to call them, ma'am. I'm not leaving."

Alex was spared having to face security. Before the nurse could even take a step toward the door, Michelle sat up and sucked in a huge breath, eyes darting left to right. "Where am I?"

Alex forgot about the nurse, about everything. How she had any more tears left she didn't know, but they flowed true. Alex darted across the room to the bed, planted kisses across Michelle's cheeks and lips, wrapping Michelle in her arms and squeezed tighter than she could ever remember.

"Oh, Michelle! I'm so relieved you're okay." Alex leant back and smoothed away the hair that had been mussed due to her enthusiasm. She carefully rubbed off some of her lip gloss smears from Michelle's lips and cheeks with her thumb. "Oops, sorry about that."

Michelle wore a groggy grin and shrugged. "I'm not. That's a great way to wake up."

Alex felt the nurse grab her gently by the elbow. "Ok, I'm going to need you to back away now. Give me some space. I need to make sure she's o— "

Alex turned to Alicia…who was no longer there. Nick was gone too. The nurse shook her head and closed the curtains of the bed.

Alex leaned, back against the wall, and slid down it to sit on the floor, hands together, eyes closed. She wasn't much for prayer, but did give thanks for this miracle. Not to God, but to the one person that made it possible. She pictured him in her mind and whispered with all the love she possessed. "Thank you, Nick. Thank you so much."

When the examination was completed, the nurse was still insistent that Alex leave. As hard as it was, Alex didn't want to antagonise the nurse further, and she was sure Michelle could tell she didn't want to leave her side.

"It's ok," Michelle smiled. "Wait outside, the car will be along in fifteen minutes."

"What car? I drove here, silly."

"Oh, you didn't, did you? Alex…" Michelle wagged her finger.

"What—" Alex was confused.

Michelle interrupted, keeping her gaze hard. "We'll sort that out. Just wait outside for the car…"

It dawned on Alex that this was some sort of message. Though she didn't know exactly what she was supposed to do, she just decided to agree. "Oh, okay."

"Fifteen minutes," Michelle repeated.

Finally, Alex clued in. "Front?"

"Back."

Alex nodded and made her way out to the elevator, escorted by the nurse. The elevator chimed and Alex stepped in, thanking the nurse, hoping her sudden happiness couldn't be seen through. There was no car here, of course. Alex climbed into her own and drove it around to the rear parking lot of the hospital and parked in a darkened distant corner and waited. She knew the police would want to question Michelle. She was, after all, the first Dream State case to wake up from the coma. But with this command to wait, Alex was sure Michelle had no intentions of talking to the police. Somehow, Michelle was escaping, and Alex didn't doubt her ability to do so for a second. The painful lump of anguish in her chest was lessening. Her Michelle was alive!

Just as she checked her watch for the sixth time, the passenger door opened and Michelle, still in her hospital gown, hopped in and gave Alex a proper hug.

"Don't you ever do that to me again," Alex mumbled into Michelle's neck, before starting the car and driving off.

"I'm sorry. It just happened. I got low, and I thought the drug was a cure. I guess I knew it was too good to be true, but I had to try. I missed Dante so much. All I kept thinking about was that connection—one that I'd never have again. And then I heard that Dream State would reverse the effect of the poisoning of my blood. I had to try it. I had to." Michelle gripped her hands together tightly in front of her as if wishing, praying she could just make the past go away.

"I can't imagine it. I'm so sorry you felt that way."

"I was…lonely, you know? It wasn't like I spent all the time picturing having sex with Dante. I just felt so alone. I kept thinking about you too."

"Why didn't you call me?"

Michelle gave a brief smile. "I guess I didn't know what to say. I felt like when I lost Dante, I kinda lost you too, just when we were getting closer."

Alex could only shake her head in sadness for her friend. "Oh, Mish… I guess it's my fault too. I thought it was inconsiderate of me to be the one to initiate contact with you, since I was with Dante and taken your place. No matter what you said, I knew it hurt you more than you let on. I wanted to be there for you, but in my head it was just so complicated. I thought I needed to give you your space. That you would call me when you were ready. I should never have let things go so long. If you had died from this, I…"

Michelle took Alex's hand. "Stop. Please promise me we'll let each other in from now on. I've lost too much already. We both have."

"I promise."

Michelle leaned over and they embraced, tears of loss turning to ones of joy, relief, renewed companionship. They would never NOT be there for one another after this, Alex knew.

"Ok." Alex sniffed, wiped away tears, grinned and threw the car into gear. "So I'm thinking I take you to Dante, but to your place first so you can get changed."

"Oh man. Undies and my own clothes would be a great start. And you can fill me in about what's been going on…"

* * *

"The door is open. That's weird." There were sounds of tense chatter coming from inside. Alex and Michelle looked at one another and crept cautiously inside. Alex tried to remain unseen as she looked around. The living area was filled with people surrounding the lit fireplace. Some Alex knew and some she'd never seen before.

"Hello girl with a boy's name."

Alex nearly jumped out of her skin. She whirled around and found Nathaniel grinning up at her. They were certainly not hidden now.

Across the room, Matt looked up but said nothing. Nearby, Melina smiled at her and blew her a kiss. Alex blushed and quickly turned her attention back to Matt. There were a group of men surrounding him that she didn't know. They sat by themselves, looking rather cross. These were probably the wolves everyone had been searching for.

Dante stepped in from a side room and called everyone to attention. He proceeded toward the fireplace and then stopped dead. He'd seen Michelle. Relief spread over his face, but he stood fast, unmoving, perhaps unsure of what to do. Michelle saved him the trouble, running to him and flinging her arms around his neck.

Dante let her hang on for a good few seconds, before easing her down, indicating for her to sit. Now was not the time, Alex figured, and sat down next to her, opposite Matt and the wolves.

"I know it is not easy for you all to be here, so firstly, thank you for taking the time and having the patience. I asked you here to tell you about the latest developments, so that together we can come up with the best course of action. By my calculations, Damien Creed, the UK's acting Alpha wolf, is just hours away. He comes for blood, and unless we come up with some sort of strategy, he will succeed. Thanks to the efforts of Clive and Lauren—" Dante indicated toward the far side of the room. "—we have managed to delay them somewhat, and we have a trace program that will tell us when they arrive."

Alex froze when she spotted her once best friend for the first time in over a year. The last time she'd seen her, Lauren had broken Matt's back and nearly torn Dante to pieces. Alex could never forget that night, could maybe never quite forgive her friend that betrayal, the horrific things Lauren had said and done. But looking at her now, Alex saw in Lauren an almost radiant beauty she didn't think she'd ever properly seen before.

Dante's speech had continued. "...also know that they have Julian and his newborn working with and waiting for them. I have spread the ashes of the Waratah around the outer perimeter of the mansion, plus along the doors of the dungeons inside, just in case Vincent had some secret entryway I'm not aware of. It should keep Julian from teleporting in, which in turn makes a full on assault more likely."

"So you're saying we should prepare for war?" Melina asked.

"We're already at war. But we'll need to be prepared for an invasion," Dante said.

"So let us meet him head on at the airport and be done with it," one of the wolves spoke up, crossing his arms.

"No," Dante looked at him before addressing the room. "I will not endanger innocent civilians in open combat. Julian will no doubt lead them here. And here is where we will make our stand. They can only approach from the north as we have miles of water behind us. They would not risk swimming across from the airport for hours when the journey on foot takes less than thirty minutes. This serves as a bottleneck we should be able to use to our advantage."

"You do not speak for us, vampire, and you most certainly would not presume to order us," Calibos spat. "I follow these four men alone and my men follow me."

"You think Creed or Julian care which of us they kill? All of us in this room are enemies. They are coming for everyone." Dante corrected. "Wolf and vampire must stand united against a common enemy. Let bygones be bygones and focus to take down a greater threat than any of our species alone could be."

"I have heard enough." One of the wolves stood up. "My name is Nathan Stryker, and I speak for all the hostages when I say we will not fight for or alongside vampires." He kept his eyes locked on Dante. "Wilson Slade was our Alpha."

"So wouldn't Nick be the Alpha now?" Alex asked, but recoiled at the death-gaze Stryker shot at her.

"The son of Slade is no Alpha of ours. He has won no victories, shed no blood and earned no respect for his pack."

"Very well!" Dante cut in, frustrated. "Your Alpha is dead, and if you will not listen to his next of kin, someone has to make a choice. We offer our strength and our cooperation. Will you stand with us or will you flee?"

"There is such a thing called respect, blood drinker. I would not presume to make a stance that would threaten the lives of these men. Lives which I hold dear. You may view death with a carefree outlook, but we have families. None of us will die for you, or for a city full of strangers that would hate and fear us."

"What about Alicia? Does she have your respect?" Alex asked.

Stryker puffed his chest with a heavy breath. "I would die for Alicia Slade. She has been a mother to us all."

"Well…she's here in Sydney. I could try calling her?" Alex pulled out her phone.

"She's alive?" Calibos bent forward, eyes as eager as a child waiting for a treat.

"You'd better be telling the truth," Stryker took a step forward.

"I've seen her with my own eyes at the hospital. She was with Nick, who saved Michelle from the Dream State coma using his blood. If Alicia wants you to stay and fight, will you?"

Stryker looked from wolf to wolf, and to Calibos, all of which gave small gestures with their heads. "Yes."

Alex looked questioningly at Dante, who made an identical movement. Alex hoped her fear couldn't be seen through as she clicked Nick's number. The fact Alicia would be with her son was the only thing Alex was sure about.

The brief moments she had seen Alicia had told Alex that the last thing her cousin wanted to do was stay in Sydney. While she didn't blame her for wanting to get Nick out and to safety, if she didn't tell the wolves to stay and fight, they were all doomed.

Chapter 44

There Can Be Only One

Alicia stood over Nick's sleeping form, struggling to get his phone out of his pocket without waking him. She'd managed by the third ring. They had gone back to Alex's apartment, the only place she could think of to provide him the shelter he needed to recover. He had only just fallen asleep.

In the hour or so before, she had been both furious and proud of him. "What were you thinking? What were you playing at? You know that could've killed you, and her?"

"I had to try." His voice had sounded like a croak, and his skin was the colour of a marshmallow.

"Why? Just for Alex? What good would you be to her dead?"

"I had to show I'm not a mistake!"

The response faltered her for a moment. "Excuse me? How could you think you're a mistake. You're my son—"

"And ever since you knew I was on the way, your life has been shit. I've heard it all my life, even when you thought I couldn't hear the two of you arguing. My parents have been in one fight after another. Hell, you've been fighting for me since before I was born."

"I've never regretted a single moment of it."

"But when does it stop? When does it end? How many more people have to die or suffer just so I can go on? Dad is dead because of me. I know I didn't kill him, but he was the only one that believed. He forced his views on me and I hated him for it. And now I have to live the rest of my life knowing that he was right, and that my last words to him were spoken in anger because of my lack of faith. I can never take them back."

"Darling, he loved you and he never doubted you loved him. You have to know that."

"That won't bring him back. And it's not just his death on my hands. All those people…I didn't know them, but it all leads to me. The only reason the vampires got access to wolf blood is because you sent them here."

"So by that logic it should be my fault. Why are you blaming yourself?"

"Because you sent them to protect me. Margaret was right. I should've said something. They would've died too had it not been for Dante, and again, because of me. I've killed! When is it my time to say *enough*? I am not a fair maiden in need of constant rescue, I am the beast that others need rescuing *from*! So with Alex, I saw one chance to actually do something right for someone else. I didn't know if it would work, but I remembered dad saying something about how we can heal. I had to try. Had to prove that I'm more than just what Margaret said."

Alicia had choked back her emotions and quickly cleared her throat. Kneeling down, she'd cupped his face. "You listen to me, Nicholas Slade, and listen carefully. I would do exactly the same things over and over again if it meant I still had the privilege to bring you into this world. You are the best thing that has ever happened to me, and my greatest accomplishment. There is only one person's thoughts and actions you have to concern yourself with, and that's yours. You saved that woman's life and I am so proud of you. But you did not owe her or Alex anything. You are not responsible for anyone else, you hear me? I know you feel guilty because of your enormous heart, but part of growing up, whether an Alpha or not, is accepting the things you cannot change or control." She had placed her palm on his chest. Thick, warm and powerful under her touch. "This is what you can control. Live the life you want, not what others expect. Be *true* to *you*."

She'd repeated the last line before Nick hugged her. She laid him gently down, the colour having somewhat returned to his face. Alicia felt confident he would be all right again if he just got a good night's sleep.

And then his phone had begun ringing.

Alicia had initially thought to just ignore the call, but when she glanced at the screen, she tapped the answer button. She would always take a call from Alex.

"Hey," Alicia whispered, stepping out onto the balcony. "He's ok. Just resting."

"Oh thank god. Michelle's ok too, I think. But that's not why I'm calling. I hesitate to bother you, but I really need your help."

"Well, I'd say you've more than earned a return favour from me. What can I do?"

"I need you to come to the mansion."

"The vampire mansion? You have to be joking."

"I wish I was. I have your mates here, the guys you sent."

"What? They are alive? I had given up hope. Are they still hostages?"

"What? Oh, no no. They are free. In fact, that's kinda the problem. Dante needs their help and they won't do anything without your say-so."

"Dante? He's your vampire friend, isn't he? Alex, I'm sorry. I know this sounds so unfair based on what I've asked of you, and what you have done for me and Nick, but I cannot, *I will not* help a vampire. Even if he's a friend of yours."

"Wait! Before you decide, please hear me out. This isn't just about Dante. The entire city is under threat. Vincent's son wants revenge."

"Dream State may have been made with werewolf blood, but it's a vampire invention and a vampire problem. I feel for the victims and their families, really I do. But I can't ask those men to lay down their lives because of Vincent's greed having predictably nasty overflow."

"There's more, though, Alicia. Vincent's son is working with a werewolf who is on his way to the country right now."

"What? Who?"

"Someone named Damien Creed. Do you know him?"

The words might as well have jumped through the phone and down her throat, for they wound themselves up into a painful ball in the very pit of her stomach. So, Creed was coming here. Maybe he was chasing her, or Nick, or both. Maybe he was coming over for the hunt, seeing as though Vincent was no longer in charge. But there was no escaping him. Nick would always be in danger as long as Creed was alive. Nick might be potentially more powerful, but right now, Creed had twenty years of training on him. Alicia needed to know more. She left Nick where he was. Sleeping, warm and safe.

"I'll be there soon."

* * *

Nick awoke to a buzzing. Short, two-burst buzzing. His phone. His temples ached as he blindly groped in the semi darkness. His fingers found the hard surface of the phone in the bed covers beside him and he clutched it and brought it to his face. 2% battery, two missed calls and a voicemail from Nicole.

He clicked to listen.

"Hi it's me. I don't know what I even want to say. Just that I'm at the airport. My flight isn't for a while but…I dunno. I'm so sorry, Nick. I can't even begin to describe how much you mean to me. What these last few weeks have meant… That night we had. You are incredible. I didn't want to say goodbye without letting you kn—"

The screen went black.

"*Oh, you have got to be fucking kidding*!"

He had already made up his mind, however. There was no time to charge the phone before he left. He grabbed his wallet and flung himself out the door. To a cab. To the airport. He just hoped he wasn't too late.

Chapter 45

The End is Nigh

"Hello, Mrs Slade." The guard opened the cab door for her, paid the driver, and led her toward the mansion.

"This way, please."

"How about you walk in front of me? I don't like the idea of you having a semi-auto at my back, thank you."

"As you like."

Alicia couldn't tell if the guard was amused or pissed, but he kept quiet and did what she asked. Stepping over the threshold, she was immediately set upon by the four men she had sent to Sydney. They knelt at once. Everyone else in the packed room she ignored for now.

"My lady," Stryker said to the floor. "I had almost given up hope, even when they said you were here, alive and well."

"Rise," Alicia looked across the room, finding Dante. "And stay there."

She moved like a bull to the vampire she had never met, yet knew very well from description. Dante Delavega was a known vampire across the world, though not with nearly as much infamy as Vincent. Dante was an anomaly. His work for human rights had made him a polarising figure, but a distant one. Australia was a very long way away from anyone who actually cared about humans enough to even consider them anything more than food. Now, though, she needed to make her point.

She lunged for his neck and lifted him as high as she could. Even the click of guns, and the snarling of her wolves and other vampires did not cause her to flinch. Surprisingly, Dante hadn't flinched either.

"I heard about what you did, vampire." Alicia seethed with hot anger. "I understand that you saved a lot of lives, including my son's. For that, I am grateful. However," she lowered him closer to her face. So close she could see her reflection in his brilliant green eyes. "If you use him for bait in an experiment again, *I will eat your face*. Do we understand each other?"

Delavega answered by gripping her wrist tight, making her release her hold. He dropped to his feet and kept his intense eyes fixed on hers. His strength was a little worrying. He held her arm at bay with almost casual ease. He had let her think she had him under control.

"We understand each other. As long as you know I would sacrifice any one of you to protect the people I care about. Do not think to come into my city and expect me to follow your wishes. You are a long way from home. And make no mistake, it is my severe wish to see you all go back as quickly as possible."

He released her then. Alicia flexed her fingers, feeling no damage. "But you have a problem you need help with. Wolf help?"

"It is a wolf that comes for all of us. I am not too proud to admit we need your help. But surely you can see we can better survive together? What sort of situation will you all be going home to? Help us end this now and take back your pack."

"Our pack was never lost, vampire," Stryker said. "It has been tainted, yes, by an unworthy usurper. One that will be dealt with accordingly. Whether tonight or another day, makes no difference. We would be fighting from a position of weakness here, not strength. This is not our home, it is not the full moon. That is why your city is the battleground."

"Dante!"

All heads turned to see a scrawny man with glasses stumble out of the elevator. "I just got word. They've landed."

* * *

"Flight Slade 1, please taxi to VIP Hangar 2."

"Roger that," Creed said, switching off the microphone directly after. He reached for his phone and clicked the number he had been told via email to enter. "We're here. Inform your master he has roughly twenty minutes before we reach the hangar. He has until then to do whatever he has planned to get us past security."

"Kay, hang on a sec."

Creed turned his lip at the response. *Teenagers.*

"What does the plane look like?"

"The big, shiny black one. Where are you?"

"Inside the terminal, waiting for you."

"And your master?"

"Outside, along the fence by now, I guess. Finding which plane is yours. He should be popping inside any minute."

But Julian was not outside the fence. Creed hung up to look out of the cockpit window to find the former Sydney prince strolling casually along the tarmac towards the oncoming plane. In the blink of an eye, he disappeared, only to reappear inside the cockpit.

"Welcome to Sydney, Creed."

"Whatever you're going to do, do it fast."

"I'm teleporting you all one by one into the terminal."

"In full view of the public, or anyone walking by?"

"Not exactly. My…son is standing guard over a secure location."

* * *

"Shall we?"

Nicole smiled, trying to hide her overwhelming fear of what to expect in the next few months, hell, the rest of her life. She and Dr Sarsky were gathered in front of the departure gate of the International Airport. She was proud of herself in many ways. She had hidden the truth from everyone and made the best decision possible for herself. But why did she feel so uneasy about it? She had worried herself physically sick the last two nights. Waking and having to visit the bathroom to throw up, then crying herself back to sleep.

She had wanted this her whole life. Hadn't she? If so, why did she have to constantly play with the strap of her carry on just to hide the trembling of her fingers. She would be getting everything she wanted, bar one. She looked around one last time, guessing there must be about fifty or more people surrounding her, and accompanied by probably the best mentor in the world, yet she had never felt more alone. It really was true, what they said about how you could be lonely in a crowded room if the one person you're missing isn't there.

Nicole gave a weak smile and picked up her bag, but did a double take. She turned her whole body and moved several steps to the side, away from the departure wall. She sucked in a breath and dropped her bag with a thud. There, slicing in and out of people, was Nick.

She didn't know what to say, what to do. Instead instinct guided her. She opened her arms, beckoning him, needing him. His arms enclosed over her and she buried her face into his chest, sobbing his name with relief.

"Thank god," Nick whispered.

"What are you doing here?"

"I had to see you before you left."

Nicole leant her head to the side to study him. His brow was sweaty, his long fringe tousled, but that face still cheered her up. His blue eyes bore into her and she was taken back to the night they shared, the feeling of him inside her. His strength but his gentleness, the way he touched her with such reverence, yet made love with such passion. That look of fierce protection, of honour, of love. "Take me with you."

Nicole wasn't sure she had heard him right. She started to speak, to question, but was halted when he took both of her hands in his. "I know I have no right to ask. What I said a few days ago still stands. I have nothing to offer you. I don't know whether I'm good enough for you, I don't know anything about the brain, but I do know that I am completely in love with you. I don't want a life of blood and killing. I want you. I can't let you go."

Nicole pulled him in, kissing him harder than she thought she was capable of. She didn't know how, but they could make it work. She could ask Dr Sarsky if Nick could help them with their project. Nick could finish his schooling over there, and she would help him during the full moon. Everything would be ok.

She leant back, looked deep into those gorgeous eyes. "I love you too."

"Aw, aint that a pretty picture?"

Nicole tensed, a frisson of terror running down her spine when she recognised the voice. Trent Miller, hands in pockets, stood there with a smug, unsatisfied look on his face. He was not alone. Behind Miller stood ten, no twelve men, all glaring at them. Two more had just appeared coming out of the men's restroom.

"Creed…" Nick stepped between Nicole and a tallish older man.

"Well, well, if it isn't Wilson's pup come to meet us."

"We don't have time for this," one of the men behind Miller said. "Delavega would be aware of your arrival by now."

"You're right." Creed took a step to the side, still sizing Nick up. "Nevertheless, this putrid wretch would be better to us dead."

"Music to my fuckin ears." Miller flashed a set of fangs and hurled a thunderous right hand. It snapped Nick's jaw, stumbling him. Nicole screamed.

"Not here!" the long haired one said. But Miller did not listen or did not care. He grabbed Nick by the shoulders of his jacket and flung him backwards, sending his whole body crashing through the departure wall, destroying the Sydney Airport logo and imploding the glass surrounds. People cried out, then scattered like ants as chaos ensued. Nick had disappeared under a mountain of concrete, steel and glass. Nicole screamed his name, choking on dust and ash. She tried to reach him, moved to dodged falling pieces of debris.

Her hand was grabbed by Dr Sarsky. "Don't. It's too dangerous!"

"I'm not leaving him! I have to save him. You don't understand"

"He's dead Nicole! He's dead. I'm sorry!"

Nicole tried to fight him off but Dr Sarsky held her wrist and tried to drag her in the opposite direction. She screamed for Nick as more and more of the roof caved in around her when with a thud, everything went dark.

* * *

Dante looked at his phone. Turn on the TV. Local news, now.

"To breaking news now out of Sydney. The International Airport is under lockdown after some kind of explosion just a few moments ago. Security footage shows a young man throwing himself into the main departure lounge seconds before the explosion. There are unconfirmed theories the attack could be terrorist related but as yet no groups have claimed responsibility. All flights have been grounded and we currently have no information on possible casualties. We will have more information on this story as it develops."

"Wait a second. Rewind that." Alicia looked stricken.

"No need." Dante turned off the set. "I saw Nick too."

"Threw himself. What are they talking about? He didn't throw himself!"

"The newborn." Dante knew it was the only thing that made sense. Miller, being a vampire, would of course not have shown up on the footage, and only a newborn could have the strength to toss a werewolf like a doll.

"What was Nick even doing there?" Alex asked. "Is he ok?"

"I don't know. He's strong but…I have to go to him." Alicia moved to go.

"There is no time. You'll never get there before they reach us here. These men are coming for all our blood. They have just used your son as a tennis ball. They will do worse to you. Will you stand with us here and now?"

"Damn you, Creed." Alicia had clearly made up her mind about something. The four wolves stood, moving closer to her, readying themselves for whatever order was given. The former Alpha mate and current Alpha mother looked at Dante, her eyes shifting to silver. "Prepare yourselves. We fight."

CHAPTER 46

BATTLE PLANS

Dante estimated the journey from the airport to Darling Point, given the speed wolves run, was about twenty minutes.

"Elements, patrol the tops of the grounds. I want you with sniper rifles on the roof. Shoot anything that approaches. We need to keep them as far back as we can. You will be our last line of defence. If they get inside, it's over."

The Elements of Night filtered up the main staircase. They numbered roughly thirty or so, but Dante wasn't fooled into confidence. While they might outnumber the wolves, they had no silver bullets. "All remaining vampires, with me."

Of the twenty or so vampires that occupied the house at any given time, only Lauren, Melina, Cassandra and Nathaniel remained. He had sent Clive back to Dante's apartment to wait the outcome of the night. As wonderful as he was in the digital world, he was no fighter. Should they lose this night, he was under instructions to delete all vampire data concerning Sydney.

The guards and servants had all fled and the vampires Vincent had instructed to leave when Dante brought Nick over, had heard what had happened to Vincent and hadn't bothered returning. Maybe they were afraid of Dante, maybe they were planning retribution. Either way, it would be Dante's worry tomorrow. If he survived.

"All right!" Melina smiled. "Let's give these bitches something to howl about. Where do you want us?"

"We'll be heading to the front lines."

"I'm ready, Dante," Nathaniel said.

"No, Nathaniel." Cassandra squeezed the boy's hand.

"But muuuummm!"

"Her orders come from me," Dante said.

"But that's not fair. I wanna fight too." Nathaniel stomped his foot hard.

Dante went down on one knee and beckoned Nathaniel closer. "My young friend, listen to me. This is not because I'm saving you from the fight. I'm saving the fight from you."

Nathaniel looked at him. "Huh?"

"Don't think I haven't noticed how fast you're getting, how much stronger you are. This is why I have a special assignment for you."

"What is it?"

He placed a hand on Nathaniel's shoulder. "Protector of the Estate. And everything in it," he said, glancing at Alex and Michelle.

"I have to protect the humans?" Nathaniel asked, his tone difficult to place.

"A job I would entrust only to you. Not even the Elements of Night are here, you notice? These women are important. I need the best."

Nathaniel looked again at Alex, Michelle, and his chest swelled with pride. "I won't let you down." He thrust his hand out and Dante shook it. Nathaniel took Alex and Michelle by the hand and walked them to the steps. "Come on, girl with a boy's name."

"As for you," Dante said, turned to Alicia. "I am no wolf. I would not presume to order your men to do anything. You have earned your right to lead, so do what you will."

Alicia nodded before addressing her men. "Those who have worked with Calibos will do so again. Assist the Elements of Night along the grounds. You four will join me and the remaining vampires on the front lines. We will give them everything we have got, but remember, Creed is mine."

"What of the newborn?" Stryker asked.

Matt cocked his gun. "He's just another fang to be pulled."

"Don't be naïve. Newborns in their first month are the strongest and deadliest of all of us."

Matt sneered. "Are you telling me the king of Sydney can't defeat a baby vampire?"

"A baby vampire crippled *you* once," Lauren said, without emotion.

Matt turned to her. "I haven't forgotten. Or that werewolf blood healed me. It was stronger than you."

"Exactly," Dante said. "None of us can match a newborn, except possibly an Alpha Wolf."

Lauren clicked her fingers. "Could we get Creed to kill him somehow? Trick him into it? He's an Alpha right?"

"Creed is not a real Alpha. He merely calls himself that," Stryker said. "He is probably the most skilled in all our pack though. But if this newborn is as strong as you say, none of us should go near him."

An unearthly howling made them all turn towards the door and their sensitive hearing picked up a dozen weapons on the roof being locked and loaded.

Dante took a breath. "Let's go say hello."

Chapter 47

The War For Sydney

Creed sniffed the air. "Get ready."

The huge wrought-iron gate of the Kent Estate loomed large when Creed called a halt. He sniffed the air. "Get ready."

One by one, his enemies appeared, leaping onto the high perimeter walls of the estate to face them. One man with a redhead and two blondes, all blood drinkers.

"I'll take you to be the new king," Creed said.

"I am. You've come far, but you will not get what you came for. Turn back and the lives of your men will be spared."

Creed laughed. "Rehearse that did you? Let us understand each other, Your Majesty. I have come far, too far for you to think you have any say over whether I get what I came for. You are but three leeches protecting a coward from the fate that awaits him. My counter offer is give me the boy and I will not take the rest of the city."

"I am not a wolf and cannot speak for them. It is not up to me to decide the fate of one of your own kind." Dante was joined on the wall by five familiar faces.

"But I can."

"Alicia. So, you've both thrown your lot in with them?"

"Anything to stop you from continuing your charade as Alpha."

"And what do you think you're doing?" Julian glared at Lauren. "You could've been something special."

Lauren scoffed. "I'm already something special, Julesie. But I sure ain't yours."

"Enough of this!" Creed had no time for these halfwits. "Where is the pretender to my throne right now? Let me think. Ah yes, buried under rubble at the airport. Some Alpha he turned out to be."

"You call *him* a pretender and a coward?" Stryker challenged, beginning to change. "You kill Wilson when his back was turned and dare call yourself his replacement?"

"Death to this false Alpha!" Alicia screamed, silver eyes raging. The wolves along the wall roared along with her.

Creed heard his loyal wolves snarl in return, ready to pounce, to kill anything that moved. He gave a loud bellow and pummelled the pavement with a growing fist, crumbling the asphalt to powder.

Two wolves leapt high, attempting to scale the fence, but were felled by sniper bullets coming from somewhere further back inside the estate. *The roof, no doubt,* thought Creed. Three more wolves surged at the female vampires, but before they could strike, the three women ducked in unison. They too were put down by bullets to the head. His seven remaining wolves were smart enough to stay low. They looked at one another and nodded at the ankles of the wolves standing on the wall. Before Alicia's wolves lost their balance, they shifted positions and jumped forward. Both sets of attackers met in mid-air, swinging with everything they had.

In the commotion, Alicia flew down, swiping at Creed. He hissed as she managed to clip his cheek with a few nails. They circled each other, each daring the other to make the first move. Suddenly, Creed felt as if he were being punched hard in the chest. The breath was knocked out of him. He fell backwards onto the pavement, still trying to suck in air.

"Oh, Dante." Julian stared up at at the king of Sydney, fangs extended. "Can this really be it then? The whole city will burn tonight and yet here we are, caring about our silly little feud. Surely you should worry about others and not just me…and how much Melina loved my dick."

The king squatted, ready. "Your father tasted like shit."

Julian screamed, popping up onto the perimeter fence beside Dante, unloading a heavy right hand. Before the king had even turned his head back, Julian disappeared and then reappeared on his other side swinging with his left. Dante blocked the blow and the both of them tumbled onto the nearest car, smashing the windshield to pieces.

* * *

"God almighty."

Alex watched the fighting unfold below her, fists flying so fast she couldn't tell if anything was connecting until a loud grunt or scream answered for her.

"They are ok, though. The Elements are doing their job."

Almost as soon as the words were out of Michelle's mouth, Alex sensed something wrong outside. Shadows from the street lights extended over the grounds, growing longer. Snaking their way quickly up the walls, blocking what Alex could see. It was as if she had put on dark sunglasses.

The noises outside changed. Suddenly the voices of those Elements of Night guards nearest her on the roof above scrambled and cursed. Alex ran to the edge of the window and looked out and around. "What the…oh my…"

Bodies were dropping past the window. Thrown down from the roof. One screamed and fell, then another and another. Out of nowhere, Elements were being tossed down, blood and bones bursting from their chests, and yet Alex could not see what was doing all this carnage. There was no one there.

"The newborn!" Michelle turned pale, confirming what Alex had guessed but didn't see. Miller leapt down onto the grounds, struggling with a soldier who had switched from a sniper rifle to an M16. It was a short struggle. The newborn wrenched the weapon free and shoved it into his stomach, pulling the trigger and blowing his back out so his corpse broke into two pieces. Alex shuddered. He had managed to kill the Elements of Night, all thirty of them, in less than a minute.

He readied the gun, and spotted Alex and Michelle staring at him. He broke into a bloodied grin, waved and aimed, ready to fire.

"Get down!" Alex crunched into Michelle just as a spray of bullets tore into the window, glass cascading all around them. Alex covered

Michelle as best as she could as the relentless savagery continued. The hot lead shredded the room, cracking the walls, spitting powdered cement in all directions.

Suddenly the shooting stopped, replaced by grunts. Alex shook her head and face free of dust, coughing. She touched Michelle's face. "You okay?"

Michelle nodded and wiped plaster dust from her eyes.

Alex crawled on her elbows to the window, peering down.

Lauren had leapt onto the newborn's back, clawing at his neck and shoulders, trying to slow him down. She dodged two shots he blindingly aimed at her before he jumped high, Lauren still clinging to him. She struck the tip of a streetlight and only then did she let go, falling to the ground in a heap as shattered glass rained down upon her. He landed nearby, pointed his gun at her head and fired, just as Cassandra swung with both hands, nails extended and knocked it free.

Cassandra struck two light blows, but as hard as she tried, he was too fast for anything severe. She leapt high to connect a knee but he dodged out of the way, bringing her down with a forearm to the jaw, cracking the back of her head open. Alex gasped, horrified to see her dispatched so easily. Fear began to take hold. She could no longer think. She could only watch the horror unfold before her.

The newborn moved over to the car Dante and Julian had fallen on moments ago and using quite some effort, picked it up by the front and staggered back over her, lifting it high in the air.

"No no no no no!" The sound of Michelle's voice penetrated Alex's daze, but she could still not look away.

The newborn struck Cassandra with the full weight of the car, causing an explosion that destroyed a part of the wall and flung them all backward.

Michelle rose gingerly and moved again towards the shattered window. "To hell with this."

"Where…?"

"I have to help. I have to do something."

Alex shook her head. Her ears would not stop ringing. Words refused to come to her tongue.

Michelle took Alex's hand, and Alex was able to will her fingers to squeeze back. They looked at each other, time stretching. Alex couldn't bare losing her again, not when she had come so close before. In that moment, she remembered how much Michelle meant to her as he eyes flicked to her lips. What she would always mean to her.

"Thank you for the save, sweet Alex. But I have to—"

Alex, still dumbstruck, grabbed Michelle's shoulders. She hesitated and then threw her arms around her. "Come back to me, please."

"You bet your cute arse," Michelle winked and raced outside to meet her fate.

* * *

Dante dug a piece of glass out of his shoulder and tried to assess the situation through the haze of pain in his head. Julian managed to wrestle out from under a car door. Alicia struggled to her feet, managing to beat a dazed Creed to standing. Melina had only just opened her eyes when she was kicked a further fifteen metres towards the mansion door by the newborn. The damn kid walked forward, one side of his body smoking, and red raw but he still smiled, otherwise unharmed. His confidence in his newborn powers was at its peak. "One down. Who's next to try? How's about you then?"

The nearest person he could find was Stryker, underneath two of Creed's wolves he had been fighting. The explosion had killed the two of them and their bodies had shielded any permanent damage to Stryker. He picked up Stryker by the scruff of the neck. Before he could respond, the young vampire plucked his voice box free from his throat, a waterfall of blood falling down his chest, tossing him aside. "Guess not. Oh well, what about you, King of Shit?"

Dante launched an attack but missed, the kid managing each time to dodge his strikes. This wasn't like his fight with Lauren as a newborn last year. She was raging, out of control. This kid was supremely calm and confident, a killing machine who clearly enjoyed it. Truly Julian's adopted son.

He now grabbed Dante by the back of the neck with his clean hand, the one used to pull Stryker's throat out at the ready, blood dripping from his fingers, when a roar pierced the sky. The earth under their feet tremored, shaking Dante out of his grip. The newborn turned towards the street as did Dante, spotting a lone figure in the dark sprinting towards the mansion. Huge. Fast.

"Finally."

The newly forged vampire stepped directly into Nick's path.

"Come on, you ugly son of a bitch. Come on." The kid stomped onto the car door Julian had discarded and caught it one handed as it tipped up on its edge. Then he hurled it like a steel Frisbee directly into Nick's chest, knocking him back to the concrete.

Nick threw the wreckage aside and got to his feet quickly, snarling a challenge to the newborn, his voice as cold as ice. "C'mon, hot shot. Afraid to get close?"

Miller cracked his neck dramatically. "You just won't stay down, will you?"

Both teens ran at each other full pelt, throwing themselves into the fight with the savagery of lions. Claws and nails ripped flesh, punches shattered bones, only for them to heal just as quick. Both boys' blood splattered the ground, but they did not stop as they battled into the street among the flaming wreckage of the car.

* * *

Alicia screamed as she pulled her leg a little straighter in front of her, repeatedly smacking her kneecap back in place, only just managing to get click it back when Creed planted a kick flush on her jaw, sending her sprawling backwards. Alicia was on her own. She tried to crawl, if not to safety, to get her bearings, but Creed would have none of it. He pursued her and dragged her back into the thickest part of the dust cloud and straddled her, knees holding her arms at her side, hands grabbing her neck and squeezing tightly. "I'm going to drag your arse back to Britain where you can watch a real wolf take care of business."

"You…are…pathetic. I will never be by your side."

"I said watching a real wolf. I have someone else in mind to be my mate. One who should've been to begin with. You were only just one of Wilson's whores…"

Alicia tried to free her arms, tried to bite him, but it was no use. Her wolf powers meant nothing, as he had the advantage of positioning and applied pressure, in short he had to do almost nothing and Alicia would surely die in less than twenty seconds. *I'm forgetting my* other *powers,* she thought, and brought her knee up hard. Creed gasped and moaned. He fell to the side, cupping his balls.

Alicia's head was spinning, and she hadn't even properly gotten any sort of breathing rhythm back, but instinct took over. Her arm found its way around Creed's neck, tightening it the way a boa constrictor would its prey as she lay on top of his back, pressing her weight on him. Creed heaved as he flung his claws to her face and head, managing to scrape her several times before she latched onto his hand with her teeth, sinking her canines into his flesh and clinging on tight. Creed screamed and Alicia, sensing victory, began to shear her fangs across his hand, partly chewing on his skin while holding the weight of her body as far back as she could, stretching his neck until finally it snapped. In a last effort, she clawed at his throat, digging her fingers deep into his skin and muscle until she touched the base of his skull and spine. Pulling hard, spilling pieces of bone and muscle tissue onto the grass, she finally rolled onto her back, exhausted and unconscious.

* * *

Dante got to a knee when Julian wrapped a thin piece of wire around his neck, yanking it with all his might. A vampire did not breathe, but decapitation was what Julian aimed for.

"You will pay for what you have done to my father."

Dante thrust himself up to stand on both feet and flipped backwards over Julian's head, landing behind him. He had sliced a huge chunk of his chin and throat but he was at last free. Before Vincent's son could teleport away, Dante jumped and pushed his knees hard into Julian's back, at the same time wrenching his jaw and snapping the spine backwards. Julian screamed, spraying blood as he fell.

* * *

Nick seethed with rage. Miller had never been anything but an utter dick to everyone, and had been even worse to Nicole. He had vowed to her that he didn't want this life, but Nick could not contain this rage any longer. Miller needed to die. Nick slammed him into the charred body of a nearby car, partially crushing it, but Miller pounded back with heavy fists, causing Nick to stagger and fall. Miller ripped off the rear door and got to his feet. He attempted another slinging throw but Nick was ready this time, and caught the door mid-air. Nick brought it down on top of Miller's head, smashing the glass over his torso. Grabbing the now empty window frame, he bashed Miller's head and face with the car door, landing thunderous blows unmercifully and relentlessly, again and again.

* * *

Melina brought down the last of the wolves in partnership with Calibos and Matt, who plugged them full of bullets as she finished them with her nails and teeth, ripping out body parts in any way they could. Creed's wolves dealt with, Melina looked to see what else needed doing. She saw Alicia, still unmoving, but alive, and heard a shout behind her. She turned to see Dante dragging a screaming Julian to the mansion.

"Trent, my son, help me. I'm injured…I can't teleport. Where the fuck are you?"

But Trent, Melina saw, was in no position to help anyone. He was on the ground, his body motionless, a crimson mess. And the Alpha was continuing to beat his fists into the newborn's body.

Dante, arm still around Julian, grabbed one of the fallen guns, and raised it over Julian's neck. Melina realised this was it. Dante was actually going to kill him.

"I only wish…I could make this more painful."

Dante cocked the gun Melina ran at him, throwing herself on top of them both.

"No!"

Dante rolled to his knees. Julian laughed. Melina held fast as Dante stood to face her.

* * *

Nick knelt beside Miller's corpse. Pieces of his bones littered the space around both of them as well as copious amounts of his blood. The red hot anger was subsiding and Nick felt a weariness creep in. A hand on his shoulder nearly made him jump out of his skin.

Alicia stood beside him, eyes alight with pride and relief. His enemy had been finally conquered, as had hers, his father's killer. Together they had avenged the deeds that had ripped their family apart. Still on his knees, Nick threw his arms around his mother, and she hugged him close, patting his hair, resting her cheek on her son's head. After a moment, she stepped back and raised her head, as did Nick, stretching his throat up to the sky. Mother and son gave a howl that both celebrated the night and mourned the loss of the man they both wished was there with them.

* * *

Dante stared at Melina, fury coursing through him. Julian continued to laugh and Lauren hobbled over, trying to see what was happening.

"You fucking bitch. Why would you stop me? You have no love for him." He thrust his hand out toward Julian.

"Alejandro, please… Forgive me."

"Forgive you? Why should I?"

"I made the go deo commitment." Melina hung her head.

Dante snapped out of his rage. "No…"

"Oh yes, Dante," Julian said, struggling to his feet. "She is mine forever. Whoever kills me, she must go after them and avenge me. So go on then. Take me. Then the two of you can have a fight to the death over it. I hope you really are ready to kill her, Dante, because should you take me out, she will have to kill you, and she has no say in the matter."

"I'll lock you up forever if that's what it takes."

"Ah, so glad you mentioned that." Julian produced what looked like a central locking car key. "I may have lost my rebellion, but I still intend to win the war."

"Julian, you wouldn't." Melina sounded terrified.

Dante peered closely at the object in Julian's hand. *What possibly could—?* And then it hit him.

"Master of the dungeons bids farewell. Happy New Year." Julian cackled, pressed the key's button, and popped away with a whip crack, as explosions rocked the grounds from beneath the foundations, flames surging up to engulf the mansion's lower level and spreading up into the night.

Chapter 48

Hope You Are Quite Prepared To Die

"What the hell was that?" Lauren asked.

Dante felt his knees shake with another explosion.

"He's destroyed the dungeons." Melina held out her arms to steady herself. "The foundations were just underneath there."

Dante bolted towards the door. There were still people he loved in that building, and he had to get them out. The flicker of flames was visible through the entry windows, and Dante called for Alex, Michelle and Nathaniel to hang on. Alicia appeared by his side, rammed her shoulder into the smoking wood. In a rush of heat and light, Dante was blown back by a burst of fire. Alicia thumped to the ground with a broken piece of metal piping lodged in her forehead and moved no more. Dante rolled as he landed, trying to douse the flames that tore at his clothes and flesh. Through the searing pain, Dante heard a thud and crack.

Melina was by his side in an instant, swatting the last of the lapping flames on his shoulders and arms. Dante tried to stand, seized his leg and crashed back to the grass. He couldn't stand.

"Alejandro, stop. It's broken—"

"Get out of my way."

She moved to run inside, presumably to help the three left inside. A gust of wind blew past Dante from behind and above, and whooshed straight toward the mansion. Melina stopped in her tracks, and the two vampires could only watch. The Alpha sailed overhead, through the space that once held the viewing window in the room where Alex and Michelle had been watching from. "We have to help him."

But it was already too late.

Fire cannoned upward and outward. Dante raised a shaking hand to shield his face against the intense heat. His arm felt unbelievably heavy. But the hardest thing was having to see the nightmare in front of him. The mansion lay in ruins, the roof and supporting walls, crumbled and burning around him. The levels were gone, leaving only a solid screen of billowing flame and heavy clouds of thick black smoke rising into the already pitch darkness of the night.

Dante laid his head back on the grass. Stunned, motionless, Lauren held either side of her face, Melina retched, coughing from smoke. It was as if time stood still for Dante, unable or perhaps unwilling to see or do anything.

His whole life and the lives of those he cared about had just come undone. Julian was alive and Melina had prevented his death because of an ancient binding ceremony. Julian, who had destroyed Michelle's life, ruined Melina's to an extent, and was still free to cause as much havoc as he wanted because Dante was forbidden to do anything about it, lest he be forced to fight the first woman he ever loved to the death.

But even with all that, nothing could be worse than this feeling right now. What good was the victory over Creed or even Vincent now? Hollow wasn't the word. Dante didn't care about winning. He didn't care about the city either. The people he did care for, were gone. And he couldn't do anything about it.

"Oi!"

Dante forced his eyes to focus. As the stars came into view, some part of Dante recognised the voice, but couldn't make himself move. Melina knelt by his head and lifted it, showing him the speaker.

Dougie. It really is you. Dante's Aboriginal mentor and oldest friend stood with Alex and Michelle, Nathaniel in Alex's arms. All were covered in soot and ash, soaking wet. She lowered Nathaniel to the ground to stand beside her. He wore the damage of third degree burns all over his small body. His clothes had been burned to a cinder and he stood there naked as the day he was born. Several bits of his skin were scarred and scabbed the colour of black cement.

Dante had a huge sense of relief, and yet not everyone was accounted for. He looked at Dougie. "The wolf?"

Dougie lowered his eyes and he shook his head. "I only saw him for a second. He threw these guys into the water behind the house, savin' 'em from the heat. I came just in time to see 'em treading water, then the whole back of the house just…" Dougie flexed his hand outward, fingers imitating the explosion. "The whole thing just crashed into the drink. I only just got 'em outta the way."

Dougie finished with a slow tone, as if sorrowful. But Dante knew there was nothing more he could do. He guessed Alex felt that way too, but the truth was too much right now.

Alicia had risen, plucking the metal out and flinging it to the side. Blood poured from the wound, over her face and Alicia staggered. Alex took a few quick steps forward but Alicia held her hand up. Dante saw Alicia and Alex look at each other for the longest time, what they were thinking was anyone's guess. The wound had partially closed, but that wasn't the wound that needed the most help.

"Creed had something else up his sleeve. I heard it in his voice. I should sort it out before it becomes another of your problems. Take care."

Alicia straightened her shoulders, turned and walked away. Moving stiffly, as if not trusting her feet to carry her. Alex made to move towards her but was halted by Michelle. "Let her go."

Alex faltered then, no longer able to hold back the choking sobs. Dante was near to tears himself, seeing her. She clasped her hands together and pressed them to her chest, lowering herself to her knees, gripping Michelle's arm who had lowered herself too.

"Melina…"

The grip on Dante's head changed as she adjusted him to look at her. "Place all the dead in the fire quickly. The authorities will be here any minute. We must leave. Get Lauren to help you."

"Lauren left as soon as Dougie arrived. The dogs and the wannabes jetted too, cowardly pricks. We are the only ones left."

* * *

Lauren made sure she took care to cloak herself, sprinting after Calibos. It wasn't a difficult task, seeing that he was supporting an unconscious Matt. She drove her shoulder into his back, forcing Calibos and Matt to the ground. Calibos was quick, rolling forward and rising with his pistol, pointing it every which way. Lauren thanked her gift again. She knew she could never be truly invisible; she could only bend light. But as long as she stood perfectly still in the shadows, she was as good as completely obscured. Just right for her next move.

She launched an upwards kick directly to Calibos's wrist, snapping it clean. She clapped her hand over his mouth to muffle his scream, and shimmered into view.

"Shhh, honey. I can't perform if there're people around…" She remembered his cocky attitude when he was ordering Matt to shoot her, and launched several punches to his head and face.

She picked him up and slammed his back into a nearby tree. Calibos spat out a glob of blood and smiled a red smile. "You were planning this all along, weren't you?"

"You should've killed me."

She flashed back to the humiliation and violation she felt when he cut open her top.

Lauren undid his belt and removed it. She unzipped him and let down his pants and boxer shorts, letting them fall to his ankles, gazing down.

"What a shame. That's a semi decent cock, pity you won't ever get to use it again."

Lauren sunk her fangs into his neck and drunk heavily. She thought about how powerless she'd felt against the kid Miller, but now she'd killed her first werewolf. She wasn't perfect as a vampire, but she was learning. And getting better.

"Move aside, dead thing."

Lauren spun around, Calibos's corpse falling to the ground at the base of the tree. She faced three Aboriginals, two men and one woman.

How the hell did they sneak up on me? "Back off. He's my kill."

"We don't care. We're here for him." One indicated Matt with a nod of his head.

"What the hell do you want with him?"

"None of ya business. We were told to get him. So we get him." The two men walked over to Matt and picked him up. The quiet ease with which they moved past her was creepy. As if she was insignificant to them.

"Are you the Forgotten?" Her voice was barely above a whisper.

"It doesn't matter. We were also told to find out what happened to Alex Hensley."

"Why do you care about her?"

"We don't. Our leader does."

"And who is that?"

"You haven't earned the right to know. Answer our question and what you will earn is the right to die another night."

Lauren wasn't sure what it was, but something in the tone stayed with her. She remembered what No-name had said those few weeks ago. How the Aboriginals could do things in Redfern that they couldn't under ordinary circumstances. They were a long way from Redfern now, but she still felt that same sense of danger.

"She's alive."

The three of them took Matt and left. Just like that. Again, a sense of complete indifference in the movements. But Lauren wasn't fooled. These were not a group of alcoholics or Centrelink no-hopers. These guys had some ability, a presence and a quiet power. More importantly, they were a serious threat.

But she would report that to Dante later. Right now, she could hear Calibos whimpering weakly, which meant he was still alive. That was good, because Lauren was still hungry.

CHAPTER 49

KEEP OFF THE MOORS

Tobias parked as close to the stone cottage as he dared. He had spotted it as he rounded the mountainside almost a mile away and followed a pebbled road until he was about fifty metres from the front door.

It was late afternoon, and yet already his breath was visible as puffs of cloudy mist. He trudged down the slight slope, through the rolling fog that covered the grounds.

While driving, he had received a call from one of Creed's men, the only survivor of the invasion. Tobias couldn't believe Creed was dead. That fact did not diminish his respect for the fallen leader, however. After all, Wilson's spoiled pup bit the bullet too. At least that was something Tobias wouldn't have to worry about. Unfortunately, Wilson's bitch wife had made it out alive.

He knocked on the thick oak door wondering what kind of weapon Creed had stashed inside. Whatever it was, he hoped it worked on a pissed off mama wolf with a serious revenge mindset. He had no doubt she would come back to the estate, and she would come for blood.

The door opened a crack, and behind it stood an ordinary woman just shorter than he was.

Tobias cleared his throat. "Radha?"

"What do you want?"

"I need to speak with you."

She looked him up and down with undisguised scepticism. "You're not the one who brings the money and it's the wrong day, too, so you can feck off."

"I was sent here by Damien Creed."

"So?"

"He's dead. He asked me for your help the last time I saw him. I could force the door open. Please don't make me."

"Well…that changes things."

She let him in, stepping aside. Tobias looked around, unimpressed. One table in the middle of the room looked like it had been recycled from a tip. Small clay decorations lined the windowsills, that were themselves dark with grime. A small fireplace to the right looked like it was one more use away from bursting into ashes. Either the money she received from Creed barely put food in her stomach, or she was saving it somewhere. *Why the hell would Creed send me here? Where the hell is this weapon?*

Tobias had had no idea what to expect, what he was looking for or why Creed wouldn't just tell him. He'd been thinking of something along the lines of a physical weapon, like a cannon or an armoury full of anti-vampire bazookas; a mini nuke. Something.

Tobias sat down and studied Radha, and truthfully saw nothing to think she could be a weapon to be used. She smelled human. Pale, Irish red hair, quite a few kilos overweight, not ugly but not striking, and not that old. Perhaps early thirties.

"So what do you want?" Radha crossed her arms, speaking quickly in her heavy Northern Irish accent. The one where even "I love you" sounded like a threat.

"Actually, I have no idea."

"Well this will be a quick visit, then."

"Look, Creed didn't tell me specifics. All he said was that I had to come here and what I was looking for would just…I don't know, *be* here. The pack is broken now, and he is dead, and a new Alpha has to be chosen."

"A new Alpha? What happened to…Slade?" She sneered at the last word like she'd sniffed something putrid.

"Creed killed him months ago."

The words brought a slow but bright smile to her face. The door creaked open and another woman entered the small house. Much younger that Radha. Barely a teen. But Tobias could not help but stare at her remarkable features and he realised she smelt like a wolf. Rich hazel eyes and wavy black hair that she flicked over her shoulder. "Who's this?"

Radha didn't answer. Probably because Tobias had risen and closed in on the girl, looking closely at her face. The cheekbones, the jawline.

"Fuck…"

He turned to Radha and then back again. Her look was enough; she didn't have to say anything or confirm it. He knew now why Creed had summoned him here. He was staring at *the weapon.* Wilson's greatest secret, the bastard he knew nothing about. And best of all, another tenth generation Alpha offspring with the strength Tobias needed. He would take her and her mother back to the estate and use them to strengthen his claim.

"This is my daughter, Talia."

"Fantasic!"

"You are way too happy…" Talia scowled.

Tobias launched into his reasons for being there, spending almost fifteen minutes in feverish abandon, stopping only when Talia began to pace the room.

"So let me get this straight. Wilson, Creed and now Nicholas are dead? The Alpha post is open?"

"Exactly. We must prepare for Alicia's return first. And you can expect the best of the best at the estate. I will ensure your complete comfort. You never have to step foot in this hovel again."

"You will ensure? Hovel? Insulting us isn't really the best persuasion, is it? And since when does anyone have to ensure the Alpha's comfort?"

"What?" Tobias laughed, not sure she understood him. "You misunderstand. You can't be an Alpha. You're a woman."

"Oh…" Talia looked down at her hand, her fingernails had sprouted, long and sharp. "You misunderstand me. I don't want to be comforted. I don't want to be an Alpha. I want to be *the* Alpha."

Tobias stared at her, seeing the brightest silver eyes he had ever encountered, the darkness around them like the blackest night. He took a fearful step back. Talia was growing, changing before him.

"It's not the full moon…it's not night-time. How? It's not possible…"

"My daughter has been changing at will since she was thirteen.

You're a fool to walk in here with your bullshit, thinking we would jump when you say. I went to the estate with her, Wilson's child inside me, and was turned away. Creed would not let me see him, and why? Because he was readying to marry an Australian bitch that very day. He shunned me but gave me a monthly allowance to ensure my silence. Out of sight and out of mind. That was and will be the last time I turn to a man for help. I cut my own daughter from my stomach. You think we owe you something? Fuck your pitiful pack aspirations and fuck Alicia. We'll bury what's left of her next to her husband. We have been waiting for a chance and we will use it to take what's ours."

Talia lunged for his chest, sinking her fist through his bones, snapping them inwards. She was the only thing holding Tobias up. His chest burned yet his fingers and toes had turned icy. He looked down, fighting for air at the blood frothing and spitting around her wrist. Right then, he knew the true meaning of fear. He realised that by letting them in on his whole plan, he had let them know the pack was weak, ripe for the picking. Talia was what Nicholas could've been, the product of her upbringing. Abandoned, impoverished and bitter.

She was hunched over him, as she'd become taller than the height of the room itself, and she had almost tripled in thickness. She was not a mere werewolf—she was the definition of a raving monster.

With barely enough time for him to beg, she pulled his heart free and he crumpled to the floor. Just before his eyes went dark forever, he saw the beast chew and swallow it whole, watching him with a superior smirk as she did so. What had he done?

* * *

"Hi, Dante." Alex knew who had called simply by the time of night. She guessed he had just woken.

"I know you asked for time, but I was wondering if you had seen the news?"

"No…should I?" It was a redundant question. Alex had clicked the TV on before Dante replied.

"I wouldn't."

"...leaving the scores locked at 18-all. And in follow-up to breaking news earlier this hour, police have confirmed the drug epidemic that has claimed over 7,000 lives is now coming to a close, with the inventor and distributor of the drug reported dead. Nicholas Slade, a teenage immigrant from England, thought to be one of over a dozen remains found in a suspected gang-related fire at a Darling Point mansion. Slade became known to police after security footage revealed an earlier altercation at Sydney Airport that caused part of the departure terminal roof to collapse, delaying flights for almost a week..."

Alex shut it off. "How the fuck can they put all that shit on him?"

"Julian, I suspect. It is a final middle finger to all of us. He has contacts in the media and Julian no doubt fed one of them a good story wrapped up in a neat bow. They don't need a body to make a ratings winning story. He had all the elements there for it... Are you all right?"

"No..." It was true. There was no point in denying it as Dante would see through it. Who was to say how long it would be before she felt ok again? Since when was there a timeframe on loss? "...but I will be."

"I understand, but please let me know if I can help."

Alex needed the phone call to stop. She felt the tears yet again and she was sick and tired of crying. "Yeah. Will do. Ok then."

"Alexandra, I know what I said, but I never meant for this to happen. He didn't deserve this. Neither of you did." Alex scrunched her eyes as her shoulders quaked. She covered her mouth but the sobs seeped through her fingers. "I am truly so sorry."

Dante saved her ending the call by hanging up first.

She couldn't speak. She wanted to be alone, she wanted to be held. She wanted to scream. She knew there was nothing more she could do, yet couldn't help question what else she could've done.

It was so hard to think about the reality that she would never see that wonderful boy again. In such a short time, he had captured her heart.

This was nothing compared to the phone call to Nicole. Alex wasn't ready to accept it herself, but there was no one else to tell her, and she needed to know.

"Alex?"

This followed a slow knock. Michelle's voice. "Honey, I know you're in there. I don't know if you want to be alone but I want you to know I'm here. Please don't shut me out. You don't have to deal with this alone."

Alex leapt up, crossed the room and pulled the door open so fast, she almost fell into Michelle's embrace. Her mind was all over the place, but as her tears flowed freely again, the fact Michelle was there meant more than she could ever say. Whatever the future held, Michelle's very presence helped her feel she could face it. Tomorrow was another day.

EPILOGUE

"Excuse me?" Dr Sarsky called quietly. "Could you do me a favour, please?"

The stewardess swept over to him in an instant. Business class staff on British Airways were probably more efficient than First in his opinion. But then again, he would never try to take advantage of that. They had a job to do, and he respected that, but this was a different situation.

"My friend has been in the lavatory for almost half an hour. Could you please check on her?"

The stewardess glanced over his shoulder, towards the facilities behind the bulkhead near the galley of the plane. "Of course, sir. Don't worry about a thing. What is her name?"

"Thank you very much. It's Nicole O'Brien."

* * *

Nicole barely registered the sound of the knocking, the pounding in her head drowning most of it out. When she did register it, she covered her mouth to stifle a sob.

"Excuse me, Ms O'Brien? Are you ok in there?"

Nicole cleared her throat as quietly as possible. "Yes, thank you. I'll be out in a minute."

She wasn't sure whether the stewardess believed her, or what she would relay to Alan before Nicole returned to her seat. So she guessed she'd better start fixing herself up.

She stood up from the toilet seat and readjusted her skirt, taking a deep breath to stem the lump in her throat that threatened to make her cry again.

She had just endured several weeks discovering the existence of vampires and werewolves. Then…Nick. How close they came to being happy. How stupid she felt for denying him, and herself, for the longest time. And then he came to meet her at the airport, to join her in the rest of her life. Only a few hours later he was gone. Leaving her alone and she never got the chance to tell him. Her body and her mind were probably still in shock.

She washed her hands and dried them. *Don't think about it.*

But how could she not? She had planned, she had been safe. She was *always* responsible. She was on the biggest journey of her life, and the most terrifying. She had ignored the nausea, the headaches and the doubts.

Nicole's eyes darted to the edge of the sink, where what she shouldn't be thinking about lay. Some part of her had not ignored, had been sensible enough to buy the test, had needed to know for sure. She could not look away from the two-line display on the small device. Despite all the precautions. *Positive.*

Her mind could not quite fathom what was growing inside her, as she wiped at her tears and splashed cool water on her face to reduce the appearance of crying. Whatever happened, whatever the future held, she would have to face it alone. As if instinct willed her, she placed a hand on her stomach and made a brief circular caressing motion. Then again, maybe she wouldn't be alone after all.

Author's Note

Thank you for reading!

Please consider leaving a review if you enjoyed Day Dreamer.

Don't forget to look up www.aaronlspeer.com and subscribe for all the latest news, promos and prizes on offer, a chance to ask the characters questions, and more!

And best of all…

Dante and Alex will return in Shadow Chaser

About the Author

I've been writing since I was around 11, and have rarely been seen without staring off into the distance or with a pen in my hand ever since.

Whatever my genre I happen to be writing at the time, I am passionate about bringing this beautiful country I live in, Australia, to light. (Hint hint...even if that includes epic fantasy and vampires)

CPSIA information can be obtained
at www.ICGtesting.com
Printed in the USA
LVHW081131131019
634028LV00050B/705/P

9 781508 895817